I0837869

CHERRY

MICHELLE ROSSA

Copyright © 2025 by Michelle Rossa
Cover design by Michelle Rossa
Paperback ISBN: 979-8-218-58390-3

All rights reserved. No part of this book may be reproduced, stored in a retrieval system, or transmitted in any form or by any means, mechanical, electronic, photocopying, recording, or otherwise, without written permission from the author Michelle Rossa.

No part of this book may be used or reproduced in any manner for the purpose of training artificial intelligence systems or technologies.

The characters, names, places, incidents and events portrayed in this book are fictitious and are the product of the author's imagination. Any similarity to real persons, living or dead, events or establishments is purely coincidental and not intended by the author.

To every woman who has suffered at the hands of a man. May the pages in this book remind you that while being nice is free, your time is not.

So be more cut-throat, be more loud, and never, ever let a man silence you again.

Also by Michelle Rossa

Shadows and Fire series
A Fate of Shadows and Fire
Guardian of Souls
Harbinger of Nightmares

Deal With A Succubus series
Cherry
Sapphire
Silver

Legacy of Cerasyn series
Captive to Twisted Torment

AUTHOR'S NOTE

This is a *dark* romance. Themes in this book are for mature audiences only, and the content warnings should be noted prior to reading. This novel contains sadism, degradation and humiliation of men, coercion, use of marijuana, attempted rape, dubcon, being roofied, mutilation of male genitalia, decapitation, gun and knife violence. This book contains explicit sexual content such as knife play, blood play, primal play, fear play, edging, orgasm denial, and snowballing.

It should be noted that **both** the FMC and MMC in this novel are morally gray characters, though one might even argue borderline morally black. This novel is not your average cutesy, vanilla love story. These characters are chaotic and sadistic.

But if you've read this far and grinned really big at all of those content warnings, then you've found yourself in the right place. So go ahead and turn the page, and enjoy. Xoxo

Chapter 1

Amelia

"Please—" His voice cuts off on a strangled grunt as I sink my seven inch heel further down onto his cheek. My red acrylic toenails press themselves into the jet black sole of my heel as the matching strap around my ankle bites ever so slightly into my porcelain skin.

I sigh audibly, rolling my eyes as I peer down at him. "Please *what*, you imbecile?"

He loosens a shaky breath, trying to lift his wild gaze up at me but my foot keeps his face cemented in place. His lips curl themselves against the crimson carpet, ironically the same shade as the color of my hair.

He manages a sharp inhale. "Please forgive me." His voice muffled as the words escape from those round, pouty lips.

Pathetic.

I hum to myself as I stare down at him, lifting my chin slightly higher. I bring my hand up in front of my face, fanning my nails towards myself as I admire my long acrylic nails. A perfect matching set to the ones on my feet.

Gods, I love Kiara. She does such a fantastic job.

At that thought, I go to reach for my cell phone on the black leather couch beside me. I open up my text threads, finding the contact marked *Ki baby*. I go to open up her thread and begin typing.

Thanks again for the set, babe. Sending you another tip to show how much I love and appreciate you. Xoxo

I swipe out of the text thread, opening my money transfer app and clicking on her contact. In the amount box, I type in one hundred and hit send. I grin at my phone as I get the confirmation pop-up that lets me know my money has been sent, and my phone buzzes a moment later with a text from Ki.

Ugh, I'm so lucky to have such an amazing client and friend. I'll do nails for you anytime. Muah xoxo

"Hello?"

I close my eyes, sighing audibly at the annoyance of this man. He showed up tonight asking for a private room, and with just one look in his eyes I knew what he wanted out of tonight.

I've noticed for some reason it's always the average looking ones that like being degraded the most. Always the ones who have seemingly normal lives, with a wife and kids at home, living in the perfect cookie-cutter house.

Mortals living the traditional human dream yet they always have the darkest, wickedest fetishes and secrets lurking beneath the surface.

And they usually come in here not even in dress code, wearing khaki pants with a half-button up shirt, like this guy. I took one look at his shoes when he arrived and scoffed to myself. He couldn't have at least put some dress shoes on before showing up to the club.

Nope. This guy showed up in some dirty ass, white sneakers that have the slightest platform on the bottom. Gods, I should have made him pay more for not *at least* trying to look presentable for me.

I set my phone back on the couch. "Right—forgot you're still here." I shrug a shoulder as a giggle slips out, a maniacal thrill coursing through my veins as I hover over him. I lower my gaze back down to him. "Do you think you deserve to be forgiven, Gary?"

He stares up at me, nearly panting as I press down harder on him. Basically suffocating the poor bastard at this point but hey, that's what he asked of me when he paid for a VIP room. To treat him like a good for nothing speck of dirt.

He manages to take a breath in before I lessen my weight. "Yes, your majesty. I do."

"And why is that?" I drawl, my gaze piercing into him. I draw him in through that mental channel, knowing if I looked in a mirror right now that the amber in my eyes would be churning even brighter.

His panting suddenly lessens as his face slackens, gazing longingly at me as I draw him in. His arms go limp against the carpet floor as if he suddenly forgot that my heel is still pressing against his alabaster cheek.

He blinks slowly. "I deserve to be forgiven because I am nothing. I am your faithful servant, and I am grateful to be in your presence."

I tilt my head, assessing. I slowly raise my heeled foot, setting it back onto the ground as I wave my hand up. "On your knees."

He lifts his face from the ground, a generous red mark now accompanying his pale skin in place of the carpet. He turns towards me as he kneels in front of my feet. Still gazing at me with those dark brown eyes.

I smirk. "Now be a servant and kiss my feet."

He lowers his face down, his lips scrunching together as he presses a kiss on top of my foot. He kisses right on top of my red toenails before lifting a hand to my ankle. His calloused fingers graze up my calf. "Thank you, Cherry. For allowing me to be graced with a touch of your soft skin." He peers his heated gaze up to me.

Ick. This sight is the furthest thing from a turn-on. But hey, he paid me a thousand dollars so it makes up for it.

He goes to reach his hand up higher when I jerk my foot out of his grasp.

Typical for a man to try and test his limits.

I turn around and go to grab my phone along with the small stack of hundreds on the glass coffee table.

"W—where are you going?" He stutters, standing himself up.

"Your hour is up." I shove the cash beneath the underside of my boob. The black leather halter top doing very little in concealing any cleavage, just enough fabric to cover my nipples. A band wraps around the underside of my breasts as my open neckline travels down to my navel. The bikini line doing everything but conceal my wide ass.

My gaze catches my reflection in the large vintage floor-length mirror mounted against the draped wall, the gold plated trim softly illuminated from the crystal light fixture above. I glance down at my outfit and how it snugs my body in all the right places. I turn to the side as my gaze lowers, smirking at myself.

Definitely a great ass.

"But it's only been fifty minutes? I still have ten minutes left!" He demands.

My grin falls as I turn back towards Gary. I give him a quick look up and down before I raise my brows. "You lost those last ten minutes when you tried to get handsy with me. You paid to be degraded and to be stepped on, feeling me up was not a part of it. So call this a...*forgiveness* fee. Actually—" I step towards him, drilling my gaze into his. I feel the sensual energy of my Succubus power heighten in the room around us. I tilt my head slightly as a smirk curves up my red painted lips.

"Give me another two hundred just for the inconvenience."

His face once again smoothes out as he nods slowly. A lazy smile appears as he lowers his hand inside his pocket. "Of course. My apologies, Cherry. For inconveniencing you with my selfish, greedy tendencies."

He pulls out two hundred dollar bills and hands them to me, his fingers clammy as they brush over mine. I take the money, shoving it with the rest as I shake my hand off.

Gross.

"You're forgiven." I wave a hand, stifling the energy altogether. "You may leave now."

His gaze roams over me as that coercive power lifts off of him. His back straightens as he nods curtly, turning to leave the VIP room entirely.

I grab my phone and exit the VIP room, leaving the frosted glass door cracked open. My heels silent against the carpeted hallway as I pass elaborate walls of red filigree detailing. Bronzed ornate molding traversing along the ceiling above.

The music envelopes the space around me, increasing the closer I get to the large awning connecting me to the rest of the club. And as I near the main floor, a sensual smile graces my lips as I await for my next willing customer.

Chapter 2

I glance down at my phone, groaning to myself as the time in the corner of my screen reads eleven o'clock. Still another three hours left of my shift.

As I make my way down the dimly lit hallway, I run my fingers through my crimson red hair, fluffing it. I pull some of it over my shoulders, letting the ends fall down past the underside of my breasts. The booming club music vibrates my skin, nearly drowning out the faint moans coming from one of the play rooms I pass.

The Playground is the only club in The Pleasure District, making it the sought-after attraction for amateur tourists wanting to check 'going to a strip-and-kink-club' off their bucket list. And—of course, the regulars who use the club as an escape from whatever shitty reality they're not finding satisfaction in, but are still too emotionally attached to to find the sense to change it.

The best part about working here? Is that the girls get freewill over what they participate in and what they don't. There's absolutely no shame to how the girls make money here, as long as it's within their own comfortability.

The Playground is composed of four main areas: the center stage for pole dancing, the private sections meant for dances, VIP rooms, and play rooms. The difference being that play rooms are usually for customers that just want to bang one out, or for when they get lucky enough to bring someone along who's down to fulfill some sick fantasy together. Play rooms are open to anyone, but VIP—well, that's where us girls make the real money.

Like tonight, making a quick twelve-hundred dollars just to step on some short guy's face and degrade him.

I chuckle to myself as I step out onto the main floor, a packed club for a typical Saturday night. I lift my gaze to see Sapphire on the main stage ahead of me, a few good-looking men occupying the sable round-backed chairs below her. The LED lights under the edge of the stage casting a dark red hue as they travel around all four sides. A vertical stage pole traveling directly up into a large mirror above, a symmetrical square that perforates out of the ceiling.

With her french-tipped manicured hand on the pole she slowly lowers herself to the sleek black laminate flooring, bending at her knees. Her long lashes lift up as her light blue eyes fixate on the man seated at the center dressed in an all black suit. Her deep blue hair turning a dark shade of purple beneath the pink moving head lights shining from above.

He watches her intently, his steady gaze not moving from hers as he leans forward in his seat. I watch as she does her usual crowd-work, a sensual graze of her fingers down the center of her breasts. His heated gaze follows its every move. Knowing that when she sets her sights on someone, she always gets what she wants.

A prowess amongst a sea of hungry suitors, looking for a temporary escape. Only Sapphire plays the game ten steps ahead of every one of them, ensnaring them into her own little trap to fuel that Succubus energy within.

My gaze travels to his wrist as he raises his hand, his index finger slowly tracing his bottom lip. A low huff gets trapped in my throat as I watch the overhead light glint off his pristine silver watch, fastened beneath a black cuff. Understanding why she's picked this one out of those three to focus her attention on.

A twenty-eight thousand dollar watch on an actually handsome man? Yeah, you're definitely grabbing Sapphire's attention.

She meets my gaze and I give my friend a sultry wink. She responds by giving me a wicked smirk before I hook a right down past the main seating area.

With each step that my heels make against the black carpet, I feel myself capture the attention of a few passerby men. Their gazes branding the side of my face as I continue in my stride. I don't feed their ego by giving a glance in their direction, I keep my gaze trained forward on the bar ahead of me instead.

Men are all about the chase, but what they fail to realize is as a Succubus, we are natural born predators at their own game. Luring them into our vicinity, rather than the other way around. Because when I don't give them the satisfaction of throwing myself into their lap like a starving lap dog, they always let their better curiosity override their composure and come crawling over to me.

Proving my theory that men cannot function properly, or live their entire desperate lives, without the attention or approval of women.

I approach a velvet bar-stool, the black material soft against my bare legs as I take a seat. I rest my forearms against the glass countertop, the crystal chandelier above the only source of light aside from the dim lights underneath the lip of the counter. I look down to the far side of the U-shaped counter, a genuine smile curving my lips when my favorite bartender comes into view.

I lean back a little, a smirk curving up my lips as I admire the brief run of his fingers through his black, buzz-cut hair. His pearly white teeth glinting even in the scarcely lit club as he smiles widely at a pretty female patron.

She smiles at him before he turns around, grabbing a martini glass. He walks over to the back wall accompanied by shelf after shelf of liquor, reaching a muscular arm up for our top-shelf brand of gin and vermouth. He turns back around to start making her drink when he catches my gaze. He gives me a quick grin before preparing her drink.

I watch him slide it over to her when he's finished before making his way down to me. I peer my gaze sidelong at the woman before meeting his again. "She's cute." I raise my eyebrows. "Did you get her number yet or are you just going to continue eye fucking her?"

He chuckles as he begins making my regular drink: a vodka cranberry. "Like how you're doing right now?"

I lazily roll my eyes, my smirk unfaltering. "Let's say we skip the part where we act like we don't feel attraction to one another and just," I lean forward into my seat, feeling my breasts rest against the glass bartop. "Get to the good part?" I nudge my head towards the woman. "She can even join us."

His golden-brown eyes contrast beautifully against his rich umber skin. His eyes fixate on my lips before meeting my gaze again. He hands me my drink, leaning in closer. "But where's the fun in that?" He lowers his gaze to my breasts, a heat eroding in his gaze as he lifts it back up to meet mine. He licks his bottom lip, his tongue gliding across his labret piercing. "I enjoy the sexual tension between us a little too much."

My gaze fixates on his lip ring, tilting my head as my seductive energy surfaces. I flutter my lashes as I look up at him. "Maybe I just want to know how that lip ring will feel in a wholly inappropriate place." My gaze pierces into his, my power reaching out for him.

He chuckles as he pulls away entirely, lowering his gaze momentarily. "Save your *tricks*, Cher. Although you don't need them for me to feel seduced by you." He winks.

I shrug my shoulders. "But it's just so fun to try anyway." I grab my drink, my lips pressing softly around the straw as I take a sip. I lower it back to the counter. "But you're right. I fear I like the fun in the tension far too much to cross that bridge quite yet."

Ace laughs. "Confident that I'll submit to you?"

"Careful. I could have you begging on your knees in a matter of seconds." I say teasingly, willing my power to the surface again before quickly forcing it down.

I suddenly feel the presence—and smell, of two men seating themselves next to me. I watch as Ace glances over to the two men before casting me a knowing look. He trains his gaze back onto them, nodding. "What can I get you two gentlemen?"

A smirk curves my lips at the two willing victims that have landed themselves right into my web.

"I'll have a beer." The man directly next to me says, his voice low and deep.

"Same." The other one's voice polarly opposite as he chimes in. As if he still hasn't hit puberty yet even though he's in his forties.

I sigh internally, taking another sip before finally turning my gaze to them. I give them both an innocent smile as my power wields to the surface once more. A grin deepening on my face as I hold my hand out, the man seated next to me grabbing it before putting my knuckles to his lips.

I smile sweetly at him as I catch him glancing at my bare legs. "What brings you boys in tonight?"

Chapter 3

Levi

My index finger idly traces the rim of my whiskey glass as I watch the man lean forward into her embrace. She reaches her hand up, running her lithe fingers through his chestnut brown hair, her shoulders relaxed as she laughs in his company. She has no idea that I've been studying her all night, waiting for the right moment—

"Anything else I can get you, Mr. Lareux?" the waitress says, interrupting my thoughts.

I glance up at her, a vague nod of my head. "I'm good for now."

"Let me know if you change your mind." She says sweetly before lifting her soft hand from my shoulder, standing herself upright before turning around. I glance at her long black hair traveling down her back, flowing against a short black dress and stiletto black heels. An attire that all of the cocktail waitresses appear to be wearing.

She looks back at me, noticing where my gaze has fallen and gives me a wink before turning her gaze forward as she walks away.

"Can you be any more subtle?" Sawyer says beside me, lifting his whiskey to his lips.

I train my gaze back onto the woman at the bar. "She's not the one I'm interested in."

Sawyer lowers his whiskey to the glass coffee table before us. He lifts his gaze to the woman in red a few rows ahead of us. "And how do you know she's one of them?"

I lift a lean leg, hooking my ankle over my knee. I rest my arms out along the chair's armrest. "Just watch." I nod my head in her direction.

Sawyer fixates his gaze back onto her as we observe.

The woman in red—Cherry, lowers her hand to the bearded man's arm, trailing her manicured fingernails along his bicep. I watch as his body goes taught, his gaze wholly fixated on her. I watch as she grins wide before leaning in close to his ear, whispering something I'm too far away to hear. I watch as his eyes go wide-eyed before she pulls back again.

The gentleman beside him watches the entire interaction, as if he's under a spell and cannot fixate his attention anywhere else.

She tilts her head and I watch as what I've been waiting for happens.

"There."

Her amber eyes glow brighter as a palpable energy pulsates around her. She says something to him, keeping her gaze locked onto him. After a moment, he reaches into his pocket, pulling out a wad of cash. Without breaking eye contact he shuffles through it until he pulls out a stack of twenties. I watch as she takes the money, counting it herself.

Four hundred dollars.

She folds the money in half before tucking it in her leather lingerie, right below her breast. The man's gaze finally breaks as his face smooths out entirely, his body relaxing as the energy around her subdues.

Sawyer lifts his whiskey to his lips. "So she is a Succubus. What does that have to do with fulfilling your job?" He turns his gaze to me, lowering his glass to hang over the armrest. "Should I suddenly be worried I've added the wrong man to my team?"

I turn my gaze to my boss, his light amber eyes shining starkly against his black shoulder-length hair. A sharp jaw to match his sharp stare. "I *earned* my bones to get here." My gaze hardens on his for a moment before smoothing out again, leaning back into my seat. I lazily shrug a shoulder. "I just think it might be interesting to have a partner who can help me easily lure them in." I smirk at him.

He stares at me, silent for a long moment as my gaze follows his index finger. He hooks it beneath the collar of his black button up shirt, pulling it away from his tattooed neck before lowering his hand back down to the armrest. "As long as you do your job, and do it well, then I don't give a fuck *how* you do it." He points a quick glance in her direction again before settling on me. "But if she jeopardizes our operations, then it's your ass who pays the price. *Earned bones* or not." He seethes as he stands himself up from his chair, his all-black attire smoothing out as the lights above glint off the rings on his fingers. He pulls a crisp hundred out of his pocket, setting it beside his empty glass before stepping out of the section entirely, declaring our meeting over.

I tilt my neck, a soft and brief crack of my bones piercing my ears before I down the rest of my whiskey. I set the empty glass down, fishing a hundred dollar bill out of my black pants before setting it beside the glass.

I lift my gaze up as I hear the scrape of a chair being pushed out, noticing Cherry leaving the two men. She turns her gaze back to them, giving them a sultry smile before turning around completely. My gaze tracks over her, roaming down to her long legs as I notice a tattoo on her right ankle. My gaze travels up to her wide hips set against a slim stomach, the leather lingerie slimming and lifting everything up in the best ways.

I take her in, eyeing her up until I reach her porcelain face. Those full, bright red lips ensnare me for a long moment before my gaze lifts to lock eyes with her.

She meets my gaze, staring at me seductively before giving me a wink. She walks towards me, her amber eyes fixed on me. As she nears my section, I can practically taste the vanilla and floral scent that wafts from her. And as I stand there shamelessly drinking it in, she walks right past me with the two men in tow at her sides.

I turn my gaze around subtly, watching her walk away as her ass bounces with each step.

I snap myself out of it completely as I fist my hand through my pocket, pulling out my cell phone as I pull up a text thread and begin typing.

I have an inquiry.

I watch as the typing bubble appears, Dex replying back a moment later.

Listening.

Cherry. Redhead ten o'clock.

I look up towards the center stage where Dex has been seated, preoccupied with a cute blue haired girl dancing on the pole above him. I watch him keep his head straight ahead on the girl on stage, knowing his eyes have just momentarily glanced over as Cherry walks past him on the left side of the stage. He leans back in his chair.

I'll have it ready in a couple hours.

I send him a thumbs up emoji as I shove my phone back into my pocket, standing up from the section and making my exit out of the club.

Chapter 4

Amelia

I shut the locker door as I walk over to the vanity table, dropping my oversized amethyst dance bag onto the chair occupying it.

Pulling out my black leggings and a loose gray T-shirt, I lower my thigh-length faux fur jacket onto the marbled vanity table. In nothing but a thong, I pull my shirt over my head as I flatten it over my stomach. I grab my cotton leggings, hooking one leg in after the other, pulling them up over my ass. I lower my feet into a pair of leather heeled boots when a familiar jasmine scent wafts towards me. A smile curves my lips. "I saw you had a particularly interested suitor tonight."

Sapphire opens her locker, stripping off her lingerie as she smirks at me. "The man liked what he saw." She tosses the fuschia pink lingerie piece into her silk black dance bag, rummaging through it until she finds a pair of mocha brown sweats. "Can't blame him, can you?"

I laugh as I zip up my dance bag before grabbing my jacket, lifting one arm through it. "But the question is did he actually tip you?"

She pulls her sweats up, tying the strings taught when she holds up the wad of cash from her locker. I watch as she fans out only hundred dollar bills across her bare chest. "The two thousand in my hand proves that he not only likes to spend leisurely on expensive jewelry but on gorgeous women as well." She winks before tossing the money into her bag.

I loop my other arm into my jacket, tilting my head. "And he didn't even pester you for a lap dance?" I loop my arm through my bag, pulling my hair free from beneath the collar of my coat. "Oh, so he's a gentleman with *class*."

Sapphire pulls a long-sleeved black T-shirt over her head before slipping her feet into a pair of beige fuzzy boots. "Best part is that I didn't even have to seduce him." She tucks her deep blue hair behind her ears, grabbing her money again as she pulls out one-fifty.

Eighty for our house mama, twenty for the DJ, twenty for the bouncer, and thirty for Janice, our club manager.

She sets it on the marbled counter before shoving the rest of her night's earnings deep into her bag. She grabs her black lapel coat, pulling it over before grabbing the tip-out fees. "He had those googly eyes for me all on his own." She wiggles her eyebrows before walking away from the lockers.

A chuckle escapes me as I zip up my jacket, following her to the little office right next to the entrance to the main floor.

We both walk in, house fee for Vivianne ready in tow. Her dark brown eyes lift up to us through her glasses as a warm smile greets her face. "I have you both on for ten tomorrow. It's game night, so you know what that means."

I hand her my house fee as I roll my eyes at the reminder. "Which means college men will be in here, who are the absolute worst tippers, so expect to have a shitty night? Got it."

An audible exhale leaves Sapphire as she hands over her fee. "Gods, I hate game night."

Vivianne gives us both a sympathetic look as she places the money into her small purse. "Better wear the school-girl skirts then if you want to make any kind of money."

I give Sapphire a sarcastic smile. "Can't wait." I roll my eyes before making my way to the door. "Goodnight, Vivi."

"Get home safe." She says before sitting back down at her desk, presumably doing whatever other clerical duties house mamas have to do.

I make my first round to the Dj, handing him his tip out before doing the same with Janice, and lastly our bouncer.

"You sure you don't want me to walk you home?" Maverick asks. An intimidating son of a bitch for a tall, handsome man. But beneath it is a teddy bear of a softy for all of the women that work here.

"I'm good, love. I'm just down the street. Goodnight." I say before turning on my heels and making the walk home to my apartment building.

The streets of The Pleasure District are far quieter now, with everyone trying to get home as bars have closed up. I look up to the cloudless sky as the moon's light shines down upon me.

As The Lofts come into view, I cut my way to the building's entrance through the alley. A mouse skitters its way across the dirty concrete, shuffling past a broken bottle. I continue my walk when I feel the presence of another behind me.

Instead of whipping my head around I continue my pace, keeping my back and head straight. I hone in on the musky cologne that wafts towards me, groaning internally at the distinct tell-tale sign of it being a man following me.

His scent creeps closer and closer, and right as I feel his fingers brush themselves around my arm I whirl around, my hand coming up to his throat.

His hand falls limp to his side as I tilt my head at the man. "Didn't anyone ever tell you it's impolite to sneak up on a woman?" I lower my gaze to his outfit before studying his face again. A grimace paints my face. "And you're not even attractive." I scoff at him as I release my hold, stepping away from him. "So what is it you thought you were after, you creepy little man?"

He brings his hand up to his throat, a dry cough escaping him as he rubs the slight indentation marks I've intentionally left on his skin. He thrusts his hand back down to his side as a vile grin curves his lips. As if my initial warning wasn't clear enough—or rather didn't frighten him enough, he advances a step towards me as he forces a laugh.

"What I was thinking," He hurriedly closes the distance between us, thrusting a hand to my coat zipper, yanking it down before jerking his hand to my breast. "Is what's a pretty thing like you doing, walking all alone at night? In these *tight* pants." He squeezes my breast once before lowering his hand down over my stomach, biting his lower lip as his hand lowers further. "Looks like you're in need of some company—"

Before he can even finish his sentence I swipe my hand clean across his neck, blood spraying my face as I sever his head right off his body.

His head collapses to the concrete as his body falls down, like a domino tumbling back. I lean over him as blood drips from my sharp talons, a feature of my real form beneath the human body I cloak myself in. A form where one would find elongated inky claws sharp enough to tear through flesh and bone. A serpent-like tail quick to lash out like a viper being cornered. Wings that hover above my head and fan wide at my sides.

The true form of a Succubus from Hell.

I retract my talons back into myself, hiding them once more beneath my human form. I tilt my head, glancing at the mouth that gapes wide open before fixing my gaze on the blood that pools itself from his neck.

I look up, fanning my gaze to both ends of the alley before I lower myself down.

I loop my hands underneath his shoulders, hauling him and leaning up against the concrete wall of some coffee shop I've never paid interest in trying. A smirk curves my lips as I dip my fingers into the crimson liquid, and begin writing a message on the wall just above his severed neck.

I admire my work before leaning over to pick his lifeless head up. I lower it down in front of his limp body, setting his head precisely into the palms of his hands, his head facing forward as he cradles it in his lap. I pat the top of his head before standing myself up, making a pouty face at him. "Looks like you were in need of someone *big* and *strong* to protect you tonight."

I wipe my hands on my leggings, cursing beneath my breath. "Now I'll have to soak these in hydrogen peroxide to get the blood out." I haul my dance bag taut up my shoulder and continue my walk to my penthouse, my heels clicking against the concrete the only noise to fill the alley.

Taking one last look at the words I've smeared on the wall with his own blood, I smile wickedly to myself before carrying on with my night.

Did you see what he was wearing? He was asking for it.

Chapter 5

Levi

Before her head can turn in my direction I step back, slipping myself back into the shadows of the exit door frame. I stand there, slowing my breathing to an almost nothingness, quietly waiting until I hear a soft thud.

I slowly peer my gaze back around, leaning up against the concrete wall as I watch as she begins writing on the wall above a now lifeless, limp Jake.

The man I was hired to kill tonight.

I'd followed him from the club, my second motive for being at The Playground tonight other than studying and observing her. I kept a far enough distance back, concealing myself in the shadows as I followed him. When I finally closed in on the alley he winded himself through, that's when I saw it.

The way he forced himself on her proved exactly why I was hired to kill him. A pathetic man who thinks he can cheat his way in life without paying the proper consequences.

Jake Larson, a middle man for weaponry that my boss had the unfortunate pleasure of doing business with. Who not only shorted Sawyer on his cut, but had the audacity to gaslight him and say that's not what the deal was.

Man had some big balls to try fucking over the Don of The Deimari Mafia.

As soon as I was about to step in and handle the son of a bitch before he could try getting his way with her, that's when she struck.

Her claws swiped through his neck like a damn blade. A clean fucking cut.

"Now I'll have to soak these in hydrogen peroxide to get the blood out."

Her voice breaks through my thoughts as I step back into the doorway. Chuckling internally to myself that out of all things that's what she would be concerned about.

As I begin to hear her heels click against the concrete, I smirk to myself as I pull out my phone, leaning around the corner of the wall. I make sure my phone is on silent and the flash is off as I open the camera app, snapping a photo of her leaving the scene. I tuck the phone back into my pocket, waiting until she's long gone before I check my surroundings, listening.

When the quietness that fills the alley confirms that no one else is out here, I slip through the alley. Keeping to the far wall and out of sight.

I approach the body, peering closer to read what she wrote on the wall. I shake my head slowly as a wicked grin curves my lips.

Damn, that's actually fucking hot.

My cock grows hard in my pants as I'm immediately insanely turned on by not only how she handled the situation, but the carelessness that she exuded for this pathetic man.

A kind of carelessness I would've exuded no less.

My phone buzzes in my pocket. I reach for it, reading the text message that Dex sent me.

And when I read the intel that Dex obtained for me on her, I grin to myself as my plan just got a whole lot more interesting. And my means of getting her to work with me just got a hell of a lot easier.

Chapter 6

Amelia

As soon as I unlock my penthouse door I dump my dance bag onto the polished wood floor. Inspecting my coat for blood before trailing it off me, I'm momentarily distracted by the sound of nails tapping against the hardwood floor as the Hellhound races towards me.

"Hi, my sweetness." I say sweetly to Rufus as I lower down to lightly scratch my acrylic nails behind his pin straight ears.

He begins sniffing at me as his nub of a tail begins wagging wildly. He huffs a low bark at me as I straighten again, finally slipping my coat off of me.

"I know, I smell." I hang it on the mounted coat rack before pulling my boots off, setting them on the entryway rug. I walk down the hallway until I reach my kitchen extending the entire left section of the room. I approach the waterfall island, setting my phone on top of the black marble design before turning the other direction for the staircase.

Rufus follows me as I walk up the wooden steps to the second level. My feet step out onto the laminate flooring before quickly sinking into my plush area rug. I walk past my bed, making my way into my connected bathroom when Rufus gives me another bark.

I look down at him, sighing as I turn on the lights. "I'm not hurt."

He stares at me for a moment before making his way across the marbled flooring to the stand-up shower. He lays himself down, taking his place as guard dog as I ready to get in the shower. My loyal companion and watchdog.

I smile at him before peeling my clothing off, discarding it in the sleek black sink. I peer my gaze up to a symphony of lights through floor to ceiling windows, displaying the best view of Lilitu City. My gaze roams over the explosion of luminescent colors against a quiet and starry winter night. My gaze lowers to the Cimiteria Sea, situated in the middle of Lilitu City as it stretches out past The Pleasure District, connecting to the coast at the edge of the city.

I lower my hand down to the cabinet below, pulling one side open as I search for that dark brown bottle. "Where are you—ah ha!" I exclaim, pulling out the hydrogen peroxide.

I set it on the counter as I close the sink drain, pouring some into the sink before submerging my clothes into the liquid, letting them soak. I twist the cap back on, setting it on top of the black quartz counter as I walk over to the standing shower, turning it on.

I step inside, closing the glass door behind me before submerging myself under the hot water. I stand there for a long moment before gently running my hands over my face, scrubbing off my makeup and the spray of blood on my face.

Once I finish, I step out onto my black plush rug, grabbing a matching towel hanging on the rack. I wrap it around my body before I use a microfiber towel to wrap my long hair up. I step out of the bathroom and head into my walk-in closet.

I turn on the light, illuminating the ivory shelves and racks within. Dresses and everyday attire beginning from the right wall, followed by all of my dance and work outfits that take up the entire middle wall. Pieces ranging from lacy hot pink two-pieces to leather bondage. Four rows of drawers stretching from the floor up, filled with more lingerie, bras, panties, and role-playing outfits. In the very middle are two large rows of floor-to-ceiling shelves of heels. Each shelf ranging from black kitten heels to fire-red seven inch stilettos.

The closet is definitely big enough to be someone's bedroom.

I walk over to the left wall, filled with comfier clothing such as robes and sleep sets. I pull a cream-colored velvet hanger off the soft golden rack, slipping the pink sleep cami and pants off the hanger before setting it back onto the rack. I pull the silk over my body before turning the closet light off, heading back into my bedroom.

I make my way back down the stairs, Rufus following behind me. My bare feet pad over to the kitchen until I approach my stainless steel fridge, opening it and pulling out a glass tupperware of left-over pepperoni pizza. I lift off the cover, gently setting the dish into the microwave and setting the timer.

I walk over to the other end of my kitchen, opening the tall pantry door. I walk inside, pulling out a bag of dog kibble. Rufus trots over at the very moment he hears the sound of his kibble hitting the stainless steel bowl.

He plops his butt down as he sits there, staring up at me and waiting. I rub the top of his head before I put the bag back into the pantry, closing the door behind me. I face him as his gaze remains on me, waiting for me to give him the command to go ahead and eat.

I wait another moment before giving him the magic word. "Okay."

He lowers his head immediately and begins chowing down as I hear the beep go off on my microwave, pulling my leftovers out and doing the same.

After I've finished, I rinse the dish off in my deep-basin sink. I open my dishwasher, setting it in before closing it again. I walk past my kitchen island and over to the floor to ceiling windows that spread down the entire back wall of my living room. I walk up to the glass, staring below at the city lights of The Pleasure District in my penthouse suite.

I hear my phone buzz on my granite kitchen island. I walk back over to the kitchen, picking my phone up and smile as I read the text that comes through.

Just saw on the news of some guy's head getting chopped off.

I begin typing as I reply to Anastasia.

Oh really?

Yeah. What's most interesting though was the message displayed above his body.

I chuckle to myself as I head back upstairs, going to inspect my clothes. Before I can send her a text back, she sends me another.

Care to explain?

I twist my lips to a half smile, typing out my response.

I don't know what you're talking about. :)

I close out the thread entirely and set my phone down onto the bathroom counter, dipping my hands into the hydrogen peroxide as I pull my leggings out. I begin scrubbing the blood I wiped on them when another text comes through.

I lean over, reading it to myself before a laugh escapes my lips. I continue scrubbing my leggings as my half-grin turns into a wide smirk.

Next time aim for the balls. xoxo

Chapter 7

The next night I'm back at the club and these hipster college guys are already pissing me off. Not even forty-five minutes into my shift did I already get a guy asking if I'd give him a lapdance for twenty instead of fifty.

I'd asked him if he was struggling and was looking for work. Once I mentioned that I was pretty sure we were still looking for someone to fill our janitor position, he called me a bitch and walked away.

I was only offended because he forgot to add *sexy* in front of it. Though the satisfaction of seeing his fragile ego crumble made up for it.

At least the guy I'm dancing for now is quiet and not trying to talk my ear off as if I'm his therapist. A rare occurrence that I quite enjoy when it does arise.

I continue rotating my hips slowly in my black and red mini skirt. Though I can hardly call this a mini skirt as almost half of my ass pokes out of it.

As the song comes to an end, I lean forward as I lower my ass down into his lap, grinding on him. My exposed breasts heaving forward as he keeps his hands firmly on the chair's armrests.

Thank gods he's not trying to get handsy.

The song blasting through the club begins to dwindle before completely transitioning into the next one. I stand myself up, turning around to face him. "You want another?"

I watch as he works on a swallow, sweat beading on the top of his brow. Awe, he's nervous.

He shakes his head, rubbing his hands on his blue jeans. "No, one is fine. Thank you." His blue eyes lock onto mine before standing himself up, my gaze falling to the bulge against his pants. He grabs his drink and hurries out of the section, slipping himself around the black velvet curtain.

A snort escapes me. "First time I guess." I lower down to grab my black bikini top, securing it back on before leaving the private section as well.

I make my way over to the bar, plopping myself down onto a bar-stool as Ace approaches me with a cranberry vodka already in tow.

I take a look down the bar and notice only one man sitting at the far end. "I take it you're having a slow night, too."

He slides the drink towards me, leaning his head as he shrugs. "It could definitely be busier. You?"

I shrug my shoulders before grabbing the drink, taking a generous sip. "Same. But who knows, maybe our luck will change." I smirk at him.

"I can make that happen."

I look to my left as a man approaches me, definitely *not* a young college kid. I stare at him, mid-sip of my drink when I lower the glass to the bar counter. I peer my gaze at him, tilting my head. "And I suppose you're here to do just that?"

I study him, recognizing him from last night. I'd seen him only briefly, but I'd definitely remember that handsome face anywhere. Those gorgeous dark-brown eyes underneath that well-groomed head of dark blonde hair, his wavy strands resting close to his forehead. My gaze lowers to that sharp jaw of his set against his sun-kissed tan skin.

He seats himself down, his forearm muscles beneath his rolled sleeves putting his tattoos on display. "I'd rather let you be the judge of that." He says through a low voice, one that carries a confidence that only few men have. He glances at Ace, ordering himself a whiskey neat.

I chuckle softly as I turn my seat towards him, fluttering my lashes up at him. "I fear you may be exerting your chances with someone who is not easily impressed." I lower my hand to my drink, bringing it up to my chest as I take a sip through the straw.

Ace brings him his drink. I watch as the man reaches into his pocket, pulls out a wad of cash and hands him a fifty dollar bill. "Keep the change, man."

Ace thanks him before taking the money. I watch from the corner of my eye as he turns towards the register, peering a glance up at me as a half smirk crawls up his lips.

I watch the man shove his wallet back into his pocket, the veins in his forearm bulging against his tanned skin. "Maybe I like a challenge."

I lift my gaze up to him, watching as he brings his whiskey to his lips, taking a drink. I huff out a noise as I cross one leg over the other, satisfied when I catch his gaze following the movement. "And your name is?"

"Levi." He goes to reach out his hand. "I hear your name is Cherry?"

I lift my hand, placing it inside of his. "You heard correctly."

He lifts my hand to his lips, pressing a soft kiss there as excitement thrums itself through my veins.

Oh, I'm going to have fun with this one.

He lowers it back down, a soft grin appearing. "Pleased to meet you."

I nod vaguely, observing him as I take another sip of my drink. I lean my elbow gracefully onto the counter, intentionally putting my hardly covered breasts on full display. I watch him, waiting for his gaze to lower but it stays fixated on my face. "So tell me, Levi. Is staring at beautiful women how you fulfill your boredom or what are your intentions for being here a second night in a row?"

He chuckles, his white teeth glinting against the chandelier above. He sips his whiskey before setting it down again. "I left last night with expectations not met that I was hoping to fulfill tonight."

"And what exactly is that?"

His gaze flickers over my face as a half grin lifts the corner of his full lips. "Spending time with you, of course."

A laugh escapes me as I lean back in my chair. "I fear you have me mistaken because I do not *spend time* with customers. Not for free that is."

He reaches into his pocket again, shuffling through his wallet until he slides towards me four hundred dollars. He glances up at me through those piercing brown eyes. "Maybe this will change your mind."

I stare at the money for a short moment before a soft grin curves my lips. I take the money and tuck it into my bikini top, watching his gaze finally dip below my face before quickly meeting my gaze again. "I guess this means we should take this party to a VIP room then." I begin to step out of the chair when he gently places a hand on my wrist, halting me.

"I wasn't paying for a VIP." He says as he stands up, lowering his hand down at his side.

My brows knit together as I look up at him. "Then what exactly were you—"

His hand comes to rest on the back of the stool, his face leaning in near my ear as he whispers. The close contact catching me momentarily off guard. "I only want a dance."

His face pulls back and I suddenly despise the thrill that courses itself through my blood. I sigh as he pulls my chair out for me, stepping back a step.

He holds his hand out as I grab it, guiding me out of the seat before lowering his hand at his side.

I decided at that moment to not question this man overpaying me for a lapdance and to run with it. I smirk at him before turning around. "Follow me."

I walk us over to the far left of the main stage. To the wall carved with several open awnings as velvet curtains part in the middle, pulled to the side to display the private sections tucked within. A room big enough to fit two—maybe three people, exclusively meant for private dances.

I approach an empty section, my hand resting on the black curtain as I nod for him to step inside. I pull the curtain closed as he seats himself down onto the leather chair, the dim lighting above creating a sensual and moody ambiance. I watch as he leans back into the chair, his legs opening ever so slightly as his arms rest casually on the armrest.

I smirk at him, an excitement eliciting a thrill in me that I haven't felt in a long, long time. "I'll tell you only once. If you grope me, I kick you in the balls and the dance is over. Understood?"

He nods his head, a grin spreading on his full lips. "Understood."

I nod my head as the song blaring in the club comes to an end. And as the next song begins, I dance for my next customer.

Chapter 8

Levi

Fuck is she gorgeous.

As soon as the next song started playing she got right into it and gods damn I can't look away.

My gaze pierces onto her red nails as they slither down her breasts, lowering behind her back as she ever so fucking slowly unties the strings keeping her bikini top together. My gaze tracks over that tiny piece of black fabric as it shimmies off her breasts and down her stomach, landing on the floor.

Her hands come up to her breasts as she massages them, taunting me before she lowers a knee in between my legs. She leans into me, her arms coming around my neck as they rest along the back of the chair. Her breasts within inches of my face as I try my fucking hardest to keep looking at her face.

Focus, Levi. Remember the plan.

I take a breath in before releasing, keeping my hands cemented onto the armrests. She leans her head in, her lips inches away from my neck and I begin to feel that energy surge between us. Like a gravitational pull that magnetizes me to her, a trap that instantly lures me in.

She takes my hand, moving it as she takes her other leg, resting her knee where my hand was. She lowers my hand to her knee, her skin buttery soft.

I go to swipe it away when she meets my gaze, stilling myself from moving it further away. "It's okay. I'm giving you permission as long as you keep it there."

I slowly move it back to her knee, keeping it there and not moving a damn muscle as I nod my understanding.

She lowers her head, fluttering her lashes at me when she begins rotating her hips. Her breasts are touching my chest now as she moves her hips above my lap.

"Is this what you imagined when you said you wanted to spend time with me?" She says, her voice suddenly coaxing me as if I'm a bee swarming towards a pot of honey.

Her breath dances above my lips as I lower my gaze to them. Knowing she's getting off on my noticing her, watching her. I chuckle deep in my throat as I slowly fan my fingers out on her thigh. "Something like this."

She laughs and damnit I'd be lying if I said it didn't send electricity through my entire body. "Good, I'm glad you found what you were—" She lowers herself completely onto my lap, her knee lowering from the armrest and my hand with it.

"Looking for." She begins slowly gyrating on my lap.

Fuck—now. It's got to be now.

"I couldn't help myself watching you last night either."

She makes a noise low in her throat, pulling her head back to look at me. A wicked smirk curves her full red lips. Lips that I would love nothing more than to kiss—

Cut it out, Levi. This is just her Succubus energy fucking with me.

"Well why watch me from afar when you could've just approached me?" She asks sweetly.

I chuckle, her hips still rotating on my lap. "I could've, but I fear I would've interrupted that little party trick of yours. It was quite interesting to see it first hand with those two gentlemen that accompanied you."

She continues slowly moving her hips, not even flinching or hesitating at my words. She tilts her head. "I think being beautiful enough to attract men doesn't qualify as a trick when they come so willingly. Like you, for example."

Oh, she's a good little tease.

"You know what I think?"

She hums. "What's that?"

I lean in closer to her, whispering. "I think you fail to realize that while most men in this club are too lust-sick to realize that you're a Succubus, I'm not."

She tilts her head, laughing. "You are a funny little man. I didn't realize you had jokes." Her hands resting around my neck suddenly begin fanning themselves through my hair. The tips of her nails gently gliding along my scalp.

I lean forward closer into her, keeping my hand right where it is on her thigh. "Oh, I'm anything but little. I think you can attest to that."

Her gaze pierces onto mine as I grin up at her, knowing she can feel how hard I am against her. A tease and a match to her own game.

"But that's not entirely what caught my attention last night. I think the real *cherry* on top was the display you made in the alley."

She finally slows her hips, rotating them slightly slower. In a split moment, she tries to hop off of me before I grab her waist, pulling her back onto my lap.

I lean in right up to her ear, whispering as my breath dances across her skin. "Don't worry, I won't tell anyone." I remove my hands from her waist and rest them on the armrest at my sides.

Instead of getting up right she stays seated in my lap. Though the anger simmering beneath her is not hard to miss. "Then what do you want? And I'd advise you to answer *wisely*, or you just might meet his same fate." She seethes.

I idly tap an index finger on the armrest as I lean back a little. "I want you to work for me."

She stares at me for a moment before she begins laughing, her chest bouncing at the movement. "Sweetheart, I'm perfectly happy here. But thanks."

"Consider it more of a...part-time gig. That is unless you want me to show the police proof of what you did."

She leans back as her gaze hardens onto mine. "You're bluffing."

I grin at her as I feel the trickle of tension seep into her body. She finally stands up, removing herself from my lap entirely. "Imagine having a great job with great income, men that have no idea what you actually are and get to use that to your advantage, with a great penthouse. What a shame it would be if The Pleasure District would find out."

She makes a harsh huffing noise. "You're blackmailing me so I can work for you and do *what* exactly?"

I stand up from my chair, approaching her. I raise a hand up to her chin as she tries to flinch from my grasp. I force her gaze back onto me. "I want you to do exactly what you're good at, *Amelia*."

Her gaze widens at the reveal of her real name, quickly hardening as anger boils beneath those amber eyes.

I lower to the ground, grabbing her bikini top and handing it to her. She whips it out of my hand.

"All I need from you is to lure them in for me. I'll handle the rest."

She rolls her eyes. "Don't tell me you're a wannabe hitman."

I step right up to her, grabbing her face and tugging her closer. "I'm *anything* but a wannabe, little red. And I would be careful how you run that pretty little mouth around me. Because it might just land you as my next target."

Amusement lights up her gaze as she laughs, her eyes churning brightly. "What a brave man to assert himself against someone of my kind, when I could kill you quicker than the rate at which your heart beat tonight as I sat upon your lap."

I let go of her chin, straightening out my black button down shirt. My hand wraps around the cuffs rolled up to my elbows, adjusting it. "You'll hear from me in less than twenty-four hours with your first assignment." I raise my hand to the curtain, going to pull it back when she grabs my arm.

She grins up at me, tilting her head as I meet her gaze. "Until you cave."

I furrow my brows at her.

She lowers her gaze to my lips before raising them again. "I will agree to work *with* you, as I do not work *for* anyone. But only until you cave into your desire for me. Then this arrangement is over."

I scoff at her. "Sweetheart, this is just a business arrangement. I know how to discipline myself against that *power* of yours."

She smirks up at me. "Really? Because your cock pressed up against your pants tonight told me otherwise." She lowers her hand before fastening the bikini top back onto her chest. My gaze betraying my restraint and tracking her movement.

She turns around, opening the curtain and clasping it to the hook on the side as we're met with the rest of the club. She turns her head around, her gaze on mine as she smiles. "Enjoy your night,

Levi." My name sounding like the smoothest taste of whiskey on her lips.

She turns back around, leaving the section entirely as I look down at my pants. I curse beneath my breath as I fix myself, tampering the bulge from my pants as I stand there and wonder what the fuck I just got myself into.

Chapter 9

Amelia

What a bold man to think he could blackmail *me*. Knowing what I am and still insisting that I take orders from him?

Pft, he has no idea what he's dealing with. But oh how I will thoroughly enjoy making him go insane by the end of it all.

At least he's actually good looking. That is a plus to this whole *arrangement*.

Last night was the first time in a long, long time that I stumbled upon someone who I didn't completely revolt, but was rather intrigued by. Dancing and entertaining men at the club is like any other job, it's just work. I go in for my shift, seduce—and sometimes degrade men to make a quick coin, and leave at the end of it. But the energy that radiated off of Levi was...exciting to say the least.

The esthetician's soft fingers apply the final product on my face, presuming some kind of sunscreen. She generously rubs it in until she lightly pats it into my cheeks and forehead. She gives me a light pat on my shoulder, her voice a soft whisper as she speaks. "All done, my dear." Her warm demeanor perfect for this kind of profession.

I open my eyes, the spa lamp hovering above me shuts off as she pushes it away from the spa bed. She leans over a small table next to her, grabbing a handheld mirror before holding it above me.

I turn my face from side to side, admiring the glow emanating off of my clear porcelain skin. A once a month facial is a necessary spa treatment for keeping me both looking, and feeling my best. I smile genuinely as I look up at her. "Thank you."

She nods before setting the mirror down. My gaze follows her warm ginger hair braided back from her face as it trails down the middle of her back.

I bring myself up to a seated position, stretching my arms out before standing up from the table. My gaze fixates on the oil diffuser at the other end of the room, a small bluetooth speaker situated next to it. Relaxing waterfall sounds play out of it, adding to the calm ambiance of the room.

I stand up and walk over to the wooden chair set against the wall beneath an awning window. I reach inside my black purse, pulling out my phone.

Nothing yet.

He said I'd hear from him twenty-four hours from last night, so I didn't expect to hear anything at noon. But still, I found myself checking anyhow.

I pull out my wallet, shuffling through the crisp hundred dollar bills until I pull two out. I shove my wallet back into my large bag before hooking it over my shoulder.

"Here." I hand the cash over to her as her rich brown eyes meet mine. "Keep the extra fifty."

"Thank you, dear." She says sweetly, a smile curving her lips before she walks over to her bag, putting the money inside.

I nod my head, tossing my long hair back behind my shoulder. "Same time next month?"

Theresa nods her head. "I'll book you in."

"Great. See you then." I say before opening the suite door and walking out into the hallway.

I pass a hallway of other office rooms, home to other small business owners leasing them. Some doors with the curtains drawn over the glass center, some with privacy film over the entirety of the glass itself. I approach the elevator doors, pressing the downward arrow for the main floor.

A faint buzzing sound from my phone prompts me to pull it out from my purse. I look at the screen and a smirk crawls up my lips, a snort getting trapped in my nose.

The elevator door opens as I step inside, hitting the glowing button for level one. The door closes as I lean back against the cool railing, opening my home security app on my phone. I pull up a live feed of a very bored Hellhound seated right in front of the camera that faces the living room.

I switch the audio on that camera to on as a sigh leaves me. "I'll be home soon, Rufus. Then we can go for a walk."

I watch the boredom leave his face as his ears twitch at the sound of his favorite word.

Well, one of them at least.

I watch as he lifts his rear, now standing up on all fours. His nub of a tail begins to wiggle, anticipation building within him. He barks at the camera as if to say *hurry woman, I want to go outside NOW*.

I laugh into the phone. "I'll be home soon." I switch the audio to mute, putting my phone back into my purse as the elevator door opens.

I step out onto the egg shell epoxy flooring. My black pointed heels clicking against the hard ground with each step. I nod at the security guard posted at the entrance, a set of glass doors to match the floor to ceiling windows of the tall building.

He opens the door for me, stepping back. "Good day." He says, smiling.

I wield my power to the surface, just for the fuck of it. I watch as his eyes soften before gazing longingly at me. I smirk at him as his shoulders slump slightly forward. "Thank you."

I exit the building, severing the magnetic cord entirely. I look back to see him shake his head, still holding the door open even after I've exited the building. He quickly lowers his hand, stepping back into his post beside the door.

I laugh to myself as my phone buzzes in my purse again. I exhale, dragging my phone out.

When I expect to see another alert of motion at my living room camera from Rufus, I find a text instead from an unknown number.

Really? The security guard?

I lift my gaze from my phone, peering my gaze casually from side to side before continuing my walk home. A smirk finds my lips again as I reply to who I can only guess is Levi. *Is stalking me part of our little arrangement now?*

The text bubble pops up, stilling momentarily until another text comes through.

I thought I'd be courteous and wait for your appointment with Theresa to be over with before having you get right to work.

My gaze freezes onto the phone screen before quickly reeling it back into a relaxed gaze. Before I can type my reply, another text from Levi pops up.

Man in navy blazer, straight ahead.

I nonchalantly raise my gaze down the street to the man holding a cup of coffee. His navy blazer open, showcasing his powder white button-down shirt. I watch him lift his coffee cup to his lips, his eyes fixating on a woman walking past him. He turns his head slightly, lowering his gaze to her ass. He turns back around, a smug grin curving his lips.

So he's a self-righteous pig. What about it?

That self-righteous pig is your first target. So lure him in like you do best.

I scoff at my phone, annoyed as I type back. *Can't this wait until tomorrow? I'd prefer to spend my days off from the club relaxing and enjoying them* by myself.

Too bad. Get it done.

I roll my eyes as I shove my phone into my purse, training my gaze up again at the man walking leisurely towards me. I look back at the coffee in his hand, rolling my eyes once again.

This really is too easy.

I look down at my faux fur coat, pulling it open before tugging my coral v-neck shirt down just enough to put my breasts further on display.

I begin walking towards him, turning my gaze down into my bag as I pretend to be looking for my phone. As I feel myself approach him, I step into him just enough to bump the coffee in his hands to splatter onto his shirt.

I whip my head up, my hand lightly coming to his bicep. "Oh—I'm so sorry!"

He pulls his shirt away from his chest, examining the mocha stain seeping into the fabric as he curses. "It's fine, just watch where you're—"

He lifts his gaze up and completely stammers on his words. Not even needing to raise my magnetism to the surface to hypnotize him.

He stares at me with his mouth gaped open as I gently, intentionally squeeze his arm. "You're right. I'm so sorry I really need to pay attention to where I'm going—"

"No," He interjects as he turns himself fully towards me. He shakes his head as his gaze glances down to my chest before raising again. That same smug smile greeting his face once more. "It's completely fine. I have other shirts in my office."

I play into the little facade and flutter my lashes at him, a fake shy smile curving my lips. I force a blush to my cheeks to make him think I'm just as starstruck as he is. "Please, you must let me make it up to you."

His gaze tracks over me until recognition flares in his face. "You're Cherry—right? From The Playground."

There you go pal, took you long enough.

I grin deeper at him as I tilt my head, running my hand down his bicep until I remove my hand entirely. His gaze tracks the movement like I suspected it would.

Gods, men are so easy.

"Yes. Have you been?" I ask sweetly.

"No, but I've heard of you. I—I've always meant to come see you but just never got the chance." He lowers a hand into his pants pocket, flexing his arm.

"Well it looks like fate has a funny way of working sometimes." I force a lighthearted laugh before I twinkle my eyes at him. "You know, I'm actually off work tonight. Why don't I buy you a drink over at Vixens? It's the least I can do." I lower my gaze to his shirt before lifting it again, training it on his lips for a long moment before lifting it to meet his gaze.

He stills for a moment, noticing where my attention landed before his voice drops an octave. "I'd appreciate that. Does ten sound good?"

I'd appreciate that? Ew, the least he could do is thank me for allowing him to be in my presence. But nonetheless, I have him locked in.

I nod slowly. "That sounds wonderful—"

"Ian." He says as he holds his hand out. I lower my hand into his before he lifts it up to his lips.

Good thing I planned on showering after taking Rufus for a walk anyway.

"Ian, it's a pleasure to meet you." I lie smoothly through a sultry tone. "I'll see you then." I give him a wink before walking away entirely. Feeling the brand of his stare on my ass the whole way down the street.

Once I've rounded the brick corner of some apartment building, I pull out my phone from my purse. Opening the text thread to Levi.

Vixens at ten. And don't keep me waiting. I'd rather not entertain the man longer than absolutely necessary.

I watch the text bubble pop up before he replies a moment later. A smirk on my face as I read his reply before slipping my phone back into my purse. Continuing my short walk back home.

I think I found you hotter when you weren't so whiny. I'll be there before you can order your second drink.

Chapter 10

Seated at the bar counter, I make eye contact with the bartender on shift tonight. A curvy woman with medium-length golden blonde hair. Nikki, I think her name is.

"What can I get ya?" She asks as her green eyes pierce into mine, a certain edginess to her stare that I can only assume is because of how packed it is in here tonight. Though to be fair, Vixens is packed pretty much every night of the week.

"I'll take a lime margarita. On the rocks."

She nods her head as she walks down the bar and prepares my drink.

As I sit in the bar chair, I keep my attention fixed straight ahead of me on the back bar wall. Keeping my composure relaxed and disinterested as I wait for Ian to arrive.

Nikki approaches me, sliding my drink towards me. "Twelve dollars." She says curtly, her gaze roaming down to the gentlemen flagging her down as he squeezes himself next to the man seated down.

I pull out a crisp fifty from my purse, handing it to her. "Keep the change."

She lifts her gaze, nodding her head once before taking the money and walking over to the register. I watch as her mauve nails tap quickly against a bright screen before putting the money in the register. She pockets the extra thirty-eight before making her way down to the gentlemen. I go to take a sip of my drink when I feel an energy approach me from behind.

"Generous of you." Ian says as he seats himself in the chair next to me. I'm immediately overwhelmed by a strong whiff of his musk-scented cologne, nearly barfing right there on the counter.

I turn my gaze to him, smiling. "I'm a generous kind of gal." I turn my chair towards him, hooking a bare leg over the other, watching as his gaze follows the movement. His gaze lifts up to my chest, my breasts nearly heaving out of this tight black dress. I reel in my revulsion as I remember I purposefully picked this dress to wear tonight, hoping that since it hugs all the right places that it'd spare me from having to do a lot of talking with this man.

He chuckles as he waves down the bartender, watching the annoyance spark in her eyes before she holds up a hand signaling she's coming. "From what I hear you're quite the opposite. I've never known a domme to be anything but."

I force a smirk up my lips. "If a client pays me to fulfill his fantasy then I don't see how that doesn't qualify me as being generous."

He leans back into his chair, his chestnut hair parted to the side and swooped back. Thankfully he omitted that tacky blazer and settled on a black suit jacket instead with black pants to match. "And what exactly do these fantasies look like?" His gaze roams over me.

I should claw those eyes from their sockets right here and now. But instead, I smile knowing the fate that is awaiting him momentarily. "That all depends. Some men like to be degraded while some," I lower a hand to retrieve my drink, bringing the straw to my lips. Taking a long drink before lowering it again, the anticipation in his eyes growing. "Like to just watch me."

The bartender comes over and takes his drink order. A whiskey sour. "And if you had to guess what kind of a man I am, what would you say?"

I feel the phone in my purse buzz, praying that it's Levi telling me he'll be here soon. I go to nonchalantly pull my phone out, keeping his gaze the entire time. I look down at my phone, nearly sighing of frustration when I see it's not Levi and Anastasia.

Missing you tonight. Xoxo

I lower the phone back into my bag but not before I notice the time reads ten-twenty.

Where the fuck is Levi?

I tilt my head, subtly willing my power to the surface. "I think you're a man who likes to watch, but I also think you're a man who likes to test a woman's boundaries."

I watch as his eyes soften, the Succubus energy holding him in place as I grab the hand that made its way to my thigh, his fingers splayed out on my bare skin. I lift his hand off me, lowering it to hang beside him. He watches me wholly, gazing at me aimlessly. Wondering if I can just keep him like this for the entire time instead of suffering to listen to him speak.

As if Levi could read my mind, my phone buzzes in my purse again. I reach for it, pulling it out when I read a text from him.

Tell the bartender you need to close out your tab.

My brows knit together as I respond. *I don't have a tab, you moron.*

Tell her it's under Levi. The basement is through the kitchen.

I glance up at Ian, still influenced by my energy and still staring at me. I lower my phone back into my purse, waiting until the bartender makes her way back around by me.

Once she approaches my side, I make eye contact with her nudging her over. "I need to close my tab."

She looks at me bewildered, lowering her voice as she leans in with her hands on the counter. As if she doesn't want to embarrass me. "You paid cash."

I lower my voice, staring at her. "My tab is under Levi."

She stares at me for a moment before vaguely nodding her head. She reaches for my drink, putting it in the sink before she discreetly swipes her hand over something next to it. She raises her hand onto the counter, laying her hand flat atop the wooden surface. Her gaze pierces mine. "Tell him I hold him to his word. I'm not in the middle of any of this."

I lower my gaze to her hand before laying my hand on top of hers, looking like to anyone else watching that I'm making a warm gesture. "You won't be."

She nods as she slips her hand away, my palm now laying on top of a cool, slender metal object.

A key.

I pull my hand away, pocketing the key into my purse as I turn towards Ian. I force a smile. "Let's go for a walk, Ian."

He nods, standing himself up from his chair before pulling mine out. I step out of it, wholly aware of the packed bar around us.

I casually loop my arm into his, my other hand coming up to his chest as I lean into him. Creating the facade that I'm just a girl about to go rail some guy in the bathroom.

I guide us to the back of the bar to a closed swinging door, light filtering through the creases of the doorway. We approach the door, pushing it open to an empty kitchen. We walk through the checker tiled floor to a locked door.

"If you wanted that much privacy, I would've just taken you back to—"

"Oh, shut up already." I say, annoyance clouding my tone as I pull out the key from my purse. I put the key into the lock, twisting the doorknob and pulling it open. My gaze lowers to the set of stairs that lead down into a dimly lit basement.

"What are you—"

"Quiet." I seethe as my gaze pierces into his, that power rising to the surface once more. "I don't know what you did to get his attention, but quite frankly I don't care." I tug on his arm, pulling us down to the first step before pulling the door closed behind us.

I pull him down the steps until we reach the basement floor, my gaze lifting to find Levi sitting in a chair at the center of the room. He instantly locks eyes with me before my gaze lowers to what he holds in his hands. To his forearms resting on top of his knees as he casually dangles a chef's knife in his hand.

Chapter 11

Levi

It takes a matter of seconds for Ian to recognize who I am, his face paling to a deathly gray hue. His lips begin to tremble as he brings his hands up to his chest, forming a praying gesture. "Mr. Lareux, I can explain—"

His stammering ceases abruptly as I stand from the rickety chair. His entire body freezes into place as I slowly advance towards him.

But not before I glance at Amelia again.

My eyes roam briefly over that tight black dress she has on before lifting them to her gaze. Her amber eyes glance down to the knife in my hands before lifting again. "Am I done here?" She asks, that snarky tone of hers doing everything except what she thought it intended to do.

"Not quite." My voice remains controlled and steady as I approach them.

I watch her gaze follow me as amusement flickers over her face before she smooths out her gaze once more.

I meet Ian's gaze, the terror in his eyes heating the blood in my veins. I inhale, drinking it in before I lay the tip of the blade across his cheek. His body starts to tremble uncontrollably as his eyes nearly pop out of their sockets. "Do you know what is going to happen tonight, Ian?"

He takes a shaky, ragged inhale in. He begins shaking his head. "Please, I—"

I shove the blade further into his cheek, puncturing the skin just enough for a trace of blood to bead to the surface. "You didn't answer the question." I purr.

He grimaces against the pressure of the knife, trembling as he gives a curt nod. "Yes."

A half-grin curves up one side of my lips. "And do you know *why* they must happen, Ian?"

A shaky exhale leaves him as he hesitates for a long moment. His lips quivering violently as he stammers over his words. "Th—there's been a misunderstanding. I—I had no idea who she was related to—"

"A misunderstanding?" I repeat slowly, each word tasting like venom in my mouth. A deep chuckle that resembles anything but humor escapes me as I lift my gaze up to Amelia, nodding towards the chair behind me. "Make him take a seat." I lower the knife and step back from them both.

She watches me for a moment before grabbing Ian's still-trembling face, forcing his gaze on her. I feel the power in her rise as her amber eyes glow vividly. She smiles sweetly as her words ooze out of her like butter. "Take a seat, Ian."

His trembling ceases as he stares at her, completely under her spell. He nods faintly before he turns around, moving to seat himself in the chair.

She looks at me, those eyes still churning brightly. "Is that satisfactory enough, Levi?"

It takes everything in me to not groan at the way she says my name, knowing full well her power is still lingering on the surface. Trying to make me cave.

Focus.

I exhale her affect, reeling myself in before turning away from her entirely. "Good enough."

I feel her power suddenly diminish before the sound of heels begin to click up the steps.

"You're not finished here." I say over my shoulder to her.

Her footsteps halt, and I can nearly feel the rage bubbling from her. "Says *who* exactly? What else do you wish for me to do? Watch?"

I turn towards her, a wicked grin deepening on my face. "If that's what you're into."

Her face blanches as anger washes over her gaze.

"But no, I need you to stay to help me carry him up the stairs."

A sultry laugh leaves her, skittering over my bones in an entirely too pleasant way. "If you aren't strong enough to carry him up then just say that."

I watch her as anger threatens to rise within me before I tamper it down, shrugging my shoulders nonchalantly instead. "It'll make for a quicker job for me." I grin at her before turning my back on her entirely, my attention now facing Ian.

I hear her stomp down the rickety, wooden steps before they halt on the concrete floor. "Hurry up then." She seethes.

Ian sits there, far calmer then moments ago thanks to her compulsion. I lower the knife I snagged from the kitchen upstairs, hoping Nikki doesn't mind my potentially messy method for killing this man.

Yet with the tarp underneath the chair, it should alleviate some of the mess. I sigh at the reminder that I don't have the time to drag his death out tonight, that unfortunately I have to make it quick.

Though he's far from deserving of it.

Usually when I'm given a job I don't ask many questions. But when I found out this involved Priscilla—Sawyer's niece, I was more than happy to take the job. Ian, a vile pig bold enough to expose nonconsensual photos of her giving him a blowjob onto an online platform, thinking he was safe from any repercussions. A damn fool wholly unaware that the same woman just happens to be the niece to the don of The Deimari Mafia.

The niece who's best friend just happens to be the bartender upstairs, giving me a perfect place to take care of him.

I raise his chin up with the blade of the knife, his eyes dulled with compulsion as I stare down at him.

"A misunderstanding, huh?" I chuckle as I press the knife in, wringing a whimper from low in his throat. "Well let me paint a *clear* picture of what happens to men like you who take advantage of women."

I shove the blade straight up through his throat, a choked noise following as blood gurgles out of Ian's mouth. Until moments later, his body falls forward onto the black tarp below as a wet thud follows.

Chapter 12

I lift the chair up and away from the tarp, setting it on the concrete nearby. Not a trace of blood stained on the wood material.

Thank fuck.

I lean down, wiping the knife's blade against his pants before shoving it into his pants pocket. I glance up at Amelia, her amber eyes boring into mine. I nod my head down at Ian as a sly grin curves my lips. "You gonna help or just stand there and look pretty?"

She huffs out an irritated exhale, rolling her eyes before looking over at the wire rack to the far wall, a box of black nitrile gloves sitting on a middle shelf. As she walks over I lower my gaze back down, beginning to undress him.

"Is that really necessary?" She asks from behind me.

I set his jacket into a black garbage bag next to me before starting on unbuttoning his shirt. I pull it out of his pants before looping his arms out of it, shoving it into the same bag. I lift my gaze to hers. "Yes." I say plainly before unbuttoning his pants.

She makes a low humming noise before leaning down in front of his head. "Fingerprints."

I pull his pants down to his ankles, lifting one leg up as I pull the pant leg free before doing the same to the other. "Precisely." I mutter.

I throw his pants into the bag before tying the bag closed. I glance over at her, noticing her kneeling above his head when I nudge to my side. "Get next to me so we can roll him up."

She moves to my side, her arm nearly brushing against mine. Through the metallic scent of him surrounding the dimly lit basement, the smell of vanilla and orchid wafts towards me. And I'd be lying if I didn't admit it was an intoxicating smell.

We both begin wrapping his body up before I tie three sections with a jute rope. One at the neck, one at the knees, and the last one at his ankles.

I lower myself to stand at his head, nudging her to his feet.

At my silent direction she moves to his feet, leaning down to lift his legs as I lean down to pick him up by his shoulders. As I move backwards up the stairs and we haul him up.

We reach the kitchen door and I halt, listening. I creak the door open, seeing it empty as I was promised it'd be. We step carefully through the kitchen and make our way out the adjacent back door.

A blast of cold air hits me as we step outside into the alley, my car parked right outside the door. We haul him out to my unlocked trunk, lifting it open with my elbow as we haul him. I lower his head and shoulders in, moving my hands down until I get down to his legs. Amelia lets go, stepping back as I haul the rest of his body in. I shut the trunk closed as I face her, holding my hand out. "Give me the key."

"It's in the basement in my purse." She goes to turn around to grab it when I hold my hand up.

"I'll get it. Just get in the car." I lower my hand but not before lowering my gaze to her still gloved hands.

"You said you just needed me to help you haul him up." She says sternly as she nearly rips the gloves off. She slams them into my hand.

I reach the back door, turning towards her as I shrug my shoulders. A grin appearing on my face. "I know. But it's not every day that I have a partner to accompany me." I turn around and open the door.

I fully expected her to be waiting in that same spot, and once I retrieved her bag to have taken off. But when I return moments later with the garbage bag of his clothes and her purse, I'm wildly surprised when I see her sitting in the passenger seat. But I quickly wonder if she's only opted to sit in my car because it's cold as fuck out here, and not because she actually wants to ride along.

Nonetheless, I find humor in the irritation creasing a frown on her face.

A smirk crawls up my lips as I lift the trunk, shedding off my own gloves and tucking them into the garbage bag before plopping it in with his body before closing it shut. I walk around to the driver's side door, opening it as I climb in and hand over her purse.

She rummages through it until she holds out a key. I watch for a moment as disdain splashes across her face as she hands it over to me, but nonetheless she leans back into the seat as she huffs out an exhale. "Where are we dumping him?"

I pocket the key into my pants, turning the ignition over as my car starts. The same smirk moments ago making another appearance on my face. "Same place where I usually dump them."

Chapter 13

Amelia

We drive up to a cargo lot on the edge of the Cimeteria Sea. The water pitch black against the night sky save for the glow of the moonlight shining above.

As he turns the ignition off I open my door, stepping out of the vehicle. "Throwing a body overboard. How original." I say lazily.

Levi hops out, closing his door as he moves to open up the trunk. His rich brown eyes like lifeless voids against the dimly lit lot. "It gets the job done." He pulls out two weighted plates, tying one through the rope around his neck, and then another one through the rope at his feet. He lays them both on top of Ian's body as he begins hauling him out.

I reach down to grab his ankles, hauling him from the trunk as we walk the few feet to the edge of the lot.

"You know, if I didn't know any better I'd say you're actually enjoying this." Levi says, a smug grin on his face.

I roll my eyes at him, and as we reach the edge of the platform, I—for a moment fantasize about pushing Levi into the water below. But I feel nice tonight, so I refrain myself from doing so. "I fear you're reading far too deep into this business arrangement of ours."

He chuckles as we both lay his body down onto the ground. We both stand up straight as he looks at me. "Maybe." He lifts a leg, kicking Ian's body forward until he rolls off the edge and down into the sea below. "Maybe not." He winks at me before walking back to the car. "I'll give you a ride home."

I watch him walk towards the car, the moon illuminating his dark blonde hair. He raises a calloused hand, pushing a loose strand back from his forehead. And because it's a particularly cold night where the thought of walking all the way back home doesn't sound pleasing, I follow him back to the car and allow him to give me a ride home.

I sigh into the heated seats, the warmth comforting my ice-pricked bare legs. I keep my gaze looking out of my window, peering up at the city lights of Lilitu. I raise a hand, inspecting my nails. Pleased at the fact that they didn't puncture those gloves and stain my nails with blood. "Who else knows?"

I feel Levi's gaze sneak a glance at me before training it back onto the road. "Just my partners and I."

"How many?" I ask. The thought of anyone other than the club employees knowing that I'm a Succubus fills me with a sense of annoyance.

"Just the inner circle." He says.

I finally look over at him as he meets my gaze. He chuckles to himself, presumably from the look of annoyance on my face. "Three. There's three of us who know."

I train my gaze forward, the nightlife dwindling down as we head into the wee hours of the night. I nod my head, electing to say nothing as I lean my head back against the headrest.

"Why do you do it?"

I groan at his perfect timing to ruin a peaceful moment of silence. "Why do you do what you do?" I retorted.

He makes a low noise in his throat, akin to a laugh that never escaped past his full lips. "It's a job."

"Out of everything else you could've picked?" I drawl.

He shrugs a shoulder, that nonchalant demeanor irritating. "And the same doesn't apply to you?"

I bite back my retort, stifling my remark entirely. I exhale long and slow, pausing for a long moment. "I'm not meant for an ordinary life. I have the ability to seduce men, and I do it well. So why not use it to my own advantage?" I lift my gaze to his before lowering it to his hand stretched over the wheel. His veins bulge from his hand like a siren's wicked delight. "Where's the dignity in having my sexuality stripped from a narrow-minded society when I can express it freely."

He glances over at me, a half grin turning up his lips. "I couldn't agree more." He faces the road again, turning the wheel to pull up alongside the curb. The awning lights of my apartment building filter through the vehicle window.

"I'm surprised."

He glances over at me again.

"Usually men want to *fix* women like me. Responding with things like 'I can take you out of the game.' Or 'you're better than that life'." I look over at him as I watch him put the car in park.

He rests his hand on the console as he narrows his gaze. "My opinion on sex work doesn't include the prejudice that most men have for it. I'm not threatened by a woman's desire to embody her sexuality how she sees fit." He shrugs his shoulders vaguely. "To be quite honest, it's also none of my business how others choose to make a living. Especially not when I kill for mine."

I watch him for a long moment as his response charges through me, a mentality that most men don't have the common sense to have.

I nod my head slowly as I unbuckle my seatbelt, tugging my purse up. I give Levi a quick smile as I rest a hand on the door handle. "Thanks for the ride." I go to open the car door.

He nods his head. "See you next time."

I get out, turning around to close the car door as my heels click against the sidewalk. I smirk to myself before turning around, sticking my tongue out at him just for the fuck of it before I walk up the short set of concrete steps towards the entrance.

I grin the whole way up as I feel his gaze slither from my back, down to my ass before I disappear behind the double front doors.

Chapter 14

Levi

I circle my way back to Vixens, parking in the alley as I hop out of my black luxury vehicle. I make my way over to the back door once more, opening it as I step inside. The overhead kitchen lights still being on tells me that she's still here, even though the club is dead quiet now.

From the doorway leading into the club, I watch as Nikki slowly ushers in. She watches me intently as if I'm going to kill her next.

Killing women and children isn't my style, but I know telling her that won't ease the tension building in her face and shoulders.

"Is it..." She trails off, glancing a nervous look at the basement door.

"It's taken care of." I say plainly. I go into my pocket, pulling out the key and handing it to her.

She holds it tightly in her hand as a heavy exhale leaves her. She nods curtly at me. "Thank you."

I nod, glancing at the basement door. I nod towards it before I turn away. "Get some bleach on those doorknobs and the chair downstairs." I push the exit door open as I head back outside and into my car.

With nothing but the silence to greet me the whole way home.

⎯⎯⎯⎯⎯⎯⎯⎯⎯⎯

Three o'clock. Don't be late.

Looking down at my phone in the middle of the gym as a text from Sawyer comes through. A vague text with just a time.

All he needs to send for me to know he has another job for me, and to meet with him to discuss it further.

I type back into the text thread, sending a thumbs up before closing it out entirely. I tap my music app, shuffling through songs until I get to a rap song. I set my phone down on the ground before leaning over to grab the metal bar. As the music blares through my bluetooth headphones, I hike the bar up close to my chest, squaring my shoulders back before releasing again.

As I continue doing my reps, the image of Amelia's dress from last night floats through my mind. I pull the bar up to my chest again, feeling the burn in my upper biceps and back muscles. Fighting to distract myself from how good she looked last night. How her long, toned legs looked and wondering how they'd feel wrapped around—

Focus, you horny bastard. This is her Succubus energy influencing you.

I do another few reps before lowering the bar altogether. Sweat drips down my forehead before I wipe it away with the back of my arm. I run my hand through my hair, wiping the memory from my mind completely as I drown it out of my head.

I stand up, walking over to the cleaning station. I grab a paper towel, spraying the cleaning solution on it before I walk back over to the seated low cable row machine.

I wipe down the metal bar as well as my bench before throwing it out in the circular trash bin. I walk back to grab my phone and bottle of water, lifting off the cap to down a few sips. I twist the cap back on before walking over to the men's locker room.

I walk down the aisle, rows of treadmills and ellipticals on my left as I look down at my phone. I turn the corner, hitting pause on the music as I lift the headphones off my ears.

I open up my locker, grabbing my gym duffel bag out and setting it on the wood bench next to me. I take a towel out, blotting my face before setting it back in. I zipper the bag closed and hook it over my shoulder as I make my way to exit the gym.

I walk out of the locker room, turning the corner when a guy slams into my shoulder.

He steps back, glaring up at me considering he's shorter than me. He curses under his breath. "Watch where you're going, man."

I ask myself at that moment if I'm going to be a villain today, or if I'm going to spare this man his life and mind my business.

I decided to just mind my business.

I nod at him before continuing my walk through the gym until I make it outside to my car.

Chapter 15

I push my front door open, closing it behind me as I punch in the six-digit security code on the alarm system. I slip off my white sneakers, setting my duffel bag on the polished wood floor before making my way to the kitchen.

I open up the stainless steel fridge, pulling out a package of chicken tenderloins and plopping it onto the counter. Rummaging through the fridge once more until I pull out a bottle of teriyaki sauce, setting it on the counter before I close the fridge.

Pulling out a frying pan from a cabinet below, I set it on the stove top and turn the heat to medium-high. I drizzle a little olive oil into the pan before I open the package of chicken.

After taking the tendons out of the chicken and seasoning it, I begin cooking it in the pan while a pouch of rice cooks in the microwave behind me. Once everything is finished cooking, I assemble the rice in a bowl first, layering the teriyaki chicken on top. Not bothering to even sit down as I lean against the cool countertop and dig in.

My phone buzzes in my pocket as I scrape the white ceramic bowl clean. I set it in the sink before reaching into my pocket and pulling out my phone, rolling my eyes at the text on the screen.

How was your little date last night?

My fingers begin typing.

It's just work.

I go to set my phone on the counter, making to walk out of the kitchen when it buzzes again. I annoyedly picked it up, reading another text from Dex.

Riiiight.

I set the phone face down back onto the counter before I make my way upstairs to shower. Amelia's words ricocheting around in my head with each step I take.

Until you cave.

I pass my king sized bed as dark grey blankets lay messily sprawled on top. I walk over to my walk-in closet, pulling out some clean clothes before walking to the bathroom.

I turn the shower dial up to hot, stripping my clothes off before stepping under the scalding water.

For a long moment I just stand there, running my fingers through my wavy damp hair. Trying to block out the way that her amber eyes glowed so bright as she looked at me. Those words falling from her lips with such surety in my inability to stay disciplined enough not to cave for her.

At the reminder of how she looked last night, my cock threatens to grow hard.

Fucking damnit.

A gruff escapes me as I force myself to dismiss the image from my mind entirely. Grabbing the shampoo I pour some into the palm of my hand, lathering it into my hair.

Blanking out the thought of her entirely.

<hr>

I drive up the long brick driveway as the electronic iron gate slides shut behind me. Each side of the driveway lined with crushed stone, trailing all the way up until it curves into a wide circle.

I drive around the curve, parking my car behind his black escalade. I step out of my vehicle, closing the door behind me as the winter air pelts against my cheek. I shove my hands into my coat pockets as I make my way to the entrance doors.

Before I can even knock the door makes a clicking noise as it unlocks itself. As I pull it open I'm immediately hit with the heat indoors.

I close the door behind me, taking my shoes off and setting them on top of the entryway rug. I shrug my coat off, setting it onto the beige chaise lounge next to the door. I head right, walking across the marbled floor before making my way up the curved iron staircase. When I make it to the top of the stairs I hear the faint sound of papers shuffling, coming from down the hall. I pass by a half-moon table set up against the cream colored walls, panel molding lining both sides of the hallway throughout.

A large iron Victorian mirror hangs above the wooden table, wall sconces to occupy each side of it. In front of the far left corner of the mirror lies a vase full of dusted pink chrysanthemums, the water inside the vase filled a quarter of the way up. My gaze lifts up to admire the crown molding at the top of the wall before looking straight ahead again.

I keep walking until I approach a mahogany door left half-opened. I knock on twice on the wood, pushing the door open all the way.

Sawyer looks up from his executive desk, his eyes momentarily piercing into mine. He lowers his gaze back down to his stack of papers, waving his hand to the oxford leather chair to his left. "Sit."

I take my seat, glancing over to the window at the opposite wall cracked open. The cold winter breeze sneaking its way through the slim opening. "Ever heard of just turning down the heat?"

He signs his signature on a piece of paper before setting it aside. "I have." He says blandly.

"It's thirty degrees outside."

He leans down to pull out a gold yellow clasp envelope from a bottom drawer, setting it onto his desk as he meets my gaze. He lazily shrugs his shoulders, his stare cold and unfeeling. "I like the fresh air."

I chuckle, shaking my head before I nudge towards the folder. "What am I working with?" Already knowing that the file inside tells me everything I need to know about my next job.

He picks it up, tossing it over to me as I catch it in my lap. "He showed up at the police station this morning inquiring about filing for a missing persons report."

I open the envelope, pulling the papers out as I glance over the black-and-white photo of a middle-aged man.

"Carson was on duty and pulled him to an interrogation room to interview him." He lowers his hand to a glass decanter filled with dark amber liquid. He twists the cap off, pouring an earful into an empty glass.

I read the name to the left of the picture. "Wesley Gray—why does that last name sound familiar?" I raise my gaze up to Sawyer's.

He raises his whiskey to his lips, taking a sip. He sets the glass down before leaning back into his leather chair. "That would be because he shares the same last name as Ian's."

I nod my head slowly, understanding settling in. "His brother."

Sawyer vaguely nods his head. He glances towards the papers I hold in my hand. "He told Carson that he didn't show up for work this morning, stating that something was wrong." He takes another drink of his whiskey, downing the remainder of it before setting the empty glass down again. "He said Ian told him he was to meet up with a red-haired broad for drinks the night before."

A sudden tremor ticks in my jaw at the way Ian described Amelia, wishing now more than ever I could recreate last night all over again.

Where I would have elected to take my time with him instead of giving him the courtesy of a quick kill.

I skim through the papers, reading through all of Wesley's basic information. Where he lives, that he's not married, has no children, and also that he works for the same company his brother Ian does. "But he failed to mention anything further?" I ask, peering my gaze up for a quick moment before lowering it back down again.

"Correct." He says coolly, lifting a leg to cross over his knee. "Carson told him he'd put a missing person report on file, and said he'd call with any updates." He pauses for a moment. "Obviously that's not what happened."

Officer Carson is the chief of police, a favored member of the Districts community. Who, in exchange for working for Sawyer by keeping his dirty work concealed from the rest of the police force, gets to know first-hand the District's crimes.

I flip to the next page, skimming through Wesley's list of bank statements knowing Dex is the one who acquired them. I scoff at myself as I see one place in particular that he frequents every Thursday night. "Well that's not a coincidence." I say sarcastically.

"Clearly." Sawyer retorts, exhaling slowly. "But quite ironic that it should be the place that your new *partner* works at."

I raise my gaze up to him, finding his stare hardening onto me. Knowing from just his stare alone that he wants this handled promptly and quietly, before Wesley starts causing too much attention. I give Sawyer a nod. "He'll be handled."

Sawyer keeps his cold gaze locked onto mine, a slow nod following. My gaze briefly glances up to the tiny silver hoops pierced on both lobes, a mixture of black studs and more silver hoops traveling up both ears. "You have not failed me yet, Levi." He uncrosses his leg from over his knee, lowering it to the ground as his gaze remains on me. "But remember that I *allow* you to have this business arrangement. Don't make me regret it." He stands up from his chair, his all black suit smoothing out as he grabs his empty glass and exits his office. Declaring this meeting officially finished.

I shove the papers back into the envelope, clasping it closed as I pull out my phone. I bring up the text thread and begin typing.

Are you working tonight?

I go to put my phone back into my pocket, standing myself up from the chair. I exit the room, making my way down that curved staircase back to the main floor.

I slip my shoes and my coat back on when my phone vibrates. I pull it out, looking down at her response.

Miss me already?

I roll my eyes, sending a quick text back before putting my phone back into my pocket.

Save the lines for someone who's desperate enough to buy into them. I'll see you at ten.

I step out into the cool crisp weather, a smirk crawling up my lips before I shove it back down.

Chapter 16

Amelia

"Sorry sir, I don't have any change to spare."

I watch the quick rise of annoyance in Levi's face, his jaw ticking as he quickly smooths it out. He lowers his hand from my wrist, leaning forward in the round-backed leather chair. "Hilarious." He says dryly, a hint of sarcasm dancing in his tone. His gaze hardens onto mine before glancing over to the private seating. "We need to talk."

I exhale an audible breath, holding my hand out. "Still have to pay up like everyone else."

He reaches into his pocket, pulling out four hundred dollar bills. "How's that?"

I take the money, shoving it underneath my garter. I smirk down at him, my gaze traveling up as he stands up from the chair. "I'm certainly not opposed to you overpaying for a dance." I turn around, stepping away as I feel him follow behind me.

I take us through the club to the unoccupied section, allowing for him to enter first before pulling the velvet curtain closed behind me. He seats himself in the leather chair, sprawling his legs out as I go to lift my top off.

"Don't bother." Levi says, waving a hand as he props his elbow onto the armrest. "This will be quick."

My hands halt their movement behind my back as my brows knit together. "You paid for a lap dance?"

He rests the tips of his finger on his defined jaw. "Technically, I paid for your time. But you can still sit if you'd like." He smirks up at me as he glances down at his lap.

I lower my hands to my sides, following his gaze down to his lap. I roll my eyes before glancing at the open armrest, a faint smirk playing up my red lips. I approach it, seating myself on the leather material as I slip my six-inch heels off. "Thank gods, my feet hurt."

I watch his eyes lower to the armrest, over my legs before quickly glancing up at me. A quick nod of his head follows to mask his sudden disappointment. "There's another job for us."

I perch my feet onto his thigh, slipping them in between his legs. He pushes his legs out, giving my feet room to rest on the seat of the chair. "Do I get the pleasure of knowing who this time?"

His gaze remains on mine. "Wesley Gray."

A low huff gets trapped in my throat. "Am I supposed to know who that is?"

"Possibly. He's a regular here every Thursday night."

I tilt my head. "You'll have to be more specific than that. I don't tend to make it a habit of *remembering* customers unless they pay me well enough."

He exhales slowly, his chest rising through the opening of his button down shirt. The tattoos on his chest peeking through the sable fabric. "He's Ian's brother, and he went to the police to file a missing persons report."

I shrug my shoulders, lowering my head slightly as boredom seeps through my tone. "He'll stop looking eventually."

Levi lowers his hand from his jaw to the other armrest, the rolled up sleeves making his veins in his forearm bulge out. He begins idly tapping his index finger. "We're not willing to wait and find out."

I watch his finger drum against the armrest before lowering further down to my feet between his legs. A smirk threatens to crawl up my face but I shove it down as I remain nonchalant. "So what's the plan, then?" I say, raising my feet onto my tiptoes, resting the heels of my feet on his thigh.

I feel his thigh tense up for a moment before forcing himself to relax again. He keeps his gaze locked onto mine, forcing himself to appear unaffected by the contact. "When he shows up Thursday, persuade him to pay for a VIP room. I'll handle the rest from there."

I fan my toes out, slowly sliding my right foot an inch closer to him. My toes an inch away from brushing up against the seam of his black pants. "I hate to spoil your fun plans, but you won't be able to *handle the rest* in the VIP room." I tilt my head as I fan my lashes at him. "I know how much you love to make a...*mess*. And we won't have the window to be able to clean the room without someone noticing."

His gaze glances down to my foot before slowly making its way up my leg. He tilts his head, shifting himself a fraction closer to me until his cock is pressed up against the side of my foot. His gaze branding itself onto my skin before finally reaching up to meet my gaze. "I promise I won't make a mess." He says, his voice deep and steady. "Not this time."

I slowly rub my foot along him, hearing a low grunt come from low in his throat. "Then how do you plan to take care of him?" My voice sultry as I fixate my gaze on him, locking him in.

His chest rises as I continue rubbing the side of my heel up against the hardness beneath until he grabs my ankle. He holds me in place for a brief moment before lifting my feet off of him, quickly turning my legs forward so I face the drawn curtain. The absence of his heavy palm on my ankle is a sudden disappointment that I hate myself for even feeling.

He stands up from the chair, inserting himself in between my legs as he leans down. The touch of his lips featherlight as they hover over my ear, the scent of eucalyptus and mint wafting towards me. I take a breath in, trying to settle the tiny bumps raising along my arms at the closeness of him now. But it does little to dispel the wicked desire that's currently burning through my veins.

His breath is warm as it gently dances along my neck, his voice low and wicked as I feel a grin form along my skin. "I'll leave that up to your imagination."

He steps away from me, his absence like the very temperature dropping in the room. He turns his back towards me and before I can say another word, he slips through the curtain as he exits the private section.

Chapter 17

I walk out of the private section and head straight for the bar, tampering the sexual frustration down.

Ace watches me approach the counter and a chuckle leaves his full lips. "That bad, huh?"

I seat myself into the chair, rolling my eyes before I force a smile onto my lips. "He's certainly a delight to be around." Sarcasm evident in my tone.

"I've seen him here a couple times now. Does this mean that you have an admirer?" He tilts his head as he leans down to grab a clean empty glass, setting it on the counter before turning towards the back wall to grab a bottle of vodka.

A snort gets trapped in my nose. "Something like that."

Ace pours two shots of vodka into the glass before setting it back onto the shelf. He turns around, grabbing a bottle of cranberry juice from the mini fridge below. "Well I'm sure eventually he'll come around." He winks.

I half roll my eyes as he hands me the drink, taking the straw into my mouth immediately to take a sip. A soft moan gets trapped in my lungs as the tart drink glazes my tongue. "I'm thinking of skipping out early tonight." I set the drink down onto the glass surface.

Ace plants his hands onto the counter, leaning in slightly. "Wouldn't blame you if ya did." He nods down to my lap, to the garter around my thigh. "How much have you made so far?"

Not even needing to pull the money out to count it as the only cash I've made so far tonight is what Levi gave me for our private section. A low exhale filters out. "Four hundred."

Ace shrugs his shoulders. "That's better than zero."

"True." I take another sip of my vodka cranberry, the drink half gone already. Perks of being a Succubus I suppose is you're not a lightweight when it comes to—well, anything. "I'll stay for another hour and see if my luck changes."

After that interaction with Levi tonight, I also admittedly *really* cannot wait to get home and use my vibrator. Teasing fucking bastard, though I can't blame him since I'm doing the same—

"Is this seat taken?"

I look over to a tall man with wavy, dark brown hair swept back into a bun, a few loose strands falling in front of his sun-kissed face. My gaze travels down to the thick extended goatee beard along his sharp jaw. My gaze lifts to meet his dark brown eyes, a smile lifting my red painted lips. "Not at all."

He nods his head, seating himself. A warm smile greets his face as he holds his hand out. "Adrian."

I lay my hand into his calloused palm, my gaze traveling up to his muscular forearms visible from his rolled up ivory sleeves. "Cherry." I say sweetly.

He squeezes gently before releasing my hand. He looks up at Ace, nodding his head "I'll take a whiskey neat, sir."

Ace nods his head before walking to the back wall to retrieve the liquor.

"If you were planning on using the '*why is such a pretty girl like you sitting by yourself*' line then I'm afraid you're flirting with the wrong dancer."

Ace brings the whiskey bottle over, pouring some into a glass. He slides it over as Adrian hands him thirty dollars. "Keep the change."

Ace nods his head and walks away entirely, but not without shooting me a quick smirk as his back turned towards Adrian.

"Actually, I planned to ask you if you were free tomorrow afternoon for lunch."

I tilt my head slightly, assessing him. "Wow, you really don't hesitate." I hook a bare leg over my other, settling back into the bar stool.

His eyes never leave my face as he chuckles. "You seem like a woman who isn't too interested in having her time wasted. So I thought I'd skip the small talk and just ask you straight out."

A laugh leaves my lips as I grab my drink, my lips finding the straw and taking a sip. My lips can't help but to form a smirk as I set the drink down again. "You would assume correctly. A man who is direct is hard to come by these days."

He rests his arm on the back of his chair. "Well I'm a man who isn't afraid to go after what I want."

My gaze lowers to his chest, a glimpse of his tanned skin visible around the collar of his ivory shirt. "And if I said no?"

"Then I would thank you for your time and tell you to enjoy the rest of your night." He says assuredly.

My acrylic nail taps idly on the glass bar top. It's a rare occurrence that I actually get approached by a good-looking man in here, not to mention one who knows how to actually talk to a woman.

Sick of the same old, weird ass pick up lines from these creeps who think that just because I'm a dancer that I'm not also a human being who enjoys being wined-and-dined and admired outside of how my body looks.

Well—that's partly false considering I'm not actually a mortal human. But whatever, the point still stands.

Not to mention it would help to distract me from the tension that's going on between Levi and I. Knowing that I have no interest in being the first one to cave. But if there's one thing I know about men, it's that they can be territorial bastards, and how fun would it be to see Levi jealous that I started to see someone else?

Because did I mention how *hot* this guy is? I'd definitely be interested in seeing where this might go, especially if Adrian is willing to show out for me in the ways I deserve.

A wicked grin threatens to curve my lips before I force it down. I drink the remaining sip left of my drink before setting it down, pushing it away from me. I step out of the stool, my clear heels hitting the carpet. I watch as his gaze stays on my face, impressed that they haven't lowered to my breasts that are nearly in his face. I rest my hand on his shoulder as I smile sweetly at him. "I don't do lunch dates." I lower my hand back to my side. "But you can take me to dinner."

He nods in agreement, a confident smile gracing his handsome face. "I'll meet you at the Gilded Flame, seven o'clock then."

I slowly nod my head, tilting my head. "I'm surprised you didn't say you'd send a car for me."

"I know working in the industry comes with certain safety practices to prevent creeps and unwanted attention in your personal life, including your home residence. I knew better than to think you'd be oblivious enough to share your location to a complete stranger like that. But as a gentleman nonetheless," Adrian goes into his dark navy blue jeans, pulling out his wallet. He flips it open, pulling out a hundred dollar bill and hands it to me. "I hope this will suffice for an Uber for you."

I take the money, the tips of my fingers gliding along the crisp bill as if he'd just pulled this money from the bank today. I lift my gaze up to him again, knowing that this will be more than enough to cover an Uber for me. But he's right—I definitely don't know him enough to have him even guessing at where I live. "This should do." I smile at him as I tuck the bill into my garter, that gaze of his still fixated on my face.

He gives me a smile. "I look forward to it, Cherry."

I lightly place my hand on his shoulder, giving him one last sweet smile before I walk away entirely. "As am I, Adrian."

Chapter 18

My hand lowers to the doorknob as a low bark travels from the other side of the wall. Knowing he sensed I was home the moment I walked up those steps to the building's entrance.

I slide the brass key into the lock, turning it as a soft click follows. I push the door open as I meet Rufus' gaze at the far end of the apartment.

"Hi my sweet and sassy boy." I say, closing the door behind me before tossing my keys onto the kitchen island.

The Hellhound makes another low bark as he stands right at the opening of his crate, just dying to get out of it and roam around freely. I've told him time and time again that if it weren't for the fact that his boredom causes him to chew on my clothing, then he wouldn't have to be in his crate while I'm gone. In which he just huffs at me in response.

But because I cannot keep myself from spoiling him, and making sure he has all the best things, I got him the biggest crate I could find. Large enough where he can walk a full, comfortable circle, and lay down and stretch his large body out without getting cramped up.

I slip off my beige boots, chucking them to the side. I shimmy out of my faux fur coat, hanging it on the back of a bar stool before walking over to Rufus. I lower down to my knees, unlocking his crate when Rufus barges out of it.

Racing out of the crate like his ass is on fire, I stumble back as the crate door pushes me backward, forcing me on my ass. My hands in an attempt to keep me upright slam onto the hardwood flooring, causing one of my nails to crack against the hard surface.

"Fuck." I seethe, bringing my hand up to my face to inspect the broken acrylic nail on my thumb. I look over to the Hellhound who sits calmly by his food bowl as if he wasn't just a lunatic two seconds ago. "You act like I starve you."

He just sits there, watching me.

I shake my head, chuckling as I look down at my nail again. Sighing, I stand up to head over to the kitchen island.

I grab my phone, opening up a text thread to Ki and begin typing.

Sooo any chance you can get me in tomorrow? I'll bring you treats xoxo

I set my phone back down onto the counter before walking over to the pantry to retrieve Rufus' dry kibble. I pour a generous amount into his metal bowl when I hear my phone buzz.

I close the kibble bag up as Rufus digs right in, plopping it back onto the pantry floor before opening up her text.

Ugh...I'm so booked already for tomorrow.

I open up the camera app, holding my thumb up to it as I snap a photo. I send it over to her with a response back. *Blame Rufus for bombarding me.*

I watch as the text bubble appears before vanishing a few seconds later. *The only time I could do it is at one, which is meant to be my* lunch break.

I begin typing when another text from Ki comes through.

Bring me a hot ham and cheese sandwich with a lemon lime soda. I'll fill you in. Xoxo

Deal. I'll tip extra. Xoxo

She sends me a pink glitter heart emoji before I close the text thread out, setting my phone back onto my counter. I head up the stairs to my bedroom, opening up the top drawer of my dresser as I grab a pair of boyshort underwear. I head into my walk-in closet, grabbing a heather grey T-shirt before I head into my bathroom.

I turn the light on, setting my clothes on the bathroom counter as I strip my leggings off, followed by my long-sleeved shirt. I plop them into my laundry hamper before I gather my hair up, clipping it up into a sand colored claw clip.

I lower my hand to the faucet, turning the hot water on as it begins filling the bathtub. Turning the cold water on just by a fraction to keep the water from becoming scalding.

I pour a generous amount of spearmint and menthol bubble bath into the water before lowering myself into the large tub. Sighing with relief as my skin meets the hot water as it soothes my minor body aches from work.

After the water has filled up to my shoulders, I turn the water off as I lean back against the ceramic surface. A slow, audible exhale fills the silent bathroom as I look up at the city lights shining through my window. My gaze lowered to the Cimiteria Sea, the murky water like a dark abyss against the vibrant nightlife of the city.

The reminder of Ian being weighed down somewhere at the bottom of that sea.

Seeing the look in Levi's gaze in that basement, the way his eyes didn't dull but instead sparked to life as he held that knife up to Ian's throat. As if hesitation and guilt were both foreign feelings for him.

I found myself standing there, observing him while masking how I really felt in that moment. That not only was I intrigued, I was also *wildly* turned on.

Far from the faked boredom I portrayed to him.

As I lay back in the tub, a smirk curves my lips at what fun this little *business arrangement* could turn into.

Chapter 19

Levi

Sweat drips down my back as I push myself harder, the pavement feeling nonexistent against my feet the faster I run. The music blaring through my wireless headphones does little to drone out the frustration that's settled within me since last night.

I turn the corner of my neighborhood, pumping my arms faster as my hair slicks itself to my forehead. The baseball cap seemingly unnecessary at this point to keep my wavy hair down.

I glide the back of my hand across my forehead as an elderly woman steps out of her home to grab the mail. She stares at me for a long moment, her eyes slightly widened before she closes her mailbox, heading back inside where I'm sure it's far warmer.

I'm sure she's thinking to herself why the fuck is this man running shirtless in forty degree weather. To which I would reply mind your damn business—

Okay, that's not true. I would probably tell her I'm a touch deprived man desperate to feel absolutely *anything* other than the sexual tension that's been caving in on me. So if running a few laps around the neighborhood in freezing weather will help tamper some of that sexual frustration down, then that's exactly what I'll do.

I mean, she has to understand. Or—does she? Do people her age even still have sex?

You know what, nevermind. Because I definitely *don't* want to know the answer to that.

The driveway to my mid-century home comes into view. I run through the opening of my wooden fence, past the tall walnut tree situated right at the entrance of my driveway.

I glance up at it, knowing well and good of the two security cameras hidden within the branches, concealed from anyone discovering them. With one covering one angle at the beginning of my driveway, and the other facing towards my front door.

I jog up the steps, searching for my keys in my navy athletic shorts. I pull them out, sliding the key into the lock as I turn it, pushing the door open.

A blast of heat rushes over me as I step inside, closing the door behind me. I shove my hand in my other pocket, lifting my phone out and hitting pause on the song currently playing. I lift the black headphones off my ears before slipping off my gym shoes.

I walk over to the kitchen as I lift my baseball cap off, grimacing as I run my hand through my sweat slicked hair. I set my headphones down on the kitchen island with my phone before I head over to the sink, washing my hands as the smell of her perfume dances through my memories again.

I shut the water off, drying my hands on the cream colored hand towel. I try to tamper the memory down as I pull out a tupperware of leftover chicken and rice, plopping it into the microwave before diving in.

The feel of her delicate foot brushing up against my cock has had my blood churning violently inside of me since last night, already having jerked myself off as soon as I got home last night to settle the tension. But she's like a damn fever that I can't cool my body down enough from, a chill that I can't shake.

A long exhale leaves me as I finish my leftovers, setting the glass tupperware into the sink as I head upstairs.

I walk through my bathroom, immediately turning the shower on. I lower my shorts off and toss them into my laundry hamper, my cock already hard as the thought of her infiltrates my mind again.

I stand under the shower, letting the water crash over me as I fight the urge to think about what it felt like to have my lips so close to her soft skin. Or how her breasts nearly brushed against my chest when I leaned into her.

My hand lowers to my cock, palming it as a low groan gets trapped in my throat. I close my eyes, unable to control the effect that this damn woman has on me.

My mind conjures up images of her kneeling before me, her body naked as water drips over her full breasts. She looks up at me, her bright amber eyes piercing into mine as she kisses just the tip.

My hand grips my cock, a slow stroke to start as my imagination takes over.

Her pretty mouth closes over my cock, her tongue slowly swirling around as her hands go to her breasts. I stroke myself a little faster, a low moan escaping me. "Keep sucking me, little red."

She smiles up at me as I stroke myself faster, her eyes so fucking gorgeous as they fixate on me. She takes me deeper as her moan vibrates my cock, cum already beading at the tip.

My hand works faster as she sucks me deeper, taking all of me down into her throat. And as the pressure builds, I begin thrusting into my hand.

I hold her face with both hands, fucking her pretty mouth as she gags on my cock. Moans tear from my lips as I come inside her mouth, spilling myself down her throat.

I ride out the wave until I open my eyes, lowering my gaze to my hand covered in cum. I regain control over my breathing as I rub my hands beneath the stream of water, feeling sated for the time being.

You will never last.

Those words slither through my mind, a traitorous taunt that is beginning to sound more like a declaration of a promise.

I just have to try to distract myself. Fuck, I'll go to the damn gym seven days a week if I have to.

Maybe I'll take up a new hobby—or just take on more jobs and preoccupy myself with killing more undeserving bastards. Yeah, that's it. Fucking Hell, I'll do anything at this point.

I grab the bar of soap, using it to wash my hands before setting it down and grabbing the bottle of shampoo. I squeeze a little into my hands, lathering it into my hair as I try to scrub away Amelia's growing affect on me.

Chapter 20

Amelia

"Oh, but you had plenty of time to snag a photo for me."

I watch as Kiara wipes the corner of her mouth, swiping the crumbs of soft french bread with her manicured thumb. She looks up at me with those rich brown eyes, nearly identical to her long curly brown hair. She tilts her head, giving me a knowing look.

I chuckle, looking down at my nails submerged in the bowl of acetone. I gently wiggle my fingers, lifting my thumb to scrape off a softened red nail. I lift my gaze back up to her. "Fine I will tonight, *mom*."

She laughs as she crumbles up the sandwich bag, tossing it into a white trash bin below her work station. She straightens her back as she grabs the lemon lime soda from her left, bringing it to her lips. "So what's the plan after dinner then?" She lifts the can up to her lips, taking a sip before setting it back down on a small table beside her work station.

I shrug my shoulders as she lifts my hands out of the bowl. "I hadn't thought of anything."

"So you're not going to fuck him?" She peers up at me, scrunching those freckles around her nose as she smirks. She wipes my hands on a towel before taking a cuticle pusher to my nails, and begins scraping off the acrylic.

"Oh you know that I don't put out *that* quickly, Ki."

"Right, because the ones you *actually* have interest in you get off on making them work for it instead."

A smile curves up my lips. "I hear no lies."

Ki laughs as she sets the cuticle pusher down, grabbing for her nail drill as she begins filing my nails. "And what about Levi?"

An exhale leaves me. "Like I said, we're just business partners."

Having told Ki a much milder version of the kind of work that I actually do with Levi, she thinks that I've hired him to be my personal bodyguard to ensure my safety both during, and on my walks home from work.

"That's what you keep saying but all I keep hearing is you're intrigued by him." She peers her gaze up, smirking before lowering it again onto my nails. "It would be pretty hot to have your bodyguard turn into a little sex friend."

My mind wanders to the last time I saw him, the way my skin felt like it was crawling out of itself as he lowered his lips down to my neck. His breath like a warm embrace as he spoke in that steady voice of his. As if I was the only one having a reaction to being that close to him.

I know that's not the case.

A faint smile curves my lips. "Yeah, I guess so. But it's looking like Adrian might be in line to take his place."

"Well he sure sounds like he knows exactly what he wants and isn't shy to go for it." She turns the drill off, setting it down on the table. "And that's infinitely hotter than a man trying to play hard to get." She grabs a rosy pink nail buffer and gets right to work.

My gaze lowers as I watch her work, the memory of being in Vixens basement watching him hold that knife up to Ian's neck resurfacing. Like watching a predator honing in on its prey, not one hint of remorse to cause his body to tense up.

I remember not being able to look away, the boredom I initially felt in agreeing to work with him suddenly revolting into something more wicked.

Something that made the fire in my veins light up like a damn christmas tree.

And until then, I had never felt anything more thrilling, more exciting than how I felt watching him kill that man like he was born for that kind of work.

An inaudible exhale leaves me as a strange feeling of disappointment churns in my stomach as I say plainly. "Indeed it is."

"They're so beautiful. Just like you." I say sweetly to Ki as I admire my new acrylic nails. A set of medium-length, french-tipped nails, squared off just how I like them.

I normally go for bold colors but tonight I was feeling a little more simple. Something a bit more on the classy side for a change.

"Careful, I might tell you to cancel your plans with Adrian and come hang out with me instead." She winks.

I grab my purse, shuffling through it until I find my black leather wallet. A laugh escapes me as I shuffle out one hundred and fifty dollars. "For you? I'd cancel anything." I hand her the cash as I stand up from my seat.

She counts it, setting it down into a small black metal box. She chuckles as she stands up to give me a hug. "Don't forget a picture."

I laugh as I pull away. "Don't worry. You'll get your damn picture." I say teasingly as I hook my bag over my shoulder. "Thanks again, babe."

"Have fun." Ki says with excitement in her tone.

I walk out of her spare bedroom where she designates for her clients. The plush carpet beneath my feet turning to hardwood flooring as I step out onto her hallway.

My pink fuzzy slippers slide quietly against the wood floor, curving the hallway corner as I step out into her open living room.

The same floor to ceiling windows except with a living room about half the size as mine. The setting sun illuminated through her opened blinds casts an orange glow on her insane number of plants. Some of which hang inside bohemian baskets mounted into the ceiling, some set on a tall black plant stand next to her burnt orange sectional couch.

On top of her glass coffee table lies books scattered messily on top, some of them with a thin piece of paper hanging out of it to notate where she left off.

I walk past her pristine kitchen. Marbled counters with small kitchen appliances neatly placed about.

I reach for her entrance door as I leave her apartment entirely, closing the door behind me. I walk down the short distance to the tall elevator door, polished and shining the reflection of myself back into it.

I press the upward facing arrow and watch as the diameter around it lights up a soft white. The elevator door opens up a moment later as I step inside. I reach for my keys from my black silk robe, a white sports bra and a pair of black flared leggings hidden underneath. I pull out my elevator key, sliding it into the lock above the golden letter P. I turn the key as the elevator begins its descent up to my floor.

I fucking love living in the same building as my nail tech—who also just happens to be my bestie. Well, the closest I've had to a friend that is.

When I first met Kiara a year ago I'd been about to walk out of the building to take Rufus for a walk. We'd made our way down to the main floor when I saw her trying to haul up a dresser by herself.

I'd raised my eyebrows and tilted my head, a snort escaping me. "Either you're extremely strong or you definitely aren't interested in asking a man for help."

She'd look up at me, startled at first before her shoulders relaxed. She'd laughed. "Usually I'm both," She'd nudged her head towards the building entrance. "But apparently the movers I paid to help move my things in said they were only under contract to get me *to* my building. That helping me move everything in would cost more."

I remember watching her, feeling anger shoot through me as these lazy bastards made this nice girl move her shit up by herself. I had to force myself to quiet that anger before a smile curved my face. "Let me go have a chat with them."

I handed her Rufus' leash as she tentatively took it.

"Don't worry. He's friendly." I'd said before I walked out of those glass doors to the two men standing near the moving truck.

They saw me coming in my tight black leggings and sports bra, immediately standing up straight as their eyes ogled my body.

Go fucking figure.

I walked up to the one with the thick black beard accompanied by a shining bald head. I willed my power to the surface as his gaze fell soft, longing.

"You will help this woman move her things into her apartment before I sever that bald head from your neck. Say you understand." I said, the Succubus energy dripping from my tone.

I'd lifted my gaze to the man next to him, slightly taller and with only a buzz cut of hair on that head of his. His expression smoothed out as I pulled him in. He'd slowly nodded. "Understood."

"Good." I looked back at the bald man again, tilting my head. "And just for her troubles, you'll treat her to one-hundred and fifty dollars worth of groceries. As your way of apologizing for your incompetence to be a gentleman."

They'd only both nodded again slowly, saying in unison. "Yes. Understood."

And this time, they didn't even let Kiara pick up a single box and moved everything up for her.

I laugh to myself at the reminder to the start of our friendship. She'd asked me how I was able to get them to change their minds. I'd told her it was just a chance of luck.

Not revealing who I am to her seems to be the best bet as many do not normally take kindly to my kind. Many people view us as just sex demons who prey on weak men and take advantage of them.

Pfft, please. As if the men who walk into The Playground and ask me to fulfill their wicked fantasies don't have control over their own lives. Yes—sometimes it's far easier to just skip all of that and just entice them to give me their money. But what else did you expect to do at a strip and pleasure club? Sit there and just *chat* with the women?

Please, save that for your therapists.

The elevator door opens up as the front door to my penthouse comes into view. I take my key out, stepping out of the elevator as I step into the small corridor in between.

I slide my key into my front door, opening it as I hear Rufus trot over to me, acting like I've been gone for five days when it's only been two hours.

I close the door behind me before kneeling down to my Hellhound. A genuine smile curving my lips as I scruff my fingers behind his ears. I lean in to give him a kiss on his nose as he tries to lick my face. I stand up again as I set my purse on my marble kitchen counter.

I slip my pink slippers off as I weave my fingers through my wine red hair, the smell of my lightly fragranced shampoo wafting through my nose.

I look down at Rufus. "What should mommy wear tonight?"

He tilts his head at me, his nub of a tail wagging.

I scrunch my lips, pondering before I walk upstairs to my bedroom, then into my walk-in closet.

Rufus follows behind me as I turn my closet light on, staring at the wall that hangs my 'nicer' clothing. Black dinner dresses, long skirts, dress shirts, things I wear for occasions such as these.

My work outfits on the middle wall next to my more modest attire, the outfits I unironically feel most alive in. Feel most beautiful and myself in.

I glance at them before training my gaze ahead on a simple black dress. I grab the velvet black hanger, pulling it out as I set it on a black chaise lounge chair. A thigh-length bodycon dress with a small back slit to give it just that little extra bit of sexiness that I yearn for.

I step out of the closet as I make my way to my vintage tri-fold black vanity. I seat myself on the cream colored stool, fluffing my hair again.

I lower myself to the curling iron cord on the carpet, plugging it into the wall. I turn it on, setting it off to the side as I pull out my drawer of make-up and begin getting ready for my date tonight.

Chapter 21

The Uber pulls up to the curb, just in front of the upscale building. I watch as a couple walks up to the walnut front doors as a male greeter lowers his head to them. He pulls the door open for them, the soft lighting above glinting off of his black silk top hat. Once they enter he closes the door, his hand going to smooth down his black tailcoat jacket. A warm and welcome smile on his pleasant face.

"Enjoy your night, ma'am." The driver says as the smell of cigarette smoke wafts from his mouth.

Thankfully he didn't dare light a cigarette while I was in the car. I would've cut out his tongue if I showed up to this date smelling like an ashtray.

I reach into my small clutch purse, a change from the large tote bag I normally carry. I pull out my phone, going into the Uber app as I enter thirty dollars into the tip amount section. A one hundred percent tip for the cost of the ride here.

"Thank you for your generosity." He says after the notification chime sound dings from his phone. His finger reaches for his phone holstered in a car mount clipped to his front air vent, swiping the notification away.

"You're welcome." I say before I hear the click of my car door opening.

The cold air drags my attention to my right, watching as a muscular hand lowers itself inside. A smile curves up my lips as I lift my gaze to who stands before me. "Thank you."

"My pleasure." Adrian says, his white teeth peeking through his smile. I take his hand as he guides me out of the Uber, shutting the door behind me as he guides us up the steps.

He loops my arm into his, my fingers brushing along his pristine suit jacket. The male greeter opens the door for us. "Good evening."

Adrian gives him a courteous nod. "Good evening, sir." He guides us into the Gilded Flame until we approach a wooden podium with a pretty blonde woman standing behind it. Her hair pulled back neatly into a tight bun as her eyes landed themselves on Adrian before falling on me. She gives me a friendly nod as she pulls out two menus. "For two?"

"Yes. Reservation for Adrian." He says calmly.

She looks down at her tablet screen for a moment before looking back up again. "Right this way."

She guides us past oval shaped tables, each dimly illuminated by a vintage lamp hanging from up above. Cream-colored table cloths lay on top of each table, each accompanied by dark red velvet bench sofas. The crimson color accentuating the dark floor to ceiling length decorative columns situated every few tables.

My black pointed-toe heels click against the hardwood floor as she guides us to a private section towards the back of the restaurant. I look up at him as he trains his gaze forward, his wavy brown hair slicked back into a bun. His beard neatly trimmed.

She stops us in front of a large round table, big enough to fit a party of ten. She smiles at us as she raises a hand out, gesturing for me to take a seat. "Someone will be with you shortly to take your drink orders." She says warmly.

I slide into the velvet bench, scooting myself down to the middle of the half-crescent shaped booth. I smile at her as Adrian seats himself as well. "Thank you."

She nods her head before walking away.

Adrian scoots closer to me, though still opting to give me a healthy amount of space. He looks up at me as a smile curves his handsome lips, the dim light above caressing his dark brown eyes. "You look exquisite."

I smile at him as I set my purse beside me, hooking a leg over my knee. "As do you."

He chuckles as he hands a menu over to me. He then grabs one for himself, turning it to the back where the drink menu is. "Did I give you enough to cover your Uber tonight?"

I lift the menu, looking at the selection of drinks. "Yes."

"Good." He sets the menu down as a man approaches our table.

"Good evening, welcome to the Gilded Flame. I'm Yanis and will be taking care of you both tonight." Yanis looks over at me as he extends a hand out before lowering it again. His blue eyes piercing into mine under his short copper hair. "May I get you started with something to drink?"

"A glass of Cabernet Sauvignon would be perfect. Thank you."

"Make that a bottle, please." Adrian says as he sets the menu down, hooking an arm around the back of the booth.

"Absolutely." Yanis gives a smile before walking away from our table.

I turn my menu over, inspecting the dinner selection. "I'm surprised you didn't order a whiskey neat or an old fashioned."

He chuckles as his cologne wafts towards me, the scent of sandalwood lingering. "Is that what men usually order?"

I skim over the steak section of their menu, my gaze landing on what I want to eat before setting the menu down beside me. I meet his gaze, tilting my head as I lower my elbow to the table. Resting my chin subtly against my fingers. "It's what men who are trying to impress me usually order." I smile.

A smile lifts his lips as he locks eyes with me. "I think I'd rather impress you in other ways."

My gaze flickers over him as heat rises within me, Yanis' approach stifling it for now.

He lowers two wine glasses to the table, filling each with five ounces of dark ruby red wine. He sets the bottle into a metal ice bucket centered at the middle of the table. "Are we ready to place our orders?"

Adrian nods his head at me, smiling. "Ladies first."

A smirk greets my face as I look up at Yanis. "I'll take the ribeye dinner. Medium rare, please."

Yanis writes my order down, nodding before looking up to Adrian. "And for you sir?"

"The porterhouse steak, please. Medium rare on that one as well." He goes to grab my menu, setting it on top of his as he hands them to the tall waiter.

Yanis takes them, smiling. "I'll put those in for you both right away. Let me know if there's anything else I can get for you both."

As he walks away, I grab my wine glass as I bring it to my lips. A soft moan escapes me as the dark red wine travels past my tongue. I lift my gaze up to him. "So what kind of work do you do, Adrian?"

He takes a sip of his wine before setting it down, leaning back into the booth. "I work in real estate. Primarily commercial."

I feel the buzz of my phone in my clutch purse beside me, faintly vibrating the seat cushion. "Interesting." I say, ignoring it. "Does this mean you dabble in buying properties as well?"

"There are a few I own in The Pleasure District."

"Hmm—" I begin as my phone vibrates again.

"Do you need to get that?" He asks calmly, glancing towards my purse next to my thigh.

A huff of annoyance escapes me. "It's probably just someone from the club asking if I'm working tonight." I lie smoothly as I look down at the screen and see two text messages from Levi.

Where are you? We need to touch base about tomorrow.

I'm busy tonight. I replied back.

I go to set my phone back into my purse when he texts me back right away.

Doing what? I know you're not working tonight.

None of your business. Xoxo

I put my phone on silent and set it back into my purse, setting the bag beside me as I meet Adrian's gaze. "Sorry about that, the girls at work can be so needy sometimes." I lower my hand to rest along his forearm. "Tell me more about these properties you own?"

Even after our plates of food arrived the conversation hardly simmered down. Only a trace amount of ruby red wine was left in the bottle between us.

A relaxed laugh tears itself from my lips as I find myself leaning in closer to Adrian. "I never would have pegged you as the stealing type."

A deep chuckle escapes his full lips. "Hey—she was the first girl I ever really fell for. I was only sixteen and was desperate for her attention."

"But she ended up not accepting it?" A giggle crawls up my throat.

"She said it was something that her grandmother would've worn and then never talked to me again."

A laugh bursts out of both of our lips, his arm now resting along my bare back.

"My mother found out and made me return the perfume the next day. From that day forward, I never tried to gift a woman perfume again."

Another laugh escapes me before I settle down once again. I go to brush an index finger beneath my eye. "Her loss. She missed out."

He catches my wrist gently, raising his thumb to wipe the tears that escaped my eye from laughing so hard. He slowly, gently swipes it away as he stares at me longingly. "None of that matters now." He lowers his hand to rest along my back again. His fingers idly tracing my bare shoulder.

I flutter my eyelashes, lowering my gaze to his lips before raising them again. My red painted lips curving into a smirk. "Are you trying to dazzle me?"

Yanis comes back to our table with the check, setting it down closest to Adrian. "Here you are, sir."

He reaches for his wallet in his black dress pants, not even bothering to look at the check. "Does this mean that I've officially wooed the one who is not so easily charmed?" He pulls out his wallet, grabbing a black card and slipping it into the pouch. He hands it back to Yanis who takes it and walks away.

I hook my leg over my knee, leaning in towards him ever so slightly. "It takes a little more than just a dinner to impress me. But you're off to a good start."

He nods his head, his gaze steady on me. "I can only hope this means you will be interested in a second date then?"

Yanis comes back to the table, two receipts sticking out of the checkbook. "Thank you both for being wonderful guests. Enjoy your night." He bows slightly before walking away.

"I can't say that I'd be opposed to a second date." I say.

He opens the check book, grabbing the pen and one of the receipts. He begins writing out a number under the tip line and I find my gaze lowering to the paper discreetly.

"I'm tipping him forty percent if you were curious."

I raise my gaze back up to him. I watch as he closes the checkbook with the receipt and pen inside, scooting it closer to the middle of the table. He faces towards me, his fingers still idly tracing themselves over my soft skin.

A smile curves up. "Good. He gave exceptional service."

His eyes heat up like pools of molten rich brown. "And do your customers treat you just as fairly?"

"Are you asking because you'd like to find out?" I asked curiously.

A low chuckle gets trapped in his throat. "Not particularly as those aren't my intentions with you." He lowers his hand from my back and gestures it in front of us. His gaze dips to my lips before raising again. "Shall we?"

I sit there for a moment letting his words sink in as that heat only builds higher within me. A smirk curves my lips as I nod my head, scooting myself down the booth before standing up completely.

He follows me out of the booth as he rests his hand on my lower back, guiding me through the restaurant. My attention fully aware on where his hand is.

We make our way to the front entrance when the host brings me my faux fur jacket. "My lady."

I nod my thanks as Adrian grabs it, putting it on me before we step outside into the frigid cold air.

I watch as a waiting Uber car sits idly a few feet down from the entrance doors, waving my hand up to get his attention. He shines his lights on me as he pulls forward.

I turn to Adrian as he raises his hand to my cheek. "I had a wonderful time tonight, Cherry." His calloused hand gently grazes my skin.

"As did I." I keep my gaze on him as I lower my hand to his pant pocket, watching his eyes bulge for a moment before realizing I'm grabbing for his phone.

I open up his contact list, putting my phone number inside and giving it to him.

"I guess this takes visiting you every night just to talk to you out of the equation."

A laugh escapes my lips. "It'll make for far easier communication." The Uber honks behind me as I look back at him, giving him a quick glare before turning back around. "Goodnight—"

Adrian pulls me in for a kiss, stifling my words completely. His hand lowers to my neck, his palm splaying along my skin as I wrap my hand around his. He pulls away a moment later, my lashes lifting to meet his gaze.

He smiles. "Goodnight, Cherry. I look forward to seeing you again soon." He pulls away from me entirely, nodding his head before walking down the street.

I watch him walk down the street for a moment before I get inside the Uber. A faint smile curving my lips as my phone buzzes in my purse. I pull it out as a text from an unknown number comes through.

Can I see you again Friday night?

Chapter 22

Levi

Where the fuck is she?

I bring the joint pressed between my thumb and index finger up to my lips, taking a long drag. Slouched in the driver seat of my car I watch as the marijuana exhaled from my lips slips through the cracked window. My gaze remains focused on the silent street ahead of me, on a set of stairs that lead straight up into her apartment building.

When I came here hours ago and rang for her unit, I figured her no answer was just her way of ignoring me. Or being a brat.

Which unfortunately doesn't deter me and only *thoroughly* arouses me.

Or just her way of getting me worked up which she exceeds spectacularly at, as well.

But when she texted me and said she was busy, I found myself unable to drive away from her building. Finding myself acting like the stalker I've apparently become for her and waiting here for her arrival home.

Some kind of fucking discipline I have.

I take another drag from my joint before discarding the roach outside my window, exhaling the remaining frustration from my system.

Thank fuck that marijuana is legal in The Pleasure District. I don't understand why it wouldn't be considering all of its medical benefits.

But let's be real, I'm smoking entirely for recreational use.

At that thought I watch as a white car pulls up to her building, twenty feet ahead of me. I sit up straight in my seat as I see through the back window a head of dark red hair before she opens up her door.

I watch as she steps out and almost find myself needing to roll up another joint. Her long legs step out of the vehicle followed by a tight black dress. She lowers at the waist, waving goodbye to the driver before she closes the door.

Fucking damnit, she looks incredible. Why couldn't she have shown up in some sweatpants and her hair tied up at least? Yet let's face it, she'd look just as incredible then, too.

As she turns around to walk up those steps I open my car door, stepping out of the driver seat as I close it quietly behind me. I quickly move over to the sidewalk as I walk the short distance up to her building entrance, watching as she slips through the double-doors.

I jog up the steps, slipping through the doors behind her as she abruptly turns around. Her amber eyes glowing brightly beneath winged black liner and shades of brown eyeshadow. "Is stalking part of our agreement now?" She says annoyedly.

"It is when it involves me needing to discuss a job with you and you're vague about when you'll be available."

She chuckles as she turns around, heading for the elevator. "I didn't realize that I needed to drop everything for you."

I find myself following her to the elevator like a damn lapdog.

She pushes the upward arrow on the stainless steel column. She gives an audible sniff as she keeps her back towards me. She huffs out a low noise. "Wow, you really were stressed about my whereabouts."

"I wasn't *stressed out.*" I lied. Because apparently I'm a pathetic fool who somehow can't maintain that mental barrier of business partners and something more.

The elevator opens and she steps through, finally turning to face me. I stand there, unsure if she's inviting me up or not. It's one thing for me to wait in my car for two hours for her but another for me to assume like a creep that I'm owed an invitation into her home.

I have to have some kind of damn sense.

She rolls her eyes, waving a hand. "Are you going to just stand there all night?"

I can't help the chuckle that gets trapped in my mouth. I nod my head, stepping into the elevator when the doors close behind me.

"So tell me this grand plan of yours." She says as she slides a key into a lock on the wall below a letter P. She turns it as the light around the letter glows, the elevator beginning to rise.

I cross my arms over my chest, standing across the room from her, leaning against the metal bar. "When you get there tomorrow night I need you to unlock the fire exit located down the hall in the VIP section."

She leans back into the wall across from me, her hands resting on top of the railing. My gaze falls to her fresh set of nails as they tap against the metal railing.

Fucking french tips *gods damnit*. What is wrong with me that I'm instantly attracted to a certain style of nail?

My gaze lowers briefly to her bare legs, noticing the sheen casting from the lights above that I presume is from some sort of body oil. I quickly raise my gaze back up to her face again before my thoughts can begin to wander.

"So that's it? I just get him into a VIP room, you slip in and...what?" She says, tilting her head. Knowing full well she caught my brief glance. A faint smirk curves up her red painted lips.

I straighten my back, keeping her gaze. "Since I can't be messy with this one, I'll need you to slip this into his drink." I uncross my arms, shoving a hand into my dark navy jean pocket until I pull out a tiny vial of clear liquid.

I close the distance between us, holding it in my hand until I'm right in front of her. I notice her stare lower briefly to my lips, the heat from her eyes lingering there.

She removes a hand from the railing, raising it to slowly grab the vial. Her soft hand meets mine and I nearly melt right then and there like a fucking starving dog.

She leans into me, taking the vial from my hands as we stand there for a moment that feels like eternity. Her eyes lower to my lips again before locking onto my gaze. Inches apart from one another, the smell of her perfume overpowers the small distance between us, taunting me in that enchantress way.

"And after I poison him, what then?" She asks, her voice low as she goes to place the vial not into her small purse, but between her breasts.

My gaze fails my self control as I follow her movement, the swell of her breasts on full display in this tight little dress she's wearing.

Fuck fuck fuck. Focus you sick bastard.

I clear my throat, forcing myself to step away from her as I lift my gaze back up to her face. The absence of her felt like a cold wind that I suddenly want to seek warmth from. I straighten my back, steadying my voice. "He'll die within moments, at which we'll do exactly what we did last time. Load him up into my car and drive him to the sea."

The elevator finally dings its arrival to her penthouse suite. I watch as disappointment flashes across her gaze before smoothing out again into an uncaring front. "Seems pretty straightforward then." She says calmly.

Too calmly.

She turns to walk out of the elevator when she looks back at me, still standing. "Is that all you needed to see me for, Levi?"

My fists tucked into my elbows clench themselves as I force myself to keep standing there. "That is all, yes." I manage to uncross my arms, leaning to push the button for level one. I step back again, nodding at her. "Text me updates as the night goes along. I'll plan to be out back around eleven."

She gives me a nod. "Sounds good, *partner*." She turns around as she opens her door to her penthouse.

Noting for a brief moment the floor to ceiling windows at the far back wall of her suite, the city lights visible through them before the elevator door closes in my face.

Chapter 23

Amelia

I pull my phone out of my purse, glancing at the text from Adrian on my screen.

Well in that case, I will come visit you Friday night then. Have a good night.

I reply back to his text, my skin still slightly on fire from a moment ago in the elevator.

Can't wait to see you. Xoxo

I set my phone down on my nightstand before walking into my bathroom. Moving my hands to the zipper at the back of my dress, I slowly pull the zipper down, careful not to snag my skin. I slip the skin tight dress off of me before throwing my dark red hair into a messy bun on the top of my head.

I lower my gaze to the vial in between my breasts, pulling it out. I hold it up to the vanity mirror light, liquid as clear as water. I set it on the bathroom counter.

I unclasp the back of my matching bra, slipping that off me too along with my lacy thong. I walk over to the shower, turning the water on before I slip myself in. Making sure not to get my hair wet while I take a long shower.

After I finish rubbing my entire body with toasted vanilla scented lotion, I shimmy a pair of brown sweatpants up my legs, tying the strings at the center of the waistband into a bow. I pull over a baggy white T-shirt before I clip my curtain bangs to each side, away from my face.

As the material of my face cleansing brush gently rubs against my skin, heat erodes my skin as I recall how it felt to watch Levi's eyes dip to my breasts. A thrill of excitement that I force myself to ignore.

I set the brush down, lowering my head to the sink as I gently scrub my face wash off. I turn the sink off, reaching for a hand towel as I blot it across my face. I focus my attention wholly on my nighttime skincare routine before shutting the bathroom light off, and slipping under the covers of my king sized bed.

My head lays against my pillow as I stare up at the ceiling. A moment later a smirk crawls up my lips as I reach for my phone, opening up my photo library to a picture I took of Adrian tonight.

Who was more than happy to let me take it.

I open up my text thread between Ki and I, sending the picture to her along with the following text.

Here's your picture as promised. He's hot and a gentleman.

I lift my gaze to the time in the corner of my phone. Ten-thirty.

My phone buzzes as I giggle at the text from Ki.

Oh he is hot ;)

He's coming to visit me at work Friday night. Maybe I might just let him get to second base ;)

I watch as another text from Ki comes through before I set my phone back onto the nightstand.

Give me all the deets Saturday morning then. Xoxo

I exhale deeply as sexual frustration plummets through me. My hand lowers to my navel, my fingers dipping just below my waistband as erotic fantasies cement themselves into my mind.

An image of Adrian's lips on someplace other than my mouth surfaces in my mind, my finger dipping lower as the image of his tongue flicking my clit illuminates my mind.

My finger lowers to the wetness already there, swirling my finger in it before bringing it to my clit. A soft moan escapes me as I rub my clit slowly to start, the images growing wilder and more erotic.

I open my legs further as my other hand sneaks up beneath my shirt, coming up to my nipple.

The image suddenly alters as Levi replaces Adrian, his eyes wholly on me as his tongue descends deep into my pussy.

Fuck, no.

I try changing back to Adrian when my own mind disobeys me, painting a picture of Levi lowering a finger to where his tongue was, cum dripping from me as he thrusts it in.

A soft moan tears from my lips as he moves his lips to my clit, closing over it as he sucks me into oblivion.

My orgasm builds intensely as I keep rubbing my clit, using my other hand to reach for my nightstand drawer. I grab the silicone toy, closing the drawer before pushing the on button.

It begins vibrating as I remove my finger and hold it up against my clit, sending me overboard as my orgasm meets my no longer quiet moaning.

My hips thrust forward as the last of my orgasm rolls through me, the image of Levi taking every last drop finishing me completely.

As my body lays limp against my sheets, I turn my vibrator off as I lift the covers from me and walk to the bathroom.

I clean off my vibrator, then myself before climbing back under the covers when I notice my phone lighting up on my nightstand. I reach for it, and my eyes bulge momentarily at the text from Levi.

Whatever you're doing, stop.

My fingers hover over the screen for a long moment.

What are you talking about? I text back, acting oblivious.

Fuck, did he really *feel* that? Normally if I want someone to feel me getting off I have to wield that Succubus power to the surface, as it takes more than just mental thought of them alone.

But clearly that wasn't the case here.

I read his reply back and a shameless smirk crawls up my face.

You know what I'm talking about. Goodnight.

I stare at my screen before deciding to send him a pink heart emoji, closing the text thread and setting my phone on the nightstand. Turning myself onto my side I pull the covers up to my chin, sighing deeply as I nuzzle myself into my cashmere sheets.

I close my eyes, the curiosity of how he genuinely reacted to that the last thing I wonder about before falling asleep.

Chapter 24

Levi

This woman is going to be the reason I go clinically insane.

It's the way she acted like she had no idea what I was talking about. When I could *feel* physically what she was doing, as if I was in the same room as her, aroused from watching her.

The intensity of the pleasure that ran through my body had me unable to do anything else but jerk off to it. Feeling my cock dripping cum onto my hand as I pumped myself to the thought of her.

I'm never going to be able to restrain myself from her if she keeps that shit up.

It doesn't surprise me that being a Succubus not only makes you more desirable, but can inflict feelings of eroticism. I just had no idea they could do it when you weren't in the same room as them.

This is fan-fucking-tastic. I'm going to cave in.

Nope, focus brother. We are partners and that can only be what it is.

I lay in my bed with my now soft cock, having cleaned myself up afterwards. I run my hand through my hair as I pull my laptop over my lap, my gray sweatpants warm from being just pulled out of the dryer.

I open up my laptop, putting in my passcode as the screen starts up.

I go to google, immediately trying to figure out how to type what I want into the search engine.

Can a Succubus ruin your fucking life?

No, not that. Hmmm...

Can a Succubus make you aroused without being near you?

Yeah, that'll do.

I type that into the search box and hit enter, finding an article pop up. I click on it, reading it aloud to myself.

"Succubi feed on the psychic, or astral forms of humans, therefore can have the ability to seduce men telepathically—Oh this is just fucking great."

I close the laptop, shoving it next to me on the charcoal gray covers. I stand up from the bed, going to my dresser to grab a pre-rolled joint and a lighter. The soft crackling of the fireplace near the far wall being the only sound to fill the room.

I walk over to the sliding glass door, meeting the cold brisk air as my bare feet step onto the heated balcony flooring. I light one end of the joint in my hand, bringing the other to my lips as I inhale in.

I exhale as I settle myself, hoping the cold air will dissolve the inferno I feel within.

Because unfortunately, I am a man who is not even remotely appalled at the fact that she pleasured herself to the thought of me. No, I am a damn bastard who finds that *insanely* hot.

Regardless of our bet on who caves first or not.

A smirk crawls up my lips at the reminder that she thought of me when she was alone, and not the man that she was on her date with tonight.

I might be a man, but I'm not an idiot. She definitely was dressed for a date tonight. The question now is *who* did she go on a date with?

I'd be lying if I didn't admit that it drove me into a well of jealousy after I put two and two together. And that my first thought was to have Dex find out who it is.

I take another hit, then another, letting the sudden ire at another man spending time with her settle as the marijuana drones it out.

I take a final hit before putting it out in the ashtray on my low patio table, leaving it inside the groove as I walk back inside where it's warm.

I close the balcony door behind me, feeling the effects coarse through my body as a wonderful calm feeling takes over.

Completely opposite from the desire of wanting to wring her dates neck.

I settle myself back onto my bed, reaching for the TV remote as I turn it on. Flipping to a random channel before I pass out moments later.

The next morning I woke up to a text from Sawyer.

Join me for lunch. Noon.

I lean back into the leather chair in his office, crossing a leg over another as I wait for him to speak.

He lifts his gaze from his desk, his shoulder length jet black hair still damp as he pushes it back with a hand. "This next job I need you to do alone." He lifts an orange envelope, tossing it to me.

I catch it in my lap, opening the clasps as my brows knit together at his order. "Any particular reason why?" I pull out the files as my gaze lowers to the papers.

"You'll know why soon."

I skim over the name, the picture and his basic info. Looking for anything that jumps out to me. I skim back to the next page and understand why he wants me to take care of this man.

A private detective currently investigating the disappearance of Ian Gray, hired by his very own brother Wesley.

"You'll need to treat this one carefully. No sudden moves. But don't wait too long."

I shuffle through the man's previous cases, all of which with success rates at putting the perpetrators away. With one area of interest that he likes to spend his time researching on.

The Deimari Mafia.

"Carson said he's known to be ruthless when it comes to cracking unresolved cases. He's tried solving jobs that have led back to us in the past. So I want him dealt with."

I shove the papers back inside, closing the envelope up before nodding my head at Sawyer. "Understood."

He nods vaguely, his gaze piercing onto mine. "How do you plan on dealing with Wesley tonight." An order rather than a question.

"Something that doesn't require any mess."

"Well hopefully after you take care of both of them, we can put all of this behind us." He nods his head curtly, glancing at the office door. "Very well then." He goes back to going through paperwork, his cue that our meeting is over.

I stand up from my seat, going to make my departure when I turn back around. "How is Priscilla doing?"

Sawyer looks up from his desk, a cold gaze momentarily appearing on his face as a loose strand of his jet black hair shifts over his dark brow. My gaze lowered to notice his sharp jaw clenching briefly at the reminder of how his niece was treated. "I've hired a therapist for her to speak to once a week." He lowers his gaze back down to his desk, reaching for a thin stack of papers. The "It seems to be helping."

I nod my head as I stare at a man who would do absolutely anything for his family. The last living male descendant of the Deimari family lineage. A man who would go to war to protect the people he loves. "Good." I turn back around and make my departure from Sawyer's office.

As I make my way downstairs a slither of a feeling makes its way through my chest. Starting from the pit of my stomach, reaching up until it burrows a home inside of my chest. A quiet calmness sharpened with a cold guttural need that feels neither forced or trivial.

A sureness that settles in its wake.

I step into my vehicle, closing the door as that feeling seeps into every inch of my mind. An internal promise now stationing itself at the forefront of my thoughts.

Of the horrific things I'd do to any man who is brave enough to take advantage of Amelia.

Chapter 25

Amelia

As soon as I get into work I do what Levi says.

After I've put all my things into my locker, I put my outfit on—which consists of a thin, sheer black, long sleeved top that ties in the front. Along with a matching sheer black skirt that goes to just below my ass, a velvet black thong underneath.

I make my way towards the VIP section, the neon sign at the center of the awning illuminated as my gaze fixates on the exit door at the end of the hallway. I pass by room after room, door after door ajar as credenza carts of clear decanters and luxurious furniture peek through the openings. Waiting to be immersed with.

I reach the end of the hallway as my thumb and index finger pinch around the lock, the cool brass biting my skin as I turn it. The faint sound of a click sounding before I make my way back out onto the main floor.

"VIP already? It's someone's lucky night." Sapphire says as her bare shoulder nearly bumps into me. Her rich blue hair magnified from the lights above as long lashes fan out beneath her bangs.

I laugh as I pull her in, giving her a friendly squeeze before pulling away. "I just wanted to check and make sure they were actually cleaned before trying to persuade a man to buy one."

"I'd imagine that'd be a safety hazard if they didn't. I don't even want to know what the locals do in those playrooms." A grimace greets her face briefly before continuing her walk up to the stage. Her hand lightly trailing up the metal railing as her clear heels click against the laminate steps. Her gaze slowly lowers to a man whistling at her from one of the leather seats below, a smirk crawling up her face as she locks eyes with him.

Sapphire—also known as Pole Princess. And for good reason, too.

She turns her head around, winking as the moving head lights above swivel around her. Casting soft hues of pink and blue against the glitter and tiny jewels fashioned into her black two-piece. "Good luck."

I give her a smirk before walking towards the bar when I see him already seated at a table, just behind the main seating from the stage.

That same, familiar russet hair. Just like his brother.

I make my slow walk over to him until I approach him. His face gradually lifts to mine, his eyes nearly bulging out of their sockets. "H-hello." He stammers as he leans back into his seat.

I smile sweetly as I take a seat on the armrest of his chair. "Hello." I purr, lowering my hand to his forearm. The touch featherlight.

His gaze roams over my face before fixating on my crimson hair, his brows knitting together momentarily before smoothing out again. I watch as the wheels turn in his head, understanding of who his brother was referring to registering on his face. I watch the not-so-subtle movement of him straightening his posture as his arm beneath my hand turns faintly rigid.

"You look handsomely familiar." I lie smoothly, working to ease the sudden tension. "Have I seen you here before?"

He clears his throat, a faint smirk gracing his lips though his energy wreaks of worry. "You must be thinking of my brother, Ian. Remember him?"

I tilt my head, leaning down closer to him, fully aware my breasts are visible through this thin piece of fabric. His gaze lowers for a moment before raising again. "Yes, he took me for drinks a few nights back. I was terribly upset when I never heard from him again." I lean a little closer down, his gaze falling to my chest again. "I guess he didn't like what he saw." I raise up suddenly, making a pouty face.

His hand lowers itself behind me, settling on my ass. The immediate impulse to break his hand surfaces, but quickly simmers at the reminder that he'll be dead in a few hours anyway. So I allow the nervous man to get a feel of a good ass, considering it'll be the last one he'll ever feel again.

"I can't imagine anyone would be displeased with you." He says, leaning forward slightly in his chair. "I'd imagine you're a lady who knows exactly how to win a man over." He winks at me.

Gross. As if the thought of being a pick-me woman just to appease a man has ever crossed my mind.

I shrug my shoulders, playing into the docile facade. "Perhaps not every man feels that way. Maybe you can ask him what I did wrong so I know what not to do the next time around."

Fake, fake, fake. Like I would ever change myself for a puny man.

"I'd be happy to, except I haven't heard from him in a few days."

I make it an effort to look surprised, a frown pulling down at my lips. "Is everything alright?" I subtly grip my hand into his bicep, releasing slowly.

He exhales. "I hope so. We're very close so it's unlike him to not return any of my texts or calls for days on end." He lifts his gaze back up to mine after having lowered it to the floor. "You haven't heard from him?"

I raise my other hand to my chest, deepening the frown as I shake my head. "After we went for drinks, he said he'd call me the next day. So we could meet again but nothing." I exhale a long breath, deepening the frown. "I probably shouldn't say this but," I lean closer to him, whispering. "He mentioned that night he was dealing with a bit of depression. So, I assumed his lack of reaching out to me had something to do with that."

Wesley raises an eyebrow, leaning a little closer into me. "That's strange—he never told me he was struggling."

I fake a heavy sigh, lowering my hand. "He probably wouldn't like me airing out his business but—no, I can't. It wouldn't be right." I begin to stand up, shaking my head as I put my hands up. "I'm sorry for wasting your time tonight, sir—"

"Wait," He grabs my wrist gently, smoothing his thumb over my soft skin. Both heat and desperation swimming in his gaze. "Please, call me Wesley."

I repeat his name slowly, intentionally. "Wesley." I slowly sit myself back onto the armrest.

He releases his hand before lowering to my back. "I would greatly appreciate anything that you tell me about my brother. Anything that could help me understand why he's gone awol."

I tilt my head, gazing at him for a long moment before I release a sigh. "Okay, I'll tell you. But promise you won't tell him I was the one who told you."

He nods his head. "Of course, dear."

I pause for a long moment, feeding into the lie. I lean in once more, whispering. "He told me he was feeling disconnected from his...masculinity because he couldn't get it up." I glance down at Wesley's pants.

He raises a brow. "Really?" Skepticism and curiosity both dancing with one another in his tone.

I nod my head as I make a slight grimace with my lips. "He said he could only get it up by being pegged."

I feel Wesley's body begin to tense up beneath my touch, his hand coming up to run itself through his hair. "That's pretty...absurd considering the things he told me he was into."

I start to see the moment that Wesley goes completely rigid, and before he can question me further I wield my power to the surface. The tension bracketing his face begins to soften as he gazes up at me.

I run the tips of my fingers along his cheek, my gaze piercing his as tiny pimples rise to the surface of his skin. The fixation on one another subtle enough it wouldn't cause extra attention from any of the other customers in this club. That anyone who did look over this way would probably think he was just admiring me. "Wesley, you want to buy me a VIP room." I purr.

He nods his head slowly, reaching into his pocket and pulling out his wallet.

"Because you want to spend time with me. Isn't that right, Wesley?" I lower my head to his ear, blowing gently onto it.

I feel him shiver with pleasure as he pulls out a few hundred dollars. "Yes, please."

I lean back, meeting his gaze again as I grab the money. His gaze softens as it trains itself on my face.

"Take me to a VIP room." He says, completely bewitched from my trance.

I nod, smiling sweetly as I stand myself up. Wesley following my lead.

I hold him by the hand, the money in the other as I guide us to the open awning. I guide him to the room furthest to the back, closest to the exit door.

My fingers splay themselves against the door as I push it open all the way. "Sit."

He walks over to the couch and gently plops down onto it, his face calm and fixated wholly on me as he waits.

I go to the cart of bottled champagne and empty glasses, pulling two out for us. I pull my phone out of my thick lace garter, opening up a particular text thread.

I'm bored with him already.

I glance at the clock in the corner of my screen as it reads ten-forty. A sigh escaping me before my gaze glances at the text back from Levi.

I'm on my way. Be there in fifteen.

I quick grin graces my face before I set my phone on the cart, lifting the vial out of my breasts. "So Wesley, tell me about yourself." Not truly interested but deciding that the silence is also too boring. Knowing that once I give this to him, he'll be out within a few moments. And Levi won't be here for another fifteen?

Ugh, what am I supposed to do with him until then?

I hear him make an audible swallow in which I turn around to face him, leaving the vial on the cart. "Are you nervous, Wesley?" I begin approaching him slowly. "Tell me the truth." I persuade through that power of mine.

He nods his head as he watches me. "Yes."

I stand in front of him, my hands coming to the sides of his face before I lower myself down into his lap. His body goes rigid as he nearly ceases breathing entirely. "Let's play a game, Wesley." I lower my hands down his neck until they rest on top of his shoulders.

A single trickle of sweat beads at the top of his brow as he nods vigorously. His cock in his pants pressing against the fabric.

"Tell me what your fantasy is," I bring my hands up to my breasts, feeling desire radiating off of him as I circle my nipples. His gaze fixates wholly on my fingers as he watches me intently. "And maybe I'll make it come true tonight."

Okay, I might not be *attracted* to the man. But I am a creature who loves to be desired. So, fuck it. Let me have my fun.

He makes another audible swallow. "I—I don't know."

"Oh, don't be shy." My fingers curve underneath my top's opening, prying it open as I free my breasts from it. Teasing him, taunting him. "Think real *long* and *hard* about it."

He exhales raggedly as his cheeks flush to a warm pink. "Um, I—I've always wanted to watch a woman—you know."

I tilt my head, surprised as I can read the truth in his words. "That's it?"

He nods his head.

"How much money do you have on you, Wesley?" Lifting myself off of his lap and seating myself onto the coffee table.

"Uh—five hundred." He chokes out.

I open my legs, wide enough for him to see that velvet thong beneath. He groans as he gasps out. "Twelve hundred. I have twelve hundred—it's all in my wallet." He nods towards it in his pocket.

A long sigh escapes me as I shake my head. "You were so close, Wesley." I reach my hand over his pocket, dipping into it until I grab his wallet. "But you had to go and lie to me. Why?"

"I don't know." He admits.

"Do you not think I'm worth paying appropriately to fulfill your fantasy?" I open up his leather wallet, counting the cash inside. Exactly twelve hundred, on top of the three hundred he already gave me.

"No—" He nearly shouts. "Please, I'm sorry."

I stand up, walking over to the cart as I check the time on my phone.

Ten fifty-five. Thank fuck.

"Let's have a glass of champagne first then." I turn my head around to look at him. "To loosen me up first." I wink before turning back around.

"Absolutely."

I pour some into each glass, setting it down while I grab the vial. I twist the tiny cap off, pouring the contents into one glass. I turn around, approaching Wesley. My power steadily keeping him calm. "Here, a gift." I hand him the vial.

He takes it. "What do you want me to do with it?" He asks.

"Put it in your pocket. Eat it, crush it into your pants. Quite frankly, I don't care." I turn back around, grabbing the two glasses as I roll my eyes. I turn back around to face him, lower his glass down to him. "I just need the evidence gone." I say plainly.

"Evidence?" He asks while simultaneously shoving the vial into his pocket, unable to do anything else as he's still under my compulsion. He lowers his hand to grab the glass from my hand, bringing it closer to his lips.

I draw out a sigh, waving a hand at him. "You'll see soon enough." I take a sip of my champagne, my gaze fixated on him. Waiting.

He slowly brings his glass to his lips, lifting it back as the liquid slides into his mouth. He goes to lower the glass down onto the coffee table.

"All of it." I command, power licking the room around us.

He does as I ask and downs the champagne. Not even a moment before he can set the empty glass down onto the table do his eyes bulge out as he drops the glass from his hand.

I quickly grab it, standing up as I set it onto the credenza cart before turning back around.

I watch as his hands come to his throat, terror blanching his face as he gasps for air. He stumbles as he stands up, hurrying towards the door when he first falls to his knees, then all the way down face first.

I watch him lie there, still as a statue as his eyes remain open, staring at the carpet below.

"Creepy." I say as I grab my phone again. Sending Levi one text, hoping he's arrived.

Done.

A moment later I hear the exit door creaking open as I fix my top, concealing my breasts beneath the fabric once again.

Like that does anything.

Levi walks into the VIP room, donned in a black jacket and black jeans. His wavy blonde hair messy and pushed back from his face as he locks eyes with me. "Ready?"

I nod, his gaze not lowering even an inch from my face.

Levi lowers himself down as we both get right to hauling Welsey's body out of the VIP room, and into the trunk of Levi's car before driving over to the Cimiteria Sea.

Chapter 26

"How are you sure nobody saw me enter with him on camera?"

Levi closes his door, cranking the dial of the heat up as he looks over at me. He glances down at my attire, a moment later taking off his black overcoat and draping it over my shoulders. I nuzzle into the thick wool material as my shivering subsides. "Because I have someone on the inside who hacked into the club's camera system. Who's also keeping an eye on things while we're gone."

I uncross my arms, feeling the immediate warmth of his jacket over my chilled skin. The smell of bergamot overpowers me as I lower each arm through each sleeve, wrapping the coat tightly against me as I shamelessly inhale the cologne in. "A partner?"

He puts the car in drive as he pulls out of the alleyway. "Something like that."

I watch as he leans his left hand over the steering wheel, his other reaching into his jean pocket. He pulls out his phone and hands it over to me. "Two-two-eight-one."

I look down at the screen as it prompts me to enter a passcode. I enter the numbers and watch the main screen pop up, a random picture of the city set as his background.

"Go to the app in the lower right-hand corner."

As I find the app I click on it, pulling up a main screen. Five camera angles show up on the screen, all live feeds of The Playground. I lower my gaze to the camera angle situated right above the VIP section entrance, angled to face down towards the hallway but too dark to see anything further.

"It's currently set on a constant loop."

I look up at him, blinking.

"It was programmed before you took Wesley into VIP. So anyone who asks won't have proof of you going in with him. Only that you went in by yourself, earlier on when you went to open the door for me."

He grabs the phone, tapping that camera angle and enlarging it. He rewinds the feed, giving it back to me. "See."

I look down at the screen, watching the moment I walked through when I got in for my shift to open the door for him. Glancing at the time at the bottom of the camera feed. I fast forward it, waiting to find me walking in with Wesley. Until I get to the exact time now, with no evidence of us entering the room at all.

I look up at him, smirking. "Nice little party trick." Exiting out of the app. "Yet it's pretty possible someone saw me walking in with him."

"Are you afraid?" He asks, turning the steering wheel as we take a left down the street.

I make a low huff noise. "Never."

"I know." He says, glancing over at me before focusing back on the road. "Besides, the few men in there had all their eyes on your friend on the main stage anyway."

I chuckle. "So you know Sapphire?"

"No, not personally. But my...partner sure has a keen interest in her."

"Why doesn't he make a move?"

Levi chuckles as he glances over at me, snuggled up in his coat. For a moment, something dances over his eyes before he turns his gaze back to the road again. "Dex won't make a move. Not yet at least."

I look back down at his phone, looking at the other camera angles. I pull up the one angled towards the main stage, watching as Sapphire dances her seductive little heart away on the pole. I squint my gaze to see a man sitting right at the center of the stage, the familiarity of him striking. A purring noise gets trapped in my throat. "Well if he's just going to sit around and watch her then he may miss his opportunity."

Levi laughs, finding myself annoyed when it does something to my belly. I force myself to shake it off as I close out the app entirely. "Dex likes to plan in the shadows and make his move right at the perfect moment." He looks over at me. "He won't miss his chance, though." He turns his gaze back to the road.

I scroll through his phone before going to his photo library. I look down at the few photos he has, mainly of landscapes and nature. I swipe to a photo of himself with who I presume is Dex, and when I try to swipe for more I find I'm at the end of his library. "Wow, a whole seven photos." I look up at him. "You have quite the fascinating life."

Levi chuckles as the light in his eyes glints. "I don't take many photos as you can see."

I open up his camera, turning the flash on as I angle the phone slightly above me. I press the circle at the bottom of the screen, the white flash blinding me momentarily as I take a photo of myself. I lower the phone, pulling up the photo. "There, now you have something."

I go to his settings, scrolling to the wallpaper section and setting my photo as his new wallpaper. I hand him back his phone as he takes it, looking down at his new background.

"Something more interesting than just the city lights."

He laughs, staring down at it for a moment before shoving his phone back in his pocket. "Infinitely more interesting to say the least."

I fight the smirk that tries to crawl up my face as he turns down another street, the container lot coming into view. He pulls forward, driving up until we're only ten feet away from the edge of the lot.

He puts the car in park as I go to open the car door. He leans over, grabbing my arm when I turn my head towards him. My gaze lowers to his lips as our faces are suddenly only inches apart.

"It's cold out. You should stay inside the car." His gaze lowers to my lips, branding itself into my red lips for a long moment. "I've got this." He says, slowly lifting his gaze back up, as if it's a challenge to do so.

For a long moment neither one of us moves, as if lost in the closeness that taunts both of us.

I nod my head slowly, lowering my gaze again to his lips. "Fine." I say, watching his gaze slowly lower.

I watch as he leans in just a hair closer, licking the bottom of his lip as I can practically taste him from here. He lets go of my arm slowly, my chest sinking as I remember to breathe correctly again.

He suddenly pulls back, looking away as he creates distance between us. My gaze tracks over him as his hand leans down to pull the trunk lever below his seat, the trunk behind me slowly swinging open as he steps out of the car.

I settle back into my seat as I watch him through the rear view mirror walk to the back of the car, the heat of his breath still lingering on my skin. I lift my hand, pressing a finger to my red lips. I shake off the heat rising inside of me, lowering my hand inside his coat as I wait in the car.

He's just a man, Amelia.

The words in my head sounding more like a delicious confession rather than a disciplinary reminder.

I watch as Levi drags Wesley out, his body wrapped in a black tarp. He drags him down to the very edge, coming back to the car to get the weighted plates.

Looping a rope through the holes he attaches them to the rope around Wesley's body, tightening it before he pushes his body over the edge with his booted foot. Down into the sea below.

Maybe he'll end up right alongside his brother. At the bottom of the sea floor, reunited once again.

A twisted family reunion to say the least.

Levi walks back to the car, seating himself down before he closes the door. He brings his hands up, rubbing his palms together vigorously. "Shit, it's cold. Soon enough the sea isn't going to be an option." He chuckles as he lowers his hands, putting the car in reverse.

I find myself glancing at his lips again before I force myself to look away. "How do you dispose of your *jobs* when the water freezes over?" I ask.

He shrugs his shoulders as he cranks the wheel, reversing until my window is now facing the river. He shifts into drive as he cranks the wheel the other way, pulling forward as we exit off the lot. "We have connections with someone who owns a funeral home."

I tilt my head at him, scrunching my eyebrows. "And you still choose to throw them over? When you could literally *burn* the evidence?"

He looks over at me, a grin curving up his full lips. "This is more fun." He faces forward again. "With cremating them it's over and done with, simple and boring."

I watch him, blinking once.

"I like to be...spontaneous." His gaze lowers to my lips once again, settling there for a moment before turning back to the road. "A good adrenaline rush." His smile deepens, one of pure wickedness that sends heat coursing through me.

I lean back into the seat, that heat rising once more within me. I inhale sharply before turning my gaze to look out of my window. As I fixate my gaze on the city lights illuminating through the car window, unable to ignore another thing we both have in common.

Chapter 27

He pulls up into the alley, right outside of the club exit door. I look down at my phone, the time in the corner of the screen reading eleven-forty.

He puts the car in park as I begin shimmying myself out of his coat. I adjust my sheer top as I look over at him, handing him the wool coat. "Thanks."

He nods, taking the coat as he begins putting it back on. He gives a half smile. "Anytime."

"So, is there another job I should be aware of right away?" I ask, fanning my lashes.

He chuckles, shaking his head. "Not at this time, but I'll let you know when something changes."

I nod my head, giving him a faint smile before I lean over to open my door. The door opens as I step one heeled foot out onto the concrete.

"Do you need a ride home tonight?"

I turn my head around, blinking.

He clears his throat. "It's pretty cold tonight. I could pick you up and take you home. If you'd like."

I watch him, contemplating for a moment as a grin crawls up my lips. "Sure. But only 'cause you asked." I step out of the car completely, lowering my head into the car once more. "I'm off at two. Don't be late."

He nods, his gaze wholly on my face as a smile creeps up his lips. "I'll be here."

I close the car door as I turn around, hurrying to the exit door as I pull the ice cold doorknob open.

I creep through the opening, the club music blasting me immediately. I quietly close the door behind me, peering down the hallway as I listen for any sound whatsoever. I look down into the room Wesley and I were in, exactly how I left it.

The room having been put back together after Levi got here as if nobody even occupied this room tonight.

A smile curves up my face as something lights up inside of me. A different kind of rush aside from the normal adrenaline of my everyday life. Using my seductress energy to my benefit, being wild and free with it.

But something about doing these jobs with Levi, it's beginning to feel less like a chore and more of a...thrill.

I straighten my shoulders as I make the exit out of the VIP hallway, back out onto the main club floor. I look to see Sapphire having seated herself beside a small section of men. Flaunting her charm and—well, obviously that Succubus energy.

I move my way over to the bar, both wanting a drink and also curious if Ace suspects anything such as—oh, I don't know. The fact that I went into the VIP hallway with a man and came back out without one.

I make it to the bar counter when I feel my phone vibrate in my hand. I glance down at the screen, smiling as I turn my phone over and seat myself down on the bar chair.

Ace approaches me, lowering his steady gaze momentarily as he gives me a smirk. "I've never seen you wear that outfit before. Your boobs look fantastic."

I flutter my lashes as I smirk at him, sighing internally of relief at no mention of me being in the VIP. I glance down the bar, noticing the amount of patrons seated here. I guess I can thank them for keeping Ace distracted. "Thanks. It's new."

He immediately has a vodka cranberry made for me as he slides it over to me. "Will we be seeing Mr. Initiative tonight?" He leans his elbows onto the counter, leaning forward.

A soft noise of appreciation escapes me as I grab the drink, bringing the straw to my lips. I take a long sip as a grin curves my lips. "No, but we will tomorrow." I lower the drink back to the counter, a strange feeling of emptiness with that statement coming and going just as quickly as it took Wesley to keel over tonight.

"And did you go to dinner with him?" His brown eyes piercing into mine.

"I did."

"*And?*" He leans in a little closer, bringing his hands up to the underneath of his jaw, curling his fingers inwards. "Are you going to make me beg the details out of you?"

"You, begging? Oh, I think I just might." I say huskily.

He steps back, gently nudging at my shoulder. "Save the teasing for the customers." A laugh bellows out of him.

I share a laugh as well, a long exhale following. "I'm afraid I have no *details* to share. We just went for dinner, he kissed me goodnight. That's it."

Ace tilts his head, playing with his lip ring as his eyebrows raise. "Oh, so he's in it for the long haul."

I shrug my shoulders. "Possibly."

"But you're bored already." He says.

I squint my eyes at him, assessing. I go to open my mouth when he cuts me off.

"I know you better than you think, Cher. I know when you're *enthralled* with a man, and when you're simply just passing the time. And you definitely don't seem enthralled by him."

I roll my eyes, sighing as I lean my head onto my fist. Thinking about the date with Adrian and how it went wonderfully. How he passed all the normal requirements, how he kept me interested and never made me feel like I had to pry the attention out of him. How *normal* he was, and how that should be refreshing to me.

Yet, a part of me still feels...bleh about him. Like there's a particular spark about us that's missing that hasn't sealed me in quite yet. Maybe I just need to get to know him a little more before that spark ignites.

Though my mind wanders to the way that Levi walked into the VIP room tonight, donned in all black like a true mafia hitman. With both precision and steadiness in his gaze as we hauled Wesley into the trunk.

How he craves that same adrenaline to life as I do, and how he's not afraid to own the most depraved, darkest parts of himself. Just thinking about those traits about him and how they mirror my own in some ways makes me feel both lit up and eager from the inside out.

The song changes in the club and I spring back to reality, Ace still standing there as the rap song blares throughout the club.

I sigh heavily again, forcing a smirk. "Maybe different is good for me." I lied.

Ace watches me as if he can smell the lie floating from my lips. He gives a huff before turning his head towards a man down at the far end, waving his hand up for him. "I guess you never know until you try." He pats the bar counter before he walks down the bar, taking the man's drink order.

I grab my drink, taking another big sip before lowering it again. Letting his words cycle through my head once before I shove all of it away, putting on my best face as I feel the eyes of someone on my back.

I go to drink the rest of my drink, setting it gently onto the counter. I slowly turn my chair around, stepping off the bar stool and begin walking casually down the main floor.

The man who had his eyes on me gently grabs my wrist, my eyes lowering to him seated in a leather chair. I turn towards him, my eyes locking onto him as that seductress comes right out to play once more.

Chapter 28

I smack the wooden paddle to his ass, a whimper escaping out of him. His body jerks forward as he kneels on all fours on the crimson carpet.

"Harder." He says curtly. His back relaxes as he lets out a ragged exhale. The white and navy striped shirt on his back quivering as a subtle shiver runs down his back.

This guy really does like being spanked.

A smirk lifts my lips as I smack his ass much harder this time, wringing a loud gasp from him.

A giggle threatens to crawl up my throat as I force it back down. Hey, I'm all into kinks. But there's just something so damn entertaining about spanking a man on all fours.

When he asked me if I could peg him I told him we don't have the right *equipment* for that here. Which honestly is too bad as I've always wanted to know what pegging someone is like. As it's pretty ironic that a man's G-spot is in his asshole yet when you mention it to them they get all mad and defensive.

Like, relax dude. You're acting like I'm the one who made you guys this way. Just get over your alpha bullshit and accept it. Better yet, start owning it.

It's too bad. He was willing to pay me three thousand for me to do it, too. Well, at least I'm making one thousand off of spanking this man until his ass bleeds.

I give him another hard spank until he yelps, his ass scrunching in his khaki pants. "Okay. Okay."

I step back, honoring his limit and walking around to stand in front of him. I lower myself down, bending at the knees. "Satisfied?" I ask, tilting my head as I grin at him.

He looks up at me, nodding his head as he slowly gets himself up onto his feet. His hand flinches to his ass as a grimace scrunches his face. "Damn, for a lady you hit hard." A laugh bursts out of him. "I don't think I'll be able to sit on my ass for a few days."

I chuckle as I stand myself up as well. "Well, you did say to hit hard so—"

"Oh, trust me. I'm not complaining." A genuine smile curves his lips, the joy painting his face one of true fulfillment. "Thank you, Ms. Cherry." He bows his head and nearly limps to the couch to grab his beige jacket.

"Now you know who to see anytime you need another fix." I wink.

He puts his coat on, giving me a wide grin. "I will keep that in mind. Goodnight." He turns around and walks out of the VIP room, his hand coming to his ass once before falling away.

What a nice guy.

I walk over to the couch, collecting the money and picking up my phone. I look down to check the time when I see a text from Levi had just come through.

I'm here out back.

A smile curves up my lips as I read one-fifty on the corner of the screen. Well, at least he's not late.

I grab my stuff and walk down the hallway, out to the main floor and head for the locker room. I see Vivianne in her little office as I enter the locker room, making my way into the small room before I head to my locker.

She looks up from her desk, a smile curving up her sweet face. She glances down at the wad of cash in my hands before a frail hand lifts her glasses off. "I see you had a decent night." She lifts her gaze again as she sets them on the wooden desk.

I pull her tip out, handing it to her. "You could say that." I smile back, nodding towards the papers scattered. "I do hope these won't keep you here all night."

She laughs as she takes the money. "Not at all, dear. Just some tedious paperwork before I skip out as well." She lowers the money into her safe box, the metal clinking together as she shuts it. "Get home safe, Cher."

"You too, house mama." I say over my shoulder before leaving the office.

I approach my locker when I see Sapphire pulling her jacket over her, already out of her work outfit. She walks over towards me, fluffing her short blue hair. "I was thinking tonight why we don't ever hang out outside of work." She makes a pouty face as she looks up at me.

I laugh, setting my cash and phone down as I pull out my dance bag, setting it on the bench. "Probably because you have a tendency to bail when we do."

She playfully swats at my arm as we both laugh. "That was one time—well, okay maybe twice." She crosses her arms as she leans herself against a locker, chuckling. "I'm sorry, I'll do better. I was just so exhausted those times."

"Just admit that you're a homebody." I smirk at her before I lift my shirt off, tossing it into my bag. I take out a long sleeved gray shirt, pulling it over me before smoothing it against my chest.

Sapphire sucks her teeth, making a humming noise. "Yeah, I really can't argue there." She hooks her dance bag over her shoulder. "Maybe that should've been my new year's resolution. Making it a point to get out of the house more."

I slip my skirt off along with my thong, tossing those into my bag as I grab a pair of boyshort underwear, slipping those on as I chuckle as I glance up at her. "It's never too late to start." I slip a pair of black leggings over, uncaring if the lines from my underwear are showing or not.

"Good point." She steps away from the locker as she steps forward. "Well, I'll see you tomorrow."

She says as she leans in to give me a quick kiss on the cheek before walking away.

"See ya, girl." I say back before closing up my locker as she makes her exit.

I grab my faux fur coat, throwing it over as I grab my tip outs for the DJ, Janice, and Maverick. I put everything else in my bag save for my phone, throwing my bag over my shoulder and exiting the locker room.

I pay each person out before I exit the club through the employee exit. I open the back door to find Levi waiting in his car for me, watching as he looks up to meet my gaze through the passenger window.

I walk towards the car, opening the passenger side door as I slide inside.

He glances at my outfit. "I can imagine that's far more comfortable." He turns the heat dial up a notch, putting the car in drive as he drives down the alley.

"Comfier, but not always sexier." I say as I set my bag down next to my feet.

He turns the wheel with one hand, turning out of the alley and onto the street. His hair laying loose as a few strands hang above his forehead. He looks over at me again, his gaze roaming before looking back onto the road. "Not always."

I look over at him, shrugging. "Whatever you say."

For a brief moment I feel his energy tense up, as if I said something to upset him. But he says nothing as he drives me the short distance home.

As we get to my street, I feel his car jerk forward. My gaze swings over to him as I sit up straight, leaning forward slightly. "What was that?"

He leans forward, his gaze on the dash as he curses. "Fucking kidding me." He releases a rough exhale as his car does it again. He pulls it over to the side of the street, putting it in park as suddenly the lights on his dash begin flashing.

Until moments later they go out completely as his car turns off.

"Um, that's not good." I say.

"It's my damn battery." He pulls the key out of the ignition as he pulls his phone out of his pocket. Swiping along the bright screen with his thumb. "I have jumper cables but no car to connect them too."

"Yeah, I unfortunately can't help you in that department."

He begins typing to someone, hitting send when moments later a text comes through. He curses again before sending another text.

"Well for such a nice car this is unfortunate."

"Batteries are no big fix, just a nuisance sometimes. It's inexpensive to get a new one." He looks at his phone once more. I watch as another text pops up before he puts his phone back in his pocket. "Dex can come jump my car but he's on the other side of town right now. It'll take him at least forty minutes to get here."

My gaze lowers to his hands for whatever reason, the veins in them bulging out. I lift my gaze, wondering if I will hate myself for the offer after I've made it. "You can come up for the time being."

Levi looks over at me, assessing for a long moment. "Nah, it's okay. I can just wait—"

"Oh, stop being modest." I say as I open the car door, stepping out before shutting the door in his face.

I watch as Levi follows suit tentatively, stepping out of the vehicle before closing the door behind him.

"Why sit out here and freeze your balls off when I have a warm place? I promise I won't bite." I start walking towards my building's entrance door, turning my head around. "Unless you ask, of course." I wink.

I watch Levi swallow as he schools his features into neutrality. He forces a laugh as he follows at my side. "You're still not getting me to cave, Amelia."

I give him a smirk as we head into my building.

The cold night air doing very little to quell the sudden overwhelming excitement coursing through me.

Chapter 29

Levi

Fuck, what am I doing?

I should've just lied to her, said I would rather freeze my balls off outside than be near her. But instead I let myself agree to coming up to her penthouse.

Stupid, stupid man.

We walk through the main entrance doors, heading for the stainless steel elevator doors when a group of three couples pile in before us.

"Hold it." Amelia yells after them as one arm comes out, holding the elevator door open for us.

We rush in as the couples part a way for us as Amelia heads to the back of the elevator, me following behind her as I plant myself at the very back of the elevator. My back against the cool railing so I have eyes on everyone in here.

A hypervigilance honed in from a young age.

"I think I drank too much tequila tonight." A blonde haired woman says to who I'm assuming is her boyfriend. I watch as he puts an arm around her, tugging her closer to him as she nuzzles herself into his thick grey coat. "I told you to slow down but you never listen." He plants a kiss on her forehead as she hums into his shoulder.

I shove my hands into my pockets, leaning against the wall as Amelia stands in front of me.

Not a very big elevator to say the fucking least.

"Which floor?" Another woman asks us, glancing at Amelia through glazed, half squinted eyes.

Amelia looks at the numbers lit up on the pad, noting the number fifteen is highlighted. She gives a vague grin, nodding. "Fifteen as well."

Smart girl.

The woman nods as she turns around and the six of them begin to talk amongst themselves. Very drunkenly, that is.

I feel Amelia sigh as she runs her hand behind her neck, lifting her deep red hair out from underneath her coat. I get a whiff of vanilla and some kind of floral scented perfume as she momentarily rubs the back of her neck, her fingers slipping just beneath the collar of her coat.

I inhale the smell of her, nearly shivering like a damn leaf against a soft breeze of wind.

I watch as she leans on one foot, her coat brushing up against me as her ass subtly pokes out. I stand completely still, keeping my hands to myself.

Dear fucking gods keep your hands to yourself, Levi.

She tilts her head slightly down to the side as she faces forward, fixing her bag up her arm as she hauls it closer to her body.

Two...Three...

The neon numbers go up ever so slowly as the elevator continues ascending up, the couples in front of us still chatting amongst themselves.

I watch as Amelia gets tired of holding her large bag up, deciding to lower it to the ground. She bends slightly as her ass presses into me. I feel her still suddenly, her hand letting go of the bag straps as she straightens herself back up again.

My head only inches away from hers, I hear her utter one faint, ragged breath and it's enough to send me spiraling into heat like a damn animal.

I feel her take a single step backwards, intentionally moving herself closer to me. She keeps her hands folded in front of her lap as she keeps her gaze forward.

Wondering if she can feel how hard I am already, and if she's appalled or just as aroused as I am right now. But as she takes another step back closer to me, that self restraint I've been keeping heavily contained slips.

I lower my head a little closer, my nose just barely brushing the side of her neck as she inhales suddenly. My gaze lowers to her hands as she fiddles with her fingers in her lap. Until she tilts her head, giving me better access to her neck.

I smirk against her skin as I slowly lower my lips over her neck, her breath hitching once more as I brush my lips against her soft skin.

Gods fucking damnit I could die happily listening to her make that noise.

Her hands unclasp themselves as one lowers to her side, the tips of her fingers slowly grazing my pant leg as she curls them inward. Wringing a ragged exhale from me as I press my lips against her neck.

My cock grows even harder at the subtle touch, completely bricked up now as her fingers slowly move over me.

I lower my hand to her waist, feeling her body tense up momentarily before relaxing into me as my fingers brush along her navel. My lips graze along her neck as her gaze remains facing forward on the couples in front of us. I press another kiss to her neck as I pull her flush against me.

Ten...Eleven...

Her hand cups my cock over my jeans and it takes everything inside of me not to whimper into her neck right now.

I raise my lips for just a moment before gliding the tips of my teeth against her skin. I raise up to her earlobe, nipping it and causing her to gasp quietly as she rocks into me. Grinding her ass into my cock as her hand cups me through my jeans.

No words shared, no sounds made other than her faint gasping and my subtle groaning. Just the two of us touching each other in a room full of people. Just two people crossing a fine line between partners and something more.

I jerk slightly into her touch as she rubs my cock slowly. I chuckle into her neck as I lower my hand from her navel down until my fingers rub over her pussy. She rocks into me as I rub my fingers over the tight fabric, the feel of her pussy lips sending me into a blind heat. Her arousal wafting towards me.

Thirteen...Fourteen...

"Do you like me touching you, Amelia?" I whisper as I nip at her neck, my thumb circling around her. A ragged exhale leaves her as she writhes into my hand, her head falling back into my shoulder. "Let them see just how much you like it."

She gasps softly as the elevator door opens, arriving at the fifteenth floor. Both of us rubbing each other as the people pile out of the elevator, not even looking back as if forgetting we were there at all. A momentary disappointment that they didn't bother to look back at us, to see the way Amelia writhes against my hand.

As the elevator door closes she removes her hand, stepping away from me entirely.

I bring my hands back to my sides as she takes her key and puts it into the lock, turning it. I hear her trying to regulate her breathing as her back remains facing me. The elevator begins ascending again as she finally turns around towards me.

My gaze immediately notices the heat lining her face, the way her cheeks are pinkened and flushed. And I'd be lying if I said it wasn't the hottest fucking thing in the world.

She steps towards me, her gaze on me wholly as I stand there waiting. She nudges her head to the elevator screen at the top of the pad, lowering her gaze again. "Looks like we're out of time." She smirks.

I bite my lip, nodding. "It appears so." My gaze lowers to her pussy, desperately wanting to know what she tastes like.

How she'd feel writhing at something other than my fingers.

Sixteen...

"Unless," She begins, quickly drawing my attention towards her. "You can make it count in ten floors—"

Seventeen...

Before she can finish her sentence I waste no time closing the distance between us. I rip open her coat as I tug her body towards mine, my hands bringing her face to mine as I press her back into the wall. Our lips press together as I kiss her, hungry and eager as my tongue glides along hers. So fucking soft her tongue is, so fucking *good* in my mouth.

I dip my hand beneath her leggings, her soft tongue gliding over mine as I lower my hand deeper beneath her leggings. I groan into her mouth as my finger glides over her wet pussy.

Fucking gods.

I swirl my thumb over her clit as I thrust my middle finger into her, curving it just right as little moans escape from her. Like music to my fucking ears.

Twenty...Twenty-one...

She starts writhing on my hand as I plunge my finger deep into her, her pussy so fucking wet as it drips down into my palm. In moments, she starts riding harder against my hand as her moans grow louder, lifting her mouth from mine as she leans her head against the wall.

"That's right, little red." I lower my lips to her neck, nipping at the soft skin there as she gasps. "Let that pretty pussy cum on my fingers."

Twenty-three...Twenty-four...

Her pussy clamps around my finger as her orgasm rocks through her, her moaning uncontained as I press kisses to her neck. She writhes against me as she rides out her release, the elevator dinging as it reaches the twenty-seventh floor.

Cum drips down my finger as her body slowly stills beneath me, her pretty face sated as she gazes at me.

I lower my finger from her, a moan escaping her as I descend out of her. The inner walls of her pussy so fucking wet—gods, I don't fucking care. I'll break my discipline to cave just to be able to feel this pussy around my cock one day.

Because suddenly I am absolutely nothing if I can't feel Amelia's sweet pussy.

At that thought I lift my hand out from her leggings, my fingers glistening of her. I put my fingers in my mouth and watch her hungry gaze lock onto me.

My eyes nearly roll to the back of my head as I taste her, sucking on my reward for making her come. My sweet, fucking reward.

I lap my tongue around my finger, savoring every last drop of her before I slowly remove my finger from my mouth. I meet her steady, hungry gaze. "Next time it'll be my tongue that you writhe against."

I lower myself down to grab her bag for her as I walk towards her front door, Amelia hesitating before she follows behind me.

I hear her fumble with her keys before meeting me at my side in front of her penthouse door. I lower my gaze to her placing the key into her door lock, her hand subtly trembling before turning the key to step into her place.

A satisfied and wicked smile curving on my face.

Chapter 30

Amelia

"Shoes off." I say to Levi before I dismiss myself and walk up to my bedroom, setting my dance bag on the carpet. Somehow managing to keep my voice steady even though my heart is still racing a mile a minute.

My mind still frazzled from the orgasm he wrung from my body in a matter of a *minute*.

My mind floats on the bargain made. Did I just cave? Did he cave? Technically not because we were just touching each other, right?

Wait, why am I even analyzing this? It's just that. A business arrangement. Nothing more.

Though at this very moment I don't care whether that's considered him caving or not. Because the way he sucked on his fingers afterwards has my skin crawling and my mind still reeling. And all I can think about is how something else would feel inside of me.

I hear him remove his shoes, setting them away from the center of the walkway. I force a long exhale from my body, calming myself before walking back downstairs. As I reach the foot of the stairs I watch him drape his coat over the back of one of my kitchen chairs. My gaze locks with his as I step back into the kitchen. "Would you like a drink?" I say casually, setting my coat on my mounted coat rack.

A smirk curves up his full lips. "Thanks, but my thirst has been sated for now."

Heat rises to my cheeks, quickly looking away as I shake it off. I tamper down the heat that rises to where his fingers were just moments ago, giving him a nod. "Fine."

Rufus barks from the living room, anxious to get out of his crate. Thank gods for the distraction.

"You have a dog?" Levi asks, leaning against the kitchen counter.

I walk over to the crate, Rufus sniffing the air between the bars. "Hellhound, but yes." I lift the crate door up as Rufus hurries out.

He trots up to Levi, sniffing a lowered hand. He begins licking it, a grimace pulling on my face. "I sure hope you're not letting my Hellhound lick my—"

"Wrong hand." He says, lifting the other from his pocket. He lowers it back into his pocket. "Besides, I washed my hands."

I raise a brow at him. "Really? Because I don't remember hearing the water running."

"You must've been too lost in your thoughts to pay attention." He smirks before leaning down to pet Rufus with both hands, scratching behind his ears.

I roll my eyes as I walk over to the fridge, pulling out a bottle of red wine and a box of leftover steak from the restaurant last night.

I set the foam box into the microwave, closing the door before setting the timer to a minute and thirty seconds. Hitting enter before I grab a wine glass from the cabinet above.

Levi stands up from kneeling towards Rufus, approaching the kitchen island as he takes a seat in one of my black swivel counter stools. His back pressing back into the velvet material as he glances around the open room, looking over towards my living room. "This is nice."

The microwave goes off as I go to grab the togo box, setting it on the counter as I peel the top back, steam rising. I scoff at him. "Were you expecting otherwise from me?" I lower my gaze to my steak, forking a piece of it into my mouth.

His gaze travels to my food before lifting up to me again. "Is that where you went last night?"

I look up at him. "Answer my question first." I say between chewing.

He chuckles. "I definitely expected you to have a luxurious style." He nods back to the food. "Your turn."

"Why so insistent on where I was last night?" I tap the fork to my mouth, a smirk playing up my face. I lower the fork, taking a sip of my wine. I lower the glass back down as I vaguely shrug a shoulder. "But to answer your question, yes."

I watch his gaze harden briefly, so momentarily you'd miss it if you weren't paying attention. His jaw ticks as he fixes his gaze. "What's his name?"

I fork another piece of steak, raising it to my lips. "None of your business." I bring the steak into my mouth, chewing as I delight in this jealous side of him.

As if he realizes it too, he loosens the tension in his jaw. Continuing on anyway. "For now." He says as his phone vibrates in his pocket, pulling it out.

I watch as he sends a text back before setting his phone on the counter. "Dex said he'll be here in twenty."

I give him a nod, finishing off my food before tossing the empty foam box into the garbage. "Lovely." I down the rest of my wine, walking out of the kitchen. "I'm going to change." I nod over to the living room. "Make yourself comfortable."

I walk upstairs once more as I step into my room, the sound of Levi scooting his chair out then back in again echoing. I close my bedroom door, walking over to my dresser as I slip my shirt off. I toss it into the laundry hamper, my leggings and underwear along with it.

I look through my drawer, about to pull out a pair of fuzzy sleep pants when a smirk crawls up my face at something far more revealing.

I grab my silk black sleep set, a pair of booty shorts with a cropped cami to match. The lining of them both trimmed with sheer lace. I pull them on, closing my drawer as I force down the smirk.

I open my door, walking back downstairs when I find Levi sitting on my couch as Rufus takes advantage of the attention that he's giving him. Once he looks up at me, his scratching behind Rufus' ears stops.

His gaze hardens on me, roaming as heat lines his rich brown eyes. That muscle in his jaw ticks once more as he forces himself to slowly continue petting Rufus again.

I go to sit on the cushion next to him, his gaze wholly on my body as it travels from the top down. Rufus scurries out of his hold as he approaches me, electing to sit in front of me now.

I lower down, petting behind his ears as I feel Levi's gaze still on me. Like a sick, hungry predator. After I feel his gaze on my exposed cleavage, he sits back on the couch, a long sigh to follow as he faces forward.

That smirk fighting its way to the surface again at his own frustration, but I keep it contained nonetheless.

I lower my hand to the remote on my glass coffee table, picking it up as Rufus moves up onto the couch, laying down on the lounge section of the couch to my left. I turn the TV on, flipping through channels. "So what do you do with your free time when you're not out killing people?"

I feel his gaze look back over at me, this time on my face. He makes a humming noise as he ponders over my question. "Go to the gym."

I look over at him. "That's it?"

He shrugs. "For the most part, yeah."

I chuckle as I turn my gaze forward again, flipping through the channels. "Well that's kind of boring."

His voice lowers an octave. "If you think there's a better way I could make use of my time I'm up for suggestions."

I look over at him again, my gaze lowering to his lips before I scoff at him. "I just think that if you had more hobbies than maybe you wouldn't need to channel your frustration into killing as much as you do."

"Let's not get it twisted, little red." He leans in a little closer, my gaze focused on the smirk curving up his lips. That damn nickname is infuriating but drawing me in nonetheless. "I don't kill just because I'm obligated to. I kill because I *want* to." He leans back into the couch, creating distance between us. "It's the second best thing I'm good at."

"And what makes the first?" I ask.

His gaze lowers to my shorts, to what's beneath. The wicked smirk on his face deepens as confidence lines his eyes. "I think you can answer that yourself."

Heat flames my skin as I roll my eyes, facing forward again as I click through the channels until I get to the one I like.

"What's this?" He asks.

"Real Dance Wives." I say as the episode starts, the girls on the screen talking as they lounge on beach chairs.

Levi chuckles as he lays his hand on his thigh, the other resting on the back of the couch. "What's it about?"

"Basically, they're all retired dancers with handsome, wealthy husbands. But she," I say pointing to Helene, a blonde bombshell. "She's actually about to tell her husband that she's leaving him for a younger man."

He scoffs at the screen. "Why would she leave him for a younger man if she's already well off? Or is the marriage failing?"

I shrug my shoulders. "She's bored, I guess. Who knows yet."

"Huh." He says, falling silent as he watches the show for a moment. "Did he cheat on her?"

"Nope." I curl my legs under me, tucking them off to the side.

"And she's seeing a younger man?"

"Yes. Only by like, six years." I say, looking over at him and smirking. "If I had to guess, it's probably that he's just better in the sack. She's been complaining this past season of how Rowan, her husband, isn't 'the same in bed anymore'. But I'm hoping to find out soon." I bring my hands up to my chest, rubbing my palms together.

"Sounds like a lame show." Levi mumbles, crossing his arms.

"Oh, you don't have to lie. I know you're secretly interested."

I hear his phone vibrate in his pocket. I glance over to see him pull it out, looking at the screen before standing up from the couch. "Dex is here."

I nod as I look up at him, standing up with him. "Okay." I set the remote down. "I'll walk you out."

We both walk over to the door as he gets his coat and shoes on. I stand there, my bare feet on the cool hardwood floor.

He looks at me. "Thanks for letting me come in for a bit."

I nod. "No problem." I go to open up my door, pulling it open as the elevator door stares back at me.

He comes up behind me, his coat brushing past my bare legs as he steps to my side. His hand lifts to my hair, pushing it back behind my ear. The tips of his fingers caressing the skin so featherlight I shiver.

His gaze pierces into mine, a soft grin curving up his lips. "Goodnight."

He tentatively lowers his hand before turning around. He hits the downward button, the elevator opening up as he steps inside.

And as he turns to face me, his eyes remain locked onto mine. As I stand there watching him until the elevator door closes in his face.

Chapter 31

Levi

The elevator descends down to the main floor as thoughts race within the walls of my mind.

She watched me until the very moment the elevator door closed. Should I have said fuck it, and stayed? Or was I supposed to leave?

Suddenly, I find myself unable to trust my own judgement. But that indecisiveness quickly subsides the moment the elevator chimes its arrival to the main floor.

The door opens up as I walk out onto the polished floor, the entryway completely silent at this hour of the night. My hand lifts out of my coat pocket as I approach the entrance doors, pushing it open with the palm of my hand as I step outside.

I walk out to see Dex standing near the hood of his car, propped up and facing the hood of mine. He looks up at the sound of me approaching, nodding as he hooks the jumper cables to his battery. A toothpick hangs out of his mouth, per usual.

His bright blue eyes squint at the corners as his mouth pulls into a wide grin. The snow that's begun to fall lightly dusts itself against his jet black hair. "Why do I get the feeling this was planned?" He peers up at me.

I roll my eyes, approaching my car door as I open it. I lower my hand down, pulling the lever for the hood. "It wasn't." The hood pops up as I close my door, moving to the front of the car as Dex props the hood up.

He chuckles. "Seems it was oddly coincidental is all." He brings the other side of the cables to my battery, hooking them to the terminals.

I cross my arms as I lean up against my car. "Should we talk about how you've been going to see the same girl for weeks now and still haven't introduced yourself?"

He forces out a laugh, nodding his head. "Fair enough." He goes to stand next to me, leaning on my driver side window. "Everything was cool tonight?"

Knowing now he's not asking about Amelia but about Wesley. I give him a nod. "All good."

He idly plays with the toothpick between his lips, lowering his gaze to his black dress shoes. "What are you doing tomorrow night?"

I shrug. "Nothing as of now."

Dex takes the toothpick out of his mouth, flicking it onto the ground. "Let's go scope out the new contract."

I turn to him. "Sawyer said it's a long burn, not a quick hit."

Dex shrugs his shoulders. "Not saying you have to finish the job tomorrow."

I sigh as a light flurry of snow lands on my cheek, my fingers brushing it away. I glance over at my battery. "So I'm assuming you know where he'll be then?" I wave my hand at him as he moves off of my car door. I open it, sitting inside as I put my key into the ignition.

"Affirmative." He says confidently.

I turn the key over, a sigh of relief when my car starts. I get out of the seat, facing Dex. "Where's he gonna be then?"

A slow grin curves up his face as he tilts his head. "Where do you think?"

He nods up towards Amelia's building before going to unhook his cables from my battery. I run my hand over my face as I make an audible sigh, stepping away from my car.

"Do men have no interests other than going to the strip club?"

Dex chuckles as he unhooks the cables from his battery. "I fear I am not one to judge in this situation."

I chuckle as I release the latch propping my hood up, closing it. "I guess not."

Knowing good and well that he's not the only one pining over a girl at that club.

Chapter 32

Amelia

Looking forward to seeing you tonight.

A grin curves up my face as I respond back to Adrian. *I'll save a dance for you. Xoxo*

I put my phone back onto my vanity table as I continued curling my hair. I wrap a large piece of my wine red hair around the styling wand, until only the very end is remaining as I hold it still.

The setting sun casts a warm, orange glow through my bedroom window as Rufus lays curled in the corner of the room fast asleep. At least until I'm finished and have to take him outside that is. Then he'll be springing awake.

I let the curled piece of hair go, falling down along my back as I continue with the rest of my head.

Thirty minutes later I turn the curling iron off, grabbing my can of hairspray as I lightly mist my entire head of hair. I gently run my fingers through my hair, fluffing it before gently brushing out the curls to give it a more natural, wavy look.

I set the brush down, glancing at my eyeshadow palettes in my clear makeup bin.

Do I want to go bold and flirty tonight, or a little more on the subdued end? I tap my index finger to my lip when I grab a palette dedicated to shades ranging from rich garnet to pastel pink.

Bold and flirty it is, obviously.

I take my eyeshadow brush, dipping it into a soft nude color to start, blending it just into the crease of my eyelid. I then dip my brush into a light mauve color, blending it right on top of the nude. The pink hues bringing out the amber in my eyes drastically.

I tap a light dusty pink color onto the center of my eyelid, lightly blending it all together.

I finish off my eyes with a jet black liquid liner, adding a thin line right in the inner corner of my eyes, a bold wing on the outer.

My phone buzzing on the vanity counter draws my attention as I cap my liquid liner. I peer down at my phone, reading the text on the screen.

Do you need a ride home tonight?

I pick my phone up, my thumb hovering over the letters on the screen as I hesitate to reply back to Levi. A sudden nervousness skittering along my skin, pricking the tiny hairs along my arms.

This is what I wanted, was to find someone else to take my mind off of Levi. So why do I feel a sudden rush of regret?

Not necessary.

I set the phone back down, unwilling to allow myself to feel guilty over my response. Something that's foreign to me when it comes to interacting with men. I direct my attention back to getting ready, pulling out my small bottle of foundation when I hear my phone buzz again. Briefly drawing those same nerves over my skin once more.

If you change your mind, let me know.

A beat of silence stills me internally, my eyes narrowed to the text until the screen goes black. I sigh to myself as I finish getting ready for the night.

I pull my outfit on before I put my clothes into my dance bag, shoving it into my locker. I take a seat on the bench as I slip my foot into my black six inch heels, fastening the sandal strap around my ankle.

I stand up again, adjusting my red one-piece bodysuit, the thong exposing my entire ass. The fabric over my nipples tailored into small diamond shapes, the same pattern traveling down until one more covers my pussy. A halter strap tied around my neck as my hair flows down in luscious waves down the middle of my back.

I tuck my phone into my garter as I begin making my way out onto the main floor, my ass jiggling with each step.

I step out onto the packed club floor, only ten minutes after ten o'clock on a Friday night. I begin my search around the room, looking for that familiar rich brown hair when I spot him in a round-backed leather chair towards the middle of the floor. A whiskey in his hand as his elbow props up onto the armrest.

I make my slow walk over, eying the back of his head, his hair pulled back into a bun. I step next to him as his gaze lifts up to me, his eyes widening as a smile curves his lips.

"You look fantastic." He stands up, leaning in to give me a kiss on the cheek before waving for me to sit down. I wait until he seats himself down before seating myself on his lap.

"Thank you." I say as I cross a leg over the other, my legs illuminated from the moving head lights above.

He goes to rest a hand on the middle of my back, leaning his head back into the chair. "Do you treat all of your guests this wonderfully or am I just special?"

I laugh huskily. "I guess you'll just have to stick around and find out."

He makes a humming noise, his gaze roaming over my face. "I sure will." He takes another sip of his whiskey, leaning the glass towards me before setting it down again. "This time I did order the typical man drink."

I laugh as I fluff my hair out, tossing some of it over my shoulder as it falls over my chest. "Does this mean you're now trying to impress me?" I peer down at him, grinning.

"In this outfit I'm afraid I might just do whatever you say." His hand idly caresses my bare back, drawing tiny goosebumps along my skin. He nudges over to one of the private dance sections. "Would you be upset if I asked to buy a dance, just to have an excuse to have you all to myself for a little while?"

My gaze roams over his lips before lifting again. I slowly nod my head before standing up. "I would not." I say, holding my hand out as he places his calloused hand into mine. I lift myself from his lap as he stands up beside me, leaning down to grab his whiskey. "Well then, Cherry. Please grace me with this honor with my first ever dance." He says as he loops my arm into his, bowing his head slightly as a grin curves his lips.

I raise a hand to my chest, my mouth slightly gaping open into a smile. "Me, taking your lapdance virginity? I'd be honored." I say with enthusiasm as a laugh escapes me. I lean into him as I turn us around to escort us over to an empty section.

My gaze lands on the curtain pulled back before my attention is drawn to two gentlemen seated at a table nearby, facing towards us. My smile falters as I lower my gaze in that direction to lock eyes with Levi, my stomach dipping into itself.

His gaze pierces into mine, my breath catching in my throat at the intensity of his stare. I force myself to continue walking Adrian to the private section as I see Levi's hand around his glass tighten, the veins in his hand bulging as a muscle ticks in his jaw.

I quickly avert my gaze back to where I'm escorting Adrian, willing the sudden unease in my stomach to lessen. I feel Adrian lower a hand to the small of my back as I remember to fix a smile back onto my face. All while distracted by the murderous look Levi had on his face when he saw me with another man.

A look not of jealousy, but of *rage* masked by a calm exterior. Conflicting feelings surface within me as Adrian and I approach the section, my hand surprisingly steady as I pull the curtain for privacy. Adrian takes a seat in the chair as I will myself to forget the look on Levi's face.

A look that made my skin crawl not only from unease, but also excitement.

Chapter 33

Levi

I'm going to fucking kill him.

"Reel it in, man." Dex says from beside me as he raises his drink to his lips.

I lower my gaze to my hand wrapped around my drink, the glass beginning to splinter at how tightly I'm holding it.

A cold rage washing over me imagining that it's his neck instead.

I quickly loosen my grip as I take a sharp inhale, releasing slowly so as to tamper my building rage.

"Remember, slow wins the race with this one."

"And suddenly that seems highly insignificant." I seethe.

"It will when you make your move too hasty. Don't fuck it all up by being impulsive just because we're learning now she's involved."

I take a shuddering inhale, willing myself to settle down as what Dex is saying is painfully right.

I lower my gaze to my hand, vaguely wiggling my fingers from the glass before I set it down on the table beside me. I glance over to the section that Amelia took him into, quickly looking away when it threatens to piss me off again. None of this would've angered me as much as it does if the man Amelia was with didn't just so happen to be who Sawyer's assigned me to take care of.

Or maybe I'd still be just as enraged. Which, if that's the case, I have a big fucking problem considering I keep telling myself I won't cave fully into her. That my discipline to remain business partners can remain intact, even though I fingered her just the other night.

And gods, I fear I would sacrifice my discipline all over again just to be able to touch her once more. Hell, I think I might even sacrifice my left nut just to *talk* to her—

Fuck, I'm down bad aren't I?

"I have to tell her." I say quietly.

"No, you don't." Dex looks over at me. "Unless you want Sawyer to place a hit on you *and* Amelia for going against his orders." Saying her name a level quicker, still maintaining a level of respect for her identity.

Fucking damnit, he's right. When Sawyer gives an order, no matter what it is, you follow it through. Unless you want to see you and everyone you love sinking to the bottom of the sea.

I grab my drink once more, finding myself glancing over to the section that she brought him into again. I take a long drink before setting it down, forcing myself to sink into the chair. Even though everything instinct firing in my body is telling me to walk over there, whip open that curtain, and put a bullet in Adrian's head for even touching her. Lucky for him the club has a strict no firearm policy, otherwise I'd have my gun holstered in my pants to tempt me. "Fine. We wait."

Dex nods his head slowly. "Has she told you anything about him?"

I remain silent, shaking my head.

"Well, I can't imagine he's told her the truth of who he is."

I curse under my breath. Fucking private investigator flirting with the clubs main dancer. The same investigator who was hired by Wesley to look into his brother's disappearance.

Not a fucking coincidence at all.

"He knows something." I say quietly.

Dex slowly nods his head. "Which means it won't be long before you get to fulfill your hit after all."

Forty minutes pass until Amelia finally walks out of the private section, Adrian in tow beside her. I glance over at her as she wraps a hand around his arm, laughing at whatever charm he's putting on for her I'm sure.

Wow, you're so jealous.

The thought comes and goes through my mind, something she would say to me if I were to question her about him.

I remember the main objective here, that he's my target and I'm under a contract to kill him. And she just so happens to be now caught in the middle of it. Though, blackmailing her to work with me is probably what got her into all of this in the first place.

Whatever. This might classify me as a selfish bastard, but I don't regret it.

I watch as she takes them both to the bar, the gentleman with the lip ring taking their drink orders as I look down at the pink garter around her creamy white thigh.

My gaze hones in on it, wondering how much he gave.

I take a sip of my third drink, Dex talking to some waitress as I pull out my phone. I pull up Amelia and I's text thread, typing.

Did he even give you enough?

I set my phone down as I watch her phone light up, she lowers her hand and holds the screen up to her face. A quick change in her expression dances across her face before she smooths it back out into her lustful, enchanting one. She types back before quickly locking her phone.

He gave me enough ;)

I take a sharp breath in, forcing myself not to clench my jaw. I smirk at my phone as I type back.

Does he know that I had my finger inside your pussy last night?

She smiles at him as he says whatever lame bullshit that's spewing out of his mouth. She glances at the phone before quickly turning her gaze back onto him.

I type another response to her.

You can ignore me all you want, little red. But I remember how the inner walls of your pussy felt clamping around me.

I send her another.

How you writhed against me.

And another.

How you were dripping onto my hand.

Adrian turns towards the bartender as she picks up her phone again, stilling as she gives a glance over my way. I grin as the color on her cheeks pinken, even under the lights of the club.

I bet your pussy is as pink as your cheeks are right now.

I watch as her stomach flexes as she inhales, one of her feet lifting up as the heel lifts off the ground. I watch as she types back to me before setting her phone in her garter and leaning in towards his ear. She glances towards me before making her way to the other side of the club.

My phone vibrates as her text comes through.

Bathrooms. Now.

I slide my phone in my pocket, watching as she makes her way under the awning with a red neon sign that reads restrooms.

"I'll be back." I say, leaning towards Dex.

"Mmhmm." He says looking at me before his attention is fixated on a blue haired girl across the way.

I stand up, making my casual stride across the club as I walk through the restroom hallway. I see the light on underneath the girls restroom, a smirk crawling up my lips as I slowly push the door open.

Amelia grabs me by my black rolled up shirt, pulling me inside before locking the door. Her hands shove me back as she pushes me up against the door, irritation and something else flashing wildly in her eyes. "What is your problem?" She seethes.

She removes her hands as she steps away, taking two steps away from me as she faces the mirror above the sink.

I shrug nonchalantly. "There's no problem here."

She whips her body around, charging towards me. That fire in her eyes cementing me in place.

"Stop texting me just because you're jealous I'm with him. *Or else.*" She goes to push me out of the way to unlock the bathroom when I grab her wrist.

My hand locks around her wrist as my other pulls her long hair away from her neck, tucking those fire red strands behind her ear. "Or else *what*?" I say, leaning my head closer to her neck as I push her chest into the door. My hips pressing into her rear as I box her in, a soft whimper escaping her lips.

Her breath hitches as her hand on the door relaxes.

I lower my index finger from her ear down her neck, trailing featherlight over her skin. I feel her breath hitch at my touch as I lower my finger down her bare back. Lowering it slowly down her spine, a thrill filling my head and my cock when her back arches at my touch. I trail my finger down until I reach her waist.

She gasps as I raise her wrist up high with my other hand, pinning it against the door. "What are you going to do, little red?"

My finger continues trailing slowly down her waist, over her round porcelain ass until my finger slides down between her cheeks. I gently lower my finger beneath her thong, tugging it up gently.

"If you want me to stop I will." I whisper against her neck before pressing a soft kiss to her warm skin. The undeniable desire rushing through me overriding any remaining tether on my discipline and common sense. "All you need to do is ask, and we'll stop." I purr against her skin, my hand ceasing its descent as I wait to advance further.

She remains quiet for a few moments, her back arching deeper into me before she presses her ass into my hips.

I chuckle against her skin as my finger continues its trek down, lowering beneath her ass until I'm gliding up over her pussy. "You wanna go on dates with other men? Fine."

I rub my finger through the wetness already gathered there, my cock hardening in my pants. I grind my hips against her rear, drilling her closer to the door.

"You wanna distract yourself from the fact that you want me as badly as I want you? Okay."

I thrust my finger inside her pussy, a breathy moan escaping from her lips as she widens her stance for me. I lower my face just below her ear as her pulse throbs erratically beneath my lips. She lets out a soft gasp as I gently nip her skin. "But let me make one thing *crystal* clear, Amelia."

I slowly plunge my finger deep inside of her, my other hand raising up to cover her mouth. Her moans now trapped beneath my palm.

"You belong to *me*."

She begins writhing against me as I grind my hips into her, pumping my finger in and out of her.

Gods, she's so fucking wet. So wet for *me*.

That thought leaves me reeling as I press kisses along her neck, my eyes nearly rolling into the back of my head the more she tells me how much she loves me touching her. With her moans, the way she shudders beneath the press of my lips. Like the most addicting drug that I never want to seek sobriety from.

I release my lips from her skin, pulling myself back enough to gaze down at her arched in front of me. Her ass pressed into my hips as my finger fucks her wet pussy. Her long hair flowing down her back like a cascade of rich red wine.

A wicked grin curves my lips as I stare down at the thin red fabric tied around the back of her neck. Her entire back and ass exposed. "You look good in this outfit, little red." I lower my gaze to the trickle of pre-cum now sliding down her thigh as it takes everything in me to not say fuck it and have my way with her right here. "You look even better in it when you're coming for me." I suddenly lower my finger out of her, her body stilling as I feel frustration building beneath her skin. That release that's been building inside of her halting abruptly.

I lower my mouth to the back of her shoulder, pressing a soft kiss there as I lower my finger down her thigh, wiping the wetness that has escaped her. I glide my finger up through it, catching it before it drips any lower before lifting my finger to my mouth.

She turns around, irritation simmering in her eyes as her gaze lowers to my lips. Watching me as I dip my finger between my lips, my eyes rolling to the back of my head as I suck every last sweet drop of her. I watch as her chest rises sharply before exhaling raggedly.

I slowly remove my finger from my mouth. "It wouldn't be very gentlemanly of me," I say, my mouth now hovering over hers. Her labored breaths clashing against my semi-calm ones. "To...ruin your outfit while you're at work. Let's save this for another time, shall we?"

I raise my head from hers, my gaze roaming her face as fury dances across her features. A smirk graces my face again as I step to the side. She tentatively steps out of the way as I unlock the bathroom door, pulling it open as the blaring club music washes over me.

And walk back out onto the main floor.

Chapter 34

Amelia

I lean up against the door, cemented in place as my breathing begins to settle.

After a few moments I quickly glance down at myself, my outfit not soiled yet from the wetness beneath as the patch that covers my pussy is still pulled to the side. I hurry to a random stall, grabbing a bunch of toilet paper as I begin wiping myself dry.

The orgasm that was building with me glistens onto the toilet paper as I toss it into the toilet, flushing it down. I look down at my thigh where some of it dripped down onto, where Levi wiped it up. How he sucked his finger—

The inferno within threatens to pool wetness below as I shove the thought out of my mind, not wanting to risk soiling my outfit.

Thank gods he pulled the fabric over as he fingered me, otherwise I'd be rushing off to the locker room to change.

I close my eyes tightly, taking a few deep breaths in and out. Settling myself and the heat bubbling over inside of me.

I am not horny. I am not horny.

I repeat to myself over and over again until I convince myself for the time being. I walk out of the stall and over to a sink, turning the water as I quickly clean myself up. I pat myself dry with more toilet paper, flushing it down again before adjusting my outfit to cover myself once more.

I walk back over to the sink, gazing at myself through the mirror as I take a deep breath. I tilt my head slightly to the side, examining my makeup.

Thank fuck he didn't smear my lipstick with his hand.

My hands turn clammy as I turn the water on again, cursing under my breath as I wash my hands and slapping some cold water on my arms to freeze the heat simmering in my body. I shut the water off, breathing in slowly and then releasing.

I fluff up my hair, willing my poker face back on before opening the bathroom door and walking back out onto the floor.

I quickly glance over at Levi sitting in the same seat, a faint smirk on his lips as his gaze dips lower. Then up again. I turn my gaze back to the bar, honing in on Adrian with his back currently facing towards me. I take one last big breath in before settling back into my seductress self.

I rest a hand along his shoulder, smiling at him as he turns to face me. "There you are. I was wondering if you'd possibly run out on me."

I force a giggle at his words, leaning up against the bar counter. I lower my hand to the buttons of his shirt, gaze lowering until I fix them back on his face again. "Me? Never." I say sweetly before he orders us a round of drinks.

***

As Adrian talks to me I find myself sneaking glances towards Levi when he's suddenly preoccupied with talking to Ace, or another man at the bar, or really just at any moment that Adrian doesn't have his attention on me.

And I hate myself for it. Because everytime I catch myself looking his way I find him staring right back at me.

Finally I turn to Adrian, resting a hand along his arm as I smile up at him. Needing to find a way to get me out of Levi's line of sight. "You know, just because you're visiting doesn't mean I'm not still working. So unless you want my attention to be taken from someone else, I suggest you make it so that I'm...unavailable."

The smell of whiskey wafts from his breath as he laughs. His eyes subtly glazed over from the liquor as he leans in a little closer. "Understandable. I think I can make that work." He grins.

He lowers his hand into his pocket, pulling out a leather wallet. He opens it up, shuffling through the hundred dollar bills inside until he pulls out one thousand. "Is this enough for your time?"

I make a humming noise as I tap a finger to my red lips. I make a playful shrug as I fan my lashes at him. "It's satisfactory enough." I go to take the money when he pulls out another five hundred.

He adds it to the pile, handing it over to me. "Well satisfactory enough doesn't cut it for me." He winks as he nods to the bartender, a gesture to insinuate he's ready to close out his tab.

Ace prints off his bill at a register, walking back over to us. Before he can set it fully onto the bar counter Adrian hands him a black card. He nods, walking away again.

When he comes back he gives Adrian the final receipt with a pen. "Enjoy your night, sir."

"Thank you." He says before opening his wallet again, pulling out a hundred dollar bill. He hands it over to Ace before turning back towards me. "You ready?" He lowers a hand to my waist.

I grin at him. "Absolutely." I turn away from the bar and guide him towards the VIP section. Catching a quick glance over to Levi to see him staring at me.

His gaze hones in on me before fixating on Adrian, a predator honing in on its next victim.

I turn my gaze forward again, taking Adrian and I down the hallway and into a vacant VIP room.

I close the door behind us as Adrian goes to sit on the couch. "I've never been in one of these before."

I face him, walking towards the couch and seating myself next to him. I curl my legs up as I tilt my head, propping an elbow on the back of the couch. "Never?"

He shakes his head as he chuckles. "I hardly make an effort to come to the club to begin with."

I lazily shrug my shoulders. "So what changed then?"

He looks over at me, resting a hand on my calf. "I saw you and had to get to know you." He grins as his gaze lowers to my feet. He removes his hand from my leg, scooting forward onto the couch. "Here."

He waves his hand for me to stretch my leg out for him. I lay a leg over him as he grabs my foot, unfastening the ankle strap until he slips my heel off. "I can't imagine you are comfortable in these things."

I laugh as he begins taking off my other one. "They're not as bad as they seem actually."

He lifts the other heel off, setting it onto the carpet as his other hand remains there. He picks my feet up, laying them over his lap as he begins massaging one foot. "The tension in your feet tells me otherwise."

He rubs his thumb into the ball of my foot, causing me to moan softly at the relief. "If only all of my customers treated me this nicely in the VIP rooms."

He chuckles as he starts kneading up my foot. "Is that what I am? A customer?"

I lift my gaze up to him as he slowly works his way up, massaging my calves now. I grin deeply at him. "Not in the slightest."

He grins backs as he continues massaging. "Tell me something that nobody knows. What you like to do for fun, anything." He says as he leans his head back into the couch.

"Hmm," I say, pondering as he kneads my soft, tired skin. Working his way up just a little higher, sighing deeply. "I really love what you're doing right now."

He laughs as his hands work on my upper calf. "No, seriously. Anything."

I rest my head along the back of the couch as I look at him. "I have a dog. He's pretty much the love of my life."

"What's his name?"

"Rufus." I say, smiling. Tempted to check my phone's home security app to check on him.

"What kind of dog is he?" He says, his hands now right above my knee. My breath hitching slightly as heat rises to my pussy again.

I contemplate for a moment a similar dog breed as I can't say what he actually is, knowing that Hellhounds aren't always accepted pets for obvious reasons.

Stupid reasons if I'm being honest.

I take a deep inhale in as he kneads my thighs. "He's a doberman."

"Ah, I see." He begins working his way up my thighs, the tips of his thumbs nearly caressing my bikini line. "That's a good breed of dog."

I watch him intently, his golden brown eyes wholly alight on my amber ones. "Indeed it is." My words come out breathy.

I lower my gaze as I watch his hands raise even higher, a moan getting trapped in my throat when the backs of his knuckles brush over my pussy. "What else?" He asks huskily. The orgasm denied from earlier slowly creeping its way back, building beneath the surface.

Frustration overwhelms me as I think of the way I dripped down my thigh from Levi fingering me, unsure of how I'd react if I let him put his hard cock in my—

I take a shuddering breath as I feel the backs of his knuckles brush against me again. Unable to tamper down the inferno building within. *Needing* to cum.

He continues as another moan gets trapped in my throat. I tilt my head, leaning in closer. "I really enjoy being topless."

"Do you now?" He lowers his gaze momentarily to my chest before raising it back to my face again.

"Yes." I hiss as I slowly climb on top of him, his hands going to my waist as I straddle him. I feel his hard cock press beneath me, taking everything in me not to ride him into oblivion just to sate my need. To distract myself from the man I want to be riding instead.

No, no, no. What is wrong with me?

I do not pine over men, nor do I find myself *craving* them like a rabid animal. Men desire *me*. They crawl after *me*.

So then why am I sitting on this man's lap, who is good looking and pays to spend time with me, but all I can think about is the one outside of this room?

The one who is my *business partner*, who I'm only under obligation to work with until he fully caves into me. The one I agreed to work with simply because I was bored.

Not because I suddenly don't mind being around him.

He licks his lower lip as he stares up at me. "I'm afraid I'm much more of a visual learner."

I focus back into the present as I feel his cock harden beneath me. I drag myself from my thoughts as I lift my hands up to the strings tied at the back of my neck. Grinning down at him. "Well, lucky for you I'm very good at demonstrating."

I slowly untie them, watching his gaze lower as the tiny strings of fabric slip down my chest, the triangles of my bodysuit covering my nipples falling down as well.

His hands grip my waist as he roams them over my ass. Leaning forward, his mouth hovers over a nipple as his gaze keeps trained on me. My breath hitches as his breath gently warms the hardened skin there. "Then I think this makes us a good pair."

He lowers his mouth, his lips closing over my nipple as a moan escapes me. His tongue twirls around it as I arch my back into him, grinding into him slowly.

He groans as my hips rock into him, sucking on that hardened peak as his hands grip my ass. He lifts his mouth, kissing in between my heavy breasts before he moves onto the next one.

Feeling that building crescendo from earlier rise quickly. The memory of his finger inside of me resurfacing as that desire builds rampantly.

This pussy belongs to me.

Wetness pools there at the confidence and coldness in his words, lighting a fire within me as I begin rocking my hips into Adrian harder.

Please, just finger me so I can finally cum.

As if he could hear the thoughts in my head, he removes a hand from my waist, slipping it beneath my bodysuit before plunging deep inside of me. He groans against me as he slips through my wetness.

I moan as he slips it in and out of me repeatedly, still sucking on my nipple as I quiver against him. My orgasm chases through me before it quickly builds over, pulsating my body entirely as I cum on his hand. My body grinding against him as his thumb circles around my clit and—

Gods, it feels so fucking *good*.

I keep my mouth closed, stifling my moans as I ride my orgasm until I'm limp against him. My breathing slowing itself down.

He removes his mouth from my nipple, a chuckle escaping him as he slowly removes his finger. "I didn't realize how wet you were for me already." He says huskily.

I will my body to settle as my breathing begins to return to normal. I force a smile on him, leaning down to kiss him on the lips. His lips part as my tongue slowly clashes against his.

We kiss for a moment longer before he slowly pulls away, looking at my face. He raises a finger to the underside of my lips, gently swiping that area. "I don't want to ruin your beautiful make-up." He chuckles.

I give him a quick grin before I lower myself back down to the couch next to him. He raises a hand, brushing my hair back from my face before leaning it on the back of the couch. His eyes roam over my face as I fight the voice inside of my head to spare me this moment, ignoring its taunting words.

That I wish it were a certain someone else touching me right now.

Chapter 35

Levi

I watch as Amelia and the fucking investigator walk out of the VIP hallway, back out onto the main floor.

My hand gripping my glass of water, intentionally chosen so I could sober myself up. So I could be alert for when he finally left.

I watch as she rests a hand on his shoulder, smiling at him as he leans down to give her a kiss on the cheek.

I tighten my fingers into the glass before forcing myself to release my grip.

"What's the plan?" Dex asks quietly from beside me.

I down the remainder of my water as I watch Adrian part his goodbyes to Amelia. My tone both steady and cold. "To observe."

Dex nods vaguely beside me as he pulls his phone out of his pocket, unlocking it until his main screen pops up. "We're good to go on our end." He says as a dark screen pops up.

A live GPS map showcasing a block down from The Playground, a small black dot pinpointing precisely over where Adrian's black sedan is parked.

"Good." Is all I say as I watch Adrian take his sweet time saying goodbye to Amelia.

While Dex and I casually get up from our chairs, throwing some cash onto the table before making our controlled exit out of the club.

We lean back into Dex's car, the tinted windows concealing us from anyone being able to peer in. I look down at my phone, noticing fifteen minutes has already passed.

How long does it take you to say fucking bye?

I look down at my phone again, for whatever reason checking to see if I missed a text from Amelia at all. I check like the obsessive bastard that I am.

Nothing.

I shove my phone back into my pocket when Dex lightly taps my forearm. "There." He whispers.

From the rearview mirror I see Adrian turning the corner, his phone held up to his ear. I watch as he takes a nonchalant glance around, noting his surroundings. "It won't take long now." He says quietly.

He continues walking to his car, parked twenty feet in front of us. He makes a low chuckle as his other hand fumbles for his keys in his jacket, a smug smirk on his face. "Give me another few dates and I'll get her to reveal where they are."

I look over at Dex as we exchange glances, turning our gazes back onto Adrian as he nears his vehicle now.

"She's a self-absorbed dancer whose language is sex and desire. All I gotta do is dangle that in her face, maybe give her a little dick and I get the answers we need."

I lean forward sharply in my seat as Dex crosses an arm over my chest, shoving me back as anger rises violently inside of me. I exhale raggedly as my gaze hones in on Adrian unlocking his car, rage setting fire to my skin as my jaw clenches.

I watch Adrian open his car door, chuckling at whoever he's on the phone with. "Yeah, I've never fucked a prostitute before. I can't say I'm too upset about getting the opportunity to experience that. But hey, it's all a part of the investigation, right?" He seats himself into the driver seat, his laugh echoing in the silence of the night before stifling behind his door closing.

My fists ball themselves against my thighs, forcing another ragged exhale out of my nose as the lights on Adrian's car turn on. Shortly after he pulls forward, driving away.

"I'm gonna fucking *kill him*." I seethe as I turn towards Dex, my gaze hard as steel.

"And you will." He confirms. A show of emotion passes over his gaze as he stares at me. "But he works with the police department, so we have to make it count *at the right moment.*"

Suddenly my anger turns into a whole different emotion. One that I'm not entirely familiar with feeling.

Disheartedness.

A *prostitute?* I fucking hate him. Amelia is a dancer and a domme. A sophisticated, street smart woman who makes money for a living by entertaining and seducing *consenting* men. Why do men stuck in the olden ages automatically presume sex workers are always prostitutes?

Not that there is anything shameful with prostitution. We all have to make our money one way or another, and quite frankly it's nobody's business how someone chooses to make money. But to say it in such a derogatory way—

"I have to tell her. I can't let her continue seeing that fucking douchebag." I say to Dex.

"You have no fucking choice, man. If you tell her and Sawyer finds out—"

"I suddenly don't give a *fuck* what Sawyer thinks."

"You *will* when he retaliates for your disobedience and you find her body dismembered in the club alleyway." His gaze hardens on me.

I take a long inhale in, suddenly hating bringing her into a situation that was supposed to be fun and exciting with her. Now wondering why I got her involved with my shit in the first place.

I shake my head. "I don't want to lie to her." I say quietly, a sudden primal need inside of me that wants to protect her. Unsure of when exactly that began, or if it was hidden beneath my cold exterior all along.

Dex sighs, finally turning on his car. "I'm afraid you don't have a choice right now."

He pulls out his phone, watching the tracker move before he sets it into the cup holder. His hand lowers to turn the heat dial on. Finally.

I never cared about anything else other than doing my job. I kill with no remorse, the capacity to feel trivial shit like sympathy and attachment aren't feelings I accompany myself with.

But suddenly those feelings are clawing their way through my sadistic walls, pining for a red haired woman whose fire for the wicked mirrors my own.

Dex puts the car in drive as he begins to tailgate Adrian from a safe distance, following him to his home.

The whole time my mind unraveling all of the horrific, yet justified ways that I'll make Adrian pay for disrespecting a woman far smarter, so far more powerful than he could've ever imagined.

Chapter 36

We follow the map until the small black dot stops at a house located in some picket-fence suburbs. Less than five minutes out from the location, we continue driving.

I pull out my phone from my pocket, having had enough of the tossing back and forth inside my head. I pull up the text thread, sending her a quick message.

You get home okay?

I stare at my phone, waiting for those bubbles above the text box to appear. My heart nearly flutters when they do, and only ease a moment later when she replies.

Yes.

I hold my finger over her text, a bubble of reaction emojis popping up. I tap the thumbs up one before I lock my phone, putting it back into my pocket.

"We're here."

I look up as Dex pulls over to the sidewalk, shutting off his lights as he puts the car in park. He looks at the map on his phone, pointing with his other hand. "He's the beige house on the right."

My gaze travels up to a beige suburban home two houses up from where we're parked. "No other cars in the driveway." I say, scoping out the exterior of the home.

Dex scrolls out of the app and into the Wifi section of his settings. "How much you wanna bet he has a lame, alpha bullshit Wifi name?"

I huff at him. "Wouldn't surprise me."

Wifi names pop up as he hits a setting on his phone that allows him to pinpoint which Wifi belongs to which home on the block.

I wonder to myself where the fuck he learned all this shit from, but hey—it comes in handy and makes him one of the best hackers in the city.

His screen flickers as he looks up at the numbers on Adrian's mailbox, looking back down at his screen. He shakes his head, scoffing as he looks over at me. "HowIMetYourWifi."

What is this guy, twelve?

I roll my eyes. "Can you get in?"

Dex smirks at me, raising a hand to his chest. "Can *I* hack into his wifi, to then allow me to hack into his home camera footage? I can't believe you just asked me that."

I chuckle as he looks back down at his phone, typing and tapping, doing whatever he's doing to hack into this guy's shit.

A minute later he holds his phone up, a live camera footage of Adrian's home appearing on screen. "Ta-da."

I lean in, looking at the eight different camera angles in and outside of this guy's home.

One angled at the back kitchen door, the kitchen itself, the living room, the living room front door, his bedroom, and then three outside. Facing the backyard, the front yard, and his driveway.

"He takes precautions, I see." I mumble.

Dex nods at the screen. "Look at this."

I look down at the angle as he enlarges the one of his bedroom, noticing the plain wooden dresser to the right of the room. The only things on top of it are a small tray of watches, and a bottle of whiskey with an empty glass. No jewelry, no vanity, and no little finishing touches to bring character and warmth to the room.

"He's not married." I say.

Dex nods as he brings up the backyard camera footage, the only thing out there being a gas grill. "No kids either."

"I kind of figured that from the one bedroom house."

Dex shrugs. "He could not have custody."

I nod. "We'll need to look further into it just to be sure."

Dex nods as we see Adrian walking into his living room, seating himself down on an ugly old leather armchair. He holds his phone in his hand, his lips moving but the phone is held away from his ear. Dex turns the audio on as we listen.

"Good, I just want to make sure you're home safe. Lots of creeps out there these days."

A woman chuckles on speakerphone. "Yes, I'm home safe." She says sweetly.

My pulse ramps up as I'd recognize that voice anywhere.

"Good. I had a good time with you tonight." He smirks as he leans back into the chair, adjusting his pants with his other hand.

"I had a great time too." She says.

"Hey, the game is on Sunday, you wanna go grab some drinks somewhere and watch it with me?"

I roll my eyes. *No* she can't go with you, you insufferable vile pig because she *works* on Sunday nights.

"Oh, I'm so sorry but I can't. I work that night."

See, told ya. A grin fights to appear on my lips.

"I should've figured. I'm sure it's a busy night for you then."

No, it's not. Because the college kids drowning in college debt, who can barely even afford a twenty dollar dinner, still come in thinking that it's okay to still be entertained by the women without actually paying them for their time. I roll my eyes again.

"Yeah, it definitely is."

For whatever reason I smile at the lie she spins.

"Well, I might sound clingy here," He forces a laugh. "But I'd like to see you again. Can I take you for lunch tomorrow afternoon?"

I wait for Amelia's reply, gnawing at the bars of my enclosure at her moment of silence. I wait at the edge of my seat until she chuckles. "Yeah, sure. That would be great."

"Great. Let's plan for one o'clock at The Brunch House. I'll Venmo you some money for an Uber."

"Sounds great. I'll see you then." She says huskily.

"Goodnight." He says.

"Goodnight, Adrian." She replies before hanging up the phone.

Adrian sets his phone onto the table beside the chair, reaching for the remote before turning the TV on. A smug smirk crawls up his face as he leans back into the chair, flipping through the channels.

Dex closes the camera footage, locking his phone. He looks over at me, narrowing his head.

I look over at him, my gaze hardening as my jealousy and discontent for her being around Adrian roils through me. "What?" I snap before fixing my gaze on the quiet street ahead.

Dex sighs. "It's not real."

I look over at him, scrunching my brows.

"I see the way she kept looking at you tonight. I know something also went down in that bathroom." He says with a knowing look. He sighs again. "She's not as interested in him as you think."

"Whatever." I say as he turns his car on, turning the heat back on again. I go to cross my arms over my chest, trying to shove down the sudden feeling of a weight pushing down on my heart.

This is my fault. I put myself in the friendzone by agreeing to terms of a business partnership that would only fall away until I caved into her. Something I was adamant about preventing.

Amelia is beautiful—Hell, that doesn't even accurately describe her. Only a fool would say otherwise.

In which case I'd *gladly* cut out his tongue for even saying otherwise about her.

But this...yearning? This is not something I'm exactly familiar with. Something that feels deeper than just attraction. It twists and mends itself within the walls of my chest and while a part of me is perplexed by it, another is eager to explore it.

I want to tell her so badly who this guy really is. I hate that I have to keep this from her. But as soon as I'm able to, I'll free her from his manipulative control. I only hope that she can believe me when I tell her who this Adrian guy really is, and possibly forgive me for killing him.

Pulling myself from my thoughts, I watch as Dex turns his lights on, putting the car in drive. An idiotic idea—and possibly an act of desperation pops into my head, drawing my gaze over to him. "Hey, can I borrow your car tomorrow?"

Chapter 37

Amelia

"That's it?" Ki asks before taking a sip of her orange juice.

I shrug my shoulders as a smirk curves up my lips. "For now."

She sets her glass down atop a maroon coaster on her coffee table, her living room blinds pulled back to let in the morning sunshine. "And he wants to see you again today? He definitely isn't playing hard to get."

A snort escapes me as I curl my legs up beneath me, sprawled slightly to the side as my pink fuzzy slippers hang over the couch. "It's just lunch."

"Yeah, until next thing you know he's asking if he can finally escort you home. Does he know where you live yet?"

"No." I say curtly, glancing at her. "That won't be a privilege he'll have for a long time yet, if he even gets to that."

Ki nods her head. "Good. I know you don't need me to tell you to be careful with being in the industry and all. But most men think they're entitled to a woman's life the moment they start taking her out on dates." She rolls her eyes. "Don't let him get too comfortable too quickly."

"You know I won't." I say, pulling my hair over to one side of my shoulder. "For now I'm just...having fun."

"As you should." She says, smiling as she stands up from the couch, grabbing her glass and bringing it to the kitchen. "You sure you don't want anything?"

I uncurl my legs, standing up from the couch. "I'm okay. I should probably get back upstairs anyway to start getting ready." I walk over to the counter as she rinses out her glass in the sink.

"At least he's taking you to lunch and not dinner."

"Yeah, nothing worse than going into work after a heavy meal and being too bloated to even want to socialize with the customers." I chuckle as she brings me in for a hug.

She pulls away as she laughs, her smile dimming as she gets quiet. "Speaking of dates," She begins as she looks at me, a shy smile appearing. "I'm thinking of asking this one girl out. I did her nails for the first time last week, and we've been texting ever since."

My mouth slightly gapes open as I gasp, a smile curving. "Why didn't you tell me you bitch."

"I don't know. I'm nervous to ask her." Kiara says, her cheeks pinking to a slight degree.

"Why wait to ask?" I say, cheering her on.

She sighs. "I don't know, I'm just not a very sociable person. I do nails for a living, and spend time at home and that's it. Plus, I only just came out a year ago so I'm not very confident in approaching women just yet."

I rest both of my hands on her shoulders, dragging her gaze up from the floor. "You deserve to be happy, and you deserve to put yourself out there. No matter how scary." I pull my hands away. "Just ask. She'd be a fool not to say yes."

Ki sighs as she nods her head. "Okay, okay. I'll ask her today and let you know what happens."

"Yes, please do." A giddy noise escapes me as I put my hands together. I look over at her microwave, the time on the display reading eleven. "Oh, I definitely have to go." I spring into action as I walk over to her door.

She follows behind me as I grab her front door knob, pulling it open as I look back over my shoulder. "Text me."

"I will." She says with a smile.

"Love you." I walk out into the hallway as she holds the door open for me.

"Love you." She says as I walk towards the elevator, hitting the upward arrow to head back up to my place.

To get ready for my date with Adrian.

I open up the Uber app, typing into the destination search bar The Brunch House as the screen loads. An option for a destination arrival of right at noon props up as I hit select, securing my ride. I watch as the screen loads as it finds me a driver, setting my phone onto the kitchen counter.

I look over at Rufus, sitting on the kitchen floor staring up at me. He tilts his head as if he's assessing my outfit.

A pair of black leggings underneath an off-white thigh-length sweater, a beige scarf wrapped around my neck to match. I lift my leather black low-heeled boots, gently wiping a piece of Rufus' dog hair off before I straighten again. Smoothing my hands over my dark beige duster jacket.

I look at him. "What?"

He narrows his chin, a low huff escaping from his nose.

"It's a cute outfit. Besides—it's cold as fuck outside."

I'm so not a winter girl.

My phone vibrates on the kitchen counter as I go to pick it up.

"Han Sum will be arriving shortly." I say aloud, my brows knitting together as I sound out the name, trying to study the photo of my Uber driver. A too-small picture of a white man with dark hair. I laugh to myself as I sound out his name again, snorting at how it sounds like *handsome.* "Wow, okay then."

I put my phone into my coat pocket as I grabbed my black purse, throwing it over my shoulder. "Be good, Rufus. Mommy will be back a little later."

I toss my hair behind my back as I unlock my front door, stepping out into the hallway as I lock my door up. I hit the elevator arrow, the doors opening right away. I press for floor one as my phone vibrates again, the doors closing behind me.

I am here, ma'am.

"Ma'am?" A smirk appears on my face. "I like him." I say, tucking my phone back into my pocket.

When the elevator makes it to the main floor I step out, noticing the all black car parked out front. I open the front door, my gaze roaming over the tinted windows of the vehicle as I approach the back door.

I open it, leaning my head down a little. "Verify your name." Making sure I get myself into the right vehicle, of course."

His head remains facing forward as he clears his throat. "Han Sum, ma'am." He says, his voice deep and steady beneath a black hat.

I refrain from giggling at the pronunciation of the name. "Good." I say, climbing in before I shut the door. I go to strap my seatbelt over me. "Hey, has anyone told you your name sounds like—"

I hear the click of a door lock, my body stilling briefly before I look up and see Levi taking off his hat, turning around to stare back at me.

"Levi—" I immediately go to unlock the car door, pulling at the lever when nothing happens.

"Child lock apparently can be effective for adults, too. Interesting." He turns back around to face forward, putting the car in drive. "The Brunch House, is that correct ma'am?" He says, enthusiasm in his voice.

"Levi, what the fuck are you doing?" I sigh audibly, irritation rising as I quit trying to pry the door open and sit back in the seat. I look over next to me, then up. "And whose fucking car is this?"

"Not important. For now, let's just focus on getting you to your date on time."

I'd be lying if I said that my heart didn't sink at his words, at him knowing where I'm going. "How'd you know that?" I ask slowly.

"Also not important right now." He turns down the street as he runs his other hand through his hair, pushing those wavy blonde strands back.

I cross my arms over my chest, exhaling slowly. "If you wanted to give me a ride to my date then why not just ask?"

He shrugs his shoulders. "This is more fun. Hey, did you know how easy it is to make an Uber account? I was approved in less than an hour." He chuckles as he pulls up to a stop light, the red glow dimmed from the bright winter day. "You'd think they'd question the legitimacy of someone named *Han Sum* but nope. Just sent me an automated response back saying *'Welcome to Uber!'*." He begins laughing deeply, the light turning green as he drives forward.

I roll my eyes. "You're insane."

His eyes gaze at me from the rearview mirror, a stare that could cement me right in place. "And you're just realizing this now?" His gaze shifts back to the road, his hand gripping the top of the steering wheel. I roll my eyes as I look out of my window, accepting my fate with Levi taking me to my date.

"You have a habit of doing that."

I scrunch my eyebrows, irritation flaring as I turn my gaze back to him. "Do what?" I seethe.

He glances up at me again through the mirror, coming to another stop light. "Roll your eyes at me." His gaze lowers again.

I scoot over to the middle seat, leaning forward as I place my hands firmly onto the seats beside me. "And what, I assume you're going to tell me to stop doing it? Like I would ever listen to—"

He turns around, grabbing my neck so quickly I can hardly blink before he has my face held up to his. So close, his lips only an inch away from mine.

His gaze bores into mine, his hand gently gripping my neck as I gasp in his hold.

"Oh, I'm not going to tell you to stop, little red." His gaze lowers to my lips, his eyes lingering there for a long moment before lifting again. "Because when I'm so far deep inside of you, I only hope you keep this same energy."

My gaze lowers to his lips momentarily, my breath hitching.

"You rolling your eyes at me doesn't taunt me with annoyance, Amelia. It only tempts me with a good time." He smirks as he lets go of his grip, turning back around as the light turns green.

I inhale deeply, rubbing my hand around my neck gently. "You mean *if* you get the chance. And—whatever happened to *my discipline is stronger than any desire for you?*"

He chuckles softly as his hand grips the steering wheel gently. "Circumstances have changed."

I regulate my breathing as I sit back into my seat, watching him through the rearview mirror. "Well, you talk a big game for someone who has to physically resist himself from touching me."

His gaze lifts to mine through the mirror. "I resist you but not for the reasons you think." He says quietly.

"We both know the reason why you resist me, Levi."

His car pulls up to a side street in front of The Brunch House, putting his—or whoever's car this is into park.

"You resist me because you know that as soon as you cave in, and this," I say, my hand gesturing to the both of us. "As soon as this happens, I'm free of my arrangement with you. And you don't want it to end because you like having me around, as more than just a pretty face to look at and someone to help you do your jobs."

He keeps himself seated, his gaze lifting as he watches me through the rearview mirror. He gives a slow nod. "And what about you? I've seen the way you watch me when I work, and not with disgust in your eyes but excitement. So just admit it, you get off on this shit just as much as I do. You can point the finger at me all you want but I'm not the only one who doesn't want this *arrangement* to end. And not just because of what we do together."

I clench my jaw as I look over through my window, watching Adrian as he makes his way to the front entrance door. He opens the door, stepping inside as he looks down at his phone. Putting it back into his jacket.

My heart does the near impossible and actually sinks for Adrian. A man I'm trying to let get to know me, and let into my life but find myself having resistance to. And not because there's anything wrong with him, but because the man in the front seat continuously holds my attention.

That for the first time in my entire life, it is not just the man being wholly consumed with me. But me being just as consumed with him.

"Then all you need to do is tell me it's no longer just a business arrangement."

I meet his gaze in the mirror, his rich brown eyes alight on mine as he remains silent.

"If you're willing to do all of this—" I gesture around the inside of the car, forcing out a pained laugh. "Just to have an excuse to see me, then say it. Like you said the other night, if you want me as badly as I want you, then say it doesn't end at a business arrangement."

I keep his gaze, waiting for him to respond. To say anything, really. But after he lowers his gaze down from the mirror, I lower my gaze to my lap. His silence everything I need to know.

I shake my head as I grab my purse, sighing. "You're right. What we do together, it excites me." I turn towards the door, holding my hand out onto the door handle as I take one last look in his direction. "But what excites you doesn't always mean it's good for you."

I feel the brand of his stare through the mirror as he lifts it to me. Waiting, until a long moment later the door clicks as it unlocks. I pause before opening it, waiting for him to say something.

To say anything that would make me decide not to go on this date.

He lowers it back to the road in front of him. Turning his head slightly to the side, not making eye contact. "Enjoy your date." He says before he faces forward again, his voice quiet and low.

I feel my chest sink inside of itself at his response, threatening to show my disappointment all over my face. Instead, I nod at his response and will a steady gaze as I open the door, stepping out of the car.

Adrian notices my arrival, a smile lighting his face as he steps out of the entryway of the restaurant. He walks down the short set of steps, approaching me as I close the door behind me.

Adrian brings me in for a hug, and I find myself glancing over to where Levi was just parked.

Noticing the car already on its way down the street as Levi drives away.

Chapter 38

Adrian pulls a chair out for me as I take my seat. His rough hands come to the neckline of my coat, draping it off of me before setting it on the back of my chair. The smell of his cedarwood cologne wafts towards me as he moves to seat himself.

"You look beautiful today." He says, a smile curving up his full lips as he drapes his coat over the back of his chair. He rolls his forest green sleeves up to his elbows, the top button of his henley T-shirt revealing a glimpse of his sun-kissed skin.

I smile as I pick up the menu. "Thank you." I flip the menu open as I explore their variety of breakfast and lunch options. "You don't look too bad yourself." I smirk up at him as my eyes lift from the menu.

Adrian chuckles, his eyes squinting slightly as a strand of his wavy hair rests loosely against his brow. "I'll take it." He grabs a menu for himself as he turns to the back of it, glancing through the drink options.

A woman with two french-tail braids approaches our table, pieces of her golden blonde hair randomly hanging out on the sides of her bronzed face. The waitress forces a smile, the exhaustion on her face evident even through her cheery voice as she speaks. "Welcome to The Brunch House, I'm Gia and I'll be your waitress for this afternoon." She turns to me, her hazel eyes stark against her tanned skin. "Can I start you off with something to drink, ma'am?"

The word ma'am floats through my mind, wanting to roll my eyes at the word entirely with the reminder of Levi's snarky enthusiasm as he said it earlier. I sigh, smiling. "A mimosa is fine."

She nods her head. "Absolutely." She turns to Adrian as I watch her work on a swallow. "And for you, sir?"

"Just water, please. Thank you."

She nods her head again. "I'll give you two a few moments to look over the menu while I go get those for you." She turns around, leaving the table entirely.

I glance down at the menu. "Water is a responsible choice." I surmise.

"I have a showing later today for a client. I can't imagine they'd be too pleased if I showed up slightly intoxicated." He chuckles.

My gaze roams over the menu before I set it down, already having decided on what I'll order. "Commercial or residential property?"

His gaze roams over the menu. "Commercial." He sets the menu down on top of mine, folding his hand on the table in front of him as his gaze lifts to mine. "All things considered I'm surprised the client is interested in this property, considering what happened not too long ago."

"The building is that bad, huh?" I ask, plopping my elbows onto the table. I clasp my hands together as I rest my chin against them.

He huffs out a chuckle. "The building itself is fine, it's what happened outside of it."

Gia returns back to our table with our drinks, setting them down. "Alright, are we ready to order?"

Adrian nods his head. "Looks like it."

She takes out a pad of paper and a pen, nodding to me as she smiles. "Ladies first."

"I'll take the french toast platter. Scrambled for the eggs."

She writes it down before nodding towards Adrian. "And for you, sir?"

"I'll have the eggs and corned beef hash, please."

She writes down his order then collects our menus. "I'll have those right up for you both."

"Thank you." I say before she walks away. I go to grab my mimosa, lifting my gaze back to Adrian. "So, spill the tea."

Adrian grabs the glass of water, the ice cubes floating at the top of the water jingling as he lifts it to his lips. He takes a sip before setting the glass down. "Well, apparently there was a murder around a week ago in the alleyway. Some guy's head was chopped off."

My poker face remains steady as I lift the glass to my lips, tilting my head as I force myself to appear shocked. "Chopped off?" I ask enthusiastically.

He nods curtly. "Apparently when the examiners arrived, they found his head resting in his hands in his lap." He grimaces as he briefly shakes his head. "They said the lines were so clean that it would've had to have been an insanely sharp blade to be able to cut through all of the bone and tissue like that."

I take a casual sip of my mimosa, widening my eyes before I set my glass down again. "Is that even possible? I can't imagine the strength it would've taken to be able to do that." I raise a hand to my chest, adding to the forced terror in my voice.

His thumbs lift up, tapping against one another as he watches me with disgust in his face. "I have no idea. It seems there's a lot of shady things going on in The Pleasure District."

Silence fills my head as I force my lips to pull down into a frown. "It's never been known to be an unsafe area, but times are changing I suppose."

He nods slowly, his gaze hardening for a moment before smoothing out again. "It appears so."

I sigh audibly as I place my hands over his. "You don't suppose these things will start happening closer to my work, do you?" I jerk them away, forcing my lips to quiver with unease. My gaze roaming over his face. "What if something happens on my way home from work—"

Adrian lifts his hands over mine, squeezing them as he pulls them back to the middle of the table.

"Nothing will happen to you, I promise." He says, his eyes dull and emotionless.

I sigh as my Succubus energy slips to the surface, just enough to smell the detest radiating off of him. I pull the energy back, nodding my head as I force a shy smile.

My gaze remains on his face as my peripheral vision catches his carotid artery ticking along his neck, the rush of adrenaline seeping out of him.

He tilts his head, smiling as that artery soothes its pace. "I'd be more than happy to start giving you rides to and from work, but I know that breaches a certain level of privacy."

I sigh, caressing a thumb along his palm. "I'll have one of my co-workers from work take me home if I feel it's necessary. Otherwise, I'll just have to be extra observant of my surroundings."

He grins, nodding his head. "As long as you're safe then I will sleep better at night."

"Awe, you really do like me, huh?"

He chuckles. "It appears I do. So much so that I was going to ask you if you were free for Valentine's Day?"

I watch him for a long moment, the brief silence interrupted as our waitress comes back with our plates of food.

I pull my hands out from his as she sets my plate of french toast and scrambled eggs down in front of me. "Here you are, dear."

"Thank you." I force a smile.

She sets Adrian's plate of scrambled eggs, corned beef hash, and toast down, stepping back from the table. "Let me know if there's anything else I can get for you two. Enjoy."

"Thank you." Adrian says as he grabs a fork. He lifts his gaze back up to me, a smirk pulling at one side of his face. "So, your hesitation either means you already have a date that night, or you just are figuring out how to let me down gently."

I huff out a chuckle as I grab my mimosa again, lifting it. "No—you just caught me a little off guard there."

"In a bad way?" He asks as he gently jabs his fork into the scrambled eggs, lifting it to his mouth.

Valentine's Day. Gods—I almost forgot that's next Friday already. A night that's either the best night to work, or what's normally the worst.

My mind stammers for a second over Levi for whatever dumb reason. Maybe I'm having a mid-life crisis, maybe I'm just too deep in my curiosity over him to really consider another man.

We're just partners, and his silence when I probed the question gave me the clarity I needed over the situation. To know that he has no intention of making an effort to keep me around, so why should I bother giving him anymore of my mental thoughts.

So then why do I feel guilty for saying yes to Adrian when it's apparent Levi won't make the move to ask me to—

Why am I even thinking about this right now? Stand the fuck up, Amelia.

I pick my fork and butter knife up, Adrian's gaze still on me as I begin cutting a piece of my french toast. A grin curves up my lips as I say sweetly to him. "Not at all."

He fights a grin on his face as he nods vaguely. "So does this mean I can have the privilege of spending Valentine's Day with you?"

I lift my fork, my french toast hanging in front of my mouth as I smile at him. "It does."

Chapter 39

As I step outside with Adrian, I find myself glancing at my phone for the third time in the past two minutes.

Finding myself overly curious as to who will be my Uber driver home. A small part of me checking if Levi's made up account name will be the one that pops up on my phone or not.

I fight the internal sigh when I get the notification that my ride has been accepted, by a different—and wholly normal name—alerting me that they will be arriving soon.

Adrian rests an arm around my shoulder, bringing me into his embrace as I shove my phone into my coat pocket. "I'm impatiently waiting for warmer weather any day now."

I snort into his hold as I lift my head up. "Well you still have a ways to go considering we still have at least another two and a half months."

He kisses the top of my forehead as he lifts his gaze up to a car approaching the sidewalk, a flash of his lights telling me that he's my Uber driver. "Yeah, I guess I'm just a little impatient."

I step away from his hold, scoffing. "Men and their desire to have things right away."

He chuckles as he holds my hands, the cool brisk wind whipping against my face as he smiles. "Thank you for coming to lunch with me." He leans forward, his lips pressing against mine.

He pulls away slowly, his gaze on me. "I'm excited for Valentine's Day."

"Me too." I say, smiling as the Uber driver honks his horn. I huff out a noise of agitation as I turn around, giving him a look before I turn back around. "Text me later." I say sweetly.

Adrian nods his head. "I will."

I step out of his embrace and begin walking to the white sedan. I pull open the back door, slipping into the back seat. "Confirm your name." I say plainly.

"Albert, your Uber driver."

"Great." I say very unenthusiastically. "Take me home, Albert."

He puts the car in drive as I wave goodbye to Adrian through my window, his grin the last thing I see before I face forward.

I cross a leg over the other, feeling my phone in my coat pocket but refraining from pulling it out to look at it. So I force my hands into my lap, and keep them there for the entirety of the ride home.

Almost eight hours later and I'm back at the club, packed with guests right off the bat.

And right away someone wants a lap dance.

I walk towards the empty private section, the guest walking behind me until I lead us into the section, pulling the curtain closed.

I step to the side as the man takes his seat into the leather round-backed chair, leaning back into it as his gaze lifts to mine. "You take your top off, right?"

I lean forward into the chair, my gaze hardening. "Rush me again and I will pry those ugly eyes right from their sockets."

His eyes widen before he nods curtly, omitting to remain silent now.

Thank gods.

I begin moving my hips slowly from side to side, that Succubus energy rising to meet me at the surface. I turn around before slowly leaning all the way forward, bending at my knees so my ass is right in his face. My fingers slowly glide down my black fishnets before standing up straight again.

I lower myself to his lap, leaning my head against his shoulder as I begin rolling my hips onto him. My mind wandering elsewhere as I do an average performance.

What should I eat for dinner when I get home? Maybe I'll just eat a peanut butter and jelly sandwich and call it a night.

This is what I get for not going to the grocery store, leaving myself with not many options right now.

I wonder what Rufus is doing. He's probably taking a nap, missing his most favorite person in the world.

I think I'm going to order him some new treats just because he's my goodest boy.

I raise my hands up to my breasts, squeezing them gently as I hear his breathing getting heavier. I lift myself from him, turning around as my hands come to my back, halting. His beady little eyes strained on my breasts.

"That'll be an extra fifty."

His gaze lifts up to me, scrunching his eyebrows. "For what?" He demands.

I shrug my shoulders. "For rushing me."

He stares at me for a moment before reaching into his jean pocket, pulling out fifty bucks. "Fine."

I snatch the money from him, lowering it beneath my garter. An exaggerated smile appearing on my lips before my hands lower to my back again. "Now we can continue."

I unfasten the black velvet bikini strings, slipping the top off of me and setting it onto a small table. My brain automatically goes on autopilot as I finish dancing to this song.

Oh! Maybe I should get Rufus those peanut butter treats he loves so much. Ugh, he'd be so happy.

After I finish, I slip the top back on, turning to find him tugging on his pants. "You have a beautiful rack."

"Already knew that." I say, picking up my phone and looking at the time in the corner of the screen.

Still a ways to go until my shift is over.

I sigh as I turn around towards him, watching him grab at his pants again.

I lean forward, chuckling as I put my hands on my knees. Slightly tilting my head. "Do you need to go potty?" I briefly lowered my gaze to his crotch area.

He immediately stops himself from grabbing at his pants a third time, standing up from the chair and nearly pushing me out of the way. "Fucking bitch." He goes to whip the curtain aside before he halts completely.

"What did you just say?"

A chill courses down my spine as I turn around, finding Levi standing there with visible anger simmering beneath his skin as he glares at the man.

"Relax, man. She's just a—"

Before he can even finish his sentence Levi has his fist around his neck, hauling him back into the private section as I quickly pull the curtain closed.

He shoves him back into the seat, his hand still wrapped around his throat as he lowers his face down to his.

I stand there watching as the veins in Levi's forearm bulge out, the tension in his back straining against his white button down shirt. My gaze lowers to the tattoos peeking out of his rolled sleeves, the black ink contrasted against the white material.

The man begins gasping for air, his gaze lifting to mine as he begins trying to pry Levi's hands off.

"Levi." I say quietly as I stand next to the chair, my gaze on him.

And as if my voice lulls him from some kind of hypnosis, he releases his grip on the man's throat entirely.

Feeling incredibly thankful for the loud club music so nobody can hear this man loudly gasping for air right now.

Levi stands up straight again, bringing his hands up to his collar, unbuttoning two of the buttons until a tattoo beneath his collarbone shows. "Do you know what this is?"

The man looks at it, a second later his lips quiver as he begins shaking in the seat. His gaze roams Levi's face wildly, panicked. "I—please. I—I had no idea." He stammers as he brings his hands up to his chest.

Levi casually buttons the shirt up again, keeping his gaze on the man as a cold stare hardens onto him. "Then you should understand perfectly that if you *ever* disrespect her again, it won't be my hand against your neck. It'll be a knife." He says way too calmly for the ire that shines in his eyes.

The man nods his head violently, his hands shaking.

"Quit your fucking shaking."

The man struggles to cease the trembling in his hands, but after a minute, he finally calms himself down enough. He nods his head. "Am I allowed to leave now?"

Levi nods his head.

The man bolts up from his seat when Levi holds a hand up to his chest, pushing him back from exiting the private section. "Actually, not quite yet."

The man lifts his gaze up to him, waiting with terror in his eyes.

"On your knees." Levi's voice being both the fluidity of a running river, and the sharp burn of a viper sinking it fangs into you.

Calm, but deadly.

The man lowers himself down to the ground, keeping his gaze on Levi.

A devious grin curves his lips, nodding to me. "Kiss her feet."

The man looks up at me quickly before lowering his mouth, planting a shaky kiss to my red-painted toes. He lifts his head up when Levi gives him a command.

"Again."

He lowers his lips, pressing another kiss.

"Again."

The man looks up at him. "How many times?"

Levi looks him dead in the eyes, absolutely no humor shining in that stern gaze of his. "Until you get the fucking message that *you* are beneath *her*, and never the other way around."

My gaze remains wholly on Levi now as warmth pools through every crevice of my body. From my cheeks down to my toes. I feel that heat radiate to my pussy as I watch the detest in his eyes. So palpable I can nearly touch it.

My gaze lowers to his hands, balled up into fists and I suddenly want to feel those hands roam over every inch of my body. Wanting to feel one of his hands balling up my long red hair while the other grips my hip while he rams into me from behind.

I loosen a breath as I turn my gaze back to the man. He nods his head before lowering his face back down, pressing soft kisses first onto my toes before roaming to the tip of my red heels. He does this over, and over, and over again. Until finally he lifts his head up before standing back up onto his two feet.

He locks eyes with Levi, nodding curtly before looking over to me. "I'm truly sorry." He straightens his posture before he draws back the curtain, and leaves the private section.

I lift my gaze to Levi. "How did you know I was in here?"

He finally looks at me, the anger in his eyes finally softening. "I saw you walk in here with him. Heard the commotion and thought to check it out."

My gaze roams over his face, suddenly finding my breathing to become uneven. I watch the rise and fall of his chest and wonder how similar to mine it must look. "Well, thank you—"

Before I can even finish Levi is on me, his hands coming up to my jaw as his mouth crashes into mine. I still for a brief moment before I wrap my arms around his neck as his tongue pries my mouth open. His tongue glides along mine as he swipes my things off the small table, pushing me onto it.

He inserts himself in between my legs as I open them wider for him, my fingers interlocking with his hair. He lowers his hands to my waist, pressing himself up against me as I moan into his mouth. His hard cock pressing up against my pussy as his mouth lifts from mine.

He breathes heavily as he whispers to me, able to hear him perfectly clear as if music wasn't blaring in the club all around us. "You make me feel fucking insane. Because you're right—" The laugh that slips from his lips pricks my skin as he grinds himself into me, a whimper escaping me. "I don't want it to end after our business arrangement. That is the very *last* thing I fucking want."

He lowers his hands to my legs, lifting them to wrap around his waist as he grinds into me, slowly to start.

"Because you are no longer just a want, Amelia."

He grinds his hips harder into me, reveling in the hardness of him rubbing up against me. He raises a hand to my neck as he pulls my face closer to his. His thumb gently sweeping over my bottom lip as his heated gaze stills me in place.

"I *need* to have you."

His lips crash into mine again, the taste of whiskey on his lips. I moan into his mouth at the feel of his cock grinding against my pussy, wanting to feel desperately how it'd feel sinking deep inside of me.

I grind my hips into him, matching his feverish pace as the table begins to sway.

His hands brace the table down, his hips stilling as his lips lift from mine. His gaze roams over my face as a smirk curves up his lips. "A pretty tight fit in here, I'd say." He grinds himself into me again, an actual *shiver* running down his body as he licks his bottom lip. "Gods, I want to feel how fucking tight it is."

A shaky exhale leaves me. "Then why don't you find out?" I say huskily.

He chuckles. "Soon." He steps away from me, his absence felt like a cold splash over my body. "The first time I fuck you won't be in a tiny private section." He lowers to the ground, picking my phone and top up as he hands both of them to me.

I take them, setting the phone next to me before putting my black bikini top back on. When suddenly he sticks a finger into his mouth, wetting it before lowering it below my lips.

He slowly glides it above my chin, his gaze wholly on my mouth until he lifts his finger away. "There." He says, looking at me before taking a cloth from the bin next to the table, wiping his mouth. He looks down at it, tossing it into his pocket. "Though it would be hot as fuck for you to walk around with your lips smeared, knowing I'm the one who caused it, I know it wouldn't be good for business."

I sit there staring at him, blinking once.

"See you soon, little red." He says before he turns around and walks out of the private section.

My fingers raise to my lips, the feel of his still lingering there. I quickly grab my phone, raising it up to my face, checking for my makeup in my camera app before walking back out onto the floor.

Where I walk out to see Levi gone, as if vanished from thin air.

Chapter 40

Levi

If I didn't get out of there I was going to fuck her right then and there, on that small pitiful piece of furniture they call a table.

Well, okay. It's not that pitiful. I'm just sexually frustrated and being overly dramatic.

I hit the unlock button on my key fob, the fog lights on my car flashing three times as I approach the vehicle. I pull the car door open, sliding inside before I shut the door beside me.

My phone buzzes in my pocket, and I'd be lying if I said I didn't get excited, expecting it to be Amelia. But when I pull my phone out of my coat pocket, I sigh as Sawyer's name pops up.

He's on the way. Don't be late.

I send him back a thumbs up emoji before setting my phone in the cup holder to my right, sliding my key into the ignition and turning my car on.

I don't even know why I showed up at the club tonight. I had no reason to be there, no business to conduct there. But I knew she'd be there, and when I saw her take that prick into the private section, something told me to wait around and make sure everything went smoothly.

I'd sat in the seat closest to the section, facing towards that closed curtain as my fingers tapped idly on my knee. Even with the music blaring throughout the club I could still hear him. Rushing her, then disrespecting her.

I'd never jumped up from my seat so fast in my life when I'd heard him call her a bitch.

I turn the dial up as heat blows through the vents, warming my ice pricked hands. I pick my phone up again, looking at the screen as if by staring at it she'll magically text me—

What the fuck is my problem? I've become a literal lunatic for this woman.

I shake my head, huffing out a ragged exhale as I set my phone back down. I switch my lights on as I drive to my original destination.

I slide open the heavy iron door, creating an opening big enough for me to slip through. I slide it closed behind me, metal scraping against the concrete flooring of this abandoned factory.

The sound of broken glass crunches beneath my black boots as the moonlight outside filters through the dirty windows high above. Soft flurries of snow begin to fall against the window panes, a heavy snowstorm projected to hit the city and only to cease early tomorrow morning.

I walk up the rusted metal stairs, a large round window at the top of the landing at the center of the far wall. My gaze lands on not only the burnt up desk, but also the man standing before it.

He faces the window, his arms crossed as he watches the snow fall. "Was meeting here really necessary?"

"It was." I say as I approach him. I waste no time pulling out the golden envelope from inside of my coat, handing it to him.

He finally looks at me, the brightness of the moon and the snow outside illuminating his blue eyes. He gazes down at the envelope, hesitating before grabbing it. He loosens the clasps as he pulls the files out. "When?"

"Six days from now."

He reads over the files, flipping the pages over to scan the backside. He puts the files back into the envelope, securing the clasps when he tucks it inside of his coat. "On Valentine's Day out of all days?"

"Does it matter?" I counter.

He huffs, a slight smirk appearing on his lips. "I guess not." His hand reaches back into his coat, pulling out his phone as it lights up in his hands. He smiles down at the screen, at what I can only presume is Sawyer's payment for his cooperation.

A substantial payment, that is.

He slips the phone back into his coat pocket, nodding. "Make it believable." He says before he turns away from the window and walks away.

His steps echoing around the empty factory are the only noise I hear until he makes his way down the steps, and out of the building entirely.

I find myself standing there watching the snowfall out of the large round window, the ground already becoming slick as it accumulates. I pull out my phone, switching to an app that Dex downloaded for me, one that's unable to be tracked.

I pull up the camera feeds inside of Adrian's home, my gaze landing on the feed to his living room. I pull it up as I watch him shuffling through paperwork, his back hunched over the coffee table with a glass of whiskey in his hands. I try peering into the screen to identify what's on the papers when a text comes through.

I immediately pull it up, a giddy feeling blossoming in my chest and a grin curving my lips when I see who it's from.

Can you give me a ride home tonight? I'd rather not ruin my shoes by walking home in the snow.

I type my response back, looking down at the time in the corner of the screen before I hit send. *Of course. I'd hate for you to ruin such pretty shoes.*

I'm off at two, be here then.

Maybe I want to come now instead.

I watch the text bubbles appear before disappearing. A few seconds later reappearing.

If you wanted round two you can just ask, you know.

I huff out a chuckle as I turn away from the window, heading towards the stairs. *You would like that wouldn't you, little red? To be able to actually feel my cock thrusting inside of you instead of bumping up against that tiny piece of fabric you're wearing?*

As I head down the stairs, I type out another text to her and hit send.

Make your money tonight, Amelia. We'll have our fun real soon.

Chapter 41

I lean my back up against the round backed chair, my gaze set on that dark red hair of hers. I told myself I wouldn't be a creep and stare at her all night, but I can't help myself.

She looks so fucking good in those fishnets. My shameless weakness. Well, these days it appears *she* as a whole is my weakness.

I watch as she rests a hand on a man's shoulder, her amber eyes gazing upon him as he watches her longingly. She smiles sweetly as he nods his head, reaching a hand into his pocket as he pulls his wallet out.

I rest my chin lightly on the tips of my fingers as I watch him pull out a couple hundred dollar bills. I roll my eyes at him, knowing she deserves far more than what he's forking up.

I take a sip of my whiskey as a familiar waitress approaches me, her long black hair trailing down her back. "Can I get you another drink, sir?"

I look up at her, nodding my head. "Another whiskey would be great. Thank you—"

"Dahlia." She says, smiling as she leans down to grab my glass, her breasts nearly falling out of her tight black dress. She smirks at me as she stands up straight again. "I'll be right back with that."

I nod again, forcing a grin. "Thanks."

She takes the glass and walks away as my gaze lands on Amelia again, only to find her staring over at me.

Her eyes churn brightly as she glances over to the waitress, her gaze hardening before locking eyes with me once more. A territorial gaze in her eyes that makes my cock hard in my pants.

Gods, that's hot as fuck.

I reach for my phone sitting on the table beside me, a half grin curving up my lips as I pull out our text thread. *Someone feeling a little jealous?*

I lift my gaze back up to her, watching her gaze fall to her phone on the bar counter. I watch her roll her eyes, picking up the phone as she quickly sends a text back. *Over Dahlia? Please.*

I chuckle to myself as I respond back. *Well it looked like you wanted to murder her just now, and I can't say that it wasn't the hottest thing I've ever seen.*

I watch her look down at her phone, a smirk fighting to pull up her lips when she forces it down. The man next to her lays a hand on her wrist, stilling her typing as he guides her attention back to him. She smiles sweetly as she sets the phone back down, leaning a little closer to him.

My insides go ice cold as I watch her fingernails trail over his chest, exposed partially by his V-neck shirt. I watch as his gaze lowers to her fingers, an exhale I can visibly see leaving his body.

I sit there, watching as she seduces him with her touch and her eyes, my insides fighting the urge to walk over there and rip his hand away that's made its way to her thigh.

He chuckles as she casually glances over at me, her gaze lowering to my fists balled up so hard onto the armrest of the chair. She lifts her gaze up to me, smiling before trailing her gaze back onto the man.

She says something to him and he removes his hand, the grip on my own loosening for a moment until I see the two of them begin to make their way over to the VIP entrance.

I watch as she sends a quick message back before disappearing down the hallway altogether.

Jealousy looks sexy on you, Levi. Xoxo

A little after one-forty and Amelia finally comes out of the VIP hallway, almost two hours later.

She waves goodbye to the man before her eyes land on me. She smiles sweetly as she tilts her head. "You really weren't kidding when you said you'd wait."

"I'm anything but a liar." I take a sniff, smelling the booze on her breath. I glance over to the man making his exit out of the club, a smirk on his face. I fixate my gaze back onto her as I step into her. "Did he play nice, or do I need to kill him?"

She giggles as she swats her hand at me, turning to walk away.

I grab her by the elbow, reeling her back to face me. Our lips only inches apart as I stare at her. My gaze lowers to her red lips, slowly working its way back up to her eyes. "I'm serious."

She watches me for a long moment, exhaling as she shakes her head vaguely. "He was *actually* a gentleman." I release my hold on her arm, stepping back. Her gaze roaming over my face.

I nod my head, adjusting my coat. "Good. I'll be waiting in the car."

She nods as she walks towards the women's locker rooms. Leaving me to exit the club and wait in my car for her.

Twenty minutes later I see Amelia exiting out of the back exit door, walking the few steps to my car. Her faux fur coat draped over her as she opens the car door, sliding inside and closing the door. "Fuck it's freezing out."

I chuckle as I turn the heat up for her. "Definitely too cold to be walking home."

She sets her purse below her seat, shimmying her coat off. I glance over at her as she pulls her long hair over her shoulder, watching as it falls over her gray long sleeved shirt. "Thank you, chauffeur." She says sarcastically.

I chuckle as I turn my gaze forward, pulling out of the alley and heading towards her building.

I turn slowly down the street, a generous layer of snow covering the streets. No one has been able to come out and plow yet. Thankfully it's a thin layer, otherwise I'd probably find myself embarrassed getting us both stuck out here.

I come up to a stop light, slowly hitting my brake as I look over to see Amelia hiking her legs up, curling them to one side. I huff at the sight. "Is that more comfortable?"

She shrugs her shoulders. "It is for now."

My left hand lays over the steering wheel as I use my right to turn the radio on.

"Leave it off. After hearing music blaring all night long I'd prefer a moment of silence for once."

I lower my hand back to the center console, the light turning green as I slowly pull forward. My car not picking up traction for a brief moment before catching, pressing slowly down on the gas pedal. "I can imagine."

"What else can you imagine?"

I scrunch my brows, looking over at her when I see that *look* on her face. The look of I want more, *need* more. I shake my head, chuckling as I turn my gaze back onto the road. "Don't do that right now."

"Do what?" She asks huskily.

I feel her hand reach over, slipping through the opening of my coat as she slowly lowers her hand down my stomach.

"Amelia." I say curtly through a ragged exhale.

"Hmm?" She asks as her hand lowers right over my pants, her hand gently squeezing what's already hard beneath.

I turn my blinker on, trying for fucks sake to focus on the slippery roads and not on her hand that's right on my cock. "You know what." I seethe.

Her hand raises to unbutton my pants before slowly lowering my zipper down, the teasing of it fucking agonizing. "Do you want me to stop, Levi?" Her hand stills as she waits for me to answer.

A ragged exhale escapes me as I find myself unable to say no to her. Gods, I definitely am not saying no to this. But why does it have to be when it's snowing out and the roads are absolute shit?

She takes my silence as an answer. "That's what I thought."

She slips my pants down as I lift my hips, helping her as she exposes my boxer briefs.

Her hand slips through the opening, her fingers wrapping gently around me and it takes everything in me to not thrust my hips forward.

"I just want to see it." She says, that sweet seductive voice raising the hairs on my skin.

She whips it out as she purrs, her hand slowly stroking me. "I knew it was big."

We come up to another intersection when the light turns yellow, lightly pressing on the brake as my hand tightens around the steering wheel. I grunt as her soft hand strokes me.

"I just want a taste." She says before she lowers her face down into my lap, my entire body stilling as I slam down on the brake.

I look up, noticing the cars on the other side of the road. Thank gods I didn't just slide us out into the damn intersection.

I lift my hips up, adjusting myself as I look down. Her deep red hair flowing around me. I take my right hand, bunching it up into my fist as I pull her head back. Her eyes looking up at me as my gaze hardens on her. She smirks as her tongue flicks out, gliding along the tip. My fist clenches a little tighter as a grunt escapes me.

Her eyes remain on me as she lowers her mouth, pressing a kiss on the tip. Pre-cum already beading at the tip as she licks it off. I curse under my breath as my gaze shoots up to the intersection lights, still on red.

Fuck, fuck fuck. What am I—

She lowers her mouth on me completely, sinking my cock down her throat as another grunt slips out of me. I blow out a shaky breath as I look over at the car next to me, finding an older man and his wife in the passenger seat. I turn my gaze forward as I try to compose myself, but all I can focus on is how wet and soft her mouth is around my cock.

Amelia begins stroking my cock again while she sucks me as I grip her hair in my hand. The light finally turns green as I force myself not to press all the way down on the damn pedal as she twirls her tongue around my cock.

Fucking gods, I'm going to get us into an accident if she doesn't slow it down.

"Amelia." I mutter out through clenched teeth as I turn down the street, her building only a few blocks away.

She ignores me as she keeps going, building up her pace a little faster as she deep throats me. As if I can't help the involuntary reaction, my hips jerk forward as I loosen a ragged exhale. My hand holding her head in place as I thrust deeper down her throat. A whimper slipping from my pressed lips.

My foot releases off the gas a little before I remember that I'm driving again. Yes—that's right. I'm still fucking driving.

I press my foot on the pedal again, praying to fucking whoever that we arrive at her building without me crashing into any parked cars on the street right now.

She lifts her mouth off of me as she looks up at me, licking her lips before she lowers herself again. This time to my balls.

She keeps stroking my cock as she kisses my balls, having no idea when she even freed those puppies either. Her lips caress that sensitive skin as I pull up to a stop sign.

I groan at how good it fucking feels. "Fuck, Amelia. If you don't get your mouth back on my—"

In the next moment my cock is gliding down her throat, a moan escaping my lips as I close my eyes. My head leaning back into the headrest.

Gods she feels so fucking *good*. I just want to live in her throat forever, feel her sucking me forever. So fucking wet, so—

My eyes shoot open as a car honks at me from behind, realizing I'm still stopped at the stop sign. I pull forward immediately as Amelia's laugh vibrates against my cock. Only intensifying that release building inside of me.

I approach her building and pull up to the side of the street, her pace quickening as I hurry and put the car in park.

I lower my other hand to her hair, forcing her head up to look at me. "Not yet." I force out.

I lower my left hand down, pulling down the lever to scoot my seat all the way back. "I want you on your knees in front of me when I come in that pretty fucking mouth of yours."

The heat in her eyes brightens as she climbs over, getting on her knees in front of my seat as she looks up at me. "Like this, Levi?" She says as she lowers her tongue, gliding it up my shaft.

I blow out a ragged breath, on the fucking edge of bursting. "Yes." I seethe, fisting my hands into her hair. "Now take it. *Please—*"

She lowers her mouth down, my cock sliding down her throat as I thrust up into her mouth. I thrust into her over and over again, taking me entirely as her eyes remain on me. Little moans that get trapped in her throat vibrate against my cock, driving me fucking wild.

I fuck her face as I hold her head in place, my body going taught as release finds me. I hold her in place as I spill myself deep into her throat, whimpers rupturing from my mouth.

I let go of her face as I ride my release, Amelia continuing to suck me into oblivion. I almost tell her to stop, that I can't handle it but am overpowered by my release that I find I can't even formulate words.

Her mouth closes over, sucking every last drop as my body shakes with release. It lasts on, and on, and on until I finish. My head ringing with how hard I'm coming, never having came this hard in my life before.

She slowly lifts her mouth off of me, her lips glistening with me as she lowers her mouth to my balls. Her tongue gliding up them, trailing a streak of my cum as I pry her head up.

I lower my mouth, meeting her halfway as I crash my lips into hers. Our tongues gliding against one another as the taste of me lingers on her lips.

I suck her tongue before parting my lips from hers. I gaze down at her, her lashes lifting as she looks up at me.

"Next time, you'll share it with me."

I wipe the underneath of her lip, watching her gaze fixate on my thumb as I suck it between my lips. Her cheeks flushed as desire brightens her eyes.

I brush her hair away from her face, tucking it behind her ear. "You okay?"

She nods, shaking herself back to reality. "Yeah."

"Good. I just wanted to make sure I wasn't too rough on you." I say, my gaze lowering to her lips before trailing my finger there. I glance up to her building, nodding towards it. "You want me to walk you up?"

She lifts herself from the floor of my seat, climbing back over to the passenger seat. "I'll be fine, *bodyguard*."

I chuckle as I tuck my cock back into my briefs, pulling my pants back up as I button them. I look over to her as she grabs her coat and her purse, facing towards me. "Well, goodnight then."

She forces a smile. "Goodnight." She goes to open the door, stepping one foot out when she turns her head over her shoulder. "Maybe when you give me a ride home tomorrow night, we can both finish at the same time." She winks.

A goofy smile lights up my face as I nod. "That can be arranged."

She smiles. "Two a.m." She steps fully out of the car, turning around as she bends down to my line of sight. "Don't be late." She closes the door before she turns around, walking towards that double-door entrance.

My face is unable to hide that goofy smile even after I've driven away, and found myself at home. And as I lie in bed for a long time, with jitters of excitement to keep me from falling asleep right away. Entirely looking forward to not the drive home tomorrow night, but to the excuse for me to be able to see her again.

Chapter 42

Amelia

The snow crunches beneath my light beige snow boots as I take two steps forward, my hands shoved into my coat pockets to keep warm. I grip Rufus' leash firmly in one hand as I wait for him to do his business.

He continues walking around in a circle with his nose pressed down into the snow, sniffing for the perfect spot to take a dump.

"Rufus, go potty." I say through the brisk cold wind that whips at my face.

He looks up at me, wagging his tail.

I nod at the ground. "It's freezing out here. Let's go." I say, pleading for him to hurry so we can venture back inside where it's warm.

He huffs at me before he goes back to sniffing for several long moments until he finally squats down.

"Good boy." I whisper, my teeth chattering.

I pull my plastic green bags out, opening both of them up as he steps away from his pile of shit. I crouch down, picking it up with one bag before dropping it into the other, tying it up. I walk over to the designated garbage bin for pet waste, dropping it in.

Rufus tugs on his leash, his tail wagging. I look down at him and where his gaze has fixated on. I frown down at him, shaking my head. "It's too cold out for a walk today, bud. We'll go tomorrow."

He huffs at me as I pull out my hand sanitizer, opening it and squeezing some out into my hands. I close it up, shoving it back inside my coat pocket as I lather my hands with it.

I look down at Rufus again, his head tilted at me in curiosity.

"Just because I don't actually touch it doesn't mean I'm not going to still sanitize my hands." I tug gently on his leash, guiding us towards the front entrance. "Let's go inside and I'll get you a treat."

His ears perk up at the sound of that word and he gets right into step as we head back inside.

As I pull the front entrance door open Rufus slips inside, I along with him. I stomp my shoes on the entry rug, shaking the snow off my boots as best I can before we head to the elevators.

I press the upward arrow button as the elevator opens up, Rufus and I slipping inside. I slide my key into the penthouse lock, turning it as the elevator begins to make its descent up.

I pull my phone out, seeing a text from Sapphire came through some time ago.

Sooo what are you dressing up as? And please don't tell me you don't know yet.

I fear I have no idea yet.

Ugh, fine. Then I guess this means you get an excuse to drag me out of the house and meet me for costume shopping. ;)

I chuckle to myself as the elevator comes to a halt, stopping at my floor as the doors open up. I remove my key from the lock and usher Rufus and I forward to our door.

I open it up, closing the door behind me as I unhook his leash from his collar. He trots over to the pantry, planting his butt down as he waits for his treat.

I send a text back to Sapphire before I set my phone onto my kitchen counter.

Tomorrow. It's a date xoxo

I slip my boots off, setting them on my entryway rug before I slip my knee length coat off of me. I hang it on the mounted coat rack before I approach Rufus.

My hands come up to his sweet little face, scratching behind his ears as I plant a kiss on his nose. "You're so spoiled." I say sweetly before opening up the panty door.

I reach for the plastic storage bin of dog biscuits, lifting the top and grabbing two of them. I close the bin again, turning towards Rufus as his gaze fixates on the treat in my hand.

I walk out of the pantry, closing the door. "Wait." I command. He stands there, perfectly still as he waits for the magic word.

I walk over to his food bowl, his gaze tracking me as I set the two biscuits into the bowl. I stand up straight again, waiting for a long moment until I nod my head. "Okay."

He hurries to the bowl, gobbling up the treats as I turn to head upstairs to my bathroom.

I turn the shower handle to hot before pulling it out. Water streams down as steam begins to fog my glass shower doors. I strip off my clothes, pooling my sweatpants and T-shirt at my feet when I hear my phone buzzing from the kitchen.

I close the shower door as I rush downstairs, finding Rufus has taken his place on his dog bed in the living room, content and happy as he lays down for a nap.

I walk over to my phone, grabbing it as I see the text on my phone. My lips curving upward at the message displayed on the screen.

A request from your chauffeur has arrived. Your driver, Levi (the most handsome man), would like to know if you will be needing his services of transportation to your place of work tonight. Please respond back with a yes to accept this invitation (preferably), or a no to decline this service.

A laugh escapes from my lips as I type back.

Yes.

I watch those three little bubbles appear right away, a reply from him showing up only moments later.

Thank you for confirming your RSVP. Levi will arrive at nine-thirty, and looks forward to servicing you this evening.

Heat pools low at his response, reminding me of having his cock deep in my throat last night. After how he treated that man for disrespecting me, and the taunting all night of him watching me, I said fuck waiting.

I wanted—*needed*, to have his dick in my mouth as soon as I got into his car. The tension between us causing that barrier of just partners to become more and more blurry the more that I'm around him.

I set my phone down, heading back upstairs to my bathroom to pull my shower door open. Steam billowing out as I step inside, the hot water pelting against my already heated skin.

Chapter 43

The city lights cast themselves through my floor to ceiling living room windows as I stare down at the streets far below me.

With all of the slush still remaining on the streets it's hard to believe that the plows actually came through this afternoon. Pft, what a pitiful job.

I turn away from the window, walking back upstairs into my bedroom as I grab a bottle of perfume, spraying it all over myself before tossing it into my dance bag. I adjust my black flare leggings, smoothing my navy crew neck sweater down. I hook my dance bag over my shoulder, turning my bedroom light off before walking downstairs to the kitchen.

I set my bag down on the hardwood floor, standing up straight again as I head over to Rufus' crate.

I stand beside it as Rufus comes walking over, ushering himself inside before I close the crate door.

I kneel down in front of the door, watching as he lays down with his head resting over his front paws. "I'll be home before you know it." I give him an air kiss before heading back over to the kitchen, my phone buzzing on the counter. I turn it over, reading Levi's text.

Your (handsome) driver has arrived. Please meet your driver out front.

I chuckle as I hold my finger over his text, sending him a heart reaction before setting my phone back down.

I turn around, grabbing my coat off the hanger before slipping my arms through it and my feet into my beige fur-lined boots. I lean down to grab my bag, hooking it over my shoulder as I grab my phone, slipping it into my coat pocket.

I step out of my door and close it behind me. I reach the elevator, hitting the downward arrow as I run my fingers through my hair. The doors open up as I step inside to make my way down to the main floor.

When the elevator door opens again I step out onto the main level floor, looking up to find Levi standing outside in front of the door.

I walk to the glass doors as Levi opens it for me. "Good evening, ma'am."

I chuckle as I step through the door, "Good evening, *sir*."

His eyes softly gazing into mine before he holds a hand out, halting me from walking further. I look down at his hand, scrunching my brows at him as I lift my gaze back up.

"Sorry ma'am, but I'm afraid I can't risk you getting your shoes or your pants dirty on the slick ground." He lowers his hand onto my back.

I laugh. "Okay, so—"

In an instant he lifts me up, carrying me in his arms. My arms instinctively wrap around his neck as he turns away, walking down the steps.

I look down at his black boots as they slush in the snow on the ground, my gaze lifting to his face as he fixes his gaze on the car ahead of us. His wavy blonde hair swept back from his face as I admire the planes of his jaw, my gaze lowering to his bare neck.

I exhale as I lean my head into his neck, feeling his body tense up as my lips brush against his skin. "Thank you for your generosity, *sir*."

I watch him work on a swallow, the second time now at that word. I smirk as I pull my face away from his neck, looking down at the ground ahead at the cleared path right in front of his passenger side door.

A path that looks like it's been cleared not with a shovel, but with someone's shoes.

He lowers slightly, pulling the car door open before gently setting me down onto the cleared path he made for me. "After you."

I look up at him, a strange emotion clogging my throat, suffocating any semblance of words to escape my lips.

I nod as I slip inside the car, setting my dance bag beside my feet as he closes the door for me.

I watch him walk around the back of the car, approaching the driver side door when he opens it, seating himself down before pulling the door closed. He leans down to turn the heat up before putting the car in drive.

"You think it'll be a busy night?" He asks, glancing over at me as he drives away from the curb.

I sigh heavily. "Most likely not."

He comes to a stop as we approach the stop sign, looking both ways before proceeding forward again. A smirk crawls up my face as I remember us being honked at last night, him being too focused on his cock deep in my throat to remember we were driving.

He looks over and catches my grin. "What?"

I vaguely shake my head, my grin unfaltering. "Nothing."

He turns his gaze forward onto the road again. We sit there in silence for a long moment until he clears his throat. "So there's a costume party at your job."

I nod my head as he turns the corner on the street. "We have one every year for Valentine's Day." My stomach suddenly knotted.

"Are you going with Adrian?"

I hesitate for a long moment, watching as my work comes into view at the far end of the street. Like a tiny pin on a map. "Yes." I say, steadying my voice.

I look over to watch him nod. No anger in his face, no jealousy. Just a slow, simple nod. As if reeling his emotions back to calculate a calm exterior.

"Are you going to say anything about that?" I ask.

He shakes his head. "I don't need to say what we both already know."

The Playground comes closer into view, those bright red neon lights casting a glow against the dark sky. He turns right, pulling down the alleyway until he parks the car right in front of the exit door.

"That I *belong* to you, right?" I say, huffing at his words as I shake my head. Fighting against my own internal dialogue that shamelessly finds myself agreeing with that statement.

That no matter what I do I can't shake my burning desire for him. That no matter who I distract myself with, he's always at the forefront of my mind.

He casually opens his door, stepping out and walking around the car until he approaches my door. He uses his foot to clear a path for me before opening my door, holding a hand out for me.

I take his hand, stepping out onto the cleared path when he lifts me up again, carrying me to the exit door. He opens it, ushering us inside of it. The looming hallway empty aside from the music blaring throughout the club.

He sets me down, his hand roaming as it glides slowly up my ass. I gasp as his lips caress against my neck, his fingers rubbing up my pussy through my pants.

"Like I said before," He starts as he rubs me slowly, his breath hot on my neck. "Distract yourself all you want. But tonight when I pick you up after your shift," He slides his hand up my ass again until he brings it to my hip. He keeps his hand cemented there as his index finger idly traces circles over my navel. Sending charges of dizzying arousal through me. "You'll be coming on *my* fingers."

A breathy moan escapes me as he presses a light kiss to my neck, his hand sliding off me as he steps away from me entirely. I turn around to face him.

He smirks at me. "See you tonight, *Cherry*." Saying my stage name with emphasis before he opens the door and walks back outside.

I stand there for a moment, my gaze on the door before I gather my sanity together again and head for the women's locker room.

Chapter 44

Levi

I went for a run for the second time today. This time at the gym on a treadmill rather than around my block.

Because well, if I don't run this frustration off I'm afraid it's going to ruin me from the inside out. Plus, it's pitch dark out so I can only imagine the kind of fear I would invoke on any random woman walking on the street at this hour of night.

Like, hey. I'm definitely not running full speed towards you because I'm going to kidnap you. I promise I'm just running for my own sanity.

My feet pound against the belt of the treadmill as I pump my arms from side to side, full on sprinting at this point.

"Are you going to say anything about that?"

Amelia's words cement themselves in my mind as I pump my arms a little faster. The real words of what I wanted to say were so close to the tips of my tongue, but I was forced to shove them back down.

All because I have to abide by my orders from the don himself.

Because if I could've said what I really wanted to say, it would've been this:

Well, considering I'm planning on killing your little distraction toy, I don't have anything to add to that considering he won't be a problem much longer. This way I can also stop getting jealous about you spending time with a man who looks like he doesn't even know where the clit is.

Sweat beads down my forehead as I continue sprinting, my breathing heavy.

Because oh, guess what? He's also a private investigator trying to solve the murders that we did together. How fucking convenient!

My feet continue pounding against the belt.

And yes, if you haven't realized by now, you drive me fucking insane. But in the best way possible. Because quite frankly, if you held a treat out for me I would probably get on my knees and beg for it like the loyal dog I am to you.

My finger presses the cool down button, slowing the pace of the treadmill down significantly as I slow down into a walk. I breathe heavily through my mouth as I brace my hands onto the handrail, feeling my heart rate go from beating a mile a minute to slowing down to a steady pace.

I clench my jaw at the reminder that Amelia is spending Valentine's Day with *him*. A reminder at my own failed attempt to even ask her if she would consider spending time with me that day and *not* as business partners.

If I had asked first instead of being too stuck in my own ways, I would've taken her to The Tower, the tallest restaurant in the city that overlooks the riverfront. She'd be wearing a dress that I bought for her, maybe a color that contrasts against that gorgeous red hair of hers. I'd pay every last dollar just to close out the entire restaurant, with only her and I sitting at that one section that faces the city below us. I'd pay the staff to fill the place with roses, the same color to match her hair. I'd say some lame jokes just in the hopes of her laughing at me, the warmth that I'd feel from that sound alone.

I wouldn't even fantasize about having sex with her. All I'd be happy to do is just spend time with her.

Because suddenly that's all I yearn to do these days. All I want to do is just be around her and it drives me fucking crazy.

No longer is it just her charming magnetism, or the fact that she's a Succubus. No, it's the way that she stands up for herself in the face of any situation. The way her eyes crinkle shut when she laughs, the relaxed bliss etched on her face even after all the pigs and undeserving men she has to deal with at work.

It was never about blackmailing her to work with me. Not even close.

I hit the off button on the treadmill, grabbing my water bottle before I step off of it. I head over to the men's locker room when long behold he's standing in front of me.

He goes to turn into the locker room when I do, glancing at me as he jumps slightly. "My bad, man. I'm apparently not paying attention to my surroundings tonight." Adrian chuckles as he lays a towel over his shoulder.

I shake it off, a casual smile appearing on my face. "It's cool. No worries."

We continue walking as my curiosity puzzles me. Why is he working out at this gym? There's another location only eight minutes away from him, but he chooses to come to one twenty minutes from his house.

I approach my locker, dialing my code until I pull my lock down. Twisting it out of the handle opening.

Adrian approaches the locker four spaces away from mine, opening his up. "You watch the game tonight?" He asks as he pulls his duffel bag out.

I pull mine out, setting it on the bench. "I watched the first half. Didn't need to watch the rest to know how it was going to end." I go to grab a sweater from inside of my bag, setting it on the bench as I lift my shirt off. Having left my coat in the car knowing I'd be too hot to wear it.

Adrian chuckles as he lifts his damp shirt off. "Sometimes a chance of luck can alter the game completely, ya know."

I toss my shirt into my bag, slipping a clean one over me. I close the locker, putting my lock into my bag before zipping it closed. "Sure. Whatever."

"I like your tattoo."

I will a poker face before glancing at him. I look down at his bare arms, his torso. "Let me guess. You're drawing up inspiration for yourself?"

He chuckles, shaking his head as he casually pulls a clean T-shirt over his head. "Merely admiring is all. Especially when one bears the mark of the Deimari."

I glare at him, curving a grin up my lips. I slowly pick my duffel bag up, gripping it in my hand. "Then I imagine you know what comes with bearing the mark then."

Adrian blinks at me, a frozen stare flashing across his face before he forces a smug smirk. "You think you know how this game will end, Levi. But I can guarantee you that this second half of this game we're playing will end with a twist."

My face remains neutral as I shrug my shoulders. "I'll be interested to see how it unfolds then." I turn my back on him as I leave the locker room altogether.

I wrap a towel around my waist as my damp hair trickles water down my neck. I walk out of my bathroom, moving to stand in front of the fireplace in my bedroom.

I knew that if he was actually good at his job that he'd be able to connect the dots between Amelia and I. Her being the last person to be seen with Ian as far as his brother Wesley knew, and me being the hitman for the mafia. Knowing Adrian's only using her to get information out of her, hoping that she'll blab to him the proof that he needs to put me away for life and take the rest of the mafia down with me.

But there's a connection to the dots that he doesn't know exists yet, that Amelia's not some meek woman who's just caught up in the wrong crowd with me like he presumes she is.

I approach my nightstand, grabbing the glass of whiskey I set out before my shower. Taking a sip before setting it down again. I unwrap the towel around my waist, slipping it off of me and putting it into my laundry hamper in my walk-in closet.

I slip a black long sleeved crew neck sweater off a hanger, pulling it over me. I flatten it down as I walked out of the closet, over to my dresser.

I open my top drawer, grabbing a pair of black boxer briefs and slipping them on. I close the drawer, opening the one below it and fishing for a pair of dark navy jeans. Pulling them out and slipping those on, too.

I close the drawer and grab my phone, looking at the time on the screen.

Just after midnight.

I run my fingers through my hair, combing through the damp strands and tousling it. I walk over to my bed, plopping onto it as I fold an arm behind my neck. Exhaling as I lean my head back, scrolling through my phone as I wait for the time to pass until I leave to go give Amelia a ride home.

I scroll through social media, seeing the same old shit until I close out of it. I gaze at my phone's home screen, the picture she took of herself and set as my wallpaper that I never bothered to change.

I chuckle as I smile at it, going to my photo album and pulling the photo up. I zoom in on her smile, on her gorgeous face and suddenly wished it was time for me to go get her.

I sigh deeply as I lock my phone, setting it on my chest. As I lay there, waiting for the time to read one-thirty and I can finally leave to go get her.

Chapter 45

Amelia

"It's actually repulsive how badly you smell." I say as I shove my fingers to my nostrils, closing them as I grimace at him.

The man scoffs at me as he shoves his hands away from the bar counter. "Whatever." As he walks away I catch him trying to sneak a sniff at his armpits, jerking his head up right as his pace quickens to the main entrance.

I hear Ace laughing behind me. Turning to face him as he grabs my empty glass. "No interest in what you can make in the next thirty minutes?"

I lower my hand to my garter, pulling out the cash I made from tonight. I count it back to myself, three hundred. "Not the worst night, but not decent enough where I care to stay any longer." I shove the money back beneath my garter as I get up from my seat. I grab my phone from the bar counter, pulling up the text thread between Levi and I and typing to him.

I'm ready to go now, chauffeur.

I stare at the screen, waiting to see the text bubbles appear. I lower my phone before turning to Ace. "I'll see you Tuesday. I'm outta here."

He nods his head, smiling. "Have a good night."

I begin walking to the women's locker room when my phone buzzes in my hand, a smirk curving my lips.

Your driver is (eagerly) on his way.

I lock my phone again when I bump into someone.

Dahlia grabs my arm, gasping with that stupid look on her face. "I'm so sorry, Cherry. I wasn't paying attention."

"Then do better next time." I say before turning away from her.

"Wait—" She calls out after me.

I close my eyes, sighing before I turn around, opening them again. "Yes?"

She twirls a long strand of her black hair around her finger, a shyness suddenly creeping into her features. "I wanted to ask you, since I've seen you chatting with him sometimes." She steps towards me. "Do you know if that blonde guy is single or not?" She smirks as she twirls that piece of hair behind her back.

Suddenly I have to restrain myself from clawing that smirk right off her face. I reel the urge down, down, down until I'm able to force a smile on my face. "I would actually steer clear of him, girl. He has chronic flatulence."

She gasps as she jerks a hand to her mouth, her eyes wide. "Oh my gods—" She pauses for a long moment before she lowers her hand, a grimace pulling at her lips.

"Yeah. It's gods awful. We're talking like every twenty minutes he passes gas. And the smell? Straight up rancid. Not even cologne can mask it."

She nearly gags as a response before she shakes her head. Lowering her hand back down to her side. "Thanks for the heads up." She quickly walks away, her long hair swishing right above her ass.

A smirk crawls up my face as I turn around and head back to the locker room.

Once I've paid everyone out for the night I head out the exit door, finding Levi's car waiting there. I look down at the ground, the streets fully plowed now.

I walk over to the car, pulling the passenger door open as I slip inside the warm car.

I close the door, setting my bag down.

"How was your night?"

I shrug my shoulders. "As good as I expected it to be."

Levi drives out of the alleyway, turning the corner onto the street. He looks over at me. "You want me to handle it?"

I look over at him, shaking my head as I scoff. "You'd really go and take care of someone just because they don't know how to tip?"

He shrugs as if it's no question what he'd do for me. "If it's something that bothers you, then yes."

My gaze lowers to his lips, lifting again as he shifts his gaze back onto the road ahead. His gaze raises to his rear view mirror for a moment before lowering again.

We ride in silence for a little while until I see him turn down the opposite street, away from my apartment. "Where are you going?"

His eyes glance up at the rearview mirror again. "Don't turn around. We're being followed."

I go to instinctively turn around when Levi braces a hand on my thigh, gripping me gently. I look up at him, leaning back into the seat as I face forward. "For how long?" I ask.

He removes his hand slowly, as if it's the last thing he wants to do. "I noticed him as I pulled up to get you."

I nod my head. "Can you get a glimpse of him?"

He shakes his head vaguely. "No." He turns his blinker on, heading down another street. "But we're about to find out."

I look through my side-view mirror, watching the car follow us down the street as they keep a healthy amount of distance behind us.

Levi turns down a street with a construction lot on the left-hand side. He keeps driving until we're past the property, pulling over to the side of the curb. The person following us pulls over three car lengths behind us, not discrete whatsoever.

Levi puts the car in park. "Stay in the car." He orders, no semblance of fucking around evident in his tone.

He hops out of the car, closing the door before walking to the car behind us. He begins backing up when Levi pulls a gun out of his pocket, pointing it straight at the man's windshield.

I open my window a crack as I listen closely to what they're saying, which isn't too difficult in the dead of night.

The car jerks to a stop as Levi rushes to the driver side door, pulling it open as he yanks the man out of his seat and shoves him to the ground.

"Please—" I hear the man plead as Levi stands over him, the gun pointed straight at his head.

I watch as Levi hesitates, lowering himself to the ground as he puts the gun back in his coat pocket. He grabs the man by his shirt with both hands, yanking him up. "You have five seconds to tell me why you're following me before I scatter your brains onto the concrete." He shoves him back down onto the ground.

The man stutters as he leans onto an elbow, his other arm bending to lift his hand to the back of his head. His arm shakes as he stares up at Levi. "He paid me to follow you. Th—that's it." He stammers.

"Who?" Levi demands.

"I—I don't know his name. I just met him earlier today. He gave me your license plate number and paid me five hundred dollars to follow you." His hand shakes as he lowers it to the outside of his coat pocket. "Please, I can prove it."

I watch Levi stare at him intently before nodding curtly, grabbing for his gun again and aiming it at the man.

He shakily pulls out a prepaid phone, his arm trembling as he hands it to Levi. "Please—take it. I don't want any trouble."

Levi takes the phone, looking at it.

"He told me to text him on that phone and let him know where you took the girl to."

My insides freeze over as I hear him stutter those last words while I watch the rage in Levi simmer around him. Like a palpable entity that I could grab onto.

Levi shoves the phone into his coat pocket, nudging the gun towards the car. "Get in."

The man stands up, tremors racking his entire body as he slides into the driver's seat. He holds his hands up as his face pales to a deathly pale shade. "Please, I did not know—"

My breath hitches as blood splatters against the windshield, the gun suppressor silencing the blow to his head.

He lowers the gun back into his coat pocket as he lowers himself into the car, reaching his gloved hand up to the windshield as he begins drawing something with the man's blood. I squint my eyes as I try to make sense of what he's writing, until he walks away and I see the words displayed perfectly clear.

Game on.

My eyes widen as he takes a handkerchief from his coat pocket, using it to wipe the blood from his gloved fingers. He approaches the car, casually seating himself down and closing the door.

I stare at him, the words unable to reach me for several moments. "Who was that?"

"Doesn't matter anymore." He says as he takes his gloves off, shoving them into his coat pocket. He pulls his phone out, going to his call log and tapping on someone's name.

I hear it ring twice before a man picks up on the other line. "Yeah?"

"Cut the feed from eighth and Hampton."

I look up, peering at the light post at the corner of the street with a surveillance camera angled towards us.

"How long?"

"The past twenty minutes. Inform Carson as well."

"You got it." The man hangs up as Levi puts his phone into the cup holder, putting the car in drive and pulling away.

"Whose Carson? And why did you write on that windshield 'game on'?"

Levi drives down the street, silent as anger brews beneath his too calm exterior.

"Hey, is there something I should know about—"

"You're staying with me tonight."

I jerk my head back as I stare at him. "What?"

"That man was following us tonight because he wanted to know where you lived."

My gaze roams over his face as disbelief overwhelms me. Why would someone want to know where I live so badly—

"It's not safe for you to be at your place alone. Not tonight at least." He turns his blinker on, turning down the street.

"Did you know who that man was? Or why he wants to know where I live? And I'm *not* staying with you. I'm not leaving Rufus." I demand.

"He can come too, of course." His gaze focused on the street ahead.

"Tell me why that man was following us." I seethe.

"I don't know." He says, his hand gripping the steering wheel as he exhales.

I watch him, noticing the tension gathering in his neck and jaw. My gaze narrows at him at his inability to look at me. "You're lying to me."

He finally glances over at me, specks of blood splattered on his face. His gaze roams over my face as I watch his chest rise and fall. "I'm handling it." That's all he says before he turns his gaze back onto the road.

"You're handling it? What the fuck does that even mean? Why won't you tell me—"

"Because I *can't*!" He yells, his gaze hard on mine as we stop at a stoplight.

I watch the anguish, the pain in his eyes and realize that there's something he's not telling me. Something he's keeping from me and it pains him greatly to do so.

But it doesn't dismiss the betrayal I feel suddenly in the pit of my stomach to be out of the loop of whatever the fuck is going on.

"If I tell you, then you and everyone you care about is dead. And it won't be by my hands."

I shake my head slowly, scrunching my brows in disbelief. "And I'm just supposed to believe that this bothers you because you *actually* care—"

"Yes!" He shouts. The magnitude of that single word felt through every inch of my body.

My gaze tracks over his face, over the deep anguish settling there.

"Yes, I fucking care." He grabs my face with his hands, jerking my face towards him as his thumb sweeps over my cheek.

I stare at the seriousness etched in his eyes as they dip to my lips. "Initially, I truly believed blackmailing you to work with me was all I cared about. That having a partner in crime would fill my life with that missing adventure, that missing adrenaline that I've been yearning for but what I needed all along was *you*."

My gaze lifts up to his eyes as they roam wildly over my face.

"Everything I do now is for *you*. And now, that is all I need in this life to feel fulfilled."

He yanks my face to his, crashing his lips into mine as I finally soften into his hold.

My hands come up to his as his tongue pries my lips open, the kiss deepening. I fall into the kiss, his soft lips consuming me wholly as I lower my hands to the center console, leaning my body forward as I begin to crawl into his lap.

A honk from behind us has me wanting to pull away when Levi keeps my face planted right where it is. He continues his exploration as I giggle against his mouth. The person behind us continues honking as we get lost in nothing other than what's going on in this car right here, right now. Until finally, the car steps on the gas and goes around us, yelling something out of his window but I find myself completely uncaring as Levi's soft lips press themselves against mine.

He smiles against my mouth, his hands anchoring themselves to the underside of my jaw and continues to kiss me as if we have all the time in the world.

Chapter 46

We finally make it to my building, electing to park down the block even though we've seen no one else following us since we left.

We walk down the neighborhood, keeping a close eye on our surroundings before we slip into the alleyway. Levi staying close by my side.

We make our way to the side of the building, approaching the exit door as Levi leans up against it. He pulls out a pin and begins picking the lock, only taking him a few seconds to get it to open. He pulls it open, allowing me to slip through before he follows behind me.

We make our way to the elevator, the door opening as I hit the button. We slip inside, the door closing behind us.

"Do you have any food at your place? I'm starving." I slide my key into the lock, turning it as the elevator begins its descent up.

"I have frozen pizza." He says as he leans up against the metal railing across from me.

I cross my arms, tilting my head. "What kind?"

He shrugs. "I think pepperoni?"

A smile curves my lips. "Perfect."

The elevator continues descending to the top floor, silence stretching between us. I glance down at his coat pocket, his hand tucked inside. "Since when do you carry a gun with you?"

His gaze lifts from the floor to my face, his expression unreadable. "I've never been without it."

"But you choose to still kill with a knife?"

A faint smirk curves his lips as his eyes darken. "I've already told you. It keeps things more interesting when I use a knife."

A chuckle gets trapped in my throat as I shake my head. I lower my gaze to my boots, turning my ankle to the side as the silence deafens around us once more. "Are you going to kiss me again?" I lift my gaze back up to his.

His gaze dips to my lips as he steps away from the railing, advancing to the middle of the elevator. His gaze lifts to mine. "Yes. Are you opposed to that?" He takes another step towards me.

A slow exhale leaves me, thinking of some kind of retort to make when all my snarky comebacks suddenly fail me. "Not particularly." I admit.

The elevator halts as the doors open up to my front door. Levi grins as he leans down to grab my dance bag, carrying it as I force my legs to cooperate and walk out of the elevator.

I slide my key into the lock and push my door open. I step to the side so Levi can get through, Rufus scratching at the bottom of his crate when he sees Levi.

"I don't know that he likes me." Levi says as he lifts my dance bag and sets it onto the kitchen counter.

I giggle as I close the door. "Trust me, that's not his 'I dislike this human' look."

Levi stands off to the side as I walk over to Rufus' crate, kneeling down in front of it. Rufus plopping his butt down as he waits for me to unlock his crate.

"No jumping, okay?"

Rufus huffs at me as he waits impatiently, excitement written all over his face. I lift the latch and Rufus pushes the door open with his nose as he trots over to Levi.

He begins sniffing him as his nub of a tail wags rambunctiously, Levi kneeling down as he holds his hand out for him.

"He won't bite. He likes you." I say assuringly as I set my coat down. "If he had a problem with you, he would've bit your hand off the first time he met you."

He nods his head as he goes to pet Rufus on his head before moving to scratch behind his ears. Rufus plops himself down onto his side, rolling over so his belly is exposed. Levi continues petting him as a smile graces his face.

I admire it for a moment, a sight that I don't see very often, before I go to grab my dance bag and head for my bedroom. "I only need a few minutes and I'll be ready to go."

I head to my room, setting my dance bag on the floor near my bed. I go to my walk-in closet and grab a different large bag. I begin shoving some clothes to sleep in, followed by a dark green zip-up sweater, a white long-sleeved T-shirt, a pair of medium-wash flare jeans, a clean thong, socks, a bra, and an extra sweater.

I set the large black bag on my bed while I grab all of my make-up necessities from my vanity, setting it into my bag before I make my way to my bathroom. Grabbing a travel bag from a drawer, I fill all of my hair and face car into it, zipping it shut and setting it into my bag.

I zip my bag almost all the way closed when I look down at my pink fuzzy slippers. I lean down, grabbing them and slipping them into my bag before I zipper it closed completely.

I walk back down to the kitchen when I see Levi taking a damp paper towel to his face, wiping off the specs of blood that splattered onto it. His gaze lowers to my large bag, chuckling. "You need all of that for one night?"

I set it onto the kitchen counter, moving towards the kitchen pantry. "Considering I'm going to need to shower at your place in the morning, yes. I need all of what's in here."

He walks over to the garbage can, pressing his foot down on the pedal as the lid opens up. He sets the paper towel in there, releasing his foot as he faces me. "Who said I was going to be nice enough to let you use my shower?" He smirks.

I roll my eyes as I open the pantry door, grabbing Rufus' storage bin of food. "Don't be a smart ass." I turn around, setting it on the counter as I grab a tupperware bin from a kitchen cabinet. Filling enough for his breakfast tomorrow since he already ate before I left for work tonight.

Levi chuckles. "Whatever you need."

I put his food container away, closing the pantry door as I look down at Rufus whose taken to waiting right next to me. He cocks his head up at me.

"Rufus, go for a ride?"

His ears perk up as he rushes to the front door, nudging his nose against his leash hanging from the coat rack on the wall.

I walk over to Levi, handing him the tupperware of dog food. "If you don't mind." I say as I go to grab Rufus' leash.

"Not at all." He says as he leans to grab my bag, carrying it in his hand.

I hook his leash up to his collar as he stands in place by my side, as he's been trained to do.

"You better not be lying about the pizza." I say as I go to open up my door, Rufus stepping out.

Levi chuckles as he steps out as well, going to the elevator to hit the downward button. "I promise it's there in my freezer."

I smile to myself as my back remains turned to him as I lock my door up. "Good." I turn around, ushering Rufus and I into the elevator as Levi follows behind us.

Once the elevator door closes I hit the button for the main level and we make our way down.

Chapter 47

We pull up to a mid-century modern home, his car driving up the concrete until it reaches the top of the driveway. I look out of my passenger window at the large wooden double-doors atop the stone porch steps, windows on each side of the mahogany wood. A large awning hangs over the porch, supported by two pillars on each end. Step lights illuminating the entrance as well as the planters on each end of the doors.

Levi turns the car off, pulling his key out. "We're here."

I open my door, stepping out onto the concrete driveway. I close it as I go to open the back passenger seat door, Rufus waiting patiently for me.

I open the door and reach for his leash as Levi grabs my bag and Rufus' dog food. Rufus steps out of the car as I close the door, walking up his steps. "Nice place." I say.

Levi shuts the door, following close behind me. "Thank you." He steps up to his front door, sliding his key in the lock and pushing the door open for us.

He steps through first, turning to the wall as Rufus and I step inside. My gaze lowers to the rug beneath our feet before raising to the alarm box, Levi punching in a code.

The light on it turns green as he closes the alarm box before shutting the door.

"Aren't you afraid I'm going to know your secret code and try breaking in?"

He chuckles as he slips off his shoes, followed by his coat as he hangs it on a coat rack. "It wouldn't be the worst thing ever if you broke into my house one night." He smirks at me as his hand gestures for my coat.

I slip it off me, handing it to him. "Thanks."

He nods as he hangs it up while I slip my shoes off. I lower myself down to Rufus, giving him a look. "Be good."

He sighs as he watches me.

I unhook his leash as he tentatively walks towards the living room ahead of us, sniffing our surroundings. I go to follow him as we pass through a short hallway. The walls void of any portraits or hanging decoration.

As I enter his living room I'm met with floor to ceiling windows that overlook a section of trees, a deck with a grill and seating as well. I approach the cream colored couch, large enough to fit about four of me on it. I run my hand along the back of the sofa as soft polyester glides along my fingertips. My gaze lowers to the distressed dark oak coffee table atop an ivory area rug. A TV remote placed at the center next to a rustic gold square dish, a white pillar candle placed at the center on top of a black iron candle plate.

I glance over to my right at the electric fireplace built into the slate stone wall, a large flatscreen TV mounted above it.

"I can turn it on if you'd like."

I look up to see Levi make his way into the adjacent kitchen, setting my bag on a kitchen stool. He approaches a stainless steel fridge, pulling out a frozen pizza and setting it onto his sleek black countertops. My stomach rumbles with hunger at the sight. "Sure."

He moves over to the stove, turning it on before making his way over to the living room. He approaches the slate wall, pressing a tiny switch on the side of the fireplace. The flames immediately begin swaying atop a long row of stones.

"Can I get you something to drink?" He turns to face me, his eyes alight on mine.

I scrunch my lips to the side as I tilt my head. "What do you have?"

He begins walking to the kitchen. "I have some red wine, whiskey, bourbon...water."

I walk over to the pristine kitchen, pulling out a kitchen island stool and taking a seat. "Water is fine."

He nods as he reaches into a cabinet, pulling out an empty glass as he walks over to the sink and fills it. He shuts the water off and hands it to me.

I go to take a sip before I stop myself. I lift my gaze up to his, finding him watching me. "How clean is the water around here?"

He stares at me for a moment, blinking once before he bellows out a laugh. "You're seriously asking me how clean my sink's water is?"

I shrug my shoulders. "And your point?"

He sighs, though the smirk from laughing remains. "I have a built-in water filter." He goes to open the bottom cabinet below the sink, holding his hand out to show a water filter system attached.

"Good to know." I lift the glass to my lips, taking a long sip before setting the glass down onto the counter. I eye that pizza again, nodding towards it. "Are you going to put it in yet?"

"Relax, woman." He grabs a pair of scissors, cutting the plastic off of it. He tosses it in the garbage as he looks up at me. "And I assume you would like ranch with it, too?"

"You'd assume correctly." I say, grinning.

He chuckles as he opens the oven door, sliding the pizza right onto the rack. He closes the door, turning towards me. "Let's go and put your things upstairs."

He leads me up his wooden floating stairs, my bag in my hands as we descend up to the second floor.

He guides me down the hallway to his room, a large king sized bed placed up against the wall.

"You'll sleep here tonight."

I look over at him, blinking. "With you?"

He walks over to his dresser, a glass tray sitting on top of the sable wood. He goes to pick something up out of it before turning back around. "I'll be sleeping downstairs on the couch."

"Oh." I set my bag on top of his dark gray sheets, glancing at the four plush pillows propped up against a black leather headboard. I lower my gaze as I run my hand along his bed.

Damn, this comforter is soft as fuck.

I step away from the bed as I watch him grab a lighter, realizing it's a joint he has in his hand. "So you do smoke."

He turns towards me, nudging his head to the side. "Sometimes." He goes to light it, pressing it up to his lips as he turns away to open up his balcony door, the brisk cool air from outside immediately filtering in. He inhales deeply, holding it before blowing the smoke out.

I walk towards him. "Are you going to be a gentleman and ask if I'd like a hit?"

He turns towards me, taking another hit as his brows raise. "You smoke?" He blows the smoke out as he hands me the joint.

I take it as I shrug my shoulders. "Sometimes." A smirk plays on my face as I take a hit, blowing the smoke out.

He chuckles as he leans up against the dresser, watching me intently. His gaze roaming from my eyes then to my lips as I take another hit, holding his gaze there until after I've blown the smoke out. "Interesting."

The taste of marijuana lingers in my mouth as I hand the joint back to him. "There's much you don't know about me, *partner*." I walk over to the bed, opening up my bag as I pull my sleep clothes out.

"Tell me something I don't know then."

I set the clothes on the bed, turning towards him. "Not until I have some of that pizza. For now," I raise my hands to my shirt, beginning to lift it off. "I'd like to get into some more comfy clothing."

I lift my shirt off over my head as Levi stands there, his feet cemented into the bedroom carpet as he stares at me. The joint nearly dangling out of his fingers as he gazes down at my exposed breasts.

I tilt my head as I lower my hands to my leggings, slipping my thumbs beneath the waistband. "Staying for the show, Levi?"

His gaze lowers to my hands, staying there for a long moment before forcing his attention back up to my eyes. "I might." His voice rich and full of dark promises.

I stand there, my hands unmoving as I smirk at him. "I'll meet you downstairs, Levi."

His gaze bores into mine for a moment before he finally nods, forcing himself to move from where he's been standing. "Take your time." He makes his exit from his bedroom, pulling the door closed.

As I finish changing out of my clothes, I look through my bag until I find my black silk pajama set. I smooth out the satiny material as I make my way back downstairs. Wondering what's in store for our night ahead.

Chapter 48

Levi

I pull the pizza out of the oven, setting it onto a pizza rack as I hear Amelia making her way back into the kitchen.

I look up and nearly drop the pizza cutting knife on my foot.

She has on this cute little black silk pajama set on with her hair pulled up into a messy bun. The first time I've ever seen her hair up before. And her face—

She must've washed her face while she was getting changed because the red lips, the dark eye make-up, all of it is gone. And in its place is this wholly perfect, porcelain face that glistens from whatever serums and creams she uses with her nightly skincare routine.

Not that she's not perfect with make-up on—

"What?" She asks, reminding me that I'm just staring at her.

My gaze roams over her clear skin, so soft and dewy I just want to press kisses all over it. "Nothing." I force out, clearing my throat as I finally go to cut the pizza. "I'm just a little stoned is all." A total fucking lie.

She giggles as she moves to stand next to me, some warm vanilla scent wafting towards me.

Did she put lotion on, too? Goddamn it smells so delicious I just want to shove my whole face into it and completely drown in it.

I've always told myself that drowning sounds like the worst possible way to die. But standing next to her while she smells like that, I couldn't think of a better way to go out in this lifetime.

That, or drowning in her sweet pussy—

"Are you gonna cut that or just keep standing there?" She asks, pulling me back once again from my thoughts.

"Right, sorry." I quickly cut the pizza up, setting it down as I let her grab as much as she wants first. Once she's filled her plate, I put a few slices onto mine as I take a seat on the couch beside her.

We both shove our faces with pizza in silence until we're both going back for seconds.

After we both finish, I take our plates and set them into the sink. I look over to see Rufus curling himself up on the floor next to the couch. His eyes alight on Amelia.

"How long have you had him for?"

"Since he was a puppy." She says, looking down at him and smiling.

"And Hellhounds, they're immortal?"

She nods her head. "So he's stuck with me for life."

I seat myself back on the couch, lifting my ankle and hooking it over my knee. "So, how old are you exactly?"

She laughs, curling her legs up as she faces me. Her head leaning against her fist as she props her elbow on the back of the couch. "Technically, I'm two hundred and eighty-six years old. But to everyone else, I'm twenty-eight."

"That makes you the oldest woman I've ever been attracted to then."

Her laugh graces my ears again as amusement glistens in her eyes. I find myself hypnotized by both.

"And what of family?"

The spark in her eyes dull as her smile slowly falters. She lowers her gaze to the couch, pain evident in her amber eyes. She raises her gaze up to me, her chest sinking slightly. "My mother and father are dead. They've been dead for over a hundred years now. I—" She works on a swallow before she continues. "I have no family outside of that."

I notice the way her frown quickly turns into a steady gaze, willing her face to regain neutrality as if to signal her disinterest in talking further about it. Instead of prying further, I narrow my gaze as I respect her boundary. "I'm terribly sorry, Amelia."

She flattens her lips as she forces a grin, nodding. "What about you?"

"My mother was a pure saint, a real woman of class and strength." I pause as memories surface in my mind. "She and my father had a...rough relationship. We lived very poor growing up, and at that time it was very unheard of for women to file for divorce. So she stayed with my dad not out of love, but obligation."

I look over at the window, the outlines of the trees staring back at me, camouflaged by the night sky. "One night my father beat her so badly that I had no choice but to take her to the hospital." I refrain from clenching my fists, remembering that it's all a thing of the past now. "She was so scared to press charges against him, so scared of what he might do next time so she lied to the doctors. Said she fell down a flight of stairs."

I look over at Amelia, her gaze wholly on me as she watches me. Sadness and something gentler swimming in her eyes as I unravel a darkness that only Dex and Sawyer know.

"Four years later he had been drinking too much and fell asleep at the wheel, causing himself to drive off a bridge and drown."

I watched her gaze lower to my hands as if she was going to reach out for them but stopped herself.

"That was the day I finally saw relief in my mother's eyes. And it was also the day I knew I'd become who I am today."

Amelia nods her head slowly. "There's a reason why I haven't seen you take jobs that involve women or children."

My gaze lowers briefly to her soft hands laid gently in her lap now.

"You don't kill just because you're good at it. You became a hitman because you hate seeing women being oppressed and taken advantage of. Because you watched your mother go through it. That's why you only take jobs that target men."

I sigh, staring ahead at the trees through the windows. "There's been many times where I've taken jobs that didn't involve the mistreatment of women. Moreover, it was just to get someone off my bosses back. But the jobs where the mistreatment of a woman is involved," I look over at Amelia. "Those I take great delight in."

Amelia reaches down for her glass of water, bringing it to her lips. She takes a steady sip before setting the glass down, turning her gaze back to me. "And what about girlfriends? Or boyfriends if you swing that way." She grins.

I chuckle as I cross my arms, leaning my head back on the couch. "It's pretty difficult to have a girlfriend when you do the line of work I do."

She nods her head. "I can understand that one."

I watch as a yawn escapes her, her fist covering her mouth before lowering her hand again.

"The majority of men look at women like me and automatically think there's something that needs to be fixed. That there has to be something mentally wrong with me just because I do the line of work that I do. That a sane person couldn't possibly be interested in sex work."

I sit there, gazing at her and remaining silent as she speaks.

She sighs. "When you're in the industry you either learn to build a thick skin, you already have one, or you fall under the opinions of others and let it eat you alive." She pauses for a moment as I watch years and years of oppression float across her gaze. The awful reminder of how at a disadvantage women are in a world that demands you to live a certain way, and shames you if you break that conformity. "Because if there's one thing people have an opinion on it's how a woman expresses her sexuality." She lowers her hand to grab her glass again, raising it to no one in particular. "And it's always the people that struggle the deepest with their own that have the most to say about it."

I watch her take a sip before setting the glass down again. "It's unfortunate we live in a world where women making a living through sex work is considered revolting and dishonorable, but the men paying for their services never receive the same reaction." I shake my head, disgusted by the complete double-standard.

She huffs out a soft noise, similar to a broken laugh that never reached past her lips. "Because 'men will be men'. Like how when a woman has sex with a man, she suddenly loses her worth and value. Looked at as *less* than. Yet when a man has sex with a woman, he's seen as more likeable, given respect for being able to *hit that*." She rolls her eyes after those last two words, forcing out a rough exhale.

I stare at her as the unfairness of how women are treated weighs heavily upon me. The unfairness I witnessed from a young age with a mother who did absolutely nothing to deserve the mistreatment she was dealt with, but endured it nonetheless because she had no other choice. Wasn't given the resources to have another option.

I gaze at Amelia and suddenly wish my mother were alive still to meet her. Knowing she would have loved to see that the times are finally beginning to change. That more and more women are reclaiming that power that rightfully belongs to them, as it never was meant to be forged into the hands of men who wanted nothing but to tame it. "It's like that's more of an insult to men than it is to women."

She whips her gaze up at me, her mouth opening before I cut her off to better explain.

"If women supposedly lose so much value by being with a man, but men gain value by being with a woman, then that just further proves that men are the ones who gain anything by being with a woman. While women gain nothing by being with a man. That the real prize is, and always will be, a woman. Which is why women can spend the rest of their lives alone and never feel like they're missing out, while men physically cannot handle being alone for any length of time."

She raises her gaze to me, leaning back up against the couch as a hint of surprise dances across her vision. After a long moment, a slow grin creeps up her face, warming her previous expression. "You have a very valid point."

I grin at her as we spend another long moment staring at one another, a sort of softness splitting open between us.

She quickly averts her gaze over to the window overlooking the trees, clearing her throat as the grin fades. "Even though The Pleasure District is better in their ways than other parts of Lilitu, it's still a man's world. And as long as the patriarchy is standing strong, women will always be seen as pawns to carry out the only thing men think they're good for: procreation. Property to be handled and controlled, and never as real individuals with rights of their own."

My heart swells in my chest, a heaviness ensuing at her words and the unfortunate truth in them. Society would be so much better if men got off their fucking high horses and started allying with and respecting women rather than fearing the limitless power they hold. The kind of power fueled by the innate strength only a woman could possess. A kind of power men fear because they know if given the chance, it could make any structure crumble to the damn ground. "Fuck the patriarchy."

She snorts as a giggle escapes from her lips, a warmth blossoming in my chest to see another grin make an appearance on her face. I watch as her eyes become glossy with tiredness. "That's what I should've written on the wall."

The memory of her slicing Jake's head off his body resurfacing, her fingers dipping into his blood as she used it to write on the alley wall above his beheaded body. I chuckle. "Maybe. Though I think what you wrote the first time was the best one."

She huffs, a smirk crawling up her lips. "I can't believe you were following me that night." She reaches her hand out, shoving my shoulder. "And I can't believe you really tried blackmailing me into working with you."

"I was technically following him." I waggle my eyebrows at her, smirking.

She lazily rolls her eyes, yawning again. "Well you're welcome for making your life easier with that one."

I chuckle as I notice her eyes getting heavy. "If you'd like to retire for the night, I won't be offended."

"No, I'm fine." She nods over to the TV. "Do you have cable?"

I chuckle, reaching for the remote on the coffee table. "Of course I do." I turn the TV on and begin shuffling through the channels, lifting my feet up and propping them up onto the coffee table. Crossing them at the ankles.

I flip through the channels until a familiar show name comes on. I peer my gaze at her as she's taken to laying down on the couch now, her body laid down the length of the couch as her head faces the TV. "If you truly care about me you'll put on my favorite show." She grabs the forest green throw blanket hanging over the top of the couch, wrapping herself into it.

I smile down at her, lifting my gaze back up to the TV as I put on Real Dance Wives.

I set the remote on the coffee table again, leaning back into the couch as a soft exhale leaves me. I still momentarily as Amelia scoots herself up the couch closer to me until she lifts her head up and rests it on my thigh. Curling into herself as she brings the blanket up to her neck, loosening a relaxed breath as she faces TV.

I fight the grin that threatens to curve my lips but lose, a giddy feeling springing to life inside my chest. I lower my hand down, gently moving her hair away from her cheek as I tuck the crimson strands behind her ear. She doesn't swat my hand away, or retort with some snarky remark at my touch.

Instead, I feel her loosening a soft breath once more as she nuzzles herself against me.

I lay my arm over the back of the couch, forcing my gaze back up to the TV as I watch two women talk to one another.

"I just don't know how I'm going to tell him. He's my husband, and he's done so much for our family. But it's just..."

"Not enough." The other woman with rich brown hair says, sipping from her glass of champagne.

The blonde woman—Helene, tears up, wiping beneath her eyes with a white handkerchief. Her mascara still intact. "We've been together since high school. Who I was back then, what I wanted, it's all changed now. We just...are two different people."

The brunette lowers a hand to the blonde woman's lap, a frown pulling at her lips.

Helene begins to shed tears, anguish painted on her face. "How did you know? That Albert was the one?"

The brunette sighs, tilting her head. "I knew because I never had to ask myself whether I knew or not. I just feel so natural, so comfortable and so myself around him. He came into my life when I wasn't even searching."

I look down at Amelia's head, my eyes roaming over her long red hair as it trails down her back and over her shoulder. Something stirring within me at the brunette's words.

I raise my gaze back up to the TV, huffing softly. "I guess you were right. She really is going to leave her husband."

At her silence I look down. I peer over her face to see her eyes shut and her mouth slightly open, Amelia fast asleep. Her chest rises and falls steadily as her porcelain face looks so peaceful.

I slowly lower my hand again to her face, gently running the backs of my knuckles along her cheek. Her soft skin brushes against my calloused skin as I do, a shy smile curving my lips as I stare down at her a moment longer.

I cradle her head into my hand, slowly lifting it as I scoot to the side, setting her head down onto the couch. I stand up, bending down as I gently scoop her up into my arms, careful not to wake her.

The blanket remains curled around her as I step away from the couch and walk to the staircase.

Her head leans into my chest as a soft exhale escapes from her lips. As I get to the bottom step I feel her hand press against my chest, her nails burrowing into my shirt as she curls her hand inward. As if she's a cat kneading on me—

Fuck, that's the cutest thing ever.

I make it to the top of the stairs, walking into my bedroom as I approach the bed. I lower myself down slightly, pulling the covers back as I slowly lower her to my bed. Her hand stays gripping on my shirt for a moment until she finally lets go, snuggling into my bed as I pull the covers over her.

I tuck her in before my hand caresses her cheek, brushing back those wine red strands as they cascade around my grey sheets. I smile at her before I head over to my dresser, quietly pulling it open as I pull out a pair of grey sweatpants. I strip off my clothes from the day, pulling the sweats on before I approach the doorway.

I look back at her, smiling faintly as I whisper. "Goodnight, Amelia." I turn around and head back downstairs.

I grab another throw blanket and plop onto the couch with it, laying it on top of me. I lay my head against the couch pillow, turning the volume on the TV down a few notches so I don't wake her up.

As I find myself watching Amelia's favorite show before I fall fast asleep as well.

Chapter 49

Amelia

I woke up sprawled beneath charcoal grey covers, Levi putting my show on being the last thing I remember before everything went dark.

He must've carried me up here last night after I fell asleep.

I tiredly glance around the room, the light from outside filtering in through his windows. I stretch my legs then my arms, his soft comforter swallowing me whole in this giant bed.

Damn is it comfy.

I rub my eyes as I sit up, the covers falling to my waist. I slip my feet over the side of the bed, stepping down onto the carpet as I make my way over to his adjoined bathroom. After I use the bathroom and wash my hands, I walk through his bedroom and make my way downstairs.

I quietly walk down the steps, assuming he's not awake yet by how quiet it is.

I approach the living room, creeping up to the couch when I see Levi laying with an arm behind his head. A blanket laying across his waist as his chest lays exposed.

Damnit, he has a nice body. My gaze lingers for a moment when I lower it to the floor where Rufus lays right up against the couch below him.

Rufus raises his head, looking at me as I give him a look. "Traitor." I whisper jokingly, though I find myself particularly intrigued by Rufus' sudden liking of another person that isn't myself.

He stretches himself up onto all fours, a yawn following as he walks over to me.

I lower down, scratching behind his ear when he steps out of my reach and walks over to the glass porch door. He turns around to face me before plopping his butt down.

Right, of course.

I walk over to the kitchen counter where Rufus' food still is along with some poop bags I brought with me. I grab one, turning around to grab his leash from where it hangs near the front door when I stop myself.

I turn around, tilting my head as I narrow my gaze down to Rufus. I raise a brow, giving him a look as if to say *if you're a good boy and stay in the yard without your leash on, I'll give you extra kibble for breakfast.*

He softly huffs at me as if to say *come on woman, I have to go.*

I chuckle quietly as I go to slip my boots on by the front door, coming back to the porch door and opening it slowly. Rufus trots out as he goes sniffing around on Levi's lawn. I close the door quietly as I stand there, hoping he does his business quickly as the brisk cold wind begins nipping at my arms and legs.

As soon as Rufus does his business I get it into the bag. I open the porch door as Rufus walks back, his paws trailing water and bits of slush from the trace amount of snow out there.

"Damnit." I mouth quietly to myself, looking at Rufus. "Stay here." I say near silently.

He looks at me, staying in place as I walk over to the kitchen garbage and toss the bag in. I go over to the sink, turning it on as I wash my hands. I dry them off on some paper towels before I grab some extra to wipe Rufus' paws onto.

As I wipe his paws and the bit of water he trekked in, I hear Levi stir awake on the couch. I look over to see him stretch his arms up, a long soft moan getting trapped in his throat as his tired eyes peel open.

He looks over at me as I wipe Rufus' paws. "Morning."

I give him a shy smile. "Goodmorning." I say, walking over to the garbage and tossing the used paper towel into there. I walk over to the tupperware of Rufus' food, grabbing it as I begin looking through his cupboards.

"Second one from the fridge." He says, his voice thick and gruff with sleep.

I open up the cupboard, finding an array of bowls in there. "Thanks." I say as I pull out a metal one, pouring his kibble into it before I set it down onto the hardwood floor for him.

Rufus begins eating right away while I set the tupperware off to the side on the counter.

I look over at Levi as he stands up from the couch, stretching once more as his muscles expand and tighten in all the right places. He walks towards me, his hair disheveled and messy. "Coffee?"

I nod. "That'd be great."

He approaches a coffee machine, taking the coffee pot out as he walks over to the sink. "How'd you sleep?" He turns the water on, filling it before shutting it off again.

"I slept well. Your bed is quite comfy."

He chuckles, the sound gliding over my skin like a sultry chill. He pours the water in, setting the pot onto the burner as he reaches into the cupboard above him. "I'm glad you found it comfortable."

My gaze narrows to his waist as he reaches his hand up, grabbing a coffee grinder. I notice the way his sweats hang low on his hips, his muscles curving and dipping downward—

My thoughts scatter as he pours coffee beans into the tiny machine, bringing myself back to reality. "Sorry for falling asleep. I was more tired than I thought."

"It's no problem." He says, looking up at me before he presses down on the button, grinding the beans into tiny bits. He pours the freshly ground coffee into the filter, closing the top and pressing the start button.

I pull a bar stool out, seating myself. "Do you think I'll have any more people following me? Or us?"

He lowers himself down to a bottom cabinet, pulling out a pan and setting in on the stove. "I'm not sure." He admits as he goes to the fridge and pulls out a carton of eggs, butter, shredded cheese, and sausage links. He sets them on the counter before he turns towards me. "I'll keep a close eye on things and will let you know if anything is suspicious."

I nod as I hear my phone buzzing down the counter, forgetting all about it until now. I lower my arm down the counter, grabbing it. I look down as the time reads eleven in the corner, a text from Sapphire popping up from an hour ago.

What time are we meeting today?

Another text sent just now.

Helllooooooooo?

I chuckle to myself as I respond.

Sorry girl, just woke up. Two-thirty okay? Xoxo

I set my phone down as I watched Levi turn the stove top on, warming the pan. "Awe you're cooking me breakfast too? What a gentleman."

He chuckles. "It's the very least I can do."

My phone buzzes as a text from Sapphire comes through.

Yesss, sounds good. Let's meet at Jamelia's. Xoxo

I hold my finger on her text, sending her a heart reaction before lowering my phone. "Well, thank you."

"Of course." He grabs a white ceramic mug, pouring coffee into it before walking it over to me. "Just let me know what time you'd like me to take you home today. Or unless you planned on staying, in which I'd have no problem with." He hands the mug to me.

I take it, setting it down. "Actually, can you drop me off at Jamelia's? I'm supposed to meet with one of the girls to go costume shopping."

He goes to his fridge, grabbing a container of creamer and hands it to me. "Sure. What time?"

I pour some into my coffee, handing it back to him. "I'm meeting her at two-thirty."

He nods as he goes to turn the sausages over in the pan. "I can do that. Is this for the costume party at your work?"

I take a sip of the coffee, sighing at both the warmth and the nutty taste. I lift my gaze to him. "Yes."

He nods slowly. "The one you're going to with Adrian?" He asks calmly.

I nod. "Yes."

He steps away from the stove, taking a sip of his coffee as he watches me. "What are you both going as?"

I watch as his eyes pierce into mine, a possessiveness lurking beneath them as he stares into my soul. I shrug my shoulders, trying to shrug off the tension simmering beneath. "He said it was up to me, but I have no idea. I was going to figure that out today."

He turns to a cupboard, grabbing a bowl from inside. He sets it down as he grabs an egg from the carton, tapping it generously on the side until it cracks. "Well I'm sure you'll find something." He dumps the egg into the bowl, adding three more until he begins whisking them.

I lower my gaze to my coffee, raising the mug to my lips as I take a long sip. My index finger taps against the ceramic as I lower the mug back to the counter."Will you be there?"

He grabs another pan from below, setting it on a burner as he turns the heat on. He turns the sausages over in the other, the smell traveling towards my nose. "I might make an appearance."

His back faces me as he uses a butter knife to scrape out some butter from the carton, plopping it into the pan.

I bite my lower lip, stifling my sudden nervousness. "Well, you should."

"And why is that?" He turns the heat off as he grabs the pan of sausage, dividing them up equally between two white plates. He sets the pan onto a cool burner as he takes the bowl with the scrambled eggs, dumping it into the other pan.

"Because they're a lot of fun." I lied.

He sets the bowl down, finally turning around to face me. He tilts his head slightly as he leans up against the sleek black counter, his hands braced on the edge of it. "That's not the real reason."

I suddenly find myself lowering my gaze back to my mug, taking another sip.

What is wrong with me? I've never, ever acted like some nervous, shy girl in front of a man before. But with him, he makes me feel so incredibly naked when he looks at me, even when I'm fully clothed. Like his gaze bears a key to my soul that could strip me entirely of every lie, every attempt at concealing how badly I want to sink my tongue into his mouth.

I force a shrug, meeting his gaze again. "That is the only reason."

He nods slowly, turning around to finish cooking the eggs. Once they're finished, he divides them onto our plates along with two pieces of toast.

He carries both plates as he approaches the seat next to me, standing behind me as his arm lowers my plate down in front of me. "Thank you." I say.

His hand raises as he releases the plate, his fingers lightly brushing my hair back behind my ear. The tips of his fingers glide lightly across my skin as he lowers his hand down to my neck, nearly leaning into his touch as he follows the trail of my hair. Tiny bumps raise along my arms as the sound of him chuckling sends heat right to my bones.

"You're welcome." He purrs as he seats himself next to me.

He looks down at the small space between us as I begin forking into my scrambled eggs. As I take a bite I feel him pull my chair closer to him until my thigh is brushing up against his, the hair on his arms tickling my pajama silk shirt.

I look up at him. "Is this really necessary?"

"Yes." He says calmly before digging in.

As we sit there in silence and eat, I constantly feel the ripples of his muscles against my arm. I force myself to think of absolutely anything else, to keep my eyes from sneaking a glance at the muscles on his abdomen on full display right now. But every time he lifts his fork his skin brushes up against mine. The silk acting as a pathetic excuse of a barrier from feeling the warmth radiating off of him.

I drink the last of my coffee as I scoot my chair out, taking my dishes to the sink to wash them off.

"So how long is this little thing with Adrian going to last?"

I continue rinsing off my plate, setting it aside in the neighboring basin. "As long as I want."

"But you don't even like him." Levi says as he stands up from his seat, walking his dishes over to the sink. He nods for me to step aside as he rinses it off.

"Yes I do. He's a nice man." I say, squaring my shoulders as I try to prove to him—or moreover myself, of the lies that slip from my lips.

He chuckles as he sets his rinsed dishes in the sink. "Just nice?"

I roll my eyes as I go to walk away from him when his hand wraps around my arm.

I whip my gaze to his when he lowers his face to mine, stealing the breath from my lungs momentarily. His gaze locks onto mine before dipping to my lips.

"When you're ready to stop playing pretend with him," His gaze lifts to my eyes again. "All you need to do is just say the word."

He lowers his lips to my ear, his breath warm against my skin as his hand lowers to my waist. My heart feels like it's jumping out of my chest as I take a ragged inhale in.

"I'll be *waiting* to give you everything you tell yourself you don't want."

He steps back from me as his eyes roam over my face, a smirk curving his lips.

"Help yourself to the shower upstairs. I'll stay down here and wait to take one until you're finished. Unless you want me to join you." His smirk deepens.

I tilt my head, playing along with this taunting game of his. "You'd like that, wouldn't you?" A sultry tone as I gaze at him. I step towards him as I lay my hand on his chest, peering up at him.

His gaze pierces into mine as I feel his chest tighten.

I gaze into his eyes as I let my power rise to the surface, his chest rising sharply before his gaze softens. I watch his jaw clench as he tries to resist my power enveloping him.

Until his hand braces itself on top of mine, my eyes widening slightly.

"You think I can't handle this?" He says as his hand squeezes over mine. "I know good and well what that power is capable of and you won't find me running away from it, little red."

He lowers his lips to my neck, his smirk curving against my ear as he presses my back into the counter. Drilling himself against me as his cock presses against my pussy. "So don't hold back. Because when I get you to myself, I won't show you any mercy."

He slowly steps away from me, making his way to the couch as I force myself to leave the kitchen. Electing not to say another word as I head up the stairs to shower.

Chapter 50

I step out of the shower, reaching for the white towel hanging on the rack beside me. I dab it all over my body as I dry myself off, setting it on the bathroom counter before I wrap my hair in my pink microfiber hair towel.

I grab my bottle of body oil, pumping some into my hands and rubbing it down my legs. I continue this on the rest of my body until I go to put on a clean thong. I pause, a smirk curving my lips as I ditch the thong for now and wrap the towel around my body. I look in the mirror as I turn around, my smirk deepening as I realize the towel barely goes to my mid thigh.

Perfect.

I pull the bathroom door open and walk through Levi's bedroom, the sound of the TV becoming clearer the further I get down the stairs. I turn the corner as I see just the top of his head peeking over the couch, his gaze fixated on the TV. I turn my gaze, paying no attention to Levi as I head straight for the kitchen..

"That was quicker than I—"

Levi's words cut off, a smirk pulling at my lips as I open the fridge door. Pretending to be looking in his fridge while his gaze brands itself into my back.

I lean onto my hip as I make a humming noise. "Hey, do you have anything other than just water to drink? And don't say liquor. I'd rather not go costume shopping tipsy."

Levi's silence causes my grin to deepen as I continue searching, taking my ever loving time.

"There might be some orange juice." He finally says curtly.

"Hmm," I say as I bend at the waist, looking down at the lowest shelf in his fridge. "Yeah I don't see it." Feeling the edge of the towel rise up before it stops just below my ass. A gentle breeze rushing beneath as I stifle the laughter that creeps up my throat.

"Then I don't have any jizz—*juice*. I don't have any juice." He stammers.

After a few long moments, I finally stand up straight again, closing the fridge as I step to a cupboard. I pull it open as I grab a clean glass, turning to glance at him. "Water is fine then."

My own tease suddenly backfires on me as I see the hungry look in his eyes, his gaze roaming over my body. I quickly reel it in, turning to face the sink as I fill my glass with water.

I turn on my heels, walking back up the stairs as I feel his gaze on me the entire way up.

I head back into the bathroom and close the door, setting the glass on the counter as I take the towel off. I begin doing my skincare when I hear a knock at the door.

"Do you need any help in there?" Levi's words travel through the door.

I chuckle softly to myself as I apply a serum to my face. "Not at this time." I say as I rub it in.

"You sure? I can help with your hair. I might not know much but I'm a quick learner." His words end on a purr as my stomach flips inside of itself.

A smirk curves my lips as I apply my moisturizer. "I think I'll manage."

"I couldn't help but notice you missed a few spots while applying that body oil of yours. I'd be happy to get the areas you missed."

I look down at myself, snorting. "I think someone is just looking for an excuse to touch me."

"No." He's silent for a few seconds before he adds, "Okay, maybe." I hear him lean up against the door. "I promise I'll be a good boy if you let me just massage a leg."

My smirk deepens as I take my hair out of my microfiber towel. Gently tussling it as I look over at the door. "I'll keep that in mind." I purr.

Silence follows from the other side of the door. After a few moments I hear Levi step away from the door as I continue getting ready.

After thirty minutes of blowing drying my hair out and getting it to the desired wavy look, I pull on my clean clothes before opening the bathroom door.

I look up to see Levi sitting on the bed. "Did you wait this entire time for me?" I walk over to my bag, setting my pajama set in there along with my hair and skincare.

Levi hesitates, an innocent look on his face as he turns to face me. "Maybe."

A laugh escapes me as I pull out my make-up bag, setting it on his dresser. I go into the bathroom, grabbing his metal framed mirror and walk back out to the bedroom, setting it on the dresser.

"There's a bigger mirror in the bathroom. Why don't you use that one?" He asks.

"Because I need natural light, and your bedroom has lots of it." I open my bag up, digging around until I find my eyeliner. I shake the tube in my hand for a few seconds before I twist the top off, applying a thin line to my eyelid.

"I'll keep that in mind." He says, his voice quiet.

I look at him through the mirror, seeing him watching me. I snort as I create a sharp wing at the corner. "Are you watching me?"

"Maybe." A shy grin appears on his lips.

I fill the line in a little before I start on my other eyelid. A grin curves my lips as I can't think of a snarky response to give him. So instead, I just settle on one word. "Okay."

I continue doing my make-up, applying my mascara, my concealer, my contour stick, all in that order until all I have left are my lips. I line my lips with a dark nude lip liner, followed by my favorite dark berry colored lip gloss. I press my lips, rubbing them gently together as the colors blend. I set everything back into my bag as I look through the mirror again.

Unable to fight my grin as I find Levi still watching me.

I close my bag up, walking to the bed. "I'm all finished in case you wanted to get in that shower now." I say as I set my make-up bag on top of my clothes, zipping my large bag up.

He shyly lowers his gaze, forcing himself to get up from the bed. "Right." He says as he walks over to his walk-in closet.

"I'll meet you downstairs." I say as I grab my bag, hooking it over my shoulder.

Levi turns towards me, smiling. "See you in a bit."

I catch myself stealing a glance towards him, watching him step into the bathroom before I leave the bedroom entirely.

Chapter 51

I look down at my phone screen as my other hand glides along the back of Rufus' fur. The time in the corner reading one-thirty.

I set my phone back down on the counter, grabbing a slice of pizza. As I take a bite I hear Levi coming down the steps.

He approaches the kitchen as the smell of him wafts towards me. Notes of spearmint and eucalyptus evident as he closes the distance between us.

"Hope you weren't planning on eating this." I say through a mouthful of pizza.

He chuckles as he opens a cupboard, grabbing a glass. "She's all yours." He closes it as he goes to the sink, filling it halfway before taking a long sip.

"Is that all you drink is water?" I ask, finishing off the last of my slice. Wiping my hands on a piece of paper towel.

"For the most part, yeah." He takes another long sip, draining the glass empty before setting it in the sink.

Well that explains why his cum *actually* tastes good. Unlike most men who taste like rancid battery acid.

I watch him go to the fridge, opening it up as he pulls out a glass tupperware. He sets it on the counter next to me, opening it as my gaze lowers down to the freshly cut pieces of pineapple inside.

Yup, that'll do it.

He plops a piece into his mouth, picking up another piece as I turn my gaze to my phone buzzing on the counter. I pick it up, a text from Adrian popping up.

Are you free tonight? I'd like to show you something.

"I figured we'll stop at your place first to drop your bag and Rufus off before I take you where you need to go." Levi says beside me.

"That's fine." I say as I begin typing back to Adrian, my fingers stalling over the letters as I hesitate for a moment.

I'm off work tonight, and though I don't have any plans, I can't help but suddenly feel guilty for spending time with Adrian when in reality there's only one man I suddenly care to spend time with.

I finish typing before hitting send, setting my phone back down.

Sure, where am I meeting you? Xoxo

Adrian sends his reply right away, glancing at the screen.

I'll Venmo you money for an Uber. Meet me at The Gallery at seven-thirty.

A moment later a notification pops up from Venmo on my phone, with an amount of eighty dollars being sent from Adrian.

"Is that Adrian?"

I hesitate for a moment. "Yes." I look up at Levi.

He nods slowly as he closes the tupperware of pineapple, moving to the fridge as he sets it back on the shelf. He closes it as he casually walks out of the kitchen. "We're leaving in fifteen so make sure you have everything together."

As we pull up outside the store, after having dropped Rufus and my stuff off at home, I pull out my phone and send Sapphire a text.

I'm here. Xoxo

I shove my phone back into my coat pocket as I try to find the right words, an issue I've never struggled with before.

A Succubus suddenly getting choked up over her own words over a mortal man? I just know if I told Anastasia about this she'd die laughing and probably tell me that's why she doesn't get involved with mortal men at all. Her words of why she'll never allow another demon, nor mortal to tie her down floating through my mind.

There are only two things I want from a man: To get laid with no strings attached, and for him to shut the fuck up.

I giggle internally to myself at her words the last time I saw her six months ago. Having told me she was bored with being in The Pleasure District and planned to venture back to Hell. Not sure if she actually went back or not.

Anastasia tends to hang around The Pleasure District for a little while then venture back when she's bored—which is often. Never having much interest in working at the club, but instead finding willing men to have sex with in one of the playrooms just to sate her needs.

The demon males in Hell are territorial bastards on steroids. Once they find another demon they are immensely drawn to, there's nearly nothing you can do or say that would keep him away from you.

And Anastasia—gods, good luck to any that try to tame her.

The sound of Levi putting the car in park jogs me from my thoughts. The majority of the drive we've both remained silent. No playful bickering, no teasing, nothing. A few words were exchanged, but nothing more.

I look over at him, trying to find some semblance of hurt in his features. Instead, I find a face void of emotion. "Thanks for the ride. For everything."

He gazes at me, nodding. "Let me know if you need a ride to and from work at all this week."

I nod my head, lowering my gaze to his hand on the steering wheel. "Let me know if anything else develops from last night."

He glances over, nodding again as he forces a grin. "I will."

I open the car door, stepping out onto the concrete as I turn around. I close the door, giving a quick wave goodbye before Levi pulls away from the curb. I sigh as I turn to face the entrance to Jamelia's.

A sudden heaviness pulling me down, but forcing myself to shake it off anyhow.

I grab the gold handle, the metal bar ice cold against my hand as I pull the door open. As soon as I step inside of the boutique, a familiar head of blue hair rushes towards me.

She pulls me in for a hug immediately, squeezing me before she steps away. "Yay, you're here." Sapphire says through a cheerful gaze. Her light blue eyes appearing even brighter against the black eyeliner smudge lightly on her lower lid.

"I'm here." I say, smiling wide as we start walking deeper into the boutique shop.

Gold mounted clothing racks stretch down the entirety of the dusted pink walls, hanging from black velvet hangers are lingerie alternating from silk to lace. Color coded sections that begin with hot pink and end with black at the entrance of the fitting rooms. Half mannequins placed every few feet on black shelves above the clothing racks, showcasing an article of lingerie from the section below.

"I got here just a few minutes before you, but I've already started to scope out what they have." She turns around, a smirk on her face as her long lashes fan up against her bangs. "So by the way, who dropped you off?"

I chuckle as I begin taking off my coat, an employee in a black dress coming by to collect it from me. "He's...a friend."

"A friend? Hmm." We make our way to the back of the store dedicated to showcasing sexy costumes. Most of them *very* revealing and meant for exotic dancers, but some of which are a little less provocative.

I approach the first rack, slowly moving costumes aside as I look through it. Sapphire steps to my right, doing the same.

"Is he hot?" She asks.

I come across a naughty nun costume, admiring the latex grommet bodysuit. Definitely a style that I would find myself wearing, but deciding against it as I swipe it over on the rack. "He's definitely good looking." I smirk.

She scoots a few hangers over before she looks up at me. "Does he have any friends?"

I chuckle. "Actually, you'd know one of them."

She turns towards me, tilting her head. "Who?" She asks.

I peer at her, smirking. "His partner just so happens to be the man who watches you dance every week."

She gasps, a mischievous grin on her face. "Partners?" She purrs. "What kind of work do they do?"

I glance over to the two women behind us, looking through costumes as well. I step into Sapphire, lowering my voice. "The kind of work that can't be discussed in public."

Excitement lights her eyes, that Succubus energy that she shares flaring to the surface for a moment before diminishing again. The two women behind us suddenly go quiet, no doubt feeling the swift change of energy in here. After a moment they resume talking amongst one another again.

I tilt my head. "Careful, or you might summon these mortal women over to us."

Sapphire smirks at me, glancing over to them. "Deep down they both want those perfect, proper feathers ruffled." She turns her gaze back to me. "Though they're not my type. I fancy a more disturbed individual."

"Such as one who spends obscene amounts of money on you but never actually talks to you?"

Sapphire nudges me with her elbow, giggling. "I think he's just shy, but something tells me he'll approach me soon."

I giggle as I continue fanning through the rack, landing on a costume that I halt on.

I remove the hanger from the rack, holding it out. A grin deepening as I admire the red suspender skirt and matching red laced cropped top.

"Oh, you have to try that on." She says as she looks at what I picked up.

I hold it up to my chest, quickly raising my eyebrows. "I'll meet you in there then."

I turn around, heading towards the heart shaped awning that leads to the fitting rooms. Two shades of dark pink, the middle layer a hot pink LED light that traces the entirety of the heart.

I walk under the awning as my feet step onto plush pink carpet, a row of dressing rooms ahead of me with dark purple curtains pulled back.

I step into an unoccupied room, pulling the purple curtain back as I set my purse onto the pink transparent plastic chair. I face the tall LED light mirror, removing my clothing as I set it on the chair on top of my purse.

"Okay, I think I found something but I'll need your opinion." Sapphire calls out as I hear her stepping into the fitting room next to mine.

"I'm sure it'll look good. You look hot in anything you wear."

I hear her hum softly. "Aww, are you trying to hype me up right now?"

We both laugh as I pull the crop top over my head. "I'm always trying to hype you up."

I pull the suspenders up my shoulders as the ends of the skirt brush along the top of my thigh. I turn around, looking behind through the mirror.

Barely covering my ass. Just how I like it.

I grab the tiny cape that comes with the costume, hooking it over my shoulders as the tips of it brush along the middle of my arms, touching just the middle of my back. I smile as I twirl my hips side to side, the skirt swishing as I do.

"Are you done yet?" I ask as I pull back the curtain, stepping out.

"Don't rush me." Sapphire says.

I chuckle as I hear her zippering up her costume, the sound of latex suctioning to her body as she adjusts it. A few moments later she pulls the curtain back, holding the end of a long black tail in her hand. "Like it?" She purrs.

She leans into the doorway, crossing a bare leg over the other. Donning a black latex bodysuit with matching latex gloves that extend up to her elbows. A mask with cat ears protruding from the top covering the top half of her face, the bottom half exposed.

I nod, smirking. "I love it."

She steps away from the doorway, her hands coming up to tug the strapless bodysuit up. "I definitely won't be on the pole in this thing though." She laughs as her gaze lowers to my costume. She gasps softly, coming closer to trace her fingertips along the edge of the skirt. "Cher, I fucking love this on you."

"Thank you." I say sweetly, genuinely smiling.

She nods as she pulls away. "Yeah, this is definitely what you're wearing." She claps her hands together, smiling wide. A little squeal slips out from her lips before she turns to face the mirror from her fitting room. She sighs. "We're going to look so hot."

I step to her side, looking in the mirror as well. The irony of this costume curving my smile into a wide grin.

Chapter 52

Levi

Once I return home I get right to work, leaving no room for my thoughts to wander about Amelia.

I hover over the blueprint Dex acquired for me, the palm of my hand pressed firmly against my kitchen table as I glance over it. I bring the glass of whiskey to my lips, taking a slow brief sip before lowering it back down to the table.

I pick up my pencil and locate the areas of interest, circling them as I make a mental note of where they're located as well.

The buzzing of my phone draws my gaze away from the map. I look down at my phone, picking it up when I see who's calling. "What's up?"

"I should be asking you the same question." Sawyer responds in a too calm voice.

I lift my palm from the table, stepping away from the map as I face my porch door. "It was necessary. He was following us."

Sawyer makes a low humming noise. "Us?"

I clench my jaw momentarily, keeping myself from sighing outloud. "Amelia and I. He was hired by Adrian to follow her, so I took care of it."

"Interesting. Because I thought I'd asked you specifically to do this one on your own." I hear the rustling of paperwork in the background, the only indication that this conversation bears no real weight to him. No real threat to my life or Amelia's.

I step closer to the glass, glancing up at the pine trees surrounding my home. Looking down at the strand of dog hair on my sweats. I pinch it, releasing it as I watch it float to the ground. "She only knows I handled someone following us. Nothing else."

"Good. I don't need you revealing who your target is, only for her to go blabbing about it to whoever and ruining our operations."

I force myself to remain calm, clenching my fist inward as I reel in my patience and remind myself that he's only doing what's best for the inner circle. That if I hadn't become obsessed with her, and drawn to her, that I would be agreeing with him. But since my discipline for keeping things professional went completely out the window, there are no limits to what I would do in order to protect her.

Regardless if she's a whole Succubus and I'm just some mortal man. The fact still stands that she completely consumes my life now, and I have absolutely no desire in staying away from her.

I nod my head, turning away from the porch door as I look down at the blueprint on my kitchen table again. "Understood." I managed to force out.

"Good. Killian tells me everything is underway, and that the day has been set."

"That's correct."

The sound of Sawyer's chuckle glides through the phone, his amusement not something many are graced with—well, ever. "Well, that's one way to make a statement." He says before hanging up the phone, leaving me to stare down at my home screen.

A soft grin curves up my lips at the simple yet large reminder of who my world revolves around now.

Chapter 53

Amelia

I arrived at The Gallery ten minutes before he said to meet him here. I shut the Uber door behind me, pulling my faux fur coat closed as I walk up the steps to the glass entrance doors.

The silver handle is ice cold against my hand as I pull the door open, the warmth as I step inside rushing to my cheeks.

The heels of my black knee-high boots click against the creamy white vinyl flooring as I advance to a blonde receptionist standing behind the front desk.

"Good evening, ma'am." Her green eyes alight on mine as her pin straight bob sways gently. "Ticket for one?"

A man sitting next to her stifles a laugh, my amber eyes slowly peering over to him. My gaze roams over his receding hairline and bushy eyebrows that are going every which way but right.

I tilt my head slightly. "Is there something I can help you with?"

He lowers his hand from his face, resting it beneath his chin as he shakes his head. Fighting the stupid smile that's curving up his pouty lips. "Just wouldn't expect someone like you to be in a place like this."

I make a vague nod of my head, my gaze lowering to the tips of his fingernails. I note the filth trapped beneath them, as if he'd spent his entire afternoon digging around in the dirt. Which, judging by the roundness of his belly, I imagine the man finds himself winded even after just one tiny flight of stairs.

I lift my gaze back up to him, fixating it on his hair for several seconds. Long enough until I see him quickly readjust himself in his chair, the uncomfortableness seeping from his energy like water from a sponge.

I lower my gaze to him for a moment before lifting my purse up onto the counter, disinterest coloring my expression. "Taking opinions from a man who can't even keep his own hair, or clean his own fingernails? I'll pass." I open my purse up, pulling out my phone as I open my text thread between Adrian and I.

The man makes a long, ragged exhale as someone advances towards us from behind me.

"Looks like you got here before I did." Adrian says, coming up from behind and kissing my cheek.

I lean into him, grinning as his beard brushes my soft skin. "Just barely." I turn around, dropping my phone back into my purse and hooking the straps around my shoulder. "I arrived only moments ago."

"Perfect." He looks up at the woman still standing there, nodding as he hands her two twenties.

She lowers the money into the register as two tickets print out. She rips them off, handing them to us. "Enjoy."

"We will." I say, glancing over at the man and giving him a wink. The ire in his eyes causing my lips to curve upwards.

Adrian and I turn away and walk through the large open awning. His arm lowers to the small of my back as he leans in closer to me. "Do I want to know why that man is glaring at you right now?"

A laugh gets trapped in my throat as we walk down the long hallway, surrounded by nothing but bare white walls to greet us. I shrug a shoulder. "Maybe he's glaring at the handsome man who gets to accompany the beautiful lady."

He chuckles as his hand idly caresses my back, the silk black material of my dress the only barrier between his skin and mine. "I'd be jealous too if I were him."

We walk down the hallway until we step through another awning, this time leading us to the main gallery room. Two rows of tall white rectangular columns line the room, each one with a framed piece of art mounted onto it.

I walk up to the first one, admiring the colors splashed meticulously across the canvas. "I didn't pick you for an art guy."

Adrian approaches my left, staring at the art before us. "I like many things. One of them including you."

I scoff as I roll my eyes at him. "Now you're just borderline desperate."

"Desperate, interested. It all sounds the same these days."

I chuckle as I step away from the painting, walking deeper into the room until I approach a familiar one.

"Ah yes, I believe everyone knows this one." Adrian says as he steps to my side again.

I glance over the three males facing towards an open landscape lacking in any vibrancy of color. All three of the males with their backs facing us, each one with large outstretched wings that span above them. Each demon ruling over the underbelly of the city where mortals are shamed for even whispering about. The part of the city most Succubi like myself, find ourselves in.

The one on the far left represented with dark shoulder-length hair and broad shoulders, his face turned towards the demon Prince in the middle as a wide smirk curves his lips. An accurate representation of Asmodeus, The Prince of Lust, to say the least.

The Prince on the far right shares a similar hair type, though his wavy strands are what tell him apart. The water droplets clinging to Leviathan's bare back are the immediate signifier that he is not only a Prince of Hell, but also the Prince who rules over the Cimiteria Sea.

And judging by his non-retaliation for the bodies being dumped into his sea, I can only assume he instead finds amusement from it.

My gaze traces over his serpent-like tail as it curls upward behind his back, his dark indigo scales enhanced with splashes of watercolor paint. My gaze then moves on to the demon in the middle, Prince Lucifer.

Many will argue and say he's the Prince of Pride because of his *"reckless"* rebellion against rigid conformity, which is true. But those who actually know his mythology view him as a divinity much larger than that.

A bearer both of knowledge and truth.

"It's said that though they remain below, that every now and then their boredom prompts them to the upper world. Where they force themselves onto women, therefore siring demon children."

I reel in the laugh that begs to crawl up my throat. For thousands of years these mortals have spun the worst ideologies possible about our kind, all fueled by a cult-like system that demands you to live a certain way—*one* way. And if you do anything that threatens the structure that's been fortified for thousands of years out of sheer fear, then you're automatically deemed as possessed and fueled by insanity.

Pft, please. The only entity that's possessing these mortals is their own self-prophecy fueled by their own fear. But there's no educating or talking to these mortals, so after a while we just started to allow them to believe what they want.

I maintain a neutral face as I look towards him, raising my hand up to my chest. Forcing my face into a state of relief. "As long as people continue to take the necessary precautions, they will stay away."

The necessary precautions being burning sage and hanging bells on your front door. We appreciate the efforts, but it takes a lot more than that to keep us away. But again, something we allow the mortals to believe for the fuck of it anyway.

Adrian gazes at me, resting a hand on my shoulder as he narrows his chin. "Indeed they will." He nods towards the end of the room. "Come, I want to show you my favorite work of art."

I force a smile as I allow him to lead us to it.

What he said though about the Princes coming up to the upper world once in a while when they're bored is true. Usually disguised in their more *desirable* human forms, as I myself do. But it's not to *sire demon children*. Usually they just want to sate their curiosity for how humanity has evolved thousands of years later.

Well, unless you're Asmodeus. He definitely shares a similar mindset as Anastasia where he takes great pride in having a very free sex life with no strings attached. So it's not uncommon to find him meandering around The Pleasure District here and there, looking for a pretty lady to *entertain* for the night. Though these mortals would never suspect a thing as they don't care to draw a lot of attention towards themselves.

We approach a painting of four men as they sit around a circular table, bottles of beer and a deck of cards laid out onto the hard surface as they each face one another. My gaze lowers to the title of the painting, a long internal sigh deafening my insides.

"It's unclear who painted this. Some say it remained anonymous because any indication of who it was painted by, would cost them their life due to an invasion of privacy."

I tilt my head to the side, adding to my faked interest.

Adrian lowers his hand down my back, lowering his head closer to my ear. "Though this was painted one hundred years ago, some say that the bloodline still lives on today. Though no one knows who exactly he is, or what he looks like."

I study the hard jaw of the man seated in the center, his piercing silver eyes narrowed on the man next to him. A familiarity that would only belong to one man involved in the same life as his grandfather.

Sawyer Deimari, the last living blood descendant of The Deimari Mafia.

I place my hand on my chest again, shaking my head slowly before I turn towards him. Placing that same hand onto his chest as I lift my gaze up to his. "Let's all hope that is not the case."

He stares at me for a moment, assessing for any bodily movements that would indicate I'm lying. Studying for any faint of worry, and sign that I know he's trying to fish information out of me.

Of course he knows. Gods, could he have made it anymore obvious? He could've at least waited until I'd *actually* warmed up to him.

Another internal sighs deafens me as I think back to the other night, to the man that was following Levi and I—

The man he was ordered not to tell me about.

"If you ever get approached by these bad men, promise you'll let me know?" He says, his face appearing sincere though I can see the anger simmering beneath.

I nod my head curtly, forcing a long exhale. "Absolutely." I step closer to him, keeping my hand on his chest.

"Good." He says as he nods to the painting next to us. "This is one of my favorites, too."

I allow him to guide me over to it as I pretend to enjoy being in his presence. Acting like I didn't just find out that the man I've been seeing as a distraction from Levi is using me as well. What an ironic turn of events we have here.

But to find out the why is because he's trying to press information out of me sends me into a quiet rage.

If Levi is assigned to take him out, then I need to know the *why* of it. Other than the fact that he's trying to catch The Deimari Mafia. There's something deeper behind it all.

I should be so angry with him for not telling me that the guy he's hired to kill is the one I've been seeing. I should be marching over to his place to tear the limbs from his mortal body for withholding this from me. But as I gaze at the man in the middle, at the sternness in his face that resembles Sawyers, the presumption of why Levi kept this from me becomes apparent. And that quiet rage simmers as something else bubbles up inside of me.

A feeling wholly consumed not by anger, but by immense enamoration for a mortal man wishing to keep me in the dark not to spite me, but to keep me from facing the don's wrath if he disobeyed his orders. Even knowing that I, a demon from Hell, am perfectly capable of executing my own wrath and need neither his protection nor his kindness.

Yet his gesture still stands as it causes a warmth to spread throughout my chest. A gesture that I realize from the time I've spent with him thus far is coming not from a place of fear for me, but from a place of genuine care.

A smirk curves up my face as I lean myself into Adrian, leaning my head up against his chest as we walk through the rest of the museum.

With nothing to fill my head but thoughts of how this is the last time that I play pretend with Adrian.

Chapter 54

Levi

I set the glass onto the counter, turning around to grab the bottle of whiskey from the cupboard above the sink. I twist the cap off, filling the glass halfway when the home security app on my phone beeps once.

Alerting me that someone's outside my home.

I slowly set the bottle down, picking up the phone as I pull the app up. Seeing if I can catch a glimpse of whoever is fucking brave enough to trespass on my property. I watch as a car drives down my driveway, away from my home as I see someone walking up to my front door.

Holding a leash to a familiar Hellhound.

I set the phone down, walking out of the kitchen and down my hallway. I watch as Amelia comes closer to the doorframe, lifting a hand to my door knob when she sees me approaching.

I pull the door open, Rufus softly barking with excitement.

"Thanks, I thought I was going to have to pick your lock and let myself in." She says as she steps inside, Rufus trailing along with her. In her arm she carries that same large bag, presuming it's been changed out from what she brought last night.

My brows knit together. "What are you doing here?" I ask, closing the door.

"I think what you mean to say is 'Wow, Amelia has graced me with her presence again! I'm the luckiest man in the world.'"

I laugh as I turn to face her. "I never said I was complaining. But I still beg the question."

She leans down to unhook the leash from Rufus' collar, wrapping it in her hands as he trots over to the living room. She glares at me, crossing her arms. "I know your next hit is Adrian."

I nod my head slowly, walking towards the kitchen as she follows me. "And what makes you think that?"

I can practically feel her roll her eyes at my back.

"Let's just say I put two and two together."

I approach the kitchen counter, grabbing my whiskey as I face towards her again. The determination in her eyes is so damn sexy that I have to force myself to take a drink, hoping to wash the effect of it away. I set the glass down, watching her. "You can't get involved."

"Like Hell I can." She snaps, her eyes hardening onto mine.

Damnit, that's even sexier.

"I need to do this on my own. You're not even supposed to know." I say, stepping away from the counter.

She grabs my arm, tugging me back as I turn my head around. "Because of your boss? I don't give a fuck about him—"

"Yeah well *I* fucking do." I seethe, turning my body fully as I advance on her. Her chest just barely brushing up against mine.

Her gaze lowers to my lips as her breath hitches in her chest. "All because you care about me." She says, sounding more like she's reminding herself of the fact.

My gaze remains on her face as I press her back up into the kitchen island. My hands come up to the edge of the counter as I lean into her, my fingers gripping the hard surface. "I won't let anything happen to you, Amelia. I know you're perfectly capable of handling things yourself. But I *can't* let anything happen to you otherwise—"

A long exhale escapes out of my nose as her eyes finally lift to mine again. A heated stare emanates from them as her eyes begin to glow. "Otherwise what?" She asks slowly.

A ragged exhale escapes me as I feel her hands come to my pants, loosening the button there. "Amelia." I breathe out.

"You didn't answer my question." She says, her voice low and sultry. She slowly lowers the zipper down, my cock growing hard against the material.

I inhale deeply before exhaling slowly. I lift a hand to her cheek, opening my hand up as my fingertips glide along her soft skin. "Because I cannot live a life where you're not involved in it. Being with you gives me a whole new pleasure to life that I never thought I could feel."

She raises her hand up to my waist again, pulling my shirt up as she places her fingers against my abdomen. It takes everything in me to not shiver at the touch.

"Just looking at you for fucks sake is everything. I don't care about our bet, our bargain, whatever the fuck it was. I never truly did."

She lowers her hand to my cock as I exhale raggedly. Her long lashes lifting as she peers her gaze up, tilting her head. "Then forget the bargain." She rubs her palm over my pants, the heat in her eyes intensifying.

She continues rubbing me slowly over my pants, my knuckles gripping into the counter as I try to reel it in.

Fuck I might just cum right here in my pants. No penetration, nothing but the feel of her soft hand rubbing against me.

"Amelia," I groan out as my pants lower themselves slightly down my hips. "I need you to be very clear on what you want from me. I need to hear you say it."

She raises her hand up until it dips below the waistband of my boxer briefs, the tips of her fingers gliding over my cock. "Well first, I want you to...how did you say it? *Show me no mercy*?"

She gently grips her hand around my shaft, rubbing me slowly. "But then, I want to explore what it means to be catered to from a mortal man. To be something other than just fucked."

A shaky exhale slips through my lips as I jerk slightly forward into her touch. "Say it."

"I want to be more than just business partners. I want you—"

Before she can say anything further I pull her hand away from my cock, lifting her dress and sinking my fingers beneath her thong. I yank it down and the smell of her arousal is strong. "Say it." I lower down, guiding each leg out of her underwear. I press a kiss to the inside of her calf as I gaze up at her.

She watches me hungrily as the amber in her eyes grow more vivid. "No more distractions."

I raise myself up slowly, pressing a kiss now to her inner thigh. She whimpers softly as my fingers graze up her thighs, my knuckles brushing along her pussy. "What else?"

She exhales as I lift her dress up her belly. "I am yours." She says breathlessly.

I waste no time and raise up onto my feet again, slipping her dress over her head until she's bare before me. Gods, her body is a fucking masterpiece. My gaze roams down as I conjure up all of the wicked things I'm going to do to her.

She gasps as I lift her up onto the counter, spreading her legs wide open for me. Her pussy glistening, waiting for me.

I push her body down and before she can even lay herself onto the counter, my mouth is on her.

Chapter 55

Amelia

His mouth descends on me as his tongue begins exploring, wringing moans from my lips.

My back arches against the hard counter, spreading my legs wider as he pulls me down onto his mouth. His hands gripping my waist as he closes his mouth over my clit.

Wetness pools from me as he sucks on it, my gaze lowering to his face as he stares up at me. I watch as a grin curves his mouth as he lowers a hand, guiding a finger inside of me slowly.

Taunting me.

I gasp when he inserts another, pleasure eroding every crevice of my body as I begin writhing against his face. My orgasm riding the surface.

He lifts his mouth off of my clit as he continues fingering me. His lips glistening as he looks up at me, pressing a wet kiss to my navel. "It's just us, baby. Let me hear how good I make you feel."

He lowers his mouth back down on my clit, flicking his tongue as I soon cannot control my cries of pleasure anymore. I writhe against him as I feel my orgasm brush the surface before it sends me fully over.

I grab his face, riding his mouth as I come undone. He slips his finger out, grabbing my waist again as he devours me. Licking and sucking every last drop of me as if I'm the sustenance to his mortal life.

As the high settles he wastes no time lifting me from the counter and hooking my legs around his waist. He flicks his tongue against a hard nipple as he carries me out of the kitchen.

His mouth moves over to the center of my chest, pressing a kiss there as a groan gets trapped in his throat. "A demon from Hell but you taste like fucking heaven." He says as he carries me up the steps.

We approach his bedroom as he tosses me onto the bed, pulling his shirt off over his head before lowering his hands to his waist. He lowers his pants to the ground as his cock presses against his briefs. I get onto my knees as I crawl closer to him.

He pulls his briefs down until his cock hangs before me. I kneel at the edge of the bed, looking up at him as I lower my mouth closer to his cock.

"Yes," He hisses. "Put that pretty mouth on my cock—"

His words end on a grunt as I close my mouth over him, swirling my tongue around him as I bring a hand to his shaft.

"That feels so fucking good, baby." He says as his hands come up to my face. One of them gathering all of my hair as he holds it at the back of my head.

I lower him deeper into my throat as I stare up at him, saliva thick around his cock.

He begins slowly thrusting into my mouth as he softly whimpers. "Take it fucking all, baby. It's all yours."

He begins to quicken his pace, my tongue swirling around him until suddenly he pulls out. My mouth makes a popping noise as saliva drips down my lips.

He pushes me onto my back as he crawls over me, his cock wet as it glides against my pussy. I moan as I writhe against him, impatient and wanting to feel him inside of me *now*.

"*Fuck*." A breathy moan following.

"That's it, little red." He says gruffly, his hand going to his cock as he slaps it against my pussy. He lowers it to my entrance, pushing just the tip inside of me. "Tell me how badly you want it."

He thrusts himself in all the way to the hilt, wringing a gasp from me at the fullness of him. He slowly pulls out until he thrusts into me again, his hand coming to my neck as he jerks my gaze up to his.

"Fuck, you feel *amazing*." He says as his eyes roll to the back of his head, a ragged exhale following. His hips ram into me as he begins fucking me harder, his hand squeezing harder into the sides of my throat. "Tell me how good I make you feel, baby. *Please*."

He rams into me as I cry out, another orgasm chasing me as I wrap my legs around him, trying to push him down further. I keep my eyes on him as I moan out his name. "Levi."

He continues ramming into me as his lips crash into mine, stifling my moans entirely into his mouth. Our tongues glide along one another's as he continues burying himself into me over and over and over again. Tingles creep along my skin the more my orgasm builds.

I feel his body tremble as he lifts his lips from mine, his lips gliding down to my neck. "*Fuck*, I'm going to cum already." He moans against my skin.

I run my fingers through his hair as he lifts his lips from my neck, looking down at me as he rams into me. I feel myself tighten around him as he groans. "*Fuck*."

I feel his body tense up as he rams into me once more, stilling as he buries himself to the hilt. He whimpers as he spills himself inside of me, my own orgasm meeting his.

I writhe against him as I cry out my release, my head pushing back into the bed. He lowers his lips to a hard nipple, sucking it as I arch my back deeper into him.

"So vocal for me." He says as his tongue trails around my nipple. My hands coming to his back as I pull him down closer, feverishly riding out my orgasm.

After a few moments he finally pulls out, panting as he raises his lips to my collarbone. He presses a gentle kiss there before laying himself down next to me.

We both catch our breath for a minute before he turns to lay facing towards me, lowering a hand to my face as he brings me in for a long kiss.

I feel him smile against my lips as his tongue glides against mine. My hand comes up to his jaw as he lowers his hand down my belly, then lower to my pussy again.

I gasp against his mouth as he inserts a finger inside of me, lifting his mouth from mine as he begins fingering me.

"This is going to be a long night, little red." His thumb lifts up to rub against my clit, causing me to arch my back as a whimper escapes out of me. "And I plan on having you cum *a lot*."

Chapter 56

Levi

I wake up to the sound of her lightly snoring beside me, one arm laid over her waist while the other rests beneath her head.

I slowly open my eyes to the sunlight filtering in from my windows, an orange glow branding the foot of my bed. I lower my gaze to her bare shoulder, glancing down to my gray bed sheet that just barely covers her breasts.

A grin curves my lips as I hug her closer to me, the smell of sex still lingering from round after round of fucking her.

My hand comes up to hers as I pull it to her chest, interlocking my hand with hers. I feel her stir beneath me as she takes a long exhale out of her nose.

Her hand squeezes mine as she stretches her legs out beneath the covers. Her rear pressing into me, not helping the morning wood whatsoever. A chuckle gets trapped in her mouth. "Goodmorning."

"Goodmorning." I say before lowering my lips to her neck, pressing a soft kiss there.

Gods, we've been at it all night and I could go another round with her right now if I wanted to. Something about being deep inside of her, how she feels around my cock. It's fucking maddening to say the least.

Like a damn fiend craving his next fix.

"I wish we could just stay in bed all day." She says sleepily, her voice like liquid ecstasy.

I press another kiss just beneath her earlobe. "I can arrange that."

She chuckles. "I have to work tonight. Plus, we need to figure out how we're going to handle our little *friend*."

"*Little* friend? Oh, so he *is* small." I say while my lips press up against her neck.

She exhales slowly. "I wouldn't know. It never got that far between us."

Oh, thank fuck. Because the thought of Amelia fucking a man who called her a prostitute behind her back would've sent me into a blind fury. That pitiful man deserves nothing gracious from her.

I nod slowly against her neck, my nose brushing up against her soft skin. I feel goosebumps pimple along her neck. "I presume you'd like to be involved in the actual execution."

I release my hand from hers, lowering it down her chest until I lay it across her belly.

She takes a shuddering breath in. "Yes." She hisses as she arches her back into me.

I press another kiss to her neck, lowering my fingers just an inch lower. "Well he'll need to think that nothing has changed between you two. For now."

"That was my logic as well. So I still plan to go to the costume party with him."

"Good." I say, my finger lowering until it dips in between her lips. Smirking at the wetness already gathering there. "What are you dressing up as?"

She takes a shaky breath in, her right leg lifting up to give me better access. "It's a surprise."

I chuckle as I open and hike her leg up, causing the bed sheet to raise before falling over her extended knee. I lower my gaze to her pussy fully exposed, exactly how I want it. I lower my hand back down as I rub my finger through her entrance, teasing her. "I do like surprises." I purr.

She moans softly as I press my finger in, gliding it inside of her. Fucking Hell she's so wet already. Now all I can think about is how good she'll feel wrapped around my cock.

I might just say fuck it and chain her up to this bed, keeping her hostage here for the day so I can do whatever I please to her. Pleasuring her over and over and over again, watching those reactions light up that pretty face of hers.

My cock grows harder at the thought as I begin fingering her. Those soft moans like music to my fucking ears.

"Okay, here's what we'll do. But first," I say as I remove my finger, lowering my hand to my cock as I slap it against her pussy. She arches her back deeper into me as I insert just the tip. "The only talking I'm interested in right now is the kind that involves me telling you how good your pussy feels."

I lower my cock in deeper, filling her halfway.

"How good *I* make you feel. So no more talk about another man in my bed."

I thrust all the way to the hilt, grunting against her neck. *Fuck, fuck, fuck* she's so warm and wet. I could think of absolutely nothing else I'd rather be doing than burying myself deep inside of her. Feeling her walls close up around me, listening to her moan because of *me*.

"So be a good girl and take all of me." I grind my hips into her rear, balls deep into her as I grunt against her. "Show me who your pussy is made for."

She takes a ragged breath in as I thrust into her again, my balls slapping against her as I continue my pace. She arches against me as I move inside of her, filling her. Fucking her. Giving her all of me as she rewards me with the sound of her moaning.

I bring my hand to her neck, holding it steady as I ram into her hard. "I'm going to fuck you so hard your legs will shake everytime you give a man a lapdance tonight."

And so I continue fucking her, drowning in the feel of her soaked pussy clamping around me with nothing but the sound of her screaming to fill the room around us.

Chapter 57

Amelia

I walk out into my kitchen as Rufus trails along behind me. I turn around, looking down at him as he plops his little butt down onto the kitchen floor.

I smirk at him as I place a hand on my hip. "Do you like mommy's costume?"

He barks at me, tilting his head.

I chuckle as I look down at my phone, a text coming through.

I'm on my way there. Can't wait to see you.

I type my response back before setting my phone back down onto the counter.

See you soon. Xoxo

Three days have come and gone just like that. Or maybe it seems that way because outside of working, all I've been doing is spending time with Levi and—well, a lot of that time spent has pretty much just been us going at it like animals.

It doesn't appear that Rufus at all minds spending the night over at Levi's. Though the poor

Hellhound has to put up with our sex-crazed selves. I laughed my ass off when I came downstairs to grab a drink of water from Levi's kitchen when I found Rufus curled up in the corner, facing the wall with his ears pinned down.

At least we're considerate and keep it upstairs. Well, most of the time.

I grab my jacket from the rack on the wall, pulling it over as I grab my purse from the bar stool. I fluff my curled hair out from beneath my collar, trailing it behind my back before slipping my feet through my heels.

A pair of black mary jane platform heels to complete the look. Though, I'm not sure they will be a smart choice for later tonight.

Fuck it, I can always buy a new pair if need be.

I fix my white ruffle ankle socks, adjusting them along with the cute white bow stitched in the back. I grab my purse as I hike it over my shoulder, glancing back at Rufus. "Be good. Mommy will be home later."

Usually I lock him up in his crate when I'm gone, but since he's been so well-behaved whenever we're at Levi's, I'm hoping he can exhibit that same behavior here.

I pull open my front door, turning my lights off before I step out into the entryway. I lock my door before hitting the downward arrow on the elevator, the doors opening up as I step inside.

As the elevator takes me down to the first floor I smooth my hands out over my red skirt, the white and black lace trim gliding across my fingertips. I flatten the two silk black bows stitched at the center of each thigh, a half-rounded square patch of white cotton fabric stitched halfway down the skirt in the center.

I lower my hand beneath my coat, adjusting my matching red mini cape before the elevator halts.

The doors open up as I step out onto the marbled floor, heading straight for the double doors to lead me outside.

Where I get into my Uber and make my way to the club.

I remove my coat as I hang it over my arm, the club music blaring and the place jam packed. I take a few steps when I hear him approach from behind.

"Ah, there you are."

I turn around to see Adrian dressed in his matching costume. The big bad wolf to my little miss red riding hood. The irony of it all utterly fitting.

I do a mocking curtsy. "Here I am." I look down at his costume which mainly consists of jeans, a red and black checkered long-sleeved shirt with a hood attached to it to resemble a wolf's head.

He looks so fucking corny, I can't.

He pulls me in for a hug and a kiss, bringing my hands up to his face as I lean into it. I even throw a little tongue in there just to really seal the act.

"We look good together. Too bad there's no prize for best costumes." He says as he steps back, checking out my costume and—well, me of course.

I pout my lips as I lift my red hood, my long hair draping down my chest. "Too bad indeed." I smirk as I grab his hand and lead us deeper into the club.

We walk over to the bar as Ace glances over at me, smirking at my costume as we approach the bar counter. "Why did I think you'd actually wear a costume that didn't incorporate the color red."

"Hey, I have to maintain a persona here." I say as I twirl a strand of my hair. "Besides, I look good in the color red."

"I see no lies told." Adrian says from beside me, seating himself as I pull my chair out to do the same.

What a turd to not at least pull my chair out for me. Gods, I can't wait to—

"What're you drinking tonight, my dear?" Adrian says as he rests a hand on my back.

I smile sweetly at him before I turn my gaze back to Ace. "Cranberry vodka, per usual."

Ace nods his head as he gets right to making the drink. I look at his costume. An all black suit fitted with a padded chest made to represent armor. My gaze peers over his shoulder to the long red cape attached to his back, a grin curving up my lips when my gaze lowers to the Mjolnir hammer set on the bar counter. "Well aren't you the most handsome Thor I've ever laid eyes on."

Ace chuckles as he pours my drink up, sliding it over to me. "Thanks for noticing." He nods over to the hammer. "I set it there purposefully because people kept asking if I was Batman with a red cape."

I laugh as I take a sip from my drink as Adrian orders himself a scotch. I watch as Ace pours it up, sliding it over to him when I hear a familiar squeal.

Her arms wrap around me as the latex rubs against my chest, her musk and floral perfume overwhelming me. "You look so good, babe." She says as she pulls away.

I turn my chair around to face her, my gaze roaming over Sapphire's costume. "As do you, girl."

She smiles before she looks over at Adrian.

He holds his hand out, nodding. "I'm Adrian."

She takes his hand, smirking. "Nice to meet you, Adrian. I'm Sapphire."

"And if my presumptions are correct you must be catwoman?"

She forces a giggle, winking at him. "You'd assume correctly." She looks over at Ace before gasping. "Honey, you look so handsome." She rushes down to the end of the bar, turning the corner to step behind the bar counter.

Ace turns around to give her a hug, smiling from ear to ear. "Thank you. So do you."

"You're not supposed to be behind there."

Janice approaches behind me as she eyes Sapphire. I turn to look at her, those beautiful green eyes piercing against her mocha brown skin. Long, wavy honey brown hair tucked behind her ears as the LED lights above glint off of her princess cut diamond earrings. I glance down to the name badge pinned to her all-black tailored jumpsuit, Club Manager engraved beneath her name.

"Sorry, Janice." Sapphire says as she lifts herself up onto the counter, planting her butt on the hard surface before lifting her legs up and around until she jumps down next to me.

Janice chuckles, shaking her head slowly. "There is never a dull moment with you." She nods her head at both of us. "Enjoy your night off." She walks away as she folds her hands in front of her lap, a classy business woman at its finest.

As my gaze goes to look away from her I spot a man entering the club, a white and black mask pulled over his face. He walks in wearing a black long-sleeved shirt, the sleeves rolled up to the elbows with black dress pants to match.

I lower my gaze to those familiar tattoos that creep up his forearm, those silver rings on his fingers that for the past few nights have become very familiar with my neck. My belly flutters as I stare at him for a moment longer.

Damn, I really hope he fucks me in that mask later tonight.

I turn my gaze back to the three of us as Adrian begins telling Ace about whatever it is they're talking about. As I fix a smile on my face and join in on the conversation.

Chapter 58

The night carries on as the music in the club continues booming. I force myself to keep my gaze on Adrian even though I can feel Levi's stare on me like a heated brand. His occasional glances over in my direction are thankfully overlooked as Adrian can't keep his eyes—or his hands off of me.

His hand rests itself on my leg hooked over my other leg, his fingers idly tracing circles on the side of my knee.

"Don't get too handsy now." I smirk as I look around us. "You'll have these men thinking I'm taken and that doesn't exactly entice men to hand me their money."

Adrian chuckles, his breath smelling like scotch. "Well what if I don't care?" He says as he raises his hand up.

Ugh, please don't make me kill you right here solely because you're pissing me off right now.

I gently lower my hand onto his, casually lowering it back down my thigh. I force a laugh, playing off the irritation simmering beneath.

"Sounds like someone is becoming a little possessive."

He shrugs his shoulders as a lazy smirk curves his lips. "I've told you from the start that I go after what I want."

I force a chuckle as a feminine laugh peers my gaze to look over in that direction.

I watch as Dahlia laughs with Levi, having taken his mask off now. My breath hitches, Adrian turning to follow the direction of my gaze.

I exhale slowly as I turn around, picking up my drink and taking a sip.

Adrian turns back around, leaning closer into me. "Do you know him?"

My hand trembles slightly as I set the glass down, shaking my head. "No, I just—" I uncross my leg as I lean forward. "I need to use the restroom."

Adrian places a hand on my wrist, stilling me into my seat. I look over at him, willing a worried look on my face.

His gaze falls to my arm that trembles beneath his touch. He raises his gaze once more, and it's evident he's trying not to appear excited that I've just revealed myself of knowing Levi. "Cherry, you're shaking."

I shake my head violently. "I'm fine."

"Is there something you're not telling me?" He asks quietly, persisting.

I take an exaggerated inhale, exhaling it out. I peer my gaze back up at him, shaking my head again. "I can't. They'll kill me."

"Who?" He asks, excitement in his tone just nearly overriding the faked concern he's giving.

"I can't say who." I quickly glance back over in Levi's direction. "Not here anyway."

Adrian loses his grip on my wrist, curtly nodding in understanding. He hesitates for a moment before turning his palm upwards, raising it towards me. "Would you like me to take you somewhere private? Where we can talk?"

I force a shaky exhale out, my gaze wildly roaming over his face. "How do I know I can trust you? I just met you." I turn from him entirely, going to grab my phone and my coat. "I'm sorry, this was a mistake—"

"I'm not a realtor."

I turn my gaze to him, watching. Waiting.

He leans in closer as I seat myself in the chair again. "I'm a private investigator."

"What?" I nearly shout.

He shushes me, making a gesture with his hand to keep it down. He tilts his head, sighing. "I've been working on a case for a while now. Particularly around the missing persons I believe is tied to The Deimari Mafia."

My eyes widen, my hand going to grip his. "You should not be telling me this. If they ask me—"

"I can protect you." He assures me, idly rubbing his thumb over my skin. He narrows his chin. "But I can only do that if you meet me halfway."

I watch him for a long moment, peering a glance over at Levi again as he talks to the waitress. I look back at Adrian, nodding my head. "There's a back exit through the VIP hallway. It'll look like I'm just taking you back there for a room."

Adrian nods. "Understood."

We begin gathering our things, I lay my coat over my arm as I guide us to the VIP hallway.

I walk us down to the far end, the red neon sign above the exit blinding against the dimly lit hallway. I push it open, peering out of the doorway before giving him the okay that no one is out here.

We both slip out of the door as it shuts behind us. He turns towards me, grabbing his keys out of his coat. "We'll head to my place. It's the safest place we can be right now."

I nod my head as he grabs my hand, interlocking my fingers with his. I gently squeeze his hand as I tug down on him. "Please." I plead.

He turns to me.

My lip quivers as my hand trembles in his. "You have to help me. I—I don't want to be in the middle of this anymore. They're *monsters*."

He wraps his arms around me as I begin to cry, pressing kisses to the top of my forehead as I shake against his hold.

He pulls away, grabbing my face and forcing me to look up at him. "I will help you. I promise."

He wipes the tears from my eyes as he gives me a shy grin. He guides me down the alley, out onto the street where his car awaits.

Driving us both to his place.

Chapter 59

I open the car door as he comes around, holding his hand out for me as I place my trembling one into his. My sobbing causing my body to shake heavily.

"They made me lure them in. I—I had no choice. They said they'd kill me if I didn't cooperate."

Adrian guides me to his front door, opening it as we both walk inside. He closes his door before turning around to face me. "Tell me everything that happened and leave nothing out."

He unbuttons his plaid shirt, revealing a white undershirt underneath as he sets it on the couch. I narrow my gaze to it.

"Sorry, I can't wear that anymore. It's incredibly itchy to say the least."

My trembling ceases as I laugh at his words, a grin fighting its way on my face.

He steps into me, placing his hand on my cheek. He tilts my head up, his thumbs gently pressing along the underneath of my jaw.

"I can, and *will* protect you. I need you to trust me." His gaze softening as his thumb sweeps across my skin.

I exhale a long breath out as I give a slight nod.

He lowers his hands as he extends one to his couch. "Sit. I'll fix us something to drink."

I make my way over to the couch, my hands folded on top of my knees as I take a seat.

Adrian walks into the kitchen, the sound of a cupboard opening and closing as I look around down at his leather couch. I pick up on the sound of two glasses being set onto the kitchen counter, the sound of him twisting the cap off of a bottle of liquor.

I peer my gaze up from the couch to the TV in front of me. Smaller than the one I have at home, but decently large nonetheless. I look down at the wood trimmed coffee table before me, a couple of folders resting atop the glass center.

My gaze raises to him as I hear him approach the living room again, carrying two glasses of dark liquor.

He seats himself next to me and hands me a glass. "I hope whiskey is alright."

I take the glass, forcing a grin. "Thank you."

I look down at the glass, raising it to my lips as I take a sip. The rich, smoky taste lingers on my tongue as I smack my lips twice at the bitter aftertaste. Looking down at the glass again, swirling the liquor inside as I tilt my head.

Adrian takes a sip as well before setting his glass down onto the coffee table. He turns to face me, resting a hand on my shoulder. "Are you ready?"

I lower my glass to the table before straightening again. I take a long exhale as I nod, and tell him everything.

I tell him about how I met Levi at the club, how he tried to coerce me into working with him. I tell him about Ian and Wesley, and who exactly Levi is.

"I had no choice but to do what he said." I stumble over my words as tears slip down my face.

He nods his head slowly as he rubs his hand on my back. "It's not your fault."

"Yes it is." I look up at him through red-rimmed eyes. My lip quivers as I loosen a shaky exhale. "If I wasn't forced to lure them in for him, they would still all be alive today."

I shed a few more tears as Adrian pulls me closer to him, his hand caressing my back.

"I will make it right for you." He says as he pulls me away, holding my shoulders gently as he gazes at me. "But in order to do that, I need legitimate evidence to put him and The Deimari Mafia away."

I nod my head curtly. "Anything. I'll do *anything* to be free of them."

Adrian's gaze pierces into mine. "I need to know where the bodies were dumped."

I bite my lower lip, my blinking slightly slowed. "They're at the bottom of the Cimeteria Sea."

Adrian sighs as he nods his head, his hands slightly gripping into my shoulders before releasing me entirely. "Thank you. I know this is all scary but we're going to make sure you're well protected."

I blink slowly at him, swaying slightly in my seat before he grabs me. "Woah—"

"Are you alright, Cherry?"

I blink my eyes, retraining my focus on him as I raise a shaky hand to my chest. "Yes—sorry, all of the drinks tonight must've gotten to me." I force out a laugh.

He gives me a half grin as he releases his hands from my shoulder, lowering one to my thigh. "Well, aside from all of the heavy talk, I hope you've at least enjoyed yourself tonight."

His hand slips up my thigh, his fingers brushing beneath my skirt. I go to push his hand away as I force out a laugh. "Of course I'm enjoying myself. I'm with you." My eyelids become heavy as I force a smile.

His hand falls away before pressing against the cushion beside me as he leans forward. "I enjoy being with you, too." He smiles as he leans in to kiss me.

He deepens the kiss as he lowers me down onto the couch, spreading my legs open for him as he lays on top of me.

I go to push him away when he continues advancing on me. "Adrian, I don't feel so good—"

"Shh. It's okay." He says as his hand lowers to his pants. "I'll make you feel all better." I hear the sound of his zipper as he lowers his hand slightly before bringing it up my thigh again.

I go to push his hand away when his other hand holds it down onto the couch. "What're you—"

"If there is anything I've been looking forward to about this case other than being the one who puts The Deimari Mafia away," He says as his fingers rub against my pussy. "Is being able to see how this tight little pussy feels. But don't worry,"

My eyes bulge out as he slips a finger through my thong.

"I'll try to go easy on you." A vile smirk curves his lips.

The widening of my eyes shrink, returning to normalcy as a wicked slowly curves up my face. I tilt my head to the side, feeling his hand still entirely as I say in a clear and steady voice. "Is that so?"

And as confusion clouds his pitifully paled face, I drive a protruded talon right into the side of his neck.

Chapter 60

My power rushes to the surface as my gaze cements itself on him, the amber in my eyes glowing vividly as blood drips from the hole in the side of his neck. He jerks up onto the couch, a hand pressing against the wound as he tries to stop the bleeding. I stand up from the couch in a calm and fluid movement.

"Did you really think I wouldn't have been able to taste the roofie you slipped in my drink?" I wave my hand out as I face him. I bend at the waist as I watch the confidence he previously had completely vanish. "Perhaps not if I were mortal. Something you *failed* to dig up about me." I stand up straight again as I fold my hands behind my back.

A wicked grin curving my lips that the true fun of tonight has only just begun.

His stare hardens on me, terror written all over his eyes as he goes to stand up from the couch when my gaze locks onto his. Power licking all around me.

"Stay seated." I order in that sensual, fluidity of mine.

He lowers himself back down as his body remains rigid against the couch. "I—I can't move."

I sigh audibly, raising a hand up until a claw taps against my red lips. "In all of your research about the hidden entities in this city, I would've figured you'd known about my kind by now."

His gaze lowers to my extended claw, my hand now turned to a blotchy coal color. I let my real form begin to take shape as his body and his lips begin to tremble. "Y—you're one of them."

I approach him, leaning down as I smirk at him. "Come on. Say it, Adrian." I say huskily. "Or shall I show you?"

I step back as I allow my real form to take over. The claws from my elongated hand protrude outward as the talons on my feet take form. I watch the terror in his eyes intensify as my human form slips away like the setting sun dipping beneath the horizon.

I feel my wings take shape behind me, spreading themselves high above my shoulders as the horns on my head curl themselves inward.

Oh, does it feel fucking good to finally wear my real form.

I stare down at him as I lower my gaze to the bulge against his pants. I roll my eyes at him, scoffing as I raise my gaze again. Even after I've punctured a hole in his throat does this pathetic man remain hard. "Such like a man. Even when I've inflicted great pain do you still get off."

Anger flairs in his eyes. "You're a Succubus." He seethes.

"Ah, so maybe we aren't as stupid as I thought."

I lower a knee down to his thighs, spreading his legs open for me. I watch as his gaze narrows quickly to his pants, his breathing ragged.

I lower a hand down to his pants, pulling them down off his hips. "This is what you wanted, isn't it?" I purr.

His chest raises sharply as I expose his cock, his hands remaining at his sides as my power keeps him in place.

I tsk at him, shaking my head. "No wonder you resort to forcing yourself on women." I look up at him, frowning as I pout my lips. "What woman would find pleasure with *this*?"

The veins in his neck bulge out as anger stems from his gaze. "You fucking b—"

"Bitch?" I laugh as I lower my hand to his cock, a pitiful excuse for one that is. "You're only fueling my ego with such compliments."

So damn small, so...skinny.

I wrap my hand around it as his breath hitches. I move my hand up slowly, pumping what little dick he has. "Is this what you imagined, Adrian?"

His gaze hardens on mine before it narrows down. Breathing raggedly as he forces himself to exhale through his nose as he jerks his hips forward.

I work him a little faster as his breathing smooths out, his eyes lowering to my cleavage as my real form bears no clothing. "My pretty mouth wrapped around your cock, while your cum drips down my throat? Is that what you planned to do while I was asleep?"

His cock jerks as pre-cum beads from the tip as I keep working him. He manages to pull his gaze away to stare at the wings behind my back. His eyes bulge out as I twitch them for him, taking pleasure in adding to the terror on his face. "No, that's not it—"

"Oh? Are you sure?" I narrow my gaze back down. "What was it you told me? That you'll *make me feel all better*?"

I feel his abdomen tighten up, both from his orgasm riding up to the surface and also from the anger brewing beneath him. His fists clenching at his sides as my power refrains him from moving.

"What's the matter? Are you not enjoying the fact that you have no control over your body right now? But...isn't that exactly what you were going to inflict upon me?"

He releases a shaky exhale as he jerks his hips forward. His head leaning against the back of the couch as a soft moan slips from his mouth.

"Looks like we're almost there." I purr.

His hips jerk up into my hand as I feel his arousal crescendoing. Until cum is spilling out of his cock, dripping down my hand.

He lets out a loud moan until his head jerks upright. A pained, shrieking cry piercing the walls around us.

As his eyes fixate wildly on his cock in my hand, severed from his body.

Chapter 61

His cries become deafening as blood spurts from where his dick just was. A clean cut with the tip of my claw.

I roll my eyes at him, annoyed with the screaming evading from his lips. "Oh, shut up already."

I shove his cock into his mouth, his eyes so wide I actually think they'll bust right out of their sockets. He gags on it as cum drips down the side of his mouth.

"You will relax." I purr.

His body ceases its violent trembling as his gagging ceases as well. As he sits there with his severed cock in his mouth.

I giggle to myself as I walk into the kitchen, washing my hands and claws once, then twice just for extra measure. I dry them off with a towel before walking over to my purse, pulling my phone out.

I step in front of Adrian, smiling as I snap a picture of him. I look down at it, giggling again before I sigh contentedly. "I love my life."

I hear the front door opening, my heart palpitating for a moment in my chest before settling again. A smirk crawls up my lips again. "Took you long enough."

I turn around to see Levi standing by the door, that mask pulled over his face again. A white mask with black see through mesh where his eyes and mouth should be.

He pulls the mask off, looking over at Adrian as he grimaces. "I thought I'd wait until you were finished with your *work of art*."

I chuckle. "I was feeling creative."

He fixes his gaze on me as it roams over my entire body, over my real form. I wait for him to show fear in his eyes, to feel the nervousness drip from his body language. But instead, he only grins wickedly at me before approaching me. "Is it strange that I find this form to be both sexy and...bad-ass?"

I snort a laugh deep in my throat as I allow my Succubus form to slip away, shifting back into my human form once more. "I'd say it's a compliment to say the least."

He presses a kiss to my lips, my arms wrapping around his neck as he deepens the kiss.

He pulls away hesitantly, his dark brown eyes piercing into mine before a wicked grin curves his lips. "Let's finish what we started. Then I want to play a game of our own. If you're interested."

"Oh?" I look down at the mask in his hands. "I do hope it involves you wearing that."

"It does." He winks before turning to face Adrian, standing there for a brief moment before setting his mask onto the coffee table.

"Tell him to spit it out." He says before he walks into the kitchen.

I lower my gaze to Adrian, willing my power to the surface. "Spit it out."

He does so immediately, coughing and gagging as droplets of his own cum splatter over himself.

I step back, holding a hand up to my lips as I grimace. "Ew. Keep that to yourself."

His gaze lifts to mine before moving to the side of the room, locking onto Levi.

He walks back into the living room with a butcher knife, twirling it in his hand as a grin curves his lips. He goes to sit on the coffee table, dangling the knife in between his legs as he faces Adrian.

I watch as anger swells in Adrian's face, trying to fight against my compulsion to keep him seated there. "If you're going to kill me then just do it." He seethes through his clenched teeth.

Levi smiles as a laugh bellows out of him. He leans forward as something cold and wicked brews beneath him. He gets close enough to Adrian until he slowly inserts the knife into his abdomen, Adrian wanting to flinch out of the way but forced to remain there and take it.

Levi tilts his head as a wicked grin curves his face. "Well, that's exactly what we're here to do."

He slowly removes the knife from his abdomen, blood pooling out. Adrian forces out a ragged breath as he grunts in pain. He peers his gaze up to Levi who pushes the tip of the knife against the other side of his abdomen. That wicked grin of his never faltering. "And I'll be sure to make it *highly* agonizing."

Chapter 62

Levi

I insert the knife into him over, and over, and over again. Starting from his abdomen and working my way up his chest. Purposefully bypassing his heart so he dies a slow, painful death.

It was torture watching him force himself onto Amelia like that. The whole time I watched my phone knowing that she was well aware he'd most likely try to drug her. Well aware that she had her own agenda for revenge. I knew it wouldn't have gotten far, but it still caused a deep well of hatred in my blood for him that I'm thoroughly expressing through this knife.

So I'm taking *great* delight in watching him suffer.

I remained silent for the entire duration as Amelia stood behind and watched, knowing she's taking delight in the retribution I'm enacting for her as well.

I watch as his face pales to a sickly white, blood pooling all around him after stabbing him eight times now. His head lolls to the side as his eyes become increasingly heavy. "Please—"

"Please what?" I ask, holding the bloody knife in my hand. "Show mercy?" I lean closer, the smell of metallic heavy in the air now. "That's not what you would've given her tonight."

I sink the knife into the base of his throat, his head jerking up as his eyes spring open.

"But thankfully for you, I'm tired of seeing your face. So I'll speed this up for the both of us now that I've had my way with you for a long while."

I sink the knife deeper into his throat, blood gurgling out of his mouth as his eyes begin to slacken. Before he stills completely and finally dies.

I pull the knife out, wiping it on his shirt. I stand up and turn towards Amelia, finding her eyes intently watching me.

I slowly stride over to her, heat coursing through my veins at the sight of her in this costume that she's willed over herself again as soon as she returned back to her human form. I smirk as I descend upon her. A different kind of predatory hunt now eroding in my blood. "Are you ready for our game now, little red?" I purr.

Heat ignites in her gaze as she watches me. "Yes." She hisses, as I trail the tip of the blade up her thigh.

I lower my gaze to the goosebumps pebbling along her skin, wanting desperately to press kisses all over them but forcing myself to wait. I slowly raise the blade until the tip is lightly brushing along the crease of her thigh. "We're going to play a little game. It's kind of like hide and seek."

She moans softly as the tip of the blade glides featherlight over her thong, right over her clit. "And how is this game different?" She opens her legs wider for me, thrilling some deranged and sick animalistic nature within me for her.

I chuckle as I lean my lips against her neck, nipping the skin there. "Because when I find you, I get to fuck you."

I feel her stomach clench as I trace that sensitive skin so featherlight. So incredibly taunting.

She exhales shakily, the hitch of her breath making my cock rock hard. "Then let's play." She purrs.

I chuckle as I pull the knife away, raising my face from her neck. My gaze dips to hers, noticing my wicked smirk matches her own. "You must stay inside the house, no venturing off the property."

I lower my lips to hers, my breath hovering between us. "You have thirty seconds," I say before stepping away from her, turning around to grab the mask from the coffee table. I pull it on, turning back around as I watch the anticipation light up in Amelia's face. Making the game all that more exciting. "Starting now."

"Twenty-nine...thirty." I finish as I open my eyes, standing up from the coffee table. The mask pulled over my face and the knife hanging from my hand. "Ready or not, here I come." I call out.

I walk out of the living room, knowing already she's not in here. That would be far too easy for me.

I walk into the dining room, bending down to look beneath this ugly ass dining table. I stand up again when I see she's not under there, making my way over to the kitchen through the open awning.

My gaze roams over the plentiful cupboards, deciding to open each and everyone of them just to draw the tension further out for the both of us. Knowing she can hear the click of each and every one of them closing.

Knowing that adding to the anticipation and fear is all a part of the game, and also adds to the love of the hunt. Something that I've never tried with any other woman before, but something that I was interested in trying with her.

Fuck, at this point I'd try absolutely anything with her. I'm down so bad she could treat me like a spec of dirt, degrade and humiliate me for even taking up space and breathing her same air, and I would say thank you.

Because as this possessiveness that I feel for her continues to grow, so does my willingness to be anything she needs me to be.

After opening each and every one, I look over at a pantry closet. "I'm going to find you, Amelia." I purr out loud as I approach the pantry closet, setting my hand on the doorknob before pulling it open.

I look around inside, no Amelia here.

I close the pantry door and turn around. I exit out of the kitchen and head down the hallway. I peek through the open bathroom, turning the light on. The shower curtain pulled closed as I approach it and fling it open. The metal shower rings scraping across the metal bar.

No Amelia in here either.

"I know I'm getting closer, little red." My voice rough as I pull the shower curtain closed once again. I turn the light off and exit the bathroom.

I walk over to Adrian's bedroom, approaching the doorway when my gaze lowers to the bed. The bed made with a hideous navy blue comforter that looks like it'd feel like stiff wool if you laid on it. I almost go to take a step into the bedroom when I halt. A wicked grin curves my lips as her arousal fills the room, dragging my gaze to the underneath of his bed.

Where I spot two little manicured feet hiding beneath the bed.

Chapter 63

Amelia

I can hear his breathing through the mask as I will myself to remain still. My blood begins pumping beneath my skin as he takes one step into the bedroom.

The wood floorboard creaks beneath his black boots, anticipation rising within me. I hear him pause as he gets to the foot of the bed. Waiting for him to say something, for him to move. But instead he just stands there, taunting me with his presence.

I go to slowly bring my legs up, curling into myself when I hear him chuckle.

"Too late for that."

In the next moment he's kneeling down and grabbing my ankles, pulling me out from underneath the bed. My back glides against the hardwood floor, gasping at the force of his strength.

I look up at Levi, the mask obscuring his face as my breathing ramps up. My arousal intensifies as he leans down to trail the blade across my chest, goosebumps pebbling onto my chest and arms. He tilts his head before releasing the blade from my skin, hauling me up with him.

He pushes me up against a wall, pressing the blade up to my chest again. "But before I fuck you, I want to do one more thing." He says.

He dips the blade to the trim of my top, lowering it down until a breast heaves out. My breath hitches as he lightly trails the blade around my nipple, eliciting a soft moan from my lips.

He trails it over to the other one, exposing that breast too as he trails the knife over it. My toes curl against the hardwood floor as he teases me, dragging his own form of torture for me out.

"Levi." A breathy moan escapes from my lips as he traces my nipple again with the blade, flicking the very tip as I shudder beneath him.

His gaze through his mask raises from my breast to my face, tilting ever so slightly. He stands there as his gaze lowers, watching the rise and fall of my chest for a long moment. "I've decided it's not enough to have my name spoken from those pretty lips." He says slowly, roughly in a voice I've never heard before. Something out of a predator who's honing in on his prey.

I feel the tip of the blade raise up my chest, over my heart before he presses it in. I flinch as he traces it downward, drawing a trace of blood to bead above the skin there as he carves the blade into my chest.

I watch as he traces the blade to my left, blood lightly trailing down my nipple as he carves into my skin. A cut minor enough that even if I were mortal, it would only remain a superficial wound. I look down at what he's traced into my chest, right over my heart.

The letter L.

"I need it to be engraved over your skin." He raises the blade, tossing it to the floor as he sweeps his index finger through the blood beading there.

He lifts his finger, lowering it to trace a heart over my nipple, my back arching at his touch. He rips the top down my body with his other hand, tossing it to the floor as he picks me up. My legs wrap around him as he turns us to the bed, setting me on top of the comforter.

His hand comes to my waist as he drills himself into me, his cock hard against his pants. "You like that?" He says roughly as he grunts against me.

He presses into me again as I moan. "Yes."

He lifts my legs straight up, bringing them together as he holds my legs at my calves. I feel his other hand lower to my pussy, rubbing me beneath my skirt before slowly lowering his face to the back of my thigh. I gasp as he lightly glides his mask there, my skin on fire as I'm wanting to feel much more—*need* to feel much more. He raises himself back up, grunting beneath his mask. "I know you do."

He pulls my skirt and thong off of me forcefully, tossing them before yanking his pants down.

His hard cock hangs between us as he lowers my legs to each shoulder, his mask rubbing against one leg as he holds my ankle. He lowers himself down, wasting no time and thrusts in completely.

I cry as he brings the other hand to my throat, squeezing it gently as he begins ramming into me. I look up at the mask that hides his face, tilting down to watch me take him. Knowing behind that mask he's enjoying every second of it.

I go to reach a hand up to him when his other hand forces my wrist back down, pushing it above my head as my legs hang over his shoulders. He raises the other one there as well as his other hand grips my thigh, his cock filling me and stretching me. The hand holding both of my wrists locking me into place as he fucks me.

My orgasm builds as I can't help the moans that evade from my lips. Levi lowers himself down closer as he whispers. "Good fucking girl. You take me so well."

My pussy clamps around him as release finds me, screaming as I cum around his cock. He grunts as he rams into me harder until he thrusts himself deep inside, staying there as I feel him spill himself inside of me.

He moans as he releases his grip from my hands and my thigh. I reach up to lift his mask off, his handsome face staring down at me when I do.

He quickly lowers both of my legs down as I bring his face to mine, our lips clashing together. My moans getting trapped in his mouth.

He slowly pulls out of me as he lowers his mouth to my nipple, flicking his tongue once there before descending on it entirely.

He sucks the sensitive flesh there as the blood drawn heart around it smudges, coating itself on his lips now.

He lifts his mouth as he stares up at me, licking his lips as he grins. He lowers himself down as his lips hover above my pussy. The feel of both of us dripping out of me. "Open your mouth."

I watch as he drinks it out of me, keeping it in his mouth before raising back up to me. His lips hover above mine as I open my mouth for him. He spits our cum into my mouth as I greedily accept it.

He licks his lips. "Now swallow."

I swallow us both down as his thumb glides along my lip before he takes it into his mouth. Sucking it.

"Good girl. Now let's finish this so we can play again when we get home."

I smirk up at him. "Deal."

Chapter 64

Levi

After we got ourselves dressed again we made our way back into the living room.

I turn to Amelia, my hand gently caressing her cheek. "Wait by the front door."

She leans into my touch before nodding her head. My gaze lowers to her chest as she steps out of my reach, at the letter I carved right above her heart. A smirk fights its way onto my lips as I head into the kitchen.

I head straight over to the stove, pulling it away from the wall as the metal pipe comes into view. I grab it, yanking it hard out of the wall as a loud crack sounds momentarily. The leaking gas begins hissing loudly as I step away from the stove, turning back around to meet Amelia by the door.

She stands there with her arms crossed over her chest, pimples raising on her bare arms. I watch as she looks over at Adrian still sitting upright on the couch, right where we left him. She turns those amber eyes back to me.

I approach her, rubbing my hands on her chilled arms. "It's a short walk, but my coat is in the car."

She nods her head as I open the door, both of us stepping outside into the cold winter night.

I watch as her heels step onto the ground, dusted with a fine layer of snow. I lean down, looping my arm underneath her legs and picking her up. Her legs dangling over my arm as my other presses up against her back

She laughs as I carry her down the driveway, her arms wrapping around my neck as I press kisses to her chilled cheeks.

We make it to the end of the driveway when she lowers her hand down into my pocket. She pulls out Adrian's phone as she looks up at me. "Can I do it?"

I look down at her, chuckling. "Go right ahead."

She narrows her gaze to his phone, going through his home screen until she taps on his home security app. The main screen pulls up as she swipes for the living room light toggle. I watch a wide grin curve her lips as she switches the living room lights from off to on. She turns her head over my shoulder at the exact moment the spark of his living room lights turning on immediately ignites the leaking gas.

A loud boom sounds from behind us as a burst of heat lightly warms my back, the erratic orange glow of the explosion visible through my car window as we finally approach it.

I set Amelia down in front of the passenger door, opening it up for her as she crawls her way inside. I waste no time by casually walking over to the driver side door, taking one look at the house on fire before sliding inside as well.

I look over at her as her gaze peers out of the window, her phone out as she takes a picture of the massive plumes of fire eroding from Adrian's home. I take a moment to watch as flames engulf his entire house, with Adrian inside. Never able to solve another case again.

Or force himself on my girl ever again.

I turn the car on, reaching in the back seat as I grab my coat, laying it on her shoulders as she puts her phone away. She nuzzles into it as she looks up at me, smiling. "Let's go home."

I can't help the goofy smile that curves my lips at the word. Doesn't matter if it's my place or hers, as my home will now always be with her, and not a place of residence.

I put the car in drive as we pull away from the crime scene, heading back to her place. Where I'm sure Rufus is waiting oh so patiently for our arrival home.

Chapter 65

Amelia closes the door behind us as we enter her penthouse. I go to set my duffel bag on the ground as Rufus rushes towards us.

I lean down, reaching my hands out as I ruffle up his ears. I smile as he tries licking my face, his excitement so damn cute.

"He really likes you, I see." She says as she takes my coat off, hanging it on the mounted rack on the wall. A warm smile curving my lips at how cute she looked snuggled up in my coat.

I chuckle as I stand up again. Watching as Amelia goes to the pantry, pulling Rufus' kibble out before pouring some into his bowl. "He's a good pup."

She laughs as she sets his kibble back into the pantry before closing the door. She lets out a long sigh as she makes her way towards her stairs. "I need a shower."

She advances up the stairs as I just stand there and watch her before finally picking my feet up and following her up the stairs. As I approach the bottom step Rufus muffles a quiet bark at me.

I turn around, nodding at him. "Your mother and I need some time alone."

He huffs at me as if to say *you two are becoming insufferable to be around now*. I chuckle to myself as he turns around to plop himself down onto her couch as I resume my venture upstairs.

I get to the top of the stairs and approach her bedroom, standing there watching her through the doorway as she slowly begins taking off her costume. Starting with her top as she lifts it over her head, finding myself slowly inching my way into her room.

She moves her hands to her skirt, bending all the way forward as she slips the skirt down her waist.

Fucking Hell I just want to smother my face in it.

I lower my hand to my pants as I begin unbuttoning them. Suddenly inching my way into her bedroom as she stands up straight again. "What a coincidence because I need a shower as well."

She turns around as heat lines her gaze, her beautiful naked body on full display. I watch as her gaze narrows lower as I slip my pants down my waist, followed by my boxer briefs. Her gaze remains there as I lift my shirt off.

Her eyes finally raise to mine as I close the distance. "You promised me we would play when we got home." She says in a deep husky voice.

I lower my hand to her waist, twirling my thumb along her soft skin as my other hand caresses lightly along her breasts.

Her breath hitches as I pull her closer to me, my lips hovering above hers as a smirk crawls up my lips. "Then let's play."

I pick her up, wrapping her legs around me as my mouth clashes with hers. Her pussy rubs against my abdomen as I set her onto the bed, splaying her out before me.

Like my own personal entree awaiting.

I pull her to the edge of the bed, pushing her legs back as I kneel down to the floor. Her pussy on full display.

I lower my lips to her clit, sucking it as she whimpers and writhes beneath me. I lift my lips off of her, grinning. "Pink. Just like I knew it'd be."

I descend my mouth on her as I glide my tongue in between her lips, wetness gathered there already. Her sweet moans fill the room as I taste her, devouring every last drop of her.

I flick my tongue on her clit as she writhes harder against my face, her pussy clamping up as her moans get louder.

At the very moment I feel her about to cum I pull my mouth away, Amelia letting out a frustrated sigh.

"Breath, baby. You're going to cum." I say as I press a kiss to her navel. "Just not yet."

I stand up as I walk over to her nightstand. "If I had to guess where you keep your toys, I'd guess they'd be in here." I pull open the drawer as a dildo appears.

A smirk curves my face as I pull out the purple toy, closing the drawer and walking back over to her again. I stand before her as her eyes move to her toy. She rolls her eyes. "There's something else I'd much rather have."

I chuckle as I tease her entrance with it, slowly sliding it up her pussy. "Yes. But I want to know what you look like when you get off to your toys."

She goes to protest when I slip it inside of her, moaning as I pull it out again. I insert it again, deeper this time, pulling it out as it glistens.

I lean down as I slip it inside again. "For the next minute, I want you to imagine my cock filling you."

A moan slips from her pretty lips as I bury it in deeper. I begin fucking her slowly with it as she tries to squirm out of my reach.

"Where are you running off to, little red?" My lips hovering above her neck before lowering to her chest.

She whimpers beneath me as I continue thrusting the dildo inside of her. "Please." She moans.

I lower my lips to a hardened nipple, kissing it once, then twice. I look up at her as I twirl my tongue around it, feeling her wetness drip down the dildo as it slips down my hand. I grin before I close my mouth over it.

She tries to squirm out of my reach again when I clamp my hand on her waist, keeping her in place. "You can take it, baby."

She starts crying as she gets close again, her sweet noises filling the room. I remove the dildo at just the right moment.

She extends a long, irritated breath.

"Good. I like it when you're angry." I say against her skin.

I set the dildo on the bed as I stand up, picking her up and wrapping her legs around me. She automatically tries to grind against me, desperate to find her release. I carry her to the bathroom, turning the light on as I walk us over to the shower.

Gods she's so wet, so fucking soft. Her skin, her tongue, her pussy.

I step inside as I set her feet on the ground, turning around to turn the water on. Water begins streaming down as I feel a hand on my abdomen.

I turn my head to see Amelia kneeling on the shower floor, her hand on my cock. I chuckle as she begins slowly pumping me. "Are you trying to torture me as I have been you?"

She smirks up at me before she presses a kiss to the tip. I nearly jump out of my skin at the touch and the way her eyes stay on mine. "Maybe." She says as she glides her tongue along my shaft. I grunt as a reaction. "Or maybe I just really like your cock in my mouth."

She closes her mouth over me as she deepthroats me, water trickling down her breasts and her face as she sucks the life out of me. An image I've been fantasizing about for months.

Fuck, I'm gonna bust.

I move my hand to her head, gathering her hair up into my fist as my cock fills her throat.

"*Fuck,* baby. You do that so well." I say roughly as I watch her take all of it.

As I feel myself getting closer I begin gently thrusting into her mouth, my body growing taught as she pulls away from me.

She smiles up at me as her mouth slides right off my cock. "Not yet."

I laugh as I haul her up, pushing her up against the shower wall as I hook a leg over my waist. I lower my hand to my cock, teasing her entrance before I thrust all the way in.

Her chest rises as she gasps, grinding into all of her wetness. I fuck her even harder against the wall as she screams for me, for the pleasure my cock is eliciting for her.

"Come on, baby." I say as I nip at her neck, grunting at the fucking overwhelming ecstacy of being inside of her. "Fucking cum for me."

She screams as her walls clamp up around my cock, matching my pace as she grinds against me. Her orgasm overtaking her as wetness drips out of her.

"Good girl." I say roughly as I feel myself riding the edge. "I know that feels so fucking good."

She continues grinding into me as I feel myself spill over, ejaculating inside of her as I whimper against my own release.

My ears begin to ring as I lose control and ram myself into her, the orgasm too fucking much and not enough all at the same time. I bite down onto her neck, stifling my own moans of pleasure. She digs her nails into my back as we frantically ride our orgasms together.

I release my teeth on her neck as I finally come down, stilling inside of her until I slowly pull out. Our breathing ragged and labored as we remained in each other's arms, catching our breaths.

The glass shower doors fog up around us as I shakily lower my hand to her leg, lowering it back to the ground. I lift my head from her neck, staring at her sated face.

I lower a kiss to her lips before taking one long exhale out, brushing her damp hair back from her face. The entire focus of my universe in the palms of my hands.

I lean my still-damp hair back into the couch as I balance a glass of whiskey on my knee, the news channel broadcasted on the TV in front of me. I run my hand through Rufus' black fur as he lays next to me, his head propped up onto my thigh.

Amelia walks out into the living room, seating herself on my right as she curls herself up into me. Exhaustion written all over her face.

I lower my hand to her shoulder and my lips to the top of her head, pressing a kiss on her still damp hair. "Are you hungry?"

She nods her head against my chest. "Starved."

I chuckle as I tuck a damp strand behind her ear. "I'll make us something to eat."

I go to get up from the couch when the news alert sound blares from the TV. I turn my gaze to the news anchor standing outside a mantled home.

"Good evening, this is Rochelle O'Connell with Lilitu City news reporting to you live with what appears to be a major gas leak in this suburban home. Officials were called to the scene and upon putting out the fire, they claim it was due to a faulty gas pipe that caused the accident. Officials are claiming that the owner who lived here was Adrian Worshire, a successful private investigator for the city police. The City Fire Marshall claims that after thorough investigation, it is concluded that the man was asleep on the couch when the house set ablaze, and suffered fatal wounds that resulted in his death."

I watch as The City Marshall comes onto screen, those striking blue eyes set onto the camera as he stands next to Rochelle.

"You weren't kidding. He does look identical to his brother." Amelia says beside me.

A smirk crawls up my face, chuckling as I watch Dexter's brother give a speech on the TV screen.

"We would like to express our sincerest condolences to this family, and would like to warn other families out there to please check your pipes. If you see anything out of the ordinary, please contact us immediately. A faulty pipe can quite literally put your life in danger."

His face remained professional and steady, a skill impeccably useful when being an asset and ally to The Deimari Mafia.

Amelia chuckles beside me. "You think his body burned to ash then?"

I shrug my shoulders faintly. "He told me we'd have an extra window of time before they got there to put out the fire." I look down at her. "So my guess is yes. Or at least enough where not much was left behind."

"I imagine if he has any sense of humor he found Adrian's severed cock entertaining."

I laugh as I stand up from the couch, walking over to the kitchen to fix Amelia something to eat. "I imagine so."

Chapter 66

Amelia

"Hey bitch, let me get a lap dance."

I stop in my stride towards the bar, a wicked grin curving my lips at his choice of words. I take a long inhale in, exhaling as an eerie calmness flows over me.

I turn around, looking down at the man sitting in the seat. Surrounded by two other men who seem to have the common sense to shy their gazes away from their friend, shame coloring their cheeks at his approach to women.

Smart decision.

I gaze down at him, lowering my hand to his scalp as I run my fingers through it. I tilt my head. "All you had to do was ask." I say sweetly.

He gives me a smug grin as he goes to get up from the chair when I keep him seated. His eyes quickly widen as the smugness on his face vanishes.

My fingers burrow themselves into his hair, appearing as if I'm running my fingers through it by anyone else watching right now. But I allow one claw to protrude to the surface, burrowing itself into his scalp just enough to prick a drop of blood.

His body goes rigid as his shaky gaze watches me.

I exhale, retracting my claw once more. "How about we get a VIP room instead?"

He exhales a shaky relief as my claw retracts itself. He goes to shake his head no when I clamp his head straight.

I coax him with my power, staring straight into his soul. "You would be honored to buy a VIP room with me."

His gaze softens as his body relaxes, his friends already having made themselves useful elsewhere and removed themselves from this section entirely.

He slowly nods as he goes to reach into his pocket. "I would really like to buy a VIP room, your majesty."

"Because you're a what?" I ask.

He responds in the same monotone voice. "Because I'm a rotten, ungrateful piece of shit who needs to learn to respect women."

I smile down at him as I release my hold. "That's right."

He pulls out a few hundred dollars, handing it to me as I look over at Levi sitting across the way. His gaze wholly on me as I nod to him. He stands up from his seat as he casually makes his way over to us.

I turn my gaze back onto the man, taking his money. "Give me everything you brought tonight just because of your disrespect."

He nods as he opens his wallet again, pulling out another three hundred dollars.

I sigh, taking it. "It'll do for now."

Levi approaches us, his dark blonde hair pushed back tonight. Donned in an all black suit, looking like the most well-dressed man in the club in a room full of college students.

Gods, I hate Sundays. But Levi sure makes up for it when he looks this good.

"You don't mind if my friend joins us, do you?" I ask the man.

He shakes his head, still under my spell. "Not at all."

I grin widely. "Great. Let's go."

He stands up as I guide us all to the VIP hallway, Levi coming up on my other side as he glides the back of his knuckles along my cheek.

"Have I ever told you how hot you are when you boss men around?"

I laugh as we approach an unoccupied VIP room, guiding us all inside. "Are you insinuating you'd like me to start bossing you around?"

"You already are a brat to me."

I laugh as he comes up behind me, pressing a hand to my navel.

"And I find I do reward you for such behavior."

A chill runs down my spine as he steps away, moving to the center of the room as he unbuttons his shirt at the top.

"Sit." I order the man.

He goes to sit in the chair when I tsk at him.

"Not there." I say, nodding to the carpet.

He nods as he lowers himself to the ground, looking up at me.

I walk around him as Levi sits on the sofa, watching me. His stare penetrates the darkest parts of my soul, fueling the most deranged parts of myself.

The parts of myself that I never have to shy away from him as he compliments them entirely. A sick and twisted love story, if there ever were one.

"Get on all fours."

The man does what I say, his hands and his knees planting firmly onto the carpet. I go to seat myself next to Levi on the couch, the man on all fours in front of me.

"Good." I say before I lift a leg up, laying my foot over his back before I hook my other leg over my ankle. I lean back into the couch as I feel the man's back arch deeply.

"Aht aht. Keep it straight."

The man immediately straightens his back, exhaling a ragged and possibly angry exhale.

A smile curves up on my face as I look down at him exactly where he's meant to be.

Beneath me.

"Shall I kill him for his disrespect?" Levi says beside me.

"Hmm, maybe later. For now I want him to see just how much of a bitch I can be."

I lean my head up against Levi's shoulder as the man below keeps my feet elevated with his back. As Levi and I begin to have a conversation amongst the two of us as if the man is not even in the room with us.

We talk about what we'll do on my day off tomorrow, Levi immediately tossing in the idea of just remaining in bed all day.

He sure does love that idea.

"So, I learned something quite interesting tonight."

I hum my response as Levi kisses the top of my head.

"That waitress—Dahlia is it? Well, when she came to bring my drink tonight I couldn't help but notice how she held her breath around me. Almost as if she was inching away from me, too."

I roll my eyes as a smirk fights to curve up my lips. I bring my hand up to my mouth to stifle the laugh creeping up my throat. "She's a strange woman."

Levi leans in towards me, the scent of spearmint and eucalyptus wafting towards me. "Strange indeed. Though before she walked away, she turned around and told me that there was nothing to be ashamed of. That there has to be some kind of remedy for chronic flatulence."

Unable to help myself I burst out laughing at the lie I spun to her weeks ago as a means to deter her interest in Levi.

Levi tucks a strand of my red hair behind my ear, a low deep chuckle escaping him. "So, is there something I should know about here?"

I shrug my shoulders, shaking my head. "I have no idea where she got that information from." I say, peering up at him as a grin curves my lips.

He snorts as he presses another kiss to the top of my head. "Next thing you know she's going to start bringing me pamphlets for support groups."

I giggle against him as I let the warmth of him carry over me, relaxing into his hold as he wraps an arm around me. Igniting everything that I am from the inside out. No need to hide who I am, no need to pretend I'm anything that I'm not.

Just two deranged individuals against the world. A sick and twisted love story if there ever were one.

AUTHOR'S NOTE

429

I want to go ahead and thank each and every one of you who has read this book. You may have found yourself laughing while reading this book, maybe even shed a tear. But at the end of the day, my hope is that you took what the underlying message of this book was: That you as a woman or non-binary human, should never, *ever* dim your light over a man. You should always stand tall in the face of criticism and smile in their face because not a damn person can keep you down. You should always strive to live your life authentically, however that means for you.♥

The trilogy continues in:

SAPPHIRE

Deal With A Succubus, Book 2

SILVER

Deal With A Succubus, Book 3
Available for pre-order now!

ABOUT THE AUTHOR

Michelle Rossa is the author of the Shadows and Fire series, and her work centers around Adult Romance and Fantasy. From writing poetry, to daydreaming fantasy worlds inside her head, Michelle has had a vast imagination since she was a child.

When she's not writing, she's most likely spending her time out in nature, snuggling with her cat Diva, or re-watching The Vampire Diaries for the millionth time. Outside of her passion for writing, she practices as a psychic medium and tarot reader. She is greatly passionate about all things astrology, the left hand path, occult studies, mythology, non-conformity to societal/gender standards, and advocating for women.

www.ingramcontent.com/pod-product-compliance
Lightning Source LLC
Chambersburg PA
CBHW020324010826
48973CB00005B/1114